Belva Plain

Author of five fabulous national best sellers: *EVERGREEN, RANDOM WINDS, EDEN BURNING, CRESCENT CITY,* and now . .

THE GOLDEN CUP

Other novels by Belva Plain:

EVERGREEN
RANDOM WINDS
EDEN BURNING
TAPESTRY
THE GOLDEN CUP
CRESCENT CITY

THE GOLDEN CUP

Belva Plain

A DELL BOOK

Published by
Dell Publishing
a division of
Bantam Doubleday Dell Publishing Group, Inc.
666 Fifth Avenue
New York, New York 10103

ISBN: 0-440-13091-3

Reprinted by arrangement with Delacorte Press

Printed in the United States of America

October 1987

10 9 8 7 6 5

KRI

Babylon hath been a golden cup in the Lord's hand,
That made all the earth drunken;
The nations have drunk of her wine,
Therefore the nations are mad.

                                    Jeremiah

It was of a famous vintage . . . when war and wine
              throve together.

                          FITZ-JAMES O'BRIEN

PART ONE

Hennie and Dan

1

All her life she would remember the somber autumn sky, how vast and high and cold it had been while the great wind raced from the East River toward Broadway. When she was very old she would still marvel, as do we all, over the randomness of things, for if she had not happened to turn just that corner, in just that hour, her whole life would have been different.

The child whose hand she held would vaguely remember cries and lurid color, a blur of savage yellow, confusion and a terror not half understood.

And another child, the one who came to be born because she had turned that corner, would hear a tale of heroism, as it grew to become a family legend, until he was sick of hearing it.

The tenement burned. Over its scorched brick walls the fire scurried and flurried, tearing as with giant claws its fibers and sinews. Out of its ruined heart there rose a spiral of flame; strong and fierce, it soared into the wind, and a bitter smoke poured over the rooftops. Powerful arcs of water shot from

the pumps to the blaze, but the fire had power of its
own.

And the watching crowd, packed tightly on the
street among the engines and great stamping fire
horses, stood waiting either for the destruction to be
complete or to be told what to do and where to go.
Sweatered and shawled in shabby brownish gray, it
hardly moved, only changing weight from one foot
to the other, shifting a baby from one shoulder to
the other. With a single voice it gave out a mournful, plaintive murmur.

Fires like this one were common enough in that
part of the city, yet these people were stunned into
disbelief. It was too soon for any of them to believe
in the truth of what was happening or to have
counted the full extent of loss, the featherbedding
and pillows, the kitchen table, the change of under-
wear and the winter coat. That would come later. It
was enough now to have gotten out alive.

There was a terrible, anguished shriek. A young
girl at the farthermost edge of the crowd, who had
been passing through the street, turned back at the
sound. She had a little boy by the hand and had
been hurrying away because she had not wanted the
child to see anything so frightful. But the cry
pierced her and she stopped.

"What is it? Is someone hurt?"

The word was carried back in relays, neighbor to
neighbor.

"There's someone left inside, somebody's baby."

"On the top floor, too."

"The hoses don't reach that far."

"There's not enough pressure anyway."

An innocent question. "Can't they go up through the next house and reach in?"

A scornful reply. "Who's going to try that, do you think?"

Now the smoke came whipping out of the fourth floor. Soon it would reach the fifth and then the top.

"Can't live long in there."

"My God, what a way to die!"

The girl was unable to pull herself away. She could hear her own heart beat.

"You're hurting my hand," the child cried.

"Oh, Paul, I'm sorry, I didn't mean to hold you so hard." And she bent to button up his little velvet collar against the wind. "We'll go, we'll go in a minute."

But she was fastened to the place where she stood. Her eyes were fastened to the windows behind which the most awful death was taking place, the death of a child. She felt the trembling warmth of the little boy's hand. What if it were he? And she looked down at the clear bright eyes, the brightest blue, and the round cheeks . . . And thought: But it is somebody's child, isn't it? And could not move away. . . .

Now with furious clangor of bells came the hook and ladder. Four horses clattered and charged, so that the crowd spread frantically apart to let them through, recoiling from the hooves and the snorting breath. The ladder was taken down, dragged to the building, and propped up against the wall; had no one known it could reach no higher than three floors? There sounded a great gasp and a collective sigh.

Stupid, stupid, thought the girl.

One of the firemen reached the top of the ladder and stood there, extending his arms in a gesture of helplessness to show that he was still a full story and a half from the top floor. Then, having shown that the task was impossible, he backed down the ladder, coughing and choking through the smoke, to join a knot of firemen gathered on the sidewalk among those onlookers who had the same opinion: There was no hope.

"Wouldn't you think," a woman ventured again, "that somebody could go through the house next door?"

"And how get across? You can see the air shaft's too wide to step over. you think anybody will try to jump across, six floors up, with nothing but a rotting cornice to hold you?"

"Anyway, you couldn't get a foothold on that ledge. It's only a couple of inches wide."

"No, whoever is in there is a goner."

"Burned to a crisp."

"They say the smoke kills you first. You suffocate."

"That's not always true. Once I saw a man in flames. He shrieked. . . . I can still hear him."

The fire began to roar. Perhaps it had been roaring all along, but the girl was only now conscious of its terrible voice. She closed her eyes. The roar was storm-wind and storm-water on the beach at Long Island, where they went sometimes in the summer, and had watched a man drown. It was a force to blow you before it like a leaf or a grain of sand. There was nothing you could do.

Someone was shoving a way through the crowd. The girl, feeling the wave of displaced bodies, had a glimpse of the back of a head of black hair and a checked woolen shirt. Standing on tiptoe, she saw a young man running, moving the sidewalk groups aside, and plunging up the steps of the next tenement.

"He's going to try," a woman said. "Can you imagine, he's going to try."

"Try what?"

"What do you think? To get in through the other building!"

"I don't believe it. It's impossible! He'd be crazy!"

"Then he's crazy."

"My God, look there! Up there!"

The young man was at the top-floor window, next to the burning building. Astride the sill, he swung a leg out into the air.

"What does he—how does he think he can—" The onlookers seemed to be whispering with that single voice again.

A foot searched for a place on the narrow cornice. It was a tin cornice; above it stood the numbers 1889. A hand went out and groped, testing the fragile scroll on the flat, fake-classic pillar, a crude bas-relief in crumbling stone. The hand drew back.

"There's no purchase there, nothing to grasp," the girl said to herself. Her breath held in her throat.

The smoke was thickening. It wreathed and curled in the scurrying wind; the fire was now making a wind of its own, which met the winds from the river, from the four corners of the earth, and fought them, swirling the smoke so that the man was almost hidden in it.

He changed to a sitting position on the sill. For a

moment he sat quite still; his legs hung down; he
wore green corduroy trousers. Then, as if he had
finally made his decision, he twisted off from the sill,
with his back to the street, his toes on the cornice,
his hands on the sill. By hand and foot he clung to
the moldering stone.

"Oh, let it hold! Let it not break off and send him
smashing to the street!"

The girl's neck ached; tense with the strain of
peering upward, she felt herself in that young man's
place. He probed now with one foot, gauging the
distance between the buildings. It was too long even
for the long legs of such a tall man—for, even from
where she stood, she could see that he was tall. So
he would need to slide to the edge of the building
and then jump, which he must have known from the
start, just as the fireman had known.

"Come back . . . don't try . . . come back."

In the burning house the windows had begun to
melt; the shattered glass fell with a musical tinkle.
Cinders and shreds of burned cloth rained gently to
the street.

Somebody spoke behind the girl. "No one can be
alive in there."

"It's not worth risking his life—"

His hand must have seized some small projection.
Inch by inch he slid along the stone face, past the
window. Far up, through the screen of smoke, they
could see him, could sense that again he was mea-
suring distance, positioned to spring. Now he
seemed to be steadying himself, assessing his balance or maybe arguing with himself as to whether it
made any sense at all to try.

You can't do it, don't you see you can't?

Silence. A horse neighed. Silence. Somebody coughed.

The girl's heart hammered. I will be sick if he falls. I should look away. Look away now! But she could not.

"It won't hold," said the talkative woman at the girl's back.

I wish you would shut up, she thought in fury.

A piece of burned paper wrapped itself like a cat or a snake around her ankle, but she did not feel it. She was feeling the fall to the street, the unspeakable seconds while the pavement rushed up.

Her full lips fell open. "Oh, God," she whispered.

He leapt. The extended arm and the leg shot across the air-space. The hand grasped; one could imagine the straining muscles of the arms and the fingernails going white. One foot jammed onto the cornice of the burning building and clung until the rest of the body, curving outward into space, could follow and right itself and steady itself.

Again the girl closed her eyes. She had a fragment of thought: No one is thinking of the child inside, even I am thinking instead of him.

When she opened her eyes, he was standing flat on the cornice of the burning building, inching himself toward the window.

Don't look down. If you look you will fall. . . .

"Thank God the window is open," the girl whispered aloud.

What would have happened had it been closed? She had not thought of that. And she wondered whether the young man had not thought of it either.

He swung himself inside. And a babble of relief and amazement broke out.

"My God, how brave!"

"Who is he? Do you know?"

"The smoke will kill him."

"It sears the lungs. All you need are a couple of breaths."

"There can't be anyone left alive in there."

"Make way! Get back, get out of the way, dammit!"

Now they were bringing up a net. A dozen men came forward to hold it.

"Dammit, out of the way!"

They waited.

"Can't survive in there. It sears the lungs."

And then he appeared at the window. He was holding someone: female, with a flapping skirt. She was not a baby: a grown child, then— He let go. The body hurtled through the air with a scream that tore the air, and bounced safe in the net, and bounced once more and was lifted out. A great cheer went up.

Then the young man, flinging out his arms, jumped too, like a boy going feetfirst into the East River on a summer day. Another great cheer of relief and release went up; laughing and clapping, the crowd pushed forward toward the hero.

But it was only an old woman whom he saved, the girl thought. No child imploring and helpless in its crib, only a very old and ugly, hairy-faced woman whimpering, with a few years left to live. Was it worth the risk of his life? And yet we are taught, she thought seriously, for she was a serious believer, that he who saves one life, saves the whole world. Still, if it had been a child's life— Well, it is done. He did it.

They had cornered him. Close to the smoking tenement, in front of a small wooden house out of the century past, he stood now panting and coughing, squeezed between a cigar-store Indian and a barber pole from which the gilded ball had been knocked off by the swinging fire hose. Thrilled and curious, the crowd pressed close to touch him and stare. Reporters were already there with notebook, pencil, and a hundred questions.

Who was he? Where did he live? Why had he done it?

"What difference does my name make? And why I did it—oh, because somebody had to. That's as good a reason as any, isn't it?"

Exhausted, he still stood straight. The girl was enthralled. A king going past in a gilded coach would have been no more enthralling. From far off, between the crowding heads, she stood and saw: vivid eyes, high cheekbones, a lock of waving hair, thick as a mane, that he kept pushing back off his forehead.

His shirt is torn and his hands are bleeding. He wants to be let alone. I would not bother you so. Go home and rest, I would say. You are the most wonderful . . . go home and rest, my dear.

"Well, sonny, what did you think of that brave man?" an old fellow asked Paul as they walked away.

"I could do that," Paul said gravely.

"Well, that's a good one! That's the way to talk! Yessir, you'll make your mother proud of you when you grow up! How old are you?"

"Four," Paul answered.

They crossed the street and Paul whispered, "He thought you were my mother, Aunt Hennie."

"I know."

It was not unusual for people to think Paul was her child when they were out together. She wished he were. There was something between them that had nothing to do with age. She could look years and years into the future and see them caring about each other. It was not a thing she talked of; people would find it silly. But it was true, all the same.

Who is this girl going home through the gathering afternoon? Her eyes tell of her that she is solitary and that she dreams. They are the distinguishing feature in a round, pleasant, otherwise undistinguished face. Leaf-shaped, they are the color of brown autumn and they match the curling hair that escapes under the brim of her feathered hat. She is eighteen years old and seems older.

Because you have large bones. I don't know how you came to be so big. There's never been anyone with your frame in my family or in your father's either, as far as I know.

Her name is Henrietta De Rivera. She lives with her family in a decent apartment house east of Washington Square's fine private brownstones, with their stoops and mounting blocks and polished railings. Her address is near enough to these things to be respectable, but too far from them to be fashionable.

On three days a week, she walks to work as a volunteer at a settlement house downtown. She teaches English to immigrants, tries also to teach them to bathe, and tries not to mind their clothes, which are sometimes very dirty, for she understands how hard it is to find the time or place for cleanliness. Her work is called "assimilation of the immigrant into American life."

Some of these people do not want to be entirely assimilated into the ways of families like the De Riveras, but the De Riveras want them to because their existence as they are is an embarrassment. Hennie is naturally aware of all that, but she does not agree with it. She does not feel superior; she feels, rather, a deep kinship. Indeed, the closest friend she has—and she has not ever had many— comes not out of the group in which she has grown up, but is a pupil in one of her English classes, an immigrant sweatshop worker only a few years older than she.

Hennie would like to be a volunteer nurse like Lillian Wald. Her parents, though, will not allow her to take training. Nor will they let her do any other labor for pay. To receive pay would make it seem that her father was unable to support her! A young lady does not work for money, even, Hennie thinks, when her family could certainly use it. But she does not say so. It is one of the many things she thinks but does not say.

"You sighed, Aunt Hennie," Paul said now.

"Did I? I'm tired, I guess. Are you tired? Are you hungry? We've had a long walk, but there'll be time for cocoa at my house before your mama comes for you."

They were passing through Washington Square. Sparrows filled the brisk air with anxious twittering. Two little girls clattered their hoops against the railings, making a rat-a-tat like drums. A lady stepped

out of her carriage, holding a little white dog, and
smiled at Paul.

"It's pretty here," Paul said.

He looked up at the dome of trees, now only
sparsely leaved; his little face was earnest; the sky,
seen through the leaves, must be a wonderment to
him, Hennie thought. Perhaps he is trying to see
God up there, as I used to do.

He was thinking not of God, but of Hennie. He
was thinking, although he did not have the words,
that he liked the hush among these houses, and the
colors, and being here with her. He loved it whenever he was allowed to visit for a day or a night. She
was so nice! She was different; he could think of the
rest of his family as "they" apart from "her," and
could love them all, for no one was ever unkind to
him, yet she was different.

She never said: "Don't bother me right now" or
"Later, Paul, I'm busy."

When she took him to the park, which wasn't
that often, usually on Fräulein's Thursday out, it
was so much better to see her sit there watching him
play, than to see Fräulein scowling over her knitting. She was always knitting some ugly gray thing
for her nieces and nephews.

"Komm jetzt! Schnell zurück!" she would call,
sounding angry; she wasn't really angry, but her
voice made it sound that way, like a bark. He
laughed, thinking of Fräulein barking like a dog. So
Aunt Hennie was much, much better. Better than
his mother, too, although he suspected he wasn't
supposed to think that. Mama didn't scold, but she
wasn't all that much fun. You could hardly ever get
on her lap because of wrinkles: *Be careful, darling;*

you'll wrinkle my skirt. Of course, he was almost five, and really didn't want to sit on anybody's lap very much; only sometimes, when he was tired, it was a good thing to do.

He could always sit on Aunt Hennie's lap, though. She would read to him about Little Orphant Annie, and then there was the one about the "funny little fellow of the very purest type, for he had a heart as mellow as an apple overripe." That's called "poetry" when it rhymes like *fellow* and *mellow.*

Aunt Hennie would hug him. "Guess who the funny little fellow is," she would say, and he would tell her he couldn't guess, although he did know.

"Why, it's you!" she would say, opening her eyes wide with the surprise, and she would hug him again.

"Did you like that man?" he asked her now.

For a moment she could not think whom he meant. "The man who climbed up on the roof, do you mean?"

"Yes. Did you like him? I did."

"Yes, he was wonderful."

"I could do that," Paul said again.

She touched his head. "I don't know that you could ever do that. Hardly anybody could." She believed in being honest with a child. "But I do believe you will do many wonderful things."

"What will I do?"

"You will learn a lot because you look carefully and you listen. You will understand beautiful things. And you will be very kind. Now let's hurry. They must be wondering where we are."

* * *

The tea service was out on its heavy tray; Hennie's mother and sister were waiting. It is a picture, she thought; they know they are making a picture. Florence must have brought the roses. She always brought them, never too many, only enough to create a perfection of pink and cream in a small silver bowl.

"Paul must have his cocoa," said Angelique, the grandmother. "And then you may take him home, Florence."

They had been comfortably chatting. The arrival of Hennie and Paul having interrupted the flow of the chat, there was a short silence while thoughts were once again collected.

"This is such a lovely room," Florence said. "All your beautiful things, Mama."

Angelique shook her head. "They belong in a proper setting. Not here."

It was true. These portraits, the lace curtains fine as a bride's veil, these Dresden dukes and duchesses bowing to each other on the whatnot, were too grand for such ordinary rooms. They recalled high ceilings, columns, and verandas. They were from another place and another life, the life that had stopped at Appomattox, eight years before Hennie was born.

How, then, could she still hear its cries and clamor in her head? It was because Angelique made them vivid. Papa, who had gone through four years of war, almost never spoke of it, nor did Great Uncle David, who had gone through even worse, though, as Angelique always said, on the wrong side. But how she clung to that old war! She wore

sorrow and anger like a worn-out coat and would
not throw it away. Perhaps she could not. Perhaps
in some peculiar way it protected her.

"Yes, it was a sorry day when we came to New
York," Angelique said now. She stood up and went
to the window, to which she was drawn a dozen
times a day. "They say it will be an early winter. All
those heaps of dirty melting snow to look forward
to."

The bleakness of the imagined wintry street was
reflected in her handsome, aging face, on which the
cheeks had just begun to sag. "Oh, when I think of
the places where I grew up! Our lovely sheltered
garden in New Orleans, with the fountain trickling!" Her voice lamented that lost, privileged
charm. "Lawns and lawns all the way to the river at
Beau Jardin before the war! Parties and servants . . ."

Slaves, but she would never use the word. And
her swift hand dismissed the little parlor that Florence, however charitably, had praised, and the
kitchen in which the latest Irish maid was humming
and chopping, the hall with Papa's bookcases—dismissed them with a gesture.

"It's dark in here," Hennie said, finding it all unbearable.

She lit the gas; the blue flame hissed and jetted.
The marble clock, suspended between gilt Corin-
thian columns, chimed the hour.

Florence stood up. "Come, Paul. Time to go
home."

"We had a good time, Paul and I," Hennie told
her.

"We saw a fire," Paul cried, "and gulls. They dive for fish in the river."

"We always have a good time," Hennie said.

"That I know." It was never clear whether Florence minded or not.

From the window Angelique watched her daughter and grandson ride away in their polished black carriage, behind the coachman in brass buttons and the fine pair of matching grays. She sighed again.

"Your father is coming down the street. Open the door so he won't have to fumble with his keys. . . . You're home early, Henry!"

"There wasn't much doing downtown."

Too often there was not. Papa had been waiting to prosper ever since he and Wendell Hughes had come north and opened their office in the cotton district near Hanover Square.

Papa was gray: gray cloth suit, skin, and faded hair. The sight of him pained Hennie.

"Not enough capital," he would say, "that's the trouble. Not enough to expand as we ought. Oh, we're managing, but it's not what I had in mind, God knows. I sometimes feel I am failing you, Angelique."

Hennie watched him all through the dinner. He ate silently. She wondered whether he heard half of her mother's and her brother's animated talk. Alfie could always amuse his mother.

"—so Mr. Hemmings turned around to see where the spitball came from, it hit the back of his neck, all squooshy, a real wet one—"

The mother wanted to seem shocked, but laughter prevented.

"Alfie, you are the limit! Now tell me, have you really done tomorrow's homework?"

Of course he hadn't. He would need to be reminded and prodded.

But he is his mother's last darling baby and will always be the darling, although his hair is no longer as yellow as canary feathers, a light mustache has begun to smudge his upper lip, and his nose will be bulbous. The twinkle of his eyes overcomes all.

When they went to the parlor, Papa laid his head on the back of his chair. He did that because he was too tired to talk. Hennie knew. They were two together, she and her father. It had been intended that she would be Henry, but she had turned out to be Henrietta instead. Still, she was tall like him, and she had his strong, separated teeth. That was supposed to be good luck, people said. Papa laughed at that and said he was still waiting.

Angelique looked up from her knitting. "Florence and Walter will be moving into the house on Seventy-fourth Street before they go to Florida. Such a beautiful house, and right near the park, which is perfect for children."

"You startled him. He was just falling asleep," Hennie said silently and angrily. She closed her book.

"Yes, wonderful," Papa said. "Wonderful to think that all their good fortune has come to them from the Werners' side, and none from me."

It was a shame for a man to feel such bitter humiliation. Hennie could not look at him.

"We didn't even have her wedding at our house," Papa said. It was the hundredth time he had said it.

"You know very well, Henry, we couldn't have

had all those people in this place," Mama answered. "I don't know why you keep harping on it."

"The South was ruined, yet I married you in your own home, Angelique."

On the wall behind Papa hung his portrait, done by an expensive artist, in Confederate gray. Proud he stood, with epaulets and braid, some sort of thing like a dagger or small sword in his hand, and a jaunty tilt to his head. Whenever he spoke of the South or of ruin, his eyes would go to the portrait. To him it was precious, but to Hennie it gave only a sense of doom, as if it were a reminder, a warning and promise that what he had lived through would have to be lived through by others, maybe by herself. Over and over again, to the end of time.

Uncle David had a picture of himself too. His was only a photograph, and his uniform was blue, but he, too, kept it where he could see it. A reminder. To the end of time.

"As to the Werners," Mama said now, "it's an even exchange and never forget that, Henry!" She broke off to cast stitches and count, her nervous hands flying. She resumed, "The Werners got rich out of the war that made us poor. They may be in banking now, but the grandfather stood behind a dry goods counter, like all the Germans, not too long ago. Don't think they aren't very much impressed by the De Rivera name, my dear!"

She was more impressed by it than Papa, who owned the name. How she talked and talked about the distinguished lawyers, the doctors and scholars, the aristocrats in Charleston before there even was a United States! What she meant to say is that although among Jews it is infinitely better to be German than one of those poor Poles and Russians downtown, it is better yet to be Portuguese or Spanish.

This makes me shrivel in my skin. So mean. And stupid, too, because her own mother's family had been German, as Uncle David liked to remind her.

Now Hennie reminded her. "Uncle David was born in Germany."

"Oh, Uncle David! Why do you always refer everything to Uncle David!"

"I don't always."

"Well, you are so much like him," Angelique said, more mildly. And she smiled to make up for the first rebuke, but the second remark was not entirely a compliment either, Hennie knew.

They thought it was ridiculous, and even Papa agreed, that Uncle David should practice medicine among the tenements and pushcarts, when he could just as easily be uptown. Angelique complained that he was an embarrassment to the family, although she was fond of him in a way. She made a mystery of his past, but it was no mystery to Hennie because Uncle David had told her about it himself. He had been a secret abolitionist in the South before the war, had shot a man, killing him accidentally, and had had to flee North for his life. He was old, nearly seventy, but you would never guess it. There was joy in his meager rooms, and nobody knew how often Hennie went to him there for his welcome.

She got up. "I think I shall go to bed. Papa, Mama, good night."

"So early?" Papa said. "Don't you feel well?"

"I feel well, only sleepy."

But mourning had lain thick in the room, like

dust. The dust lay on the furniture, the walls, the ceiling, and everything between the walls; the man with the newspaper dropped by his chair, the woman frowning and knitting; it was as if they—we —were all waiting for something. More money, so that they might be what they had been. But what they had been was nothing Hennie wanted.

In her own room she could shut the sadness away. The things in it were friends. They spoke to her. The doll with the china head had a winsome face, reminding her of the sunny birthday when Uncle David had brought it, a dozen years ago. Books filled the shelves. *Robinson Crusoe, Alice in Wonderland, The Old Curiosity Shop*—all were friends. Their covers were neat, although they had been read and reread. She liked things to be neat, but spare, without excess. In her jewelry box lay a gold bangle bracelet and a seed pearl necklace; they were her treasures and she craved no more.

She lay down in the dark. It was growing cold, with chilly air seeping around the edges of the bed; the quilt made a warm pocket in which she curled, loving her little room. The wind that had been so fierce in the afternoon had died away, so that the night was still. The street was quiet except for the occasional clip-clop of a horse and a voice calling good night.

Suddenly it was too quiet. It was still early; there ought to be more life. And she thought of the streets where her settlement house people struggled in dirt and disorder, such as no human being should endure. Yet there was more real life there. Was that nonsense?

She knew she was thought to be too emotional.

She could not bear the mew of a starving cat in the areaway, to see horses struggling to pull a bus uphill on ice, while the driver lashed them. Poor things! Poor things! she used to cry, when still a child.

Too emotional, they said. Well, she was never her mother's favorite and she had always known that, too, for no gift or smile or kiss can hide a truth like that from a child.

Oh, her mother could be so gay with Alfie! He had "personality," or rather, many personalities to suit the moment. Mrs. Hughes, the wife of Papa's partner—a hearty fool, in Hennie's opinion—called Alfie a "young gentleman," which was, of course, her highest praise. She wouldn't think he was one if she could see him mock her with his sputtering laugh while he tucked two pillows under his coat behind and before.

And her mother could be so confidential with Florence! But Florence had always known how to tie a blue sash on an old white summer dress and turn herself into a beauty, which she was not. When *she* had been eighteen, like Hennie now, the invitations in their lovely thick envelopes had piled up on the table in the hall. People remembered Florence, people from Sunday school at temple, or people met during a week at the shore. Walter Werner proposed to her two months after they were introduced and married her on her nineteenth birthday.

So Hennie was caught between the sister and the brother. So easily could she vanish under their waves, a little skiff capsized in their wake, if she were to let it happen! But none of that was any fault of theirs. It was simply that they were determined people and she was not.

"You only think you are not," her friend Olga
corrected her. "You have never tried to find out."

Their friendship was unexpected—or perhaps not
unexpected, for Hennie needed to be wanted and
Olga was honored that her teacher sought her out.
They had met on the street one summer evening
after class; it had been early, still light, and on sudden impulse Hennie had proposed having a cup of
coffee together. Olga had piqued her curiosity. Married to a worker like herself, confined to a drab and
bitter life, she had not lost her eager imagination.
As fast as Hennie lent books to her, she came back
for more.

From discussion of Tolstoy and Dickens they
came to the personal. Olga told of the shame and
horror of Russian persecution, and of the long, hard
months of the escape and voyage and the struggle in
New York. Hennie told something about her family,
and in some fashion, from what Hennie did not say
rather than from what she did say, Olga came to
understand her position in that family. The imagination that took her to Dickens's England took her
into Hennie's home.

She had never physically entered that home.
Clearly felt by both girls, although never put into
words, was the unsuitability of such a visit. Their
friendship was better left on neutral ground, removed from the tenements to whose resentful occupants Hennie would seem to be a mere sightseer,
and removed as well from the polite and curious
scrutiny of Angelique.

Hennie was wide-awake. She felt suddenly a restless energy. These random thoughts of her friend
led now, possibly through a natural association of

Olga's mean street with the one on which that afternoon's miracle had taken place, back to her own emotion. As never before in her life, she had been dazzled. She wanted to feel like that again. . . .

In the gray shadows of the room, his image floated, vague as an unfinished sketch. Yet it was certain that she would recognize him: vivid eyes, a careless dark wave of hair. Absurd fantasy! What had he to do with her life? She was a foolish romantic, an embarrassment even to her most secret self.

And yet . . . there was so much happening in the world. Meetings, partings, lovers . . . life. Why not to her?

Because . . . absurd fantasy . . . that is why not.

Then one day she saw him coming out of Uncle David's office. He was running down the steps, tossing off his forehead that long, loose wave of hair that would not stay in place. He wore the same green corduroy trousers; it seemed to her very touching, very masculine, not to know better than to wear such an ugly color. She watched him stride away through the crowded street.

What a fool you are, Hennie! A ridiculous fool, she thought, and stood there arguing with herself, trying to decide, encircled by jostling customers in front of a pushcart piled with bananas.

A shove brought her to herself. She turned around and went up the stairs.

Uncle David had apparently just made a pot of tea. Cup in hand, with feet propped on the ink-spotted desk, he had settled down for an hour of rare solitude. But the smile he gave to Hennie was genuine.

"Sit down, pour a cup for yourself. Sorry I've nothing else to offer, but I forgot to market yesterday. And so how are you?"

"Fine, Uncle David, fine."

"So, tell me what's going on in the family! I feel guilty, I've not seen your parents in more than a month. But I get so busy here, the days rush into each other." And through the open door, he glanced toward the little waiting room, in which the stiff chairs were lined up on all four sides. His sigh spoke of both weariness and satisfaction, here in his sanctuary, furnished as it was with a baby scale, a shelf of dusty textbooks, a yellowed human skull, medicines, bandages, and splints.

"So, tell me, how are they all?"

"The same. My parents still worry about Alfie. He's not doing well at school and says he won't go to college. He wants to make money instead."

"Leave him alone, then. He's a perfectly sound young man who knows where he wants to go. They'll never make a scholar out of him, don't they see that?"

"And Florence is moving. I saw the new house; it's lovely, right off Central Park West."

"Ah, yes, the Jewish Fifth Avenue. Well, good. That's what she wanted. It's nice to see people get what they want. And you, Hennie, are you getting what you want?"

"How does anybody know what he really wants, Uncle?"

"A Jewish reply! Answering a question with a question." He set the cup down. "Philosophically, you're correct. A large question, the aim of life—ah, most of us die without ever knowing that! But I'm talking about the small question, what you do with your life day by day and whether you are satisfied—more or less."

It pleased her that he should have so serious an interest in her. Yet, to a certain extent, she saw through his concern, for surely her parents must have talked about her, just as she had heard them talk about Alfie.

She began, "Well, you know I am happy with what I am doing. I feel I'm helping at the settlement—"

"Outside of the settlement," the old man interrupted.

"Oh, I read, I go to the library once a week. I must read three books a week, good ones. And I have been taking out books for Paul. You know what he said to me the other day? 'I wonder what my ancestors think of me when they look down from heaven.' Imagine a child of his age having a thought like that! He's a beautiful child. I think he'll be somebody unusual when he's grown."

The old man did not let her slide into evasions but forced her to answer directly. "Yes, yes, but we were talking about you, not Paul. What about your social life?"

She flushed. " 'Social life!' It's stupid, Uncle David! People trading invitations . . ." And she mocked, " 'Have you been asked to the so-and-so's? What! You haven't? What a tragedy! You could have shown off your new fur cape, your—' "

Again Uncle David interrupted. Interruption was

a strange habit for a man who was otherwise so courteous.

"I understand what you mean, I of all people. But it isn't entirely like that, Hennie. Don't sneer at all of it. It's not healthy to set yourself so apart." He spoke very gently. "Be honest, Hennie, you've re-treated from it for some reason that I don't understand. You make no effort. Is it possible that you don't feel pretty? Is that it?"

Your dress is correct, there are no pimples on your face, you are not disfigured; but you are awkward, your feet are awkward, your tongue is awkward, and you sit with the women when your dances are not taken.

"I don't know exactly," she murmured.

There is something one has or one doesn't have. Easy grace, that's what's lacking. Easy grace.

"You'll be a fine-looking woman, Hennie. It's too early yet to see it, but it's there. Some women mature late, that's all. Do you know," David said, leaning forward, carefully studying the wall behind Hennie's head, "do you know, you remind me so much of your grandmother Miriam? Her qualities seem to have skipped a generation. Your mother is not at all like her. That's not to say there's anything wrong with your mother," he added quickly.

"I know."

"She had endurance, Miriam. Strength. Bravery."

A rush of words, unplanned, came suddenly. "Speaking of bravery, Uncle David, I saw something stupendous a few weeks ago. I saw a man rescue a woman out of a fire. I'll never forget it. He climbed up on the cornice six floors above the street. It was horrible! And so wonderful! You should have seen it, you would not believe a man could do that. It was—he was offering his whole life for a stranger."

"Oh, I know who it was. I know him."

"Do you really? That's odd, I thought I recognized him on this street just a while ago when I came in."

"Daniel Roth! He was just here. I took care of his hands."

"His whole life," Hennie repeated with awe.

"He's a very unusual man."

She remembered something. "Daniel Roth . . . I thought I saw that name on the bulletin board at the settlement house. Daniel Roth to play the piano at our children's Thanksgiving festival. Do you suppose that's the same one?"

"Oh, yes, he plays piano pretty well and it's the kind of thing he would do. He's a teacher. Teaches high school science downtown here. Something of an inventor-scientist, too, keeps a little lab, lives in back of it or upstairs."

Tilting in the chair, Uncle David reached for his pipe. He struck a match, lit the pipe, puffed, took it out of his mouth and examined it with exasperating care while time ticked away.

He chuckled. "Oh, Dan's something special, all right! I've known him awhile. He's a fighter, a scrapper. Right now, he's gotten mixed up with tenement reform." He paused, reflecting for a minute, unaware of Hennie's rigid, impatient attention, with her hands clasped around her knees.

"Yes, yes, a scrapper. Carrying the fight to the legislature. Works with Lawrence Veiller, an interesting man, an aristocrat born with a strong conscience. Worked in a settlement house, like you. You've heard of Veiller and read Jacob Riis, I suppose?"

"I've read *How the Other Half Lives.*" But she did not want to hear about Riis or Veiller.

"Men like them, they looked out"—here Uncle David waved his hand toward the window—"and hated what they saw. You know, it's an outrage, Hennie, that they permit these dumbbell tenements, no courtyard, no light or air. But worse than that, fires, like that one the other day. Stairway right in the center, draws the fire up like a rocket; it shoots through the building, people don't stand a chance."

So he must have railed against slavery in the South. Youth, fired with indignation, burst for a moment out of the old shell, with its spotty skin and false teeth thick as earthenware plates; for a moment the eyes sparkled and Hennie, seeing what he had been, felt pity. Still, she wanted to bring the conversation back to Daniel Roth.

Uncle David's tongue was quicker.

"Yes, Hennie, yes, and you've seen the girls standing in doorways waiting for men. Oh, you're old enough for me to talk about those things, although your parents would be shocked and wouldn't forgive me. But they're life, and we must look life in the eye. When a girl is desperate to get out of a rotten hole and there's no other way, at least no other way she can see—" The clock struck the quarter hour again. He stood up, bustling. "Let me put these cups away. It won't do to have patients come in and see dirty cups. Oh, yes, we were talking about Dan, weren't we? I suppose it's not becoming of me to say, but—oh, it's in the family, and you'll

excuse a little boastfulness if I tell you he reminds
me of myself? Except that I was never that good-
looking. Of course, he's not observant; I doubt that
he ever goes to a synagogue, which is regrettable,
but still I mustn't hold that against him."

He talks too much, it's a symptom of old age,
Hennie thought lovingly as she went out. And she
thought, The Thanksgiving festival. I shall be there.

The settlement house lay in the center of an irregular quadrangle bounded by Houston Street, the
Bowery, Monroe Street and the East River. Five old
houses, once the homes of affluent merchants, had
been renovated into classrooms and workshops,
where cooking, dancing, sewing, debating, carpen-
try, civics, and the English language were taught.
An ample playground had swings and sandboxes.
The reception rooms were furnished with donations
from the homes of what were called "The uptown
ladies": solid black horsehair sofas, cuspidors and
overstuffed chairs, fire screens and glass-fronted
bookcases, kept locked to safeguard rows of gold-
stamped classics: Plutarch's *Lives* and *The Decline
and Fall of the Roman Empire.* Over the fireplace in
the central reception hall hung a large mirror
framed with gilded plaster nymphs and cherubs
holding a cornucopia brimming with grapes. It had
been an unwelcome wedding present to Florence
and Walter Werner.

On this evening, all the lights were on and the
building was crowded. The assembly hall had been
decorated with Pilgrim symbols, pumpkins and
dried speckled corn being part of the process by

which the shawled women, the bearded men, and
their children from the *stetls* and the Pale were to be
turned into Americans. On the stage, Governor
Bradford and Elder Brewster in black breeches and
high-crowned black cardboard hats declaimed with
dignity, bowing to Squantum and assorted squaws
in striped blankets and chains of beads. Massasoit
was a red-haired, ruddy-cheeked twelve-year-old
only a year out of Minsk, whom Hennie had
brought in less than that year to fluency.

The piano was on the far side of the stage from
where Hennie sat. The gas lamps were turned down
as he came in—for she saw that it was Dan Roth.

He made a slight bow and struck the keys. He
played the simple music with pleasure, looking up
now and then to nod encouragement to a faltering
child; he was enjoying himself.

Again she heard her own heart beat. And she sat
quite still with her hands folded on her dark silk lap,
thinking: I shall probably do nothing. The play will
end, he will leave, and I will go home.

There were speeches. Various ladies, wearing
pince-nez on chains, thanked one another for their
cooperation. Miss Demarest, the director, expressed
appreciation to all, and in her bird-voice thanked
Mr. Roth especially for his assistance with the music.

Everyone rose and those who could sang the non-
denominational Thanksgiving hymn "We Gather
Together to Ask the Lord's Blessing." They were
invited to the adjoining hall for coffee and cake. It
was over.

Still Hennie did not move. Someone tapped her
on the shoulder.

"What is it? Are you sick?" asked Olga.

The room was empty.

"I was only—only thinking," Hennie flushed.

Olga was disbelieving and concerned. "But of what, all alone in here?"

"That man who played the piano—my uncle knows him, I think. I was wondering how to talk to him, whether I should."

"How to talk? You open your mouth, you say 'How do you do, I think you're very good-looking and my name is—' "

Laughter eased the tension in Hennie's chest. "Olga, you make it so easy."

"It is easy. Seriously, if you want to talk to a person, just go and do it! The worst that can happen is that the person won't like you and if he doesn't seem to, then the devil with him, you'll try somebody else another time."

So Hennie got up and went inside to Daniel Roth. He was standing among the buxom uptown ladies in their good suits, with gold watches pinned to their lapels, and he looked as if he wanted to get away, just as he had when the reporters besieged him after the fire.

"You know my uncle," she said, "Dr. David Raphael. I'm Henrietta De Rivera."

"I certainly do! He's one of my favorite people." The smile was warm.

"He admires you too."

She did not know that her flush and her timid excitement were becoming. She would have liked to say something gay about the evening, but could think of nothing more, and was confused.

The uptown ladies, seeing that the guest of honor

was occupied, moved away. The evening was ending. Sleeping infants were awakened and hoisted onto their fathers' shoulders. Children were fastened into their coats and people were going home. But they were faceless and anonymous to Hennie. They fell away like shadows. She was alone in the room with Daniel Roth, who was looking down at her.

He said, astounding her, "Come out and have coffee with me, will you? It's early yet."

Such things do not happen. Extravagant fantasies do not come true. In a daze, she took the arm that he offered and they went out onto the street.

It was a mild fall night, a rare, brief reprieve of summer, with a milky sky over the rooftops. He led her toward East Broadway.

"We can have coffee there, or tea. Do you live near here?"

"No, near Washington Square."

"What brought you down here tonight, then?"

"I work at the settlement."

"One of those generous uptown ladies?"

"Not especially generous. I haven't any money to give. I just teach English to greenhorns."

"That wasn't nice of me."

"What wasn't?"

"My remark about uptown ladies. It was sarcastic. I'm sorry."

She had missed the sarcasm.

"What else do you do?"

"Sometimes I have a cooking class. Not that I'm so good, but I like to cook. I like to bake. It's relaxing."

"You need to relax?" He sounded amused, so that she thought she was being foolish.

"I guess so. Sometimes," she said lamely.

She was beginning to feel uncomfortable with her hand in the crook of his elbow, and made as if to remove it, but he tightened her arm against his side, imprisoning her hand.

"You don't mind taking my arm?"

"Oh, no, I didn't mean—"

Again she fell silent. If she had chattered, he told her later, it would have turned out differently between them.

"Your parents won't worry about your being out?"

"No. A group of us usually walk home together, so it's safe."

"You'll be safe with me, Henrietta."

"I'm called Hennie."

"That does suit you better. And I'm called Dan."

The darkening streets were still astir. A horse plodded back to the stables, pulling an empty wagon. Children spilled raucously over the stoops, and sewing machines whined like tired voices from open ground-floor windows.

"Listen," Dan said. "They're still working. I don't know where the strength comes from. Heat, cold, asthma, work and work."

"That's what Uncle David says."

"Yes, he knows. And cares. That's why he stays down here. It would surely be easier to move uptown."

"Is that why you teach here too?"

"Yes," Dan answered shortly.

East Broadway was light. Streetlamps glowed

across the wide avenue, while lamps in the tall windows of pleasant homes revealed quiet families sitting in parlors, or still at their supper tables.

Dan released Hennie's arm. "In here. It's a café. I'll bet you've never been in a café before, have you?"

"No." Nor out with a man, especially one to whom her parents had not introduced her.

"We'll find a quiet table; it's early enough. By midnight it will be so noisy, you won't even hear yourself think, let alone talk, what with the gypsy fiddler and all the Russians arguing."

They sat down. Wooden tables without cloths crowded close.

"But it's clean," Dan assured her, following her glance. "Or reasonably so."

A waiter brought two glasses of hot tea.

"You can have coffee instead. It's the Russian style to offer tea, and in a glass. You didn't know that, I think."

"I'd heard of it."

Her hands felt cold. She curved her palms around the hot glass, aware that he was regarding her with a studied gaze, and wondering what his thoughts were. Perhaps he regretted the impulsive invitation, given only out of politeness because she was Uncle David's niece. Looking down, she could see his hands resting on the table. She could see the forked vein in the wrist that was turned on its side. It seemed an intimate thing, that small blue vein.

Some men came in, speaking volubly in Yiddish. Dan pointed one out.

"He's an actor. He may be a star before long. This is a famous place for the Russian intelligentsia.

Journalists, poets, socialists—they all come here. The Orthodox have their own places. I go to all of them and belong to none. I like to observe, I'm curious."

"You're not Russian, then?"

"I was born in New York. In Yorkville, Eighty-fourth Street on Third Avenue. The Bohemian neighborhood, German-speaking."

Her fingers were playing now with a fork.

"You keep looking down," Dan said abruptly. "Why? Does it frighten you so to be looked at?"

"No. Why do you ask that?"

"Because you blush. Don't be ashamed. It's charming."

She looked up. "I can't help blushing. I hate it." Then something loosened inside her. "I saw you when you rescued the woman at the fire. I wanted to go up and tell you how wonderful it was."

"Why didn't you?"

"I suppose I'm timid. And I saw that you wanted to get away."

"You're right, I did. They'd have made a circus out of it, if I'd let them. Tell me, how old are you, Hennie?"

"Eighteen." She did not know whether that would seem too young to be interesting, or too old to be as inexperienced as she must seem.

"I'm twenty-four. You seem older than eighteen. You're very, very serious."

"I guess I am. It's one of my faults."

"Why, whoever tells you that?"

"Oh—people."

He considered. "Well, there's nothing wrong with that. Living is a serious enough business, God

knows. Especially living around here. Did you know
they found out later there were three babies left in
that building that day? They found the bodies after
the fire had burned itself out."

Hennie shuddered, and he went on, "I get in a
rage when I think of people getting rich out of owning such rat holes! I want to tear them all down or
blow them all up!" He broke off. "Excuse me. I
want to change the world. I make myself ridiculous."

She said gently, "You're not ridiculous at all."

"Yes, I am. I'm listening to myself talking too
much. That's odd, too, because I'm often criticized
for being too silent. But when I get excited about
something, then I don't know when to stop talking."

Florence taught: Always allow a man to talk
about himself. Encourage him. Men love that. And
feeling ashamed of using such a trick, Hennie said,
"I like to hear you. Tell me about yourself."

"There's nothing much to tell. Anyway, I
wouldn't know how to begin."

"At the beginning. Where you grew up."

He laughed. "Let's say I was surrounded by ci-
gars. The trash cans on the sidewalks were always
full of tobacco leaves. But my father wasn't a cigar
maker, he was a tailor. My mother was dead. I don't
remember her."

He stopped, as if the sudden memory had halted
him. She thought she saw, in the pained contraction
of his forehead, something more than a natural regret over a mother. He knew a fundamental melancholy. It surprised her that she could so quickly
recognize something of herself in a stranger, differ-

ent as they were, his face so mobile and hers so quiet.

"That's not all," she said, wanting to recall him from wherever he was.

"What else do you want me to tell you?"

"You could tell me what you wanted to be."

"Be! Well, there was a while there when I had some grandiose ideas about music. When I was a kid, my piano teacher used to praise me, so I began to have a silly vision of myself at a concert grand, you know, dressed in white tie and tails—me, in a tailcoat! Taking bows, with the audience on its feet, going wild." He frowned. "Anyway, I got over that. Well, I didn't want to be a lawyer—all that haggling and arguing—and, unlike half the boys in the neighborhood, I didn't want to be a doctor, either. But I did like science. I did chores in a chemistry lab one summer and that decided me. So I went to City College and now I'm a science teacher." He made a small, embarrassed grimace. "I do my little experiments on the side."

"What do you do?"

It was working, Florence was right. A man wanted to talk about himself.

"You've heard of Charles Brush?"

"I'm afraid I haven't."

"He developed the carbon arc light. I like to study things like that and the power of electrical resonance and . . . oh, many things . . . it's hard to explain."

"Don't try. You might as well talk to me in Bulgarian."

He laughed. "Well, it's just that I admire men who have ideas, men like Edison and Bell—you know. I've got notebooks filled with ideas, most of them not much use, probably. Though I did invent something pretty good once. . . . I'm boring you."

"Of course you're not! What was the invention?"

"It was an electric arc lamp that could burn longer than the old ones."

"What happened to it?"

"It's being manufactured. I got five hundred dollars for it. A friend of mine has a cousin, a lawyer, and he sold it for me. The five hundred came in handy right then, helped make my father's dying a little more comfortable." Dan's jaw tightened. Then he turned to her with an apologetic smile. "I still have crazy dreams that I'll discover something marvelous, like sending messages around the world by air, or maybe using electrical machines to diagnose disease. Crazy, you know. Who am I, after all?"

"It's not crazy. You're only twenty-four. You can't tell yet what you'll do."

"It's no matter if I never do. At least I can do some good by teaching, I hope. There's so much intelligence here on these streets, waiting to be unlocked and set free! It would be easier, though, one could do so much more in the school if the life outside were better. That's where science comes in, science and socialism."

"You're not a socialist!" Hennie had never met an actual socialist.

"My sentiments are. Not officially. I don't care about politics, which would shock the political types at these tables. I'm not with any party. I just like to get out and try to do things that need doing."

"You really do remind me of Uncle David."

"Oh-ho, that's a real compliment! I can't begin to

tell you what I think of him. Honest, simple, good. You know, sometimes I think he has second sight, that man, and can read your mind. Well, I don't actually mean that, but he is rare, that you have to say. Rare."

"I think so too. In the family, you know," Hennie said shyly, "they think he's awfully odd. You should hear the discussions at our house! My father and my sister's husband always vote Republican, you see. They think Uncle David's a wild-eyed radical, but I don't find him so."

"Then your family must find you odd, too, and radical?"

"I think they do. They love me, but I think they do."

"Is it lonely for you in your house, then? I imagine it must be."

"Yes. A little."

They looked candidly at one another. They made solemn appraisal, eye to eye. The contact must have lasted a minute, a long time for eyes to meet without turning away. And Hennie had an extraordinary sense of startling reality, sharp and clear, as if she had just waked up to that reality, which made trivial and insignificant whatever she had known until then.

Dan pushed his chair back. "Come," he said, "it's late, and I don't want your parents to be furious that I kept you out."

The night had deepened. It was beautiful, with fantastic dark blue clouds in the pale sky, a night to walk and walk and not go home. Here and there, at the street corners, a knot of youths jostled and smoked wherever the light from a candy store fanned out onto the sidewalk. On the top step of a meeting hall an orator was exhorting a small crowd.

"Christian mission to the Jews," Dan remarked.

"Let's stop, it should be interesting."

"No." Dan was firm. He led her by the elbow. "It can get very nasty. There's always somebody who's roused to fury one way or the other. I wouldn't want you to be there. As for me, I never could understand all this passion about religion. A lot of foolishness, don't you think so?"

"No." No "tricks" anymore, nothing but the truth.

He asked her curiously, "You're a believer, then?"

"Yes . . . there has to be something." She looked up. The clouds were dispersing, opening the wide sky to a million stars. "All of that, and we down here, can't be accidents. Beethoven, or men like your Edison, can't be just accidents."

He was looking down at her now, paying gentle attention to her; the look on his face, the lovely night, the solemn subject, all filled her.

"Are you observant, then, Hennie?"

"Yes, but not like Uncle David. He's Orthodox. We go to Temple Emanu-El."

"I've left all that behind me, but if ever I were to be observant, I'd have to be Orthodox."

They had reached the entrance of Hennie's building. A wind rose, rustling the last leaves from the trees. Dan looked up and down the street.

"I wonder," he said slowly, "how anyone can believe in Him. Such misery. And the worst of all are the wars."

"Those are not God's fault, but ours," she said.

"You should talk to Uncle David. You admire him so much."

"I do, I do. Yes, it's a good thing to be a believer —if one can. And it suits you, Hennie." He turned her face up to the light. "Such a kind face. And lovely eyes, grave eyes. I want to see you again. May I?"

There was such a catch in her throat that she could only nod.

"I shall call on your parents. They will expect that. Good night then, Hennie."

She fled upstairs. Tears came to her eyes, the softest, most bewildering tears.

He is like nobody else in all the world.

"Do you remember when we talked about Dan Roth, Uncle David? Well, I've met him. It was two weeks ago when he came to the Thanksgiving festival, and I've seen him twice since then. We went to the Aquarium and to Central Park last Sunday." She heard her voice, faster and higher in pitch than usual.

The old man's untidy eyebrows rose. "He came to call on you? Met your parents?"

"Of course. How else would I get to go walking out with him?"

"Whatever did they talk about?"

"Oh, things. Nothing much, just the usual polite things."

But there had been questions, leading questions, and it had all come out, about the tailor father, and the struggle, and teaching school. Angelique had

asked the most questions, so courteous always, with
the small smile and the nodding head.

And Dan had been the same, answering with the
same small smiles and nods, a proper minuet of
nodding heads, so that you would have thought
they must be despising each other, and yet neither,
afterward, had said anything except "He's an intelligent young man" and "Your parents are gracious
people."

"He has invited me to the opera. I don't think
Mama wants me to go, but she can't very well refuse, since he invited me in her presence."

Uncle David took the pipe out of his mouth.
"What you're telling me is that your parents—your
mother—didn't like him."

"Of course they would prefer someone like Walter."

It was what they had not said after Dan had left,
the words they had not used that mattered: family
background, meaning, at bottom, money. Money
for things to handle and hold, as when Angelique
moves the candelabra after dinner or fingers her
pearls.

"They do make quite a contrast, don't they, Daniel Roth and my brother-in-law?"

Uncle David's response was a surprise. "There is,
after all, nothing that wrong about Walter Werner."

"I didn't mean that there was, but I do prefer
Dan's sort of man."

"Oh, I agree. Yet things—people—are not all that
simple."

The remark was trite, a statement of the obvious.
Still, there was a strange ring to it.

* * *

They went to hear *Rigoletto*. Florence and Walter, undoubtedly at Angelique's instigation, went with them. Walter had insisted on providing the four seats in the fifth row at the center.

"I sit in the top balcony, when I don't stand," Dan remarked.

Above them, the Diamond Horseshoe glittered and spangled; there was much back-and-forth motion up there, visits among the boxes, late arrivals and second-act departures.

"That's Mrs. Astor," Florence said, offering her opera glasses to view a large, bejeweled lady.

Dan whispered, "Now I know where the expression 'Astor's pet horse' comes from."

Hennie laughed and was grateful that he had whispered. The remark would have been a dreadful affront to Florence, for whom the Mrs. Astors of the world were objects of veneration.

Later, Walter took them all to supper at Delmonico's. Although Hennie had at first refused to borrow her sister's evening cloak, she was now relieved that her mother had made her accept it, for the room was a flower garden of satins and velvets, and of white shoulders belonging to women so exquisite, it was hard not to stare. Hennie had been there only twice before.

"Well, what do you think of it?" Walter asked. He had a paternal manner toward Hennie. His eyes, magnified by his glasses, were penetrating.

Disliking him, she blurted, "I'm not sure what I think, Walter. It doesn't seem quite real to me."

And he had laughed, with that cool, not un-

friendly laugh, the head tilted, considering her as
though she had said something witty.

And she went on—why did she persist?—"Oh,
it's beautiful, but it's like a play, do you see what I
mean, as if everyone were acting a part. A play or a
ceremony."

"Now that," Florence said, irked, but certainly
not as sharp-toned as she would have been if Dan,
the outsider, had not been there, "that is really nonsense, Hennie."

Dan came to Hennie's defense. "I understand exactly what Hennie means by 'unreal.' Yes, I do."
And he looked around. The lofty space was filled
with animation: laughter, swirling dresses, popping
champagne corks, scurrying waiters, lavish furs
draped on the backs of chairs. He continued slowly,
"There's a sense of true value, of truth worth,
among the workers. There's so much waste here,
more food than can be eaten, more and too much of
everything. I have been determined all my life never
to fall into the trap of wanting luxury. Once you
begin, there's no end to what you will find necessary, even when you don't deserve it."

His head went up as he said it. There was not a
man in the room to compare with him. Hennie had
not failed to notice the women who had glanced at
Dan when he walked in, their glances lingering an
extra fraction of a second. People looked at him, not
at her. And for an instant something cold fell in her
chest, a weight, cold and heavy, so that she had to
force herself to raise it.

"You must remember," Walter admonished, "that
these people worked for what they have, or their

parents or grandparents did. And they do provide employment. They keep the country moving."

Dan was stubborn. "Spending on armaments, that's what really keeps the country moving, as you put it."

"You don't think we should be armed?" asked Walter.

And Hennie thought, as she felt an accumulating tension, why are we talking like this?

"We are spending like madmen," Dan said. "Still, there are hopeful signs." He went on, "That a blind despot like the Czar should call for a limitation of armaments is hopeful."

The dialogue was a ball, thrown and immediately returned.

Walter replied, "I wouldn't place too much hope in that. I don't trust them in Europe, any of them."

"Without some trust in the good intentions of one's fellow man there can be no future."

"If we are all to disarm, just as we are, that must mean everyone is satisfied with things as they are. Do you suppose France is content to let Germany keep Alsace-Lorraine? In my opinion, Germany has no right to it."

When Dan raised his eyebrows, Walter laughed, a slight superior laugh.

"Do I surprise you? You must be thinking that because my parents are German-born, I am a Germanophile? No, I assure you. I am of another generation."

"German, French, or whatnot, it makes no difference. They are all murdering thieves."

Dan's voice, although low, resounded. People at

the adjacent table looked, and looked away. And Dan continued.

"Yes, the common man is taxed to pay for their monstrous weapons, advanced models, year after year, with money that could be used for electrification, clean power, to take the load off the human back. I myself, in my small way, have been working on—" He stopped. "I'm sorry. This isn't the time or place."

But Walter insisted, "You have to have weapons." His neat mouth firmed. "It's naive to think otherwise. Would you put your life's savings on the table and leave the front door open?"

"You have to make a beginning," Dan responded.

Now Florence intervened. "Mr. Roth is right, Walter. It isn't the time for all this serious talk. We've come to enjoy ourselves."

"Call me Dan. And scold me. I began it."

"I will call you Dan, but I will not scold you." Florence smiled charmingly. "I think you have a very interesting point of view, and I'd like to hear more sometime. But right now, I don't mind telling you, I'm starved. Shall we order?"

Let us have no rough edges. Smooth. Smooth. She was right to do that, Hennie knew. But Dan was right too.

Water and oil don't mix. They would never like each other, any of them.

The winter blossomed. The ice-cold sky reflected its pure blue in the snow meadows of Central Park, and the tinkling bells of jolly sleighs sounded in the streets, while snow sprayed under the runners. At

the St. Nicholas Rink, Hennie, in new striped
woolen stockings, whirled with Dan: a couple together, striding and sliding in rhythm.

Oh, enchanted city! Every passerby smiled approval. The man on the freezing corner, who sold a
flower for Hennie's lapel, handed it over as if it were
a gift. At the settlement, her most rowdy, unmanageable children were really only normal rascals, after all. People were so friendly, so good. One could
love everyone.

"It shows on your face," Olga said one evening,
after an English class.

"What shows?" Hennie pretended not to understand, but she knew quite well; she had told Olga,
having had to tell someone, and this girl—with the
poor thin, white-faced young husband bent all day
over a sewing machine—knew about love.

At night, Hennie sat at her window and dreamed.
She had such longing for him, for his thick hair,
shining as animal fur, for his sad mouth, his
rounded eyelids, his beautiful hands. Such longing.

"It's been a long time since you were here," Uncle
David said. "What have you been doing?"

She wanted to seem casual. "I've been seeing your
friend Daniel Roth."

"Oh? Where do you go together?"

"Walking. Skating. We went to the opera with
Florence and Walter. Heard *Rigoletto*. It was marvelous."

"Ah, yes . . . and how did it work out?"

Uncle David had a way of fixing you with his
gaze, demanding an honest answer. So, dropping

the careless manner, she replied, "Walter insisted on buying the seats and Dan didn't like that very much."

"I should imagine not. He's independent, if he's anything at all."

Uncle David paused, looking thoughtful. In a moment he would fumble with the pipe, preparing what he had to say. He struck a match and blew it out.

"Yes, yes, it's a strange business, this man-woman thing. Making a choice, I mean. How does one ever know? And one's whole life is in the balance." He struck another match, lit the pipe, puffed, and removed the pipe. "Maybe that's why I never married. My sister, your grandmother, how much do you remember of her, Hennie?"

You never knew what unexpected direction a conversation with Uncle David might take. He could be exasperating.

"Not much. She used to sing a German song when I was very little: 'Du Bist wie eine Blume.' "

" 'You Are Like a Flower.' She remembered that from her own childhood. Yes, a remarkable woman. She had tremendous courage, as I always tell you."

And I don't need to hear it again, Hennie thought.

"Maybe you didn't know she had made the wrong marriage. She lived in misery with your grandfather for years."

"I didn't know."

"Well, I don't suppose there's much use in resurrecting these things. It's just that sometimes one remembers, and it can be painful to remember."

Her mind was filled with today, the cold, glittering afternoon, and he was talking about people long dead. His tone was rueful, which she did not want, because it did not match the energy within her.

The old man began to clean his pen on a rag. His forehead was thoughtful; his hands went round and round. After a minute or two he remarked, "I suppose you find him very handsome?"

She was startled. "Who?"

"Why, Roth of course, who else? You didn't think I meant Walter Werner, did you?"

"Well, you were talking about my grandfather." She laughed, then answered lightly, "Oh, yes, don't you think so too?"

"I do. And so does every woman who comes in sight of him, Hennie."

"What can you mean?"

"What I say. All the women run after him. I've known him a while, you see, and I—"

"Am I running after him?" Hennie's face prickled with the sudden heat of an intense blush. "Do you really think I would run after anyone, Uncle David?"

"No, you're not bold enough, my dear."

Not bold. But tenacious, Papa says. You never give up, in your quiet way.

"Other women are bold enough, though, Hennie. And that's the trouble."

"I don't know what you're trying to tell me, Uncle David." Something hardened in her. Fear or anger, or both.

"He has too much charm for his own good. Some people are born like that. It's as if they had a magnet in them."

The glitter of light beyond the window hurt her eyes. She moved the chair.

"I don't see what difference all that makes," she said.

Don't you? Don't you?

"What if other women look at him? He can't help that, can he?"

Again there was that slow business with the pipe. He does that because he has to think of an answer. And she waited.

"You see how it is, Hennie. There are men who can't resist. They can't be faithful to one woman. Yes, they love their wives, but still they can't resist."

"And you think . . ." Her voice was queer, falsetto. "You think Dan is like that?"

"Yes, I do. Don't go falling in love with him, Hennie. Please don't."

She was silent, stricken, disbelieving.

"Are you in love with him, Hennie?"

She was still silent.

"He won't do for you. I must tell you. Listen to me, Hennie, my dear. He loves women too much. That's his failing."

"After all the fine things you said about him!"

"Yes, and they were all true. But what I'm telling you now is true too."

"Now you tell me! Why just now?"

"I never thought before that it would be necessary."

She despised him, sitting there with his pipe and his pen and his skeleton on the shelf. He was old, and old people hated the young when they looked at them and realized what they had missed, what it was now too late for them to have. . . .

"I see that you're angry at me."

"I am. You have no right. You're spoiling . . . spoiling," she stammered.

"I don't want you to be hurt, that's all," Uncle David said gently.

"I won't be hurt. Or is there something else you're not telling me?"

That Dan had committed some crime . . . no, no, impossible.

"There's nothing more, I swear, but what I've said. Believe me, Hennie, I'm telling you something your mother wouldn't tell you. She wouldn't think it 'nice.' But I know that an unfaithful husband would break your heart. There are many women who can live with that, but I don't think you could." The old man gave her a smile, which she did not return. "Let me not make too much of this, though. A man comes to call a few times . . . that doesn't mean you'll be married. I only wanted to warn you. No harm done, I hope."

She would not look at him. How dare he? A man was falling in love with her, she was certain of it. She drew herself up, smoothing her skirt; the womanly gesture reassured her.

Old man, old man, what do you know?

Oh, the damp first air of spring, the damp soft air! The Italian organ-grinder played "Santa Lucia" with passionate longing, grinding it out from one street into the next. Girls played hopscotch and boys shot marbles on the sidewalks. Dan and Hennie rode a tandem bicycle, singing, through Central

Park. They walked across the Brooklyn Bridge and watched the sailing ships come up the river.

"Imagine! Around the Horn from China!" Hennie cried.

Dark yellow men on the deck, men in miniature from where they stood far above in the wind on the bridge, were hauling rope. She turned to face Dan.

"What does it make you think of? Tea? Silk? Red lacquer?"

He bent down to her. Tall as he was, he always had to lean down. "Of you. I can see myself in your eyes. Did you know they've got green in them?"

"Dan! They're brown."

Staring back into his eyes, she could see herself reflected. She was easy with him now; it seemed impossible that she could ever have been wary. He had done that for her.

"But there's green all the same," he insisted. "Not like any other eyes I've ever seen. You're not like any girl I've ever known, either."

She countered cheerfully. "How many have you known?"

Banter, light and happy, while the heart pounds.

"Oh, dozens. Hundreds, maybe. No, seriously, Hennie, you're different from all of them. I'm in love with you. You know that, don't you?"

She wanted to prolong the marvel of suspense. "You hardly know me!"

"Four months, almost. That's long enough. Anyway, I know my own mind. The question is, do you?"

"Do I—"

"Know your own mind? Love me?"

The wind almost bore her faint voice away.

"I love you."

"Darling Hennie." His lips moved on her cheek. "We'll have good years together, a good life. Darling Hennie."

How wrong you were, Uncle David.

"You are seeing so much of Daniel Roth," Angelique remarked one day.

"Not just of him! I told you, there are always seven or eight of us together when we go skating or riding. Friends of his, other teachers." She elaborated. "They're a sort of club—for cycling—and sports."

Her mother looked at her doubtfully. "Well, of course, I know you wouldn't go about with any young man unchaperoned."

Dan was not used to chaperonage. Among East Side intellectuals, teachers, and writers, that sort of thing was ridiculed. So it became necessary for her to lie at home.

Oh, if they knew what was going on! She thought of that rent-strike meeting at which he had spoken with such passionate and righteous conviction, a hero on the platform. Standing there in the crowd, looking up at him, she'd had a flash, an incongruous picture of her parents and herself at the dinner table in Florence's house: the timid maid passing the platters, Walter's pink-shaven cheeks above the stiff collar, an array of silver forks.

She had, of course, known her people in the classroom, but had had to imagine where they lived. Now she saw.

"The rent for those foul holes is twelve dollars a

month," Dan told her. "Sure, they get a lodger who pays sixty-five cents a week, but bread is fifteen cents a day at least, milk four cents a quart, a pound of meat twelve cents. No wonder they eat so many pickles. They're cheap and they fill you up."

She came to know every miserable street. Her sharpened vision picked out details that had once been only a blur. Listening to Dan, she felt a new rise of surging, painful indignation. Strange that she had perhaps heard the same words often enough in the mouth of Uncle David, but never with this immediacy.

"It's like Zola," she observed.

"You've read Zola? That's pretty daring for a girl your age." He spoke with admiration.

They walked through Bottle Alley onto Mulberry Street. Rags blew on the clotheslines overhead; a hawker offered a worn coat for fifty cents; on a plank laid across two ash barrels, piles of fish lay rotting in the sun, as spring warmed into summer. Here no organ-grinders played, for there was no one to throw pennies to them.

"Look," Dan said, "at that boy reading there on the stoop. There's no place inside for him to do his schoolwork. Frustrating. I am frustrated as a teacher."

Riding the Second Avenue elevated, they could see into the second-floor rooms where the "sweaters" worked.

"Like animals in stalls," Dan said. "Tubercular old men, and children who soon will be, cooped up together. See the belt on your dress?"

Hennie looked down at the narrow belt.

"It came from a place like that. Somebody working ten or twelve hours a day for five dollars a week or less made it."

"I know. I have a friend, Olga . . ."

Oh, it was wrong! Wrong! And Mama complains that it's not easy to be poor, as if she had any idea what being poor is.

Between Grand Street and East Broadway lay a scrap of park, gray cement between the gray tenements, with some benches under a scrawny tree that drooped in the heat of fading summer. They sat for a while without speaking. Dan looked off into the distance. She wondered what he could be seeing in that arid place.

"I'm proud of you, Dan," she said, suddenly very moved.

"Proud? What have I done? I've done nothing yet."

He took her hand. The warmth of their two hands sent soft waves sweeping through her body. She felt the warmth of her own hair on her neck, was aware of her breasts, and thought of their bodies entwined.

"We've known each other almost a year," she said. "It seems longer."

The sky dimmed. Dan pulled his hand away.

"It's late. We can't just keep sitting here," he said, almost angrily.

"Why not? It's peaceful."

"Because. Your parents will be asking questions."

"I don't care."

"You don't mean that. There's no sense looking for trouble."

They walked slowly, lingering. The streets were

emptying, children were called in, horses clumped back to the stables.

Hennie pointed. "That's your street, isn't it?"

"Yes." After a moment, Dan said, "I'd ask you in . . . but I have the lab in back of a machine shop, and a room upstairs . . . it's a mess."

She was silent.

"The room is, I mean. The lab I keep spick-and-span. Couldn't work otherwise."

Her heart was heavy and despondent, with all the warm glow cooled. Yet she had to say something; what she said must be neutral and light.

"You know, I've never really understood what you do in the lab."

"Oh, one thing and another, as the ideas come."

"I don't even know what electricity is!"

"Don't let that worry you. Nobody knows what it is. We can use it, make transformers and generators, do things with it, but what it is . . ." He shrugged. "If you're religious, you can say God made it. Otherwise, you can just say it's some sort of energy rushing around the universe, and let it go at that."

She thought: As if I really care about electricity or whether God made it or anything except—what I care about.

They arrived at her house. He stood looking at her.

"I wish we could go home together," he said. "I'm so sick of always leaving you here. Kissing you quickly before anyone sees, walking home alone. It's such a waste. I wish we could be in a room together with a closed door."

She wanted to ask: "Yes, when?" But she kept still. Her eyes filled with quick tears.

"It's only money. I'm afraid of the future, of having nothing for you. Every damned thing is money," he said bitterly. "Even love costs money in this damned world."

She wanted to shut his words out. Like a key, they opened a door onto a gloomy space into which she did not want to look.

"We'll find a way," she said. "I'm sure we will."

Alfie came into her room. Thirteen now, he was becoming a person, a *Mensch,* as the Germans said. Sometimes, especially when their parents were out of the house, he would wander into her room and lie on the floor on his stomach, doing homework while she read. He could say surprising things, too, showing a power of observation with which his parents did not credit him.

"I heard Mama and Pa talking about you last Sunday," he informed her.

Brushing her hair, she could see him in the mirror. He had given himself an expression of importance.

"Mama wants Pa to speak up to you."

"Speak up? About what?" She turned quickly, knowing.

"You know what. About Dan."

"Mr. Roth, you mean. You're not grown up enough to call him Dan."

Why did she chastise the boy? You kill the messenger who brings the bad news, that's why.

"Aw," he said, "I can call him Dan if I want to. Don't you want to hear what they said? Then I won't tell you."

"I'm sorry, Alfie. Tell me, please."

Mollified, he explained, "Well, Pa said, 'No, that's a foolish tactic. Let the thing wear itself out,' or something like that. And he said, 'The girl's bewitched, anybody can see it.' And he said, 'Nothing will probably come of it anyway.' And Mama said, 'Yes, but it's been a year, he's wasting her time.'"

"Anything else?"

"Yes. Mama said you really have been looking so much prettier lately. And she said that Florence could introduce you to lots of people, but you always say no. Do you?"

"I suppose I do."

She felt a weakness, an inner trembling. Soon they would really begin to press her for an explanation.

Alfie's humorous eyes crinkled with curiosity. "Because you're in love, that's why. You let him kiss you, I'll bet." And he gave his sputtering laugh.

He is thinking about what comes after kissing, just as I do.

"Alfie! Don't be fresh."

"I don't care if you kiss him, you know. I like him. He's smart. I hate school, but I wouldn't mind being in his class, you know?"

"He is very smart. He invented something, some kind of light, or tube or something that burns longer than they ever did before."

"Really? He must be rich, then."

"Oh, no, he got almost nothing for it."

"Then he was cheated. He shouldn't have sold outright. An income is what you want."

"Alfie, I don't mean to insult you, but you don't

know anything about business. You're only thirteen."

"A ten-year-old would know better than that!"

"Well, anyway, Dan doesn't do these things for money. He does them for the pleasure, for curiosity about the way the world works. He's a true scientist."

"You going to marry him, Hennie?"

She had a need to talk about what had filled her all these months with such joy and such expectancy.

"I want to trust you, Alfie. Can I trust you? I've not told anyone."

He was pleased. "Not Florence?"

"No. Only you. Because I know you won't tell till I'm ready."

"I won't tell. Are you going to marry him, then?"

"Yes," she said softly.

"When?"

"I don't know . . . soon."

There was deep loneliness in the room after Alfie went out, a sadness deeper than the melancholy of separation, because tonight for the first time it was tinged with fear. She tried to comfort herself with sleep, but sleep only brought a terrifying dream. Dan was standing beside her in some place with a vaulted ceiling, full of crashing music and echoes; he was opening his lips, saying something she could not hear; he had to repeat it over and over before she understood.

"I will never marry you, Hennie," he was saying, while behind his shoulder Uncle David nodded mournfully and wisely.

2

Hennie put the book away. It was no use trying to concentrate. Her eyes, looking into the farthest distance, came to rest on the fringe of spring-green leafage that screened the stone gleam of the mansions on Fifth Avenue, across the park. The weather was fine and fresh; a spirited breeze rippled through the shrubbery; everything was new and restless and beautiful, making you want everything. She had a feeling of panic: This was all being wasted. Days like this were slipping by, and she was doing nothing with them.

People passed. An old man and his wife walked arm in arm, with their homely faces turned to the sun. Big dirty boys jostled and shoved, on the way home from school; raucous and laughing, one doubled over, holding his stomach.

On the opposite bench sat a young woman; it was plain, in spite of her concealing, modest coat, that she was expecting a baby.

She's not much older than I am, Hennie thought. Perhaps not older at all, and from what I can see of her face when she looks up from the magazine, she's no beauty.

Yet someone wanted her enough to spend the rest of his life with her, and now there would be a child. . . . A dreamy smile touched the young woman's mouth. She was thinking of the child. No, she was thinking of the man who had given her the child. . . .

A life made out of two. Of Dan and me. Hennie was shaken. Longing and terror that it might never be—these shook her. And in her mind's eye, closing her seeing eyes, she saw Dan's dark head; saw, too, a baby's head, damp and fuzzy; she felt the baby, warm, curved, curling on her shoulder . . .

"I'm back, Aunt Hennie!"

She opened her eyes. Paul sat on his little bicycle with the pride of a conqueror.

"Well, you had a long ride, didn't you? It's time to go home, you know. Time for your piano lesson."

"I don't want to play piano," Paul protested.

"Ah, but it will be fun to know how when you grow up," she said. "I have a friend who plays just beautifully."

"I know! It's Dan!"

"Dan? You must call him Mr. Roth."

"He said I could call him Dan."

"When did he say that?"

"The time we met him here in the park, near the lake, and he took me rowing."

That had been one Sunday afternoon last year. Now the second year was well along.

"Where does Dan live?"

"Oh, far from here. Downtown."

"Let's go to his house."

"But I told you we have to go home."

"Then take me to his house next time."

"Well . . . we can't. He hasn't got a house."

"Everybody has a house!" Paul cried scornfully.

"No, everybody hasn't. Not big enough for company, I mean."

"Oh, you mean like Grandma's house, where you live? All flat, with no stairs?"

"Much smaller than that."

"I like Grandma's elevator, except the ride's not long enough. I'd like to be an elevator man when I grow up; then I could ride up and down as much as I wanted."

"Oh, yes, that would be lovely!"

At the corner of the street they could see halfway down the block; trunks were being carried up from the areaway of the Werners' house and loaded onto a wagon.

"Look, Paul, there go your things on the way to the mountains! Aren't you excited?"

"Yes, and we're taking the canary and the cook's cat, too, this year, Mother promised. They can ride all the way in the train, just the way we do."

Florence was at the front door as the wagon departed.

"What a mess it is going away," she sighed. "Such a rush! All this furniture to be covered and the windows boarded up for the summer. And the seamstress is still upstairs working on my summer dresses, with only two more weeks to go. I don't know what I'll do if she doesn't finish them. Well, come in, sit down, you must be exhausted."

"No, we had a nice time, Paul and I. It's a lovely day."

The hall was somber. The stained-glass window next to the door turned the outdoor light to a dreary mauve, spilling it over the golden oak woodwork and the fleur-de-lis wallpaper.

In the parlor, more stained glass in an enormous chandelier laid another gloom, wine-colored this time, over the sepia photographs of Michelangelo's *Moses* and Rembrandt's *Night Watch*. In front of the sofa, the tea wagon stood ready.

"I want cake," Paul said immediately.

"It's time for your piano lesson in fifteen minutes," Florence objected. "Go up and wash your hands, dear. You may have cake after supper."

"I'm afraid I promised him some on the way home," Hennie said meekly.

"Oh dear, you'll spoil the child. Well, all right, then, take a chocolate cookie, it won't make so many crumbs, and go upstairs and ask Mary or Sheila to wash your hands. That's a good boy.

"Yes, you will spoil him," Florence repeated when he had left the room.

"I don't mean to. It would be hard to 'spoil' Paul anyway. He's far too intelligent for that."

Florence looked at her. "You should have a dozen children, you're the type."

Hennie gave the expected modest smile. A sudden physical weakness hit her, so that her hand, accepting the teacup, trembled. The airless room, with its potted palm and its "Oriental nook" under the striped canopy, was stifling. She felt like crying and fought the first gathering of tears by straining her eyes toward the hall, toward the stuffed peacock on the newel post.

It was fortunate that the room was so dark.

"You really should come to the Adirondack place with us, Hennie. With Alfie going, it will be so nice. Why don't you?" Florence's hand fondled the arm of a new chair; it had mother-of-pearl inlay; it must feel slick and expensive.

"It's awfully far" was all Hennie could think to answer.

"Nonsense! What difference does that make? You'll sleep on the train and in the morning, there you'll be at the lake. You can't believe how beautiful it is, wild and beautiful. At night the loons call, and everything smells of pine, even your blankets. You'd love all that."

Why is she so insistent? Why should it matter whether I go or not? But I do know why. And she knows I know.

"Walter's parents are so hospitable, they'll make you at home right away. But you've been at their place in Elberon, so you know how they are. Except this is so much nicer, even though I admit Elberon is convenient, with Walter commuting to work by ferry; only, this summer they want us to spend a month with them in the mountains. They're really so good to us. I'm lucky to have in-laws like them. I pray you'll be as lucky, Hennie."

Yes, Hennie thought, I believe she does pray for me.

Security and satisfaction had softened Florence. The nervous impatience that Hennie remembered had come, very likely, from anxiety about her future; it had vanished entirely in the years of her marriage.

"Do come, Hennie!" Florence looked kindly at her sister. "If you don't, you'll only have to argue your way out of two weeks at some boring mountain hotel with Pa and Mama. Two weeks in a rocking chair on a veranda. How I always hated it! Those huge, shingled piles with turrets and miles of corridors and old people doing nothing all day but sitting and eating and then sitting some more."

Hennie collected herself. "I'm so busy at the settlement right now, you see. I've started a cooking class, did I tell you? And I hate to just abandon it in the middle."

Florence jumped up and went to the little desk between the front windows.

"That reminds me, I almost forgot! Walter left a check for the settlement, for you to give in your name."

"Oh, thank him for me. No, I will write to him myself!" Hennie cried, and felt ashamed of her mental image of Walter, that *stick,* with his bowler hat and spats. "It's so generous of him! Five hundred dollars!"

"Walter is generous," Florence said primly. "The Germans are, you know, even though Mama still likes to look down on them. But the Germans have a conscience, they know what anti-Semitism is. People like the De Riveras have been in America so long—Sons of the American Revolution, the Knickerbocker Club and all—that they've forgotten. Of course," she continued with high amusement, "now that the Germans have gotten rich, they are socially acceptable."

Hennie folded the check into a neat square and put it in her purse, repeating, "It's so good of Walter."

"Well, he admires your work. Bringing these peo-

ple into American life, making them Americans of
Jewish faith. The sooner they lose their foreign
ways, the better for them and for us all, Walter be-
lieves." Florence was complacent.

What are we doing? Two sisters talking generali-
ties, concealing what is really on our minds.

Florence poured another cup of tea and stirred it.
Round and round went the pretty spoon. After a
minute she said lightly, "I read in the paper that
Lucille Marks is being married. Isn't she the Marks
girl you went to school with?"

"No. Her sister, Annie."

"Somebody named Dreyfuss. A graduate of Har-
vard Law. I wonder if that's the Boston Dreyfuss
my friend Hilda knows? I must ask."

Florence had almost total recall of the social columns. Now she paused, studied the teaspoon, and
finally, having made a decision, looked up frankly at
her sister.

"You won't go away because of Daniel."

Hennie, forcing herself to meet Florence's gaze,
was surprised to see, not the challenge she had expected, but a rather soft concern.

"I guess so," she said, beguiled into admission.

"What's happening, Hennie? I don't want to pry,
honestly I don't. But I've had a hard time keeping
Mama from exploding. She doesn't understand
what's going on."

" 'Going on!' Good heavens, I've known him a
little more than a year—"

"Almost two, dear."

"Do they want marriage on sight?"

"Hennie—they don't want you to marry him at

all. That's what they're worried about. You must see that."

"Then what do they want? Him to propose and me to refuse him?"

"They suspect you're seeing more of him secretly than you admit to, but they can't prove it, and that's why they haven't really raised the roof."

"I don't see him all that much. I do run into him at the settlement. There's nothing wrong with that, is there? He's been giving free piano lessons to a few of my children."

"Very commendable of him." Florence added quietly, "You have also been meeting him in Central Park, haven't you? Paul said something. And Walter saw you once on his way home from his parents' house."

Hennie flushed. "Well? What if we did meet a couple of times in the park? One would think he had planned to—to attack me there."

"Hennie! What an awful thing to say! You shock me! But just listen to me and don't be angry. I'm only trying to help you."

"You don't like him, either. Don't deny it. It won't be any use, because I know you don't."

"I've been as nice to him as anyone could be, the few times I've been with him, and so has Walter. You can't say we haven't been."

"Yes, but he's not your style."

Florence did not reply at once. Then, laying her hand on her sister's arm, she spoke with a married woman's dignity and the authority of experience.

"Hennie, I see you don't want to talk about it, so I'll say no more, except that you don't fool me. Just remember, these are your best years. A girl hasn't

got all the time in the world, and that's all I have to
say . . . will you stay to dinner?"

Hennie stood up. "I'm not dressed up enough for
your house," she said, hearing the petulance in her
own voice. "Paul got chocolate on my skirt just
now."

The sarcasm did not escape Florence. "We are
not Buckingham Palace here, after all," she said re-
proachfully. "And there is no one coming to dinner,
except a young man from the office to go over some
last-minute business with Walter. A rather nice
young man, too, come to think of it. You might do
well to stay. I'll lend you a dress if you want to
change."

But Hennie had to go. Something was jumping
alive in her chest. Something had to be done. She
couldn't stay waiting this way any longer, waiting
for something to happen. In the mirror over the
hatrack her face was sallow. "It's the light from the
stained glass," she said to herself. "No, it's not, I
look awful; I look weary, worried and furrowed."
She pinned her hat on.

"Think about the mountains, anyway," Florence
said. Her face in the glass was younger than Hennie's, smooth, troubled only because of Hennie and
for no reason of her own. "If you change your mind,
let me know."

Hennie rode the omnibus, clattering over the cob-
bles down Fifth Avenue. Past the Vanderbilt man-
sion and the imitation châteaux, the gray granite
and white marble, and past the Croton Reservoir on
42nd Street, they rattled and swayed. Block after
block of tidy brownstones stood behind their neat
squares of lawn and iron fences. She glanced at her

watch. In each neat parlor, no doubt, the tea service was now being cleared away. All was orderly.

Oh, there was much to be said for order! For the solid roof beneath which everyone knew what was expected of him, for the place that is there today and will be there tomorrow. The table and the child. Yes, and upstairs the room with the door that can be shut and locked, and in the center of the room the bed in which one never has to lie alone.

Why, why so long to wait? Meeting always in public places, in parks and restaurants, walking, walking until it became too dark, too cold, or too late to stay any longer. And a thought made her hand fly involuntarily to her lips: Was he perhaps, after all, the kind of man who wouldn't marry? Things Uncle David had said . . . Not possible! And the thought terrified her, as would a robber confronted in an alley; like a robber, it robbed and fled.

The horses pulled to a stop at Washington Square. Among the last remaining passengers, she stepped out into the fading afternoon. For a moment or two she stood beneath the gold-green shimmer of the trees, holding an idea as if in the palms of her hands. She looked east toward home. She ought to go home. But there was a need to know. . . .

At last she made up her mind, and walked away with quick, decisive steps.

She has not meant it to happen this way. But then, neither had he. She has only meant to ask him what is to become of them and whether he really means to stay with her, because he has been so vague about it and this panic has taken hold of her. That's all she has meant.

But they come together. That which, in ignorance and desire, she has so long imagined, now happens.

He opens the door and is astonished to see her. Suddenly she is appalled at her own boldness, but it is too late to turn back.

He has been working; there is a light under some sort of burner in the room behind him.

"I'm disturbing you," she says.

"No, no, I was just finishing. I was going upstairs."

He turns off the burner. They stand there looking at each other.

Then, "Will you come up?" he asks.

He opens the door at the top of the stairs and stands aside to let her go in. This is where he lives. . . . His bed is the first thing she sees there, his naked bed. She looks away. But the room is too small to avoid it. Between the bed and the bulk of an ugly upright piano, there is just enough space to pass. There is a pile of clothing on a chair. When he removes it, there is a pile of books beneath it. He stands there holding the clothes and the books, looking for a place to put them all down. Since there is no place, he puts them back on the chair. He apologizes for the mess, and they both sit down on the edge of the bed.

They don't say a word. The window is open, so that the life of the street rushes in: wagons rattle, a door is slammed, a child wails, two angry men threaten one another. And yet the street is remote. They are insulated from it behind the walls. The room is an island.

He kisses her. The kiss is different from past kisses, softer, and also harder, because they are alone, no one is watching, and there is plenty of time. She does not want it to end.

His hands quiver on the buttons that go all the way down her back. There is no question now about what is to happen. Often she has thought that she would be afraid, and has a flash of surprise at herself because she is not. Instead, it is all simple and clear, all decided. She will let him do whatever he will with her; she will wait for whatever happens.

Piece by piece, he takes off her clothes. She is warm, warm and weak, but she is strong, too, in the way she clings to him.

She can't stop, she can't wait.

The last thing she hears is the sounds of the organ-grinder, the opening bars of some banal, familiar tune that fades as quickly as it began, along with all the noises and voices in the world; everything fades, even the afternoon light; the circle draws in, shrinks to a single point where they lie.

He brought a woolen robe to cover her. It was almost dark, a blue dusk, with a great peace in the room. It was entirely natural to be there.

"You're so beautiful," he said. "Your perfect neck and shoulders. One would never guess. Your clothes hide you. You ought to wear lower necks and brighter colors. Why don't you?"

"My mother always says I don't look well in bright colors."

"Your mother's wrong. I wonder why she does

that to you. Maybe she doesn't even know why, herself."

"You don't like my mother. Don't try to hide it. I understand."

"I could like your father. But even he, I'm sure, thinks you could do better than me."

She had a vision of long years ahead that could be turbulent and should be tranquil. And she tried to explain.

"It isn't only snobbishness, although there's too much of that. But they've been crushed down. The war did it to them."

"Tell me about it. You never have."

"They were ruined. My grandfather was killed, fallen from a balcony during a soldiers' raid. My mother knelt on the grass all night beside him while he died. She was only a girl."

She felt a sudden wave of love and pity for her mother. And she went on, "Some day I'll tell more. How the lovely house was sold. It didn't bring nearly what it was worth, Papa says, but they had to sell it, they couldn't afford to keep it up. But he'd been wanting to go North anyway."

"Dear Hennie, I'm so glad he did!"

She thought of something. "Isn't it amazing that you and Uncle David knew each other? If you hadn't, I could never have gone up to speak to you."

"What a grand man he is! I hope he thinks half as much of me as I do of him."

"He told me wonderful things about you," she answered.

Someday, maybe, she'd tell him what else Uncle David said, and they'd laugh about it together. Old people, they'd say. . . .

She went behind the door to get dressed. Strange that the removal of her clothes had been so natural, while their replacement was embarrassing!

"Hennie, there's something I want to tell you," she heard him say.

He will tell me when we shall be married.

"I only want to promise you that you needn't worry. I'm very careful. You won't become pregnant."

Why, all at once, this trembling shame? Because . . . the consequences of all that sweetness could be so fearful. . . .

"Hennie, did you hear me? I said don't worry. Trust me."

"I will. I do."

"Listen to me, I know you. You'll go home and have a bad conscience. But you mustn't. We've done nothing wrong. Can there ever be anything wrong about love?"

"No," she whispered.

"Of course there can't."

When she awoke the next morning, the thought flooded in instantly: I am different because of what happened yesterday. It seemed impossible that this difference, this great change, was not visible. Yet her father read the *Times* at breakfast and her mother hurried Alfie off to school; everything was as always, the cereal, the iceman's bell, and the mailman's whistle. But all that day, whenever she passed a mirror, she stared at herself.

After that, it was arranged between Dan and Hennie that whenever she could find plausible time,

she would come to him. Arriving early, she would
watch quietly while he finished his work in the orderly laboratory, so different from the room in
which he ate and slept. Here, properly arrayed, were
papers, tubes, coils of wire, filaments and tools.
Sometimes Dan tried to explain what he was doing.

"This is an amplifier. And here, this is hand-
drawn copper wire, much stronger than ordinary
copper wire—"

She had no idea what all this meant; the words
passed over her head, acknowledged by a vague
smile. Always and only there was the longing for
him. He was so absorbed; with narrowed eyes, head
on one side, he'd whistle thoughtfully and pause to
think, completely at ease with himself. Always at
ease with himself and everyone. He spoke as he
pleased, dressed as he pleased—she had to laugh
inwardly, thinking, as she watched, how amusing it
was that, caring so little about his own dress, he yet
had that quirk of noting how a woman looked or
ought to look.

"That yellow thing is very good on you." He
would turn suddenly. "I'm finished. Let's go upstairs and take the yellow thing off."

She liked to bring food, to make or bake something at home on the pretext of taking it to the settlement house. She tidied the room as best she
could, for Dan was careless and never threw anything away, whether old clothes, letters, or cracked
dishes. Doing these things, she felt the marvel of
making a life together in daily work and trust.

She felt as good as married. Almost.

The months flowed easily into one another and
Dan was happy; he talked no more of longing to be

in a room with her behind a locked door. Hesitating to mention marriage, and wishing she could hide her flushed face, since, after all, it was the man who ought to be the eager one, or so the novels all said, she nevertheless brought up the subject.

"You see, I have to get some money ahead," Dan replied.

"I'm a simple person, Dan, you know that. I don't want a lot. I'm as simple as you."

"We may be simple, but even so, we can't live here in this room, can we?"

Glancing at the narrow bed, the single chair, and the milk bottle on the windowsill, she had to concede that.

"Darling, I wish it could be tomorrow. But I shall have to get a little ahead."

"How is that to be done?" she asked, keeping her tone steady.

"I don't know. I don't know. Look about you. More soup kitchens, bank failures, unemployment. This is a full-blown depression, Hennie. True, I get a salary, but till I met you I saved very little. I always gave so much away, and now the need for giving is greater than it ever was."

"You're still giving?"

"Not much, though it's hard not to when I see my kids coming to school half asleep because they've been up late making artificial flowers. But I'm trying, I really am. Just be patient."

Alfie went to the Werners' Adirondack camp and came back to entertain them at dinner with ac-

counts of canoe trips and cookouts with trout he
had caught.

"It's called 'roughing it in comfort.' You should
have gone, Hennie. You'd have had a great time."

Alfie knew how to enjoy the pleasures of luxury.
Nothing was ever wasted on him.

"I'm sure I don't know why she didn't," Mama
said. Serving the dessert, she dropped the spoon into
the pudding with a stern splash. "This insufferable
heat! Hanging around the settlement house all summer! Nobody stays in the city who has a chance to
get out of it, except Hennie. Well, charity is one
thing, but there's no need to be a martyr for it."

Alfie promptly reversed himself. "Oh, Ma, it
wasn't all that wonderful. And everybody doesn't
like the mountains, anyway."

Dear little Alfie, once a nuisance, and suddenly a
grown-up ally! Tears pressed the back of Hennie's
eyes. She was in terror that they might fall, one
slow, piteous drop after the other, forcing her to flee
from the room and later to face questions. Questions . . .

The happy family at dinner. You could make a
nice lithograph and put it in a gilded frame on the
parlor wall: the father in his dark suit, the presiding
mother, the jolly schoolboy son, and the marriage-
able daughter.

Oh, if they knew! Schemes and possibilities
whirled through Hennie's brain. Maybe Papa could
offer Dan a job that paid more than teaching? No,
he wouldn't take it. He loved to teach. Anyway, Pa
had no job to offer. If ever there were one in that
struggling partnership, it would go to Alfie.

Pictures floated through her brain. White weddings. Music, blessings, and safety. Above all, safety . . .

The months revolved and fall came again. She bought a copy of *The Scarlet Letter*. My God, what cruelty! But that, after all, was two centuries ago, wasn't it?

It's not all that different now.

She rarely stopped in to visit Uncle David anymore. When she did, he never mentioned Dan, which made her wonder what he knew or suspected. Maybe nothing at all.

At the settlement house, Miss Demarest, with an expression both curious and envious, dropped remarks about "you and your young man." She must have seen Hennie walking in the neighborhood with Dan. Even in a city as enormous as New York, one could not go unnoticed.

Having a painfully growing need to confide in someone, she was almost prepared to take Olga out for coffee some evening and trust her. But then, one day, somehow their conversation took a turn that made confidence impossible.

"In Russia we had nothing," Olga had said. "We still have nothing. But as long as I am with my husband, everything is bearable."

"Did you know each other a long time before you were married?"

"We grew up in the same village, but we didn't really know each other . . . and then all of a sudden it happened. You know how it is . . . we decided to get married."

Hennie's thoughts moved gingerly, like fingers not quite daring to touch.

"But surely you loved, you knew love, for some time before you were married?"

Olga looked up. "Knew love? You don't mean that we slept together? Why, he would never do that before we were married. He's not that kind of man."

Hennie flushed. "I didn't mean that," she said quickly. "Of course not."

She was, then, entirely alone with her secret.

"We haven't seen much of Daniel Roth lately," Angelique observed.

Dan hadn't been at Hennie's house in weeks, since now they met elsewhere.

When Hennie did not reply at once, her mother inquired, "Has he stopped courting you, then?"

"Courting! That's ridiculous. He's my friend. Everything is not 'courting,' as you put it, Mama."

"A man is either interested in something permanent or he is not. It's as plain as that. And if he is no longer interested, I can tell you plainly that your father and I will be much relieved. We'll be sorry for you, but you'll get over it and be all the happier."

Hennie said coldly, "You were going out at ten o'clock, weren't you? Well, you're late, it's ten after."

A man is either interested in something permanent or he is not.

Eileen was singing in the kitchen, her song rising freely now that the lady of the house had gone out. Hennie went into her room and shut the door against that strong, cheerful voice.

* * *

When had she really felt the beginning of the drift?
It was impossible to know precisely when. A drift
was just that: gradual and vague, veering like a
night breeze.

Women glanced, inviting, and he responded.
Nothing came of it really, except that whenever it
happened, she felt left out and afterward, reflecting,
humiliated by her own jealousy. She knew one
thing: never to let him know that she saw or cared,
lest she become that ridiculous creature, a suspicious and possessive woman.

They had been at a beach picnic to celebrate the
end of the school year; that had been one time.
There had been a lively group of teachers with wives
and daughters. It was a marvelous day, too cool for
bathing but perfect for walking on the hard sand
near the water's edge.

We are in line, somehow arranged by twos, to the
jetty and back. I find myself with Mr. Marston, the
Latin teacher. Dan is ahead of us with the daughter,
Lucy Marston. She is about my age and is as noisy
as my brother Alfie. Does she really think that her
explosive laughter is alluring?

Mr. Marston keeps talking about his wife, recently dead, and of the responsibility he has to be
both mother and father to Lucy. I am sorry for him,
but I am bored with his troubles, although I offer
the proper sympathy. My eyes are on Dan and the
girl ahead. After all, I can't help seeing them, can I?
The wind carries their voices away, all except her
giggling treble, so I don't know what they are talking about, but I can see by Dan's enthusiastic ges-
tures that he is happy.

When she stumbles in the sand, he offers his arm and they go on walking that way. When we arrive at the jetty and make the turn to go back, I shall manage, I think, to walk back with him. But, still arm in arm, they swing about. Her brown hair has gold streaks. It's beautiful hair. She has a pug-face like a doll's, pretty but stupid. She doesn't stop talking. Dan likes quiet women, he says. He can't bear chatter, he says.

It's time to eat. Some people have brought blankets to spread on the sand. I sit on the rocks beside Dan. Lucy Marston wanders uncertainly holding her plate, looking for a place to sit. Dan calls to her.

"Over here! There's room."

He moves to make a place for her on his other side. I do not know if it is truly he who has invited her, or she who first made certain that he would. Something has been felt between them. Why doesn't she find a man of her own?

I try to see the girl through Dan's eyes, which are now so bright that the clear whites are almost blue. I study her, saying nothing, while they talk as if I weren't there. She has a lively energy that I don't have. She raises her arms above her head to stretch, and arches her back as if she were in bed; her body is an invitation and a promise. If I see it, surely Dan does. I imagine that he is imagining her in bed, and I feel such a terrible, frenzied jealousy that I could smash my fist into her face. . . .

Was that day the beginning? Hennie dared not ask.

From time to time, Dan mentioned the girl. The mother's death had been such a brutal shock. Lucy and her father had come home to find her dead in the parlor. She had never been sick. Terrible. Mr. Marston was a changed man. But Lucy was so spirited, he was lucky to have a daughter like her to cheer him.

From time to time, though, Dan mentioned other women too. The new assistant at the library. A red-haired nurse at the settlement. So really it must be just a kind of game. A game of the eyes, of compliments and admiration. That was what Uncle David had seen and failed to understand.

Yes, Hennie assured herself in moments of optimism, it is his way, harmless in spite of being painful to me. I will have to accept it. He must be loosely held and then he will always come back.

And yet the second year was ending.

On the Sunday before Thanksgiving they went for an afternoon walk in Central Park. The day was hazy, the air warm and still, vaguely depressing in a season that ought to be brisk.

People wandered slowly; children kicked at the piled leaves along the paths. A little group had gathered to watch an old man feeding pigeons; earnest as a farmer going about his labor, he dipped his hand into the sack and scattered the grain.

"Out of place in the city," Dan observed. "Look at his rosy cheeks."

"He's the same old man Paul watches when I bring him to the park."

And lines of a Stevenson poem, memorized at school, came to her suddenly, something about country places.

"Where the old plain men have rosy faces
     And the young fair maidens
          Quiet eyes."

My eyes are not quiet, she thought.

They walked on. They had spoken very little all
the way. Presently Dan remarked that it was so
warm, one scarcely needed a coat, that it was amazing weather, but that they would probably make up
for it with tons of snow in January.

"I suppose so," she answered.

A flock of sparrows rushed up out of the grass at
their approach.

"Funny, nobody feeds them," Dan remarked.
"Not pretty enough, I suppose. I call them the poor
people because the Lord made so many of them."

You don't even believe in the Lord, she thought,
without replying.

Why are you doing this? Talking about sparrows,
when we should be talking about ourselves? Tell me,
say it, get it over with. Say: I'm tired of you, I've
changed my mind.

Dan was staring at her. They had come to a stop
in the middle of the path.

"What is it, Hennie?" Impatience crept into the
voice of concern. "You look miserable. What's bothering you?"

Humiliation stripped her naked in the park.
Surely every passerby could see her naked misery.
As if he did not know!

Her lips were so dry that she could feel them
sliding over her teeth. "A mood, I guess."

"Well, you're entitled to a mood. I'll forgive you,"
he said lightly.

Forgive me for what? she cried silently. How dare *you* forgive *me!* Oh, God, Dan, won't you understand? I need to know where I'm going!

They went on again, breaking the silence now and then when it became too heavy, with some desultory remarks about things passing: a pair of handsome collies, or a maroon barouche containing three girls in identical white feathered hats. They came out onto Fifth Avenue among the Sunday strollers, elegant pairs on their way to tea at the Plaza, and affable families taking the air after midday dinner. They caught the omnibus downtown.

"I forgot to tell you," Dan said, "there are some cousins of my mother's coming in from Chicago. They'll be staying at a hotel, since I surely have no place to put them up, but naturally I'm obligated to take them around the city. They've never been here. So the next week will be a busy one for me."

"Yes, of course," Hennie answered quickly.

When they got off at the last stop, she said, "You needn't walk home with me. No, really, I know you've got things to do."

"Not coming back with me?" Dan asked without urgency.

"No, my sister's coming to tea. Walter's got one of his Sunday meetings."

He did not insist.

"As a matter of fact, I can use the time. I've a pile of papers to go over." He smiled. "Cheer up, Hennie. The world hasn't come to an end."

Oh, turn the knife in the wound!

"I'm very cheerful, I'm quite fine, don't worry about me," she said, walking away.

I will not look back to see whether he is looking after me. I will not. But I have lost him.

She had, in fact, not been expecting Florence; the sight of the familiar carriage and dappled grays at the curb was a surprise. She went inside with a sense of dread, hoping there was other company in the house so that the conversation would have to be impersonal. But Florence and Angelique were alone in the parlor with the inevitable tea service between them. How would New York life be conducted without the tea service, the important gossip, the marriages arranged for the sons and daughters?

"Where is Papa?" Hennie inquired.

"Taking his Sunday nap. My goodness, you look so pale!"

She answered without thinking, "It's getting cold, a wind's come up."

"Cold!" Angelique said. "And Florence has just been complaining of the unseasonable heat! Where have you been, Hennie?"

"For a walk in the park."

Over Hennie's head, as she sat down, the glances passed and vanished.

"Do try this cake." Florence passed a plate. "My new cook made it. She's Irish, but surprisingly good. They are not famous for their cooking, as we all know. I do wish I could afford a French chef. Walter's parents have one and he's marvelous."

A congress of nations, Hennie thought. French chefs, Irish maids, and German governesses. An English butler would be the ultimate, but that's beyond the Werners' reach . . . Why do I pick on my sister's foibles? Because I'm wounded and I need to lash out at somebody, that's why.

The conversation that Hennie's entrance had interrupted was now resumed.

"The furniture was all Louis Seize. Half the women wore tiaras. You can't imagine what a scene it was. I have been telling Mama about the Brocklehurst dinner. Another world, not Jewish, of course. I was really flattered to be invited, although it was a business thing, I don't delude myself. The apartment must cost heaven only knows what. Twenty rooms on Fifth Avenue. I know Walter's cousin pays one hundred a month for seven rooms on Fifth Avenue, so this one must have cost . . ." Florence's voice trailed off in awe. "Right near the Harmonie Club they are."

"I have never been in the Harmonie Club," Angelique remarked wistfully.

"You wouldn't like it, Mama. Naturally I have to go because of Walter's parents, but it's so German! The Kaiser's portrait in the hall! And it's just this year that German stopped being the official language. I wish it would stop being the official language in my in-laws' house too. After all, they've been forty years in America. And they still think of themselves as German. Carlsbad and Marienbad every other summer."

"It must be tiring to do so much traveling." Angelique sighed. "Still, I wish your father could—"

"What do you wish I could?" Henry inquired, coming in.

"Travel, my dear, you haven't had a real vacation in years."

"I keep inviting you," Florence declared. "Why not come to Florida with us this winter? And you come with them, too, Hennie." She swung round in her chair and faced Hennie. "Now, listen, I want your promise, your solemn promise, that you'll come with us this winter."

Hennie's palms were wet. Sickening, dizzying speckles of light flashed in the air.

"I'll try," she answered weakly.

She felt ill. Her stomach heaved. She had been feeling like that quite often this last week or two.

"What do you mean, you'll try? What else have you got to do?" And when Hennie did not reply, "Or will you have something else to do?"

The question opened new possibilities in the room.

"Let us not beat about the bush any longer." Angelique clipped the words. "You have been seeing this Roth, and no one else, for too long."

Hennie bowed her head. In the line of her vision were shoes: Florence's slim pointed toes, Papa's feet —in scuffed boots, he needs new ones—planted on the rug, and her mother's foot tapping.

"What have you to say about it? Anything, Hennie?"

What have I to say? Only that I love him, I would die for him, and he does not want me anymore.

"Hennie! Why are you looking like that, as if the end of the world had come?"

Funny, that's what he said, the end of the world hasn't come. She raised her head and put out her hand.

"I would like some tea, you haven't given me my tea." Maybe it would settle her queasy stomach.

They had planned this conversation. This was no spontaneous thing. They had been waiting for her. It was for this that Florence had come on a Sunday.

Now they made a semicircle around her, as in that engraving of the stag, cornered finally by the hounds. There was no way out, and hating them for what they were doing, she knew they were right.

"What do you want of me? What do you want me to say?" she cried, shouting into the decorous room.

"We only want to know what's going on," Angelique said. "Have we no right to know, no interest in you?"

Don't be sick on the carpet.

"All Mama means," Florence said quietly, "is whether you have any—any understanding."

This day had been too much, everything was too much, unbearable. Hennie's look appealed to her father, begging him to stop this, to release her. But his head was down, reaming his pipe. He was not going to help, and for the first time she had no pity for him.

"We know," continued her mother, "that you have been seeing him more often than you admit. You may think you have been fooling us with your denials. Yes, for a while you did, we believed you, but all that has come to a finish, Hennie. It's time for you to speak frankly, for all of us to speak frankly."

Oh, the little room where we took our joy, and how we loved each other!

"There is nothing to speak frankly about," Hennie said. "Nothing at all."

"Perhaps your father should speak to him and find out what all this 'nothing' amounts to."

This was not even decent, the hounds were ripping at her.

"No, no," Hennie cried, adding then very faintly, "he needs more money. He can't afford—"

Angelique set her cup down. "What? Then he is looking for a rich wife?"

"Mama, how can you say such a thing? Of all people! Dan cares nothing for money. He has no interest in wealth—" The words choked her.

"But you just said he needs more, so he has to care. Don't be a child," Angelique said, and touching Hennie's arm, spoke with surprising gentleness. "Listen, Hennie dear, it takes money to run a home, you're seeing that it does. Even a once-a-week cleaning woman costs a dollar and a half. How is he to get it, does he say?"

"He's a teacher. The salary is small."

"People do live on teacher's salaries, though," said Angelique, reversing herself.

Hennie did not answer. Someone walked in the apartment overhead and the crystal drops on the chandelier tinkled lightly. There was no other sound in the room. They were waiting for Hennie to say something.

"I can't talk now," she said. "I don't feel well. Can't you see that I'm miserable?"

"Yes, and that's just why we're talking now, because we do see and have been seeing," answered Angelique.

"I'm miserable because I'm coming down with a cold, and I only want to be let alone!" Hennie shouted, causing them all to draw back.

It crossed her mind that they had never heard her shout *at* them. Her voice had suddenly become a weapon. They all stood up. Florence went to the mirror to adjust her hat, on which a small bird, brightly blue, perched above a wreath of veiling.

She spoke into the mirror, in which she could see Hennie. "We only mean your good, dear. But I see that this is not the best time to discuss anything. Another day, then."

Hennie stood at the window watching the bird and veil, the sable muff and velvet sleeves, disappear inside the carriage. She felt her father's hand on her shoulder.

"May I talk to you, Hennie? Only for a minute, then go lie down."

Angelique had taken the tea tray into the kitchen, this being Eileen's free afternoon.

"Not now, Papa."

He could have come to her rescue! Perhaps he had been too tired. He was always tired.

Her father spoke quickly. "I don't want anyone to hurt you, Hennie, that's all. I know your mother and your sister care about things that don't interest you, but they do care about you. You may not like the way they show it, but they love you. You know that, don't you?"

She nodded. The quiet tone and the warm touch of his hand brought the sting of tears. This time they brimmed over. She caught her father's hand and laid it against her cheek.

"This is all wrong, Hennie."

"What is, Papa?"

"I don't know the man."

"You don't like him?"

"I don't know him, I tell you. And I've let you be too free. I shouldn't have allowed it all this time. I don't know why I did."

But I know why. Because you knew I needed to
be loved and you didn't want to spoil it. Yes, I
know.

"Don't worry about me, Papa, I'll be all right."

Later in her room, in the early evening after the
spasm of sickness had passed, she sat down at her
desk and began to write. The words came of themselves.

"Dear Dan, I know you have grown tired of me. I
won't plead or ask for any explanation. A person is
perfectly free to love and to stop loving. Only be
honest with me and say so."

She dipped the pen. The ink slid across the paper,
making smooth curves and loops; how odd it was
that a pattern of arabesques so light and easy could
spell out such a breaking! And how was it possible
for another human being to be so much a part of
you as to break you in half by leaving you?

"I will make no scenes," she wrote.

He would tear this open when the mail came, or
perhaps the letter would be waiting under the mail
slot when he got home. Then he would sit down by
the window at the table on which the crumbs from
his breakfast roll would still be scattered, and would
tear it open and read, feeling—feeling what? Relief?
Guilt? Sorrow, or all of these? And would do what?
Come running to her in remorse? No, it would not
be that. He would say, "Yes, yes, it's true, and I am
so terribly sorry, but it's over; this is how it happened. I'm in love with Lucy Marston—or somebody."

Her heart pounded, her head pounded, yet the
pen moved on, offering her sacrifice, giving everything away.

"There will be no blame. What I did I did to myself. There's no use pretending something you don't feel, and if you don't feel anything for me anymore, you can't help it. But you mustn't lie to me. It is not fair to lie to me."

After signing the letter, she sat for a while, sat up very straight and stiffened her back; she was filled with a deep, mournful pride in her ability to bear so much pain. Then she lay down, exhausted, and slept.

In the morning she tore the letter up.

There was a chill in the household. Angelique spoke of ordinary things, as though nothing had happened. Yet all her words came out like a rebuke: We are observing the natural decencies, as you see, but do not think we have forgotten. We are only waiting.

Hennie was starved for food. Five times during one afternoon she went to the kitchen, raiding the icebox, then the breadbox, tearing off the bread in a hunk, so that even Eileen looked astonished. She ate a chicken leg from the previous night's dinner, drank a glass of milk, and ate an apple. When her stomach was empty, she felt sick.

One morning she vomited. The fine machinery of her body was definitely out of order. She wished she had more knowledge . . . On the other hand, she wished she had never gone peeking into Uncle David's textbooks. . . .

Oh, my God, it can't be! It's something else. Dan said it wouldn't be. So it isn't.

She had not heard from him. She thought of

walking downtown, playing a game, a dangerous
game with herself: How far will I go toward his
house before I turn back? This was the hour when
he sat near the window correcting papers. He could
look down into the street; she could not risk the
humiliation of having him see her searching for
him. . . .

One morning she was sent to the grocery store. A
strange thing happened: She forgot what she had
been sent for. Among the barrels of oatmeal and
coffee she stood trying to recollect, feeling faintly
dizzy. It was still early and the store was empty.
Mr. Potter was being patient. Nevertheless, she felt
painfully embarrassed.

"Well, now, what could it have been?" he asked.
His red hands, resting on the counter, looked like
raw beef; a sickening thought.

He looks like a gnome. I wish I could tell him
everything. I must be crazy.

"What could it be?" he repeated. "Let's think.
Sugar? Bread?"

Sugar, yes, sugar! It all came back to her: a bag of
walnuts for Sunday's cake, and butter.

The butter had begun to melt. Along the sides of
the crock it swam in fat yellow globules. Slick,
greasy butter. Her mouth filled with water. She had
to shut her eyes from the sight. Hurry, hurry! She
was going to be sick.

Out on the street again, her reflection jumped out
of Mr. Potter's plate glass window. She looked like a
pouter pigeon. Of course! Of course, she was laced
too tight, that's why she had been feeling so ill.
That's why she was sweating as though it were still
August.

She stood at the curb, trying to decide whether to go home with the bag of groceries, or to find out once and for all . . .

She went downtown. On Uncle David's street the pushcarts in double rows stood piled with suspenders, caps, aprons, and potatoes. A horseless carriage, an unusual sight on such a poor street, came rattling to a halt when the bicycle chain came loose from the rear axle. The peddlers cursed, and a frightened horse tore away, pulling his wagon, while a pair of boys who should have been in school jeered at the luckless owner of the new contraption: "Get a horse! Get a horse!"

The confusion, lasting no more than a minute, printed itself on Hennie's mind. I shall remember this, she thought queerly, although none of it has anything to do with me: the frightened horse and the dazzle of light on the dangling chain.

Uncle David's door was open, but the office was empty. She sat down to wait, picked up last week's copy of Frank Leslie's *Illustrated Newspaper,* and was unable to read. Without moving, almost frozen, she waited for, and also dreaded, the sound of Uncle David's footsteps on the stairs.

"In a doctor's eyes," Uncle David said, "the body is only a machine. Like the horseless carriage to the mechanic. That's all there is to it."

She could not look at him. With the fingers of one hand she smoothed the nails of the other. Pink nails, neatly rounded and glossy as shells.

"From what you tell me," Uncle David said

gently, "it's pretty clear what's the matter. But I shall need to look, all the same."

Burning, burning shame. Wherever does one find the courage to do this?

"Just lie down and put the sheet over yourself. I shall step out. When you're ready, call me."

She lay quite still. The corset, the corset cover, the chemise and the petticoats lay on a chair. They looked ashamed, limp and exposed like that in a strange place. She closed her eyes so as not to see them, or the ceiling or anything. She called out.

When the sheet was lifted, cool air swept over her and she felt cold metal. Her hands were clenched.

I am not here. I am somebody else.

The sheet was drawn up again.

"Get dressed," Uncle David said. "We'll talk afterward."

His voice was dry, without emotion, and she knew he was suppressing a terrible anger. So it was true.

Now panic shook her. A panic as awful as if she had been tottering on a cliff in a roaring wind, or as if she had been lying alone in an enormous house at night, with footsteps coming up the stairs. She made herself stand and fasten her clothes and tie her shoes. Tears poured; she wept without making a sound.

When Uncle David returned to the room, he said softly, "Don't cry, Hennie." All the anger had gone out of his voice. But the tears still slid down her cheeks.

The old man looked away. Drab, sorry sparrows, hunched in their feathers, Dan's poor people, cheeped on the windowsill. The old man watched them while he tapped with a pencil on the desk, making a little marching rhythm. After a minute he spoke.

"Will you tell me about it, Hennie?"

When she opened her mouth, no sound came until, straining, she was able to whisper, "I can't."

"All right. I suppose there's nothing to tell . . . it happened, that's all. At least you love each other, and that's what matters."

Yes, in his practical way, he was thinking as he always did, All right, it happened; now we must think of what to do about it. And this, along with the absence of reproach and the swallowing of what must surely be his outrage, could have been such comfort, such strength on which to lean and take hope, except for those few words: *At least you love each other.*

Her tears stopped. In desperation she looked around the room, at the books and the medicines on the shelves. She made a vague gesture.

"Isn't there some medicine—something?"

"Pe-Ru-Na?" David's smile was a rueful twist of the lips. "It will cure almost everything. But not this." His eyes rested on Hennie, touching her softly, softly. "You will have to be married," he said. "Right away. Really, right away."

Hennie bowed her head.

"Right away," Uncle David emphasized. He asked then, "Does he know anything of this?"

Hennie shook her head.

"You must tell him today, Hennie."

Why so proud? Put your head on this old man's shoulder and cry it out: Oh, Uncle, you told me there are men who don't stay with one woman, you told me.

"I will say the baby came early. No one will question it when I say so. I will take care of it, Hennie. Now you're in this, you must brave it out."

"I don't know how I can do that, Uncle David."

"You will."

"You're more sure than I am, then."

"You will do it because you have to."

His warm, firm hand, as he helped her with her coat, paused to press her shoulder. Opening the door, he reminded her, "Dear Hennie, the main thing is, at least you love each other. Just keep thinking of that."

She waited for Dan on the stairs. While, in the half darkness, he searched for the keyhole, she blurted what she had to tell.

"Dan, I am having a baby."

What plans she had labored over during these last hours! Whether to berate him for his neglect of her, or to beguile him with lace at her throat and a charming hat, or to seize his hands and be tender, or to weep, or somehow to make him jealous (how, you fool, how?)—repeatedly she had considered all of these and discarded them. Now, after all, she had crudely and simply flung the words *I am having a baby.*

The door slammed back against the wall. He threw his coat—she had mended a burn-hole he had made in it at the lab—over the back of the chair and slid his armful of books into a pile on the table. She saw him catch his lip under his teeth.

"How do you know?"

"I went to Uncle David this morning."

"Good God, not to him!"

"Why not to him?"

He struck a match to light a cigarette. The flame went out in his shaking fingers.

"Was he sure? Is it definite?"

"It's definite."

How many times had she come running up the stairs to this room, running to find the door wide open and Dan with his arms outstretched and a glowing face, mischievous, bright with expectation! They stood now with the width of the room between them. He struck another match and held it to the gas bracket; a weak light seeped out into the dusky afternoon.

"What did he say? Was he in a rage?"

That we must be married right away. That the important thing is, we love each other.

"He didn't say very much."

"He must have said something." Dan looked down at the floor. "I should think he'd want to kill me."

"There wouldn't be much point in that, would there?"

"I've ruined his good opinion of me—of us both."

"I don't know. Mostly, I think, he's just sorry."

Sorry. Sad, yet more than that. "A sorry sight," one says, by which one means something sad indeed but also pitiable because it need not have been. . . .

It came to her, in her misery, that she was thinking like an English teacher; she felt the absurdity of a smile on her lips.

Dan caught the smile. He's afraid I'm going to be hysterical, she thought as he came to her.

"Sit down here, take off your coat, maybe you should lie down . . ."

She glanced at the bed and, moving past it, sat down in the chair at the window.

She felt Dan's hand on her shoulder.

"Don't be afraid, Hennie. We'll have to be married quickly, that's all."

His voice came to her as if it were an echo; she had a queer feeling of unreality. And as if another voice, not her own, were answering, she heard, "You don't want to."

"Hennie, I do! For God's sake, I do! It's just a little sooner than I—but we'll manage, it will be all right." And he repeated, pleading, "Don't be afraid."

"All this time . . . you said we couldn't afford it. And then you didn't talk about it at all anymore."

"I suppose I was afraid of the responsibility. The bills, the rent, I kept putting it off. Don't think I haven't felt guilty. It would have been better for you if you'd met someone else, not me."

Hennie put her face in her hands. Better to have met someone else, he said. She felt blank exhaustion; everything just stopped. Everything.

"Hennie, look at me. I'm not proud of myself. Hennie, don't cry. Please, I can't bear your tears."

"I'm not." She raised her head. Like death, he looked. This had brought him down. And she felt a vindictive triumph.

"You'll get over my tears soon enough. Miss Lucy Marston will help you do that."

"What in the name of creation are you saying?"

"I should think it's pretty clear."

"She has nothing to do with this! What can you be thinking? A girl . . . a pretty girl . . . there are dozens of them . . . everywhere . . . can a man not talk to a girl without somebody's thinking that—" he stammered, and stopped.

It would be good to believe him. Maybe it was the truth.

She stood up and, pulling the curtain aside, looked down at the lamplighter, who, moving along the street, made one sallow circle of light after the other in the growing darkness. Except for him, the street was empty.

Dan urged, repeating himself, "We shall have to be married right away, Hennie."

She spun around.

"No. I don't want you to marry me because we 'have to.' " Something rose in her, something heedless and strong, a surge of defiance that rose above the exhaustion. "I'm worth more than that. I won't live with a man who will throw this up to me every time we have an argument."

"We never will."

"Never have an argument? That's ridiculous. How can you think that?"

"I meant I would never 'throw it up to you.' You have my word."

"Your word isn't good enough anymore."

He asked quietly, "Then, what do you want?"

Leaning her head against the icy pane, she thought, I want it to be as it was in the beginning. I want you to look at me the way you did when we stood on the Brooklyn Bridge and you said, "I love you, we'll have a good life."

"Hennie, talk to me! Look at me. If you won't marry me, what will you do?"

"I don't know." She heard her own laugh, an ugly broken sound. "Kill myself, I suppose."

"My God, Hennie!"

"What difference would it make? You think I'm playacting to get your sympathy? Or threatening you, though I can't imagine for what? No, it's quite true that it would make no difference. My family, you, the whole world would go on, wouldn't it, without me in it? Oh, they would cry whenever they thought of me; your conscience would torture you —for a few weeks—and it would be talked about among all my family's friends: 'What do you think, the De Rivera girl, they say she . . .' 'Oh, no, not possible!' 'Oh, yes, my dear, I heard'— Then it would all be just as before. But I, at least, would have nothing to trouble about."

The words lifted her, making her stand tall before him. And she meant every one of them. All at once her anger made her powerful.

She horrified him. "Hennie! Ah, don't talk like that!"

He put his arms around her and laid his cheek on her hair; his warm breath, his murmur, hovered over her head.

"Don't talk about dying. Please. You terrify me."

Rigidly she stood, her body resisting his tight hold. Not a word had he said about the two weeks of silence, or the indifference before that.

She became aware that he was controlling a sob.

"I know I don't always do what I ought. I'm not

good enough for you. I know that. Look up at me, Hennie, do."

He lifted her chin so that she was forced to see the tears in his eyes.

"I never meant to hurt you. I'm not always the easiest person to get along with. I blunder, I'm not as considerate as I should be. But I'll do better, believe me."

"I wish I could."

"You can! Trust me. And I'm so sorry. God, I'm so sorry!"

You could not be lying and look like that. No, you could not.

"Trust me, will you? From now on?"

She was quite still, wanting, considering, hesitating.

Then his tears broke her. The great hard lump of grief in her chest broke open, little pieces shattered and burst in her throat with cries and tears.

She wept. "I don't want to die! I didn't mean what I said!"

"Of course you didn't. You're going to live. Darling Hennie."

He kissed her hair. Their tears ran together on her wet cheeks. His mouth came down on hers; they clung to each other. She was bathed in his heat. All the terror, the fear, the wrath and pride, melted away into a merciful relief.

"You're so good, so brave."

"I don't know."

"Well, you are. Lovely and brave."

For long minutes they held each other. And at last Hennie smiled. Tenderly, with the familiar gesture, she pushed the stray wave from his forehead.

"I'll take care of you, Hennie. I'll talk to Uncle David—even if he wants to kill me."

She was able now to laugh.

"He won't want to kill you."

"I'll take care of you. Don't be afraid of anything. I'm here. I'll always be here."

Yes, yes, forget everything, ask no more, go back to the beginning.

Angelique frowned. "I can't understand the sudden haste. Or why your father is going along with Daniel's insistence."

"Papa's happy for me."

"The whole thing's a puzzle. All of a sudden your father has such good things to say: He's so cultured, he's a scientist. What does that matter?"

Hennie thought, It's because Papa knows how sad I've been. Or can it be possible that he suspects the truth?

Florence said, "If you'd wait until spring, we could have the winter to get properly ready. There's no reason to hurry so, now that you're engaged."

"Florence, we don't want to wait."

"Well, then, we shall have to rush the invitations. You'll come down my stairs, Hennie, I'll have ropes of smilax on the banisters . . ."

"You're very dear to want to go to all that trouble, but I would rather have it very small, here at home."

"It would be beautiful in Florence's house," Angelique said, "I really think you should accept her offer."

"It would make Papa happy to have a wedding here. It really would."

"Perhaps she's right," Florence agreed reluctantly. "You know it has always hurt him that I wasn't married from our home."

Angelique sighed, and Hennie thought, She has no enthusiasm. If I were marrying someone she approved of, she would not be so tired. And she felt a queer pity because her mother was disappointed.

"At least let me help you with your clothes," Florence said, bright with energy and kindliness. "White velvet, perhaps? Or maybe not velvet, the season's so short for it. Brocade or watered silk would be better. Something you can wear afterward to formal dinners and get some use out of. You're always so practical."

"I doubt we shall be going to formal dinners."

"Well, you're certainly not going to hibernate in the heart of New York! So, we'll go on Monday. Begin on Broadway with Lord & Taylor. McCreery's after that. Walter and I have decided to give you a check to start you off."

Hennie scarcely heard. All was being taken care of. She was being taken care of.

True, one night she woke up with pounding heart from a nightmare in which she was carrying a baby —so heavy it was!—and standing outside of Dan's door at the top of those steep stairs, ringing and ringing, and he would not answer, and in terror she knew he would not marry her. . . .

Waking slowly, she felt for the ring, the chip of a diamond that had belonged to Dan's mother. She liked to twist it on her finger, to feel it as promise and proof. Then she laid the hand on the place where the secret life lay curled and waiting, the life Dan had put there, that tied them together.

Incredible relief swept over her, like the gratitude of one who has been saved from drowning.

For a long time she lay there, smiling in the dark.

The boy Frederick, named after Dan's father and immediately called Freddy, was unusually large and strong, Uncle David informed the family, for a seven-month baby; they were very lucky that the birth had gone so well.

The family came to the hospital, Hennie's parents, and Florence and Walter with little Paul.

"We've sent a carriage to the house," Florence said. "A dark blue British carriage fit for a crown prince."

Hennie and Dan had already bought a perfectly good wicker carriage with a parasol, advertised for thirteen dollars in the Sears catalogue. They would simply return it. One couldn't hurt Florence's feelings.

"I don't think you'll take me to the park anymore," Paul told Hennie.

"Of course I will! Why shouldn't I?"

"Because you have him, and you won't love me anymore."

Everyone laughed, except Hennie, who reached for Paul's hand. "I will love you both. You'll help me with Freddy and teach him, because you'll always be the big boy. And Freddy will love you. You will love each other all your lives."

"But you will love him more," Paul said seriously, "because he's yours."

How wise Paul is! Already he sees things as they are and can accept them. He is blessed, thought Hennie, and did not answer, but held the child's hand until he left.

Then she was alone with Dan and the baby, who lay in a basket next to the bed. Dan knelt to bring his face on a level with hers. He had brought roses and a little cloth cat.

"You and this boy." His voice wavered. "I don't deserve you."

She stroked his hair. "Don't say that. It's not true."

"Yes . . . these last months, being together, I've seen all the goodness in you. I'm ashamed of some of the things I've done. You don't know how I—"

Intensely moved, she whispered, "I don't want to hear. We're together, that's enough."

He straightened up. "All right. You know what I did just now? Bought concert tickets. There's a new piece by Debussy, *Afternoon of a Faun.* They say it's beautiful. We'll have dinner and celebrate when you're well again."

"Well again? I'm well now, I couldn't be better."

When Dan went home, she was left alone with the baby; a little mound under a white blanket, he slept on his stomach, revealing only half of a mottled face and some tan hairs on a naked skull. One hand lay above the blanket; the tiny fingers were trying to grasp the smooth sheet. The lips moved, and leaning closer, Hennie could see a flicker of the white perfect eyelids; it seemed to her that he might be dreaming of food. For minutes, propped on her elbow, Hennie observed this marvel she had made.

The shifting sun poured drowsy heat into the room, and she lay back on the pillow.

Incredible that he had been alive, only a few hours before, inside her body! At the same time she was amused at herself; surely every woman, giving birth, must feel the same astonishment. As if there were anything original in it!

At any rate, he's here and I'm here. We're a family with a future, and I know at last who I am.

3

It is the last night of the year, indeed the last of the century, and there is in the air the splendid tension that precedes a holiday, along with the regret that comes from leaving a familiar place.

Hennie looks around at the gathered family. We were together in the last hours of the nineteenth century, we will say, years from now; we will talk about it and there will be something elegiac in the telling. For a moment she sees herself in some far-off year to come—old, sitting in some vague room in a large chair, probably a wing chair, with her feet crossed and her spotted hands folded—and shakes herself free of the image.

All evening she has had a lovely sense of well-being. All is orderly in the home; there is enough of everything but not too much. Only the silver tea service, one of several that Mama's mother had buried in the woods during the Civil War, is out of place: rotund, filigreed, and gadroon-edged, the pots and kettles stand on the plain Mission table.

"Mission furniture?" Florence questioned when they bought it. "That square, homely stuff?"

"Dan doesn't think it's homely."

"It has no true style. It's a fad for the masses."

"It's made for the people, solid and simple. That's why Dan likes it."

She has never wanted the things that Florence and Mama want. It is wrong to own so much that one doesn't need. Besides, clutter depresses her.

Dan has made their rooms cheerful. He has painted the walls and ceiling white, quite out of style when dark flock wallpaper is the fashion. But rich dark colors close in on you, while white opens out to the world, to sun and air. The apartment is sunny. From the kitchen window, Hennie can look down on the green yards around the prosperous homes of East Broadway, half a block distant. She has sewn sheer curtains and Dan has built bookshelves. It gives her pleasure to watch the shelves fill up, for books are their one extravagance. They look neat in their rows; neatness has always given Hennie a sense of comfort and completion.

Fortunately, there is a large closet in the back hall where Dan, who has no such need for tidiness, can toss his belongings; papers and pamphlets along with every letter he ever received spill out of shelves and boxes onto the floor. Hennie smiles to herself now; the closet is a reflection of Dan—large, careless, free, and bold.

Her eyes move to the old upright on which he has begun to give piano lessons to Freddy. Her eyes tend to rest on everything that is Dan's. And that fine sense of well-being comes over her again.

They have eaten well: turkey and turnips, potatoes, rolls and homemade jellies. Now, with dinner over, fruit and cake are to be served on the round table in the parlor.

"An excellent dinner," says Hennie's mother. "I do admire the way you've learned to manage. I grew up not knowing how to boil water and, for goodness' sake, everybody knows I still can't do it! Yes, an excellent dinner, although I must say one does miss greens in this climate, having to wait till summer for a taste of something fresh. Unless, of course, one can afford hothouse vegetables and fruits. Oh, wherever did you get those?" she exclaims as Dan comes bearing a small pyramid of oranges in a bowl.

"A present from Florence and Walter," he replies.

Angelique is pleased. "Florence thinks of everything, doesn't she? Too bad they couldn't be here, but they had a formal dinner to go to. There are some obligations one just can't refuse."

Alfie comes galloping down the hall with Freddy on his shoulders; the child's skinny legs in their black cotton stockings dangle over Alfie's thick chest.

"Did you know I saw elephants at the zoo?" he cries. "They eat with their nose!"

"No," Paul corrects. "They only pick up the food with their long noses. The mouth is underneath, don't you remember?"

Freddy laughs, showing perfect little teeth. He has a short upper lip, quick to tremble with every emotion.

"If I hadn't seen him when he was a minute old," Dan likes to say, "I would swear he's not ours. He's too beautiful."

This is praise; yet there is something doubtful in it. Although he is fair-haired, the child is unmistakably Dan's son; the cleft chin, the rounded forehead, and the heavy-lidded eyes are Dan's. But he is small for a six-year-old, fearful and frail.

"I want to see the elephant again, and the monkeys," Freddy demands now as Alfie puts him down. "Paul, you said we could get peanuts for the monkeys."

"It's too cold in the winter. We'll go back to the zoo when spring comes."

Paul is Freddy's favorite love. After him comes Uncle Alfie. He has no bond with any child of his own age; Paul and Alfie are beloved because they are gentle with him. Hennie understands that clearly, but she does not speak of it to Dan. For some reason, perhaps because she fears Dan will not like to hear it, she keeps the knowledge to herself.

Alfie, setting Freddy down, catches Hennie's look and gives her a jolly wink. Alfie is happy; he is almost always happy, but more so tonight, because he has brought with him the girl he wants to marry, the serene Emily, daughter of the formidable Hugheses, whose opposition to the marriage looms like a mountain. His own parents' opposition looms, too, although it makes not quite as high a mountain.

Emily stands at the desk in the corner where Uncle David is showing her a book of Matthew Brady's Civil War photographs. Courteously, she listens to the enthusiastic old man. Her pale hair, caught high by a tortoiseshell comb, crowns her symmetrical Saxon face; she is placid and somehow ageless. She looked like this when she was a child and will not look very different when she is old. Now, with her head bent over the book, her slender neck is pitiably tender.

It is all too complicated, Hennie thinks, when it deserves to be so simple. Only wanting to be together! Yet some force in the world seems to want to keep people apart. In this case, it is religion. In my case . . . I don't know. We never talk about it. She closes her eyes for an instant, as if to blot out the thought.

Then she looks back at Emily. They must decide soon; Alfie must not make her wait. It is the cruelest thing for a woman. Hennie's lips move involuntarily, angrily, without a sound, upon the word: *cruel.*

She comes back to the moment and begins to cut the cake.

"It's a Russian cream cake, and it's the first time I've made it. I hope it's good. One of my old pupils —my friend Olga—gave me her mother's recipe. I made an extra to give to her; she has no place to bake, no place for anything, really, since her husband died. Tuberculosis, as usual. She and her little girl, a darling child, have to board. I've never seen the place, but I can imagine it. Here, take this plate, Paul."

"I'll need a bigger piece than that," Paul complains.

"I don't know where you put it," Angelique remarks fondly. "It's a good thing you don't run to fat like your Uncle Alfie."

Paul runs a finger inside his Buster Brown collar. His mother has made him dress up for this visit and he has arrived to stay the night at the Roths', wearing his best clothes, complete with a Windsor scarf tied in a flopping bow, more suitable to his parents' parlor, certainly, than to this one.

Paul is almost a man. Contained within the form
of the twelve-year-old boy is the design of the man
he will be. He has a thoughtful, rather formal expression, contradicted every now and then by his
lively curiosity. One might say—and people do—
that he looks aristocratic. How Dan despises the
word! thinks Hennie, who does not often use the
word herself. Nevertheless, it does describe Paul.
One sees it in his posture and in his steady gaze, so
strikingly blue in the dark face. Spirit and strength
are there.

Suddenly troubled, Hennie tries to recall what he
was like six years ago, at the age Freddy is now.
Paul was bolder. Without fear he approached
strange dogs; he sailed his boat in the Central Park
lake, fell in, and was pulled out laughing. Whereas
Freddy hangs back . . . he is perfectly healthy,
rarely sick, but he won't play and wrestle, even with
Dan.

She wonders whether he is perhaps a musical genius. Dan says he has talent. Or is she merely the
doting mother of an only child?

Oh, the world is so tough! On East Side streets
rove gangs of homeless boys, some as young as
Freddy, sleeping in hallways, running errands for
pay in pennies, to the saloons and worse places than
saloons. A merciless world. The child would never
be able to survive in it. Thank God, he will not have
to. Strange, that when she considers such a possibility for Paul, who most assuredly will never even
have to pass through such streets, she can quite easily imagine him set down in that world and somehow coping with it.

Now Freddy challenges Paul: "I'll beat you at checkers."

They get out the board and lay it on the floor.

"Paul is so patient with Freddy," remarks Angelique. "But then, neither of them has a brother."

And why Paul hasn't got one, why Florence doesn't want more children, I'll never understand! Hennie's thoughts are bitter. In her place, I would have five children. The time Dan said he would not let it happen, it did. Now for six years we have been wanting another, and nothing happens.

"Yes," Angelique continues, "it's too bad Paul hasn't a brother, then he wouldn't be bothering you at your house so often."

"Mama! He doesn't bother! He likes it here and we want him."

Surely she must know that Paul isn't attracted to this house just to play with his little cousin! Of course he is amused by the younger boy, but he really comes because he loves the style and the freedom of their home. Dan, a fine teacher, makes him feel important. She can see them at the kitchen table talking while she is cooking, talking about politics, electricity, the opera, the labor movement, and everything under the sun. Dan is vigorous and earnest, making patterns in the air with his hands as he illustrates and explains. Paul is eager and impatient, sometimes argumentative. Always they are in the kitchen, because the fruit bowl and coffeepot are there and because Dan is most comfortable in the kitchen. She wonders whether he and Freddy, when Freddy is twelve, will be the same with one another.

Now she becomes aware that Uncle David is looking at her.

"What are you looking at, Uncle?"

"At you. You've grown so pretty. But then I always said you would."

She is not "pretty." It is true, though, that a change has been made in her; she has acquired a bloom, so that one is now more than ever aware of her rich hair and her leaf-shaped eyes. Dan has done it, it's he who has taught her. She remembers standing with him at the window of the salon de coiffures, looking at the model heads with their winsome faces, and being urged to go in. Dan likes a woman to be well-groomed; he points them out, the vivid ones, the smooth ones . . . And each time a tiny chill of fear darts through her and is suppressed.

"You do look well," Angelique, who has overheard, says critically. "It's a wonder, too, hard as you work keeping the house, caring for the child, and still giving time at the settlement house to your poor families."

"I only do what I like," Hennie answers mildly.

"Well, you are two busy people," Mama says. She is leading up to something. "Florence mentioned that Dan is being made head of the science department."

"It's not official yet, that's why we haven't talked much about it."

"And he's still doing his experiments?"

"Oh, yes, he spends every spare minute in his lab. Right now he's working with high-voltage transformers—way too much for me to understand, I have to admit."

Mama speaks in her dry voice of polite disapproval. "It must be fascinating. Still, there's no money in it."

Uncle David speaks up. "I'm sure he doesn't do it for that reason, Angelique."

"But you could make a lot of money if you wanted to, Dan," Alfie says.

Dan seems to be amused. "How is that, Alfie?"

"Well, I'm no scientist, but from what I read, there's a lot of stuff being done like the stuff you talk about. There was something in the paper about sending electricity through the air, some fellow's idea, and J. P. Morgan's building a tower somewhere on Long Island for it. Two hundred feet high. Fellow stands to make a fortune, I should think."

Paul is interested. "What do you mean, sending electricity through the air?"

"Talk through the air. People will hear you miles away, that's what I read. Sounds impossible, doesn't it?"

"It's not impossible," Dan says quickly. "It will come sooner than you think."

"Well, then, I'm right!" Alfie cries. "Why don't you try to sell something like that, Uncle Dan?"

Dan answers him, "Those men are geniuses. I'm no genius, neither financial nor scientific. I just plod along and I'm satisfied that way." He is shutting Alfie off, nicely but definitely. "Now, how about making that lemonade you and Emily were talking about?"

None of you in this family, except Uncle David, understands him, Hennie thinks. Not you, Mama, who measure things by what they cost. Nor you, Florence, with your dull, tailored man who "provides so well." Can you ever know what it is to look

at your man across the room in a crowd and catch
his eye and be so proud? Proud because he's worth
more than any other man there? Or to wake up
sometimes in the middle of the night with him lying
there next to you, and feel that flooding sweetness
that is so sweet you could almost cry with it?

The sound of Dan's laughter comes now from the
kitchen, where he has followed Alfie and Emily. His
laughter has a special note of gaiety that tells her he
is enjoying himself enormously.

He comes back now carrying the pitcher, and
pours two glasses for Papa and Uncle David. He is
good to them both, especially to Papa, who is growing old, going downhill faster than Uncle David.

"That Alfie certainly knows how to pick a girl,"
Dan says. "She's a fine one, all right. Heads are
going to turn when he walks in with her, wherever
he goes."

Angelique reproves him. "Fine she may be, but
hardly our first choice, as even you can understand."

"Oh, yes," Dan says, "and I'm sure you understand that your son isn't her parents' first choice,
either."

"Choice? They're in terror that something will
come of it every time Alfie crosses their doorstep!"

Dan shrugs. "Perhaps nothing will. At his age a
man can expect ten love affairs before he's through.
If he is ever through," he adds mischievously.

Uncle David's glass has traveled halfway to his
mouth; he sets it down with a clink.

"Any man worth his salt knows when it's time to
be through." He snaps the words. "Either keep a

woman's trust or leave her alone in the first place. Either or, and no two ways about it."

Dan makes no comment but busies himself with the pitcher and the tray. Uncle David brings the glass back to his lips. Over the rim his old eyes catch Hennie's for a fraction of an instant before concealing themselves again behind the protection of his glasses and his hanging gray eyebrows.

What have they meant to say, those kind, clever eyes? Anything new that Hennie does not know? Or have they revealed only a flickering recall of words once spoken, and never spoken since? Probably so. When the darting doubt pays its unwelcome visits— just now and then, and mostly in the chill of a night of poor sleep—Hennie keeps it to herself. It is essential to her peace that doubt be stifled. Talking about it would only make it more real. . . .

Angelique is caught up in her own worries.

"I certainly hope he'll have another love affair, as many as he wants. I've nothing personal against Emily, but"—here she becomes indignant—"I would despise one of those drab interfaith marriages with a judge officiating or, worse yet, God forbid, a clerk at City Hall." She sighs. "But what can we do? You may be sure we've talked to Alfie, but we can hardly tie him up and lock him in the house."

"A man is a rebellious animal," Dan says. "The more you try to tie him, the harder he'll try to get away."

There is no answer to that, and no one makes any, not even Uncle David. The mantel clock strikes the half hour.

"Thirty minutes to go before the twentieth century begins," says Alfie.

"Half past eleven! Oh, Freddy's falling asleep over the checkerboard," Hennie says. "Dan, he belongs in bed."

"Let him see this new year in. It's something he'll remember."

"Yes, you're right," Hennie agrees, and is struck again with a feeling for the drama of the hour. "What a splendid century it will be! I feel great events coming, although I can't imagine what!"

"Ah, but the last one had its splendors too," says Uncle David, who is thinking how little of the new century he will live to see. "It had its causes and its heroes—"

"And it goes out in shame," Dan interrupts, "with a dirty war in Cuba."

"True, true." Uncle David sighs.

"However," Dan resumes briskly, "I don't lose confidence. This twentieth century will be better, Hennie is right. The young will make it better."

The clock rattles, lurching toward midnight. They open the windows and lean out into the freezing air. The city is almost as light as day; every light —gas, electric, or candle—must be ablaze. Down in the street, a crowd is massed. Tin horns squawk and blare; whistles shrill and someone beats a drum.

Suddenly a tremendous shout goes up, a roar like thunder or surf, as if every throat in the city has opened to hail the first of January.

"Twelve o'clock. Nineteen hundred," Dan says.

For a moment they are all stilled. Then the spell breaks. There are kisses and toasts. Freddy is woken up and, held in his father's arms, is allowed a sip of wine. Coats are collected as the gathering breaks up. Alfie and Emily have embraced without embarrassment. Henry and Angelique have decorously kissed each other. Hennie and Dan, looking into one another's eyes, decide to wait until the house is quiet and they are alone.

Their bodies, joined and now released, have made a golden heat in the winter night. Dan laughs.

"How wonderful it is!" he says. "Do you ever think how really wonderful it is?"

"Yes, always," she whispers seriously.

She marvels that they have given one another so much joy, that she has given it to him, and can again, and will.

"No one would think, to look at you, that you could be like this," he tells her. "You do look like such a lady, you know."

"Surely not prim?" She is anxious, for he despises primness.

"Not prim, just very earnest, very correct. But that's all right." He chuckles. "Let people think what they want of you. *I* have you. *I* know you."

She kisses his neck. "You do have me. Always. You and only you."

"Well," he says in mock indignation, "I should hope so! If any man thinks he can—well, he's risking his head!"

But you? she thinks.

Hands that linger a little too long when hands are shaken or a coat is helped on; eyes that call and answer, that sparkle and glint—

No, no! You imagine things, Hennie; you remember too much; after all this time, here in this home that you've made together, with your beloved child asleep under this safe roof, here in your husband's arms, you still remember. But you mustn't, you can't. In the name of wholeness or sanity, in the name of life, you can't. You must insist to yourself that everything is exactly what you want it to be.

"Hennie?"

"Yes?"

"Dear heart," he says.

Dear heart. This is his loving name for her.

"We've come a long way together."

"Yes."

"You're a marvelous woman. You're so good for me. You make peace for me." She *is* good for him. She knows it's true.

"The boy had a good time tonight, didn't he?"

"Oh, yes, he felt important."

Dan yawns. "If we go to sleep right now, we can wake up early enough to start the day right, if you know what I mean."

She knows. "Oh, haven't you had enough?" she asks, moving closer.

"It's just that they say what you do on New Year's Day, you'll do every day all year. That would really be nice, don't you think so?"

Now Hennie laughs. "Very nice, darling."

No, there is no doubt that she pleases him. A man can't pretend. If she were only sure that she is the only one. . . .

Stop it, Hennie. Stop it right now.

"I'm falling asleep," he says.

"Me too."

She closes her eyes. The warmth makes her drowsy at last. She seems to be seeing pink through her lids as sleep comes. Why, it's nine whole years since the fire that changed their lives! And still they love each other, and always will.

Of course they will . . . Won't they?

4

Beneath the pastel shimmer of the time that has come to be known as the Belle Epoque, with its sensuous, curvaceous art and its exotic music, under all the lavish beauty, the bottom seethed, sullen and dark.

A long line of anarchists, beginning with the assassins of the Italian king, the Austrian empress, and the American president, brought terror to Europe and America. Groups less radical but equally determined—socialists, suffragettes, and advocates of disarmament—met and marched, petitioned and wrote. Crusading journalists and novelists exposed the corruption of the cities, the filth of the stockyards, the evils of child labor, and the brutalities in the Pennsylvania oil fields.

In New York City there were rent strikes and meat strikes. Housewives rioted in the streets and poured kerosene on overpriced meat. Twenty thousand shirtwaist workers struck for decent wages and conditions.

"They're working seventy hours a week for less than five dollars! It makes me sick to wear this Gib-

son Girl thing," declared Hennie, plucking at the
spiraling white ruffle on her shirt. "Do you know,
Dan, they have to pay for the chairs they sit on? Pay
for their own needles and their lockers and put up
with . . . advances . . . from the men besides?"

"Oh-ho." Dan laughed. " 'Advances,' hey?"

"How can you laugh? It's outrageous! Here, help
unbutton me. How is a woman supposed to get in or
out of this thing with all these slippery little buttons
down the back? Unless she has a lady's maid or a
husband to help her to bed."

Dan's face appeared in the mirror above her head
as he bent to the buttons.

"Indignation becomes you," he said, and kissed
the back of her neck.

"Oh, Dan, I feel this more than I've felt almost
anything! It's personal. I know so many of the girls.
They almost all come into the settlement; they're so
young and here alone, just off the boat, lots of them
from Italy this past year or two."

Dan was abruptly serious. "They ought to union-
ize, of course."

"I know. But they all hope to get married and
quit, so the union organizers haven't ever gotten
very far with them. And then I think of Olga. She's
not well; I'm afraid it's . . ." She paused, reflecting. "You know, I ought to be doing something."

"You? What can you do?"

"I could picket, for one thing. I could at least do
that."

In the second month of the strike the girls still
marched outside the factory. Two by two they

paced, carrying their defiant placards; their defiant
songs in Yiddish and Italian rang with vigor. When
one dropped out because of sickness or discouragement, two came to take her place.

Oh, it was cold! The January wind slashed around
the corner of the street at which, after fifty paces,
they turned and walked back.

Hennie came every day while Freddy was at
school. Whenever she could, she found her place
beside Olga Zaretkin.

"You ought to take my coat," she said one day.
"It's a lot heavier than yours. You're shivering."

The girl's thin coat was held up protectively
around her throat, leaving her thin wrists bare between sleeve and glove.

"Not at all! Why should you do that?" Olga was
indignant. "I don't need—" The words were cut off
by a spasm of coughing.

"I wasn't trying to embarrass you. Let's not quibble, Olga. Your coat's like paper and you're sick."

There was no answer. They trudged, their feet
squelching in the mucky brown snow. The wind
fought with the placards borne high on flimsy
sticks, trying to wrench them out of numb hands.
An automobile passed deliberately close to the curb;
girls squealed and jumped to escape the spattering
slush, while the driver laughed with contempt. But
a workman on top of a wagon tipped his cap as the
vanguard of a small procession reached the corner
for the fiftieth time that day, wheeled, and turned
back down the block.

"Olga," Hennie persisted. "You shouldn't be here
at all. You should be seeing a doctor."

"What good is a doctor if I can't make a decent

living? No, this comes first." Olga had a faint accent, no more than a Russian countess who had
learned English from her governess might have.
"Besides, I know what's the matter with me anyway."

Indeed, one did not need much knowledge of
medicine to recognize tuberculosis, the East Side
killer. The pink-petal flush, and that peculiar luminous beauty of the eyes, were both as typical as the
cough.

"Of course, I know you haven't been feeling well,
you've told me—"

"Come, Hennie, call it what it is!"

"But . . . you never know, a doctor might—"

"Might what? You said before, let's not quibble."

She is going to die as her husband did; she knows
it quite well. In a few more months she will be too
weak to get out of bed. She will lean over the side
and spit blood. The fever will mount. The end will
come too slowly, unless she gets pneumonia out
here first. Then it will come sooner and more mercifully.

They walked in silence to the end of the block.
Hennie glanced down, for Olga was much shorter
than she; most women were! Still, Olga's steps kept
pace: one-two, one-two, turn at the corner and back.
The second hour and the third. Why? Since she
would certainly not see the benefits of this strike, if
there should ever be any! Surely it would be easier
for her to join with the poor frightened handful of
scabs who, protected by double ranks of burly
toughs, went scurrying into the building every
morning.

"I worry so about Leah." The wind muffled the

sound so that Hennie, not sure she had heard, asked Olga to repeat it.

"I worry about Leah. She's only eight and a half."

"No family here at all?" Hennie asked, although she knew the answer.

"Not here, not there. The ones over there are dead. Killed when they burned our house."

Immediately Hennie saw it all: orange flames and black figures, pursued and struck down. She heard shots and wailing and the final silence when it was over. She felt now Olga's silence of recollection. It was necessary to speak, to make it bearable.

"I haven't seen your Leah in so long . . ." Hennie was guilty and ashamed. She had been concerned with so many things that she had neglected her friend.

"I wish we had a good place to live. It's not right for her this way, living with strangers. They're good people, they struggle, with five children. They sew pants, the whole family, even the children work. Oh!" Olga cried. "What will become of Leah?"

And now she looked Hennie full in the face, while her question hung in the cold air between them. One had to look away from such terror, such anguish; one had no answer.

"She's smart, she's good at numbers. I suppose she could grow up and be a cash girl," Olga said. "They take them as young as twelve, for one dollar seventy-five cents a week, a sixteen-hour day . . . she'll be pretty, too, which is another worry. I don't say so because she's my child, I'm not a fool. But you'd know what I mean if you saw her. Don't look at me, she doesn't look anything like me."

"There's nothing wrong with the way you look," Hennie said gently.

Olga pinched her lips into the shape of a suppressed smile, full of bitterness. The smile said: That was a stupid remark. It had nothing to do with the case and you are stupid, too, if you are trying to make me feel good. I am talking about life and death, don't you understand? All this was in the bitter smile. And Hennie did understand, and was rebuked.

"I don't know what to tell you, Olga," she said honestly then. "I wish I did. God knows. All I can say is, I'll try to keep an eye on her."

Keep an eye on her! What did they mean, those banal, weak words?

"I don't know now whether I'll be able to help," she continued. "Maybe if we win in this place, conditions will change and they'll pay a living wage, with decent conditions, some sort of future."

What did that have to do with a child, alone in the world?

"It will take a long time. A long time to pass laws. And scabs—"

Hennie interrupted, relieved to change from the subject of Olga's child. "There haven't been any in over a week."

She gazed up at the building. The grimy windows were blank, with drawn shades. A prison. A gray stone mountain. A house where everyone has died. Hennie shuddered and shook herself. Then she spoke briskly.

"That may be a good sign, that they're not going to try anymore. It's not working out for them.

Maybe they're going to give in, partway at least, enough to meet and talk. There'll be a union . . ."

They turned again at the corner. The block seemed to be growing longer and longer. How many more times before the relief arrived? It was too much trouble to take off gloves and fumble with freezing hands for her watch. No matter, anyway. When the time was up, she would know.

It was so still. The sounds of shuffling feet and passing traffic grew remote in the women's ears. A numbness began to possess them. They moved mechanically, gasping with the cold. One by one, they had stopped singing and talking. Speech only used the energy they needed now to move their feet: up and down, turn, stamp, shuffle, and trudge. The day wore on, the whole long, gray unbroken day.

It shattered into a thousand pieces.

When the smash came, the narrow column wheeled about. On the instant, without seeing, the strikers knew what it was that had come pounding at their backs. They had seen it before.

From around the corner, with savage, insane cries, as if the sound of their voices could strike its own terror—which it could—came a dozen or more men on the half-run. Street thugs they were, of the familiar type that loiters in bars and pool halls. Huge-shouldered in jackets and sweaters they came; they fell upon the women, shoved them, beat them with raw fists, swore at them, and scattered them.

They wrested the flimsy cardboard signs out of frozen hands. Some of the women, thus pushed off balance, fell screaming; others, small as they were in contrast to their attackers, put up an astonishing fight. In Italian, in Yiddish, in English, they screeched their righteous rage; they used their small fists, kicked and beat at their attackers with the frail sticks and placards on which they had demanded justice.

The street came alive. Windows on the other side, which had revealed no signs of life all day, were raised; from every one heads poked, crowding to the sight of the struggle below.

And rushing to the factory door, heads down, with furtive glances at that struggle, went a file of pathetic shamefaced women, some old, some young, all desperate for work. The door opened briefly to admit them and closed behind them with an echoing clang.

Now the hired toughs were driven into fury. They had not expected such desperate resistance from the striking women. They had not expected to be kicked and scratched, had not expected such united strength. And they brought fuller force to bear; out of nowhere came bricks and clubs, as well as shrill calls for the police.

In the confused chaotic struggle, Hennie had been slammed against the factory wall, at the rear of the flailing mass. She had lost sight of Olga, but suddenly, through a tangle of knees and shoulders, she saw the familiar red woolen hat on the pavement and Olga sobbing on the ground beside the hat. A man's knee pressed her down, grinding into her chest, while her frantic hands scratched at his face.

There was no thought in Hennie, only a crazy rage on behalf of her friend. She leapt. She tore at the man.

"You savage, you ape, you're not fit to live!"

She clawed him, kicked his ankles, and pulled at

his shoulders to topple him; but he was too heavy and she couldn't move him. She heard herself howling like an animal. Why, why was he doing this to Olga, frail as a bird, not half his size? Because he loves it, loves her pain and her sobs.

Hennie bit him. She sank her teeth into his earlobe and bore down. She heard him scream, was flung off, and felt a blow on the side of her head that dropped her on the ground.

How long she lay there, she did not know; it could not have been long before the women were bested. The brawl could not have lasted more than five minutes. She awoke to a clear instant of unreality, thinking: I must have fainted, I never fainted before in all my life, but that's what I must have done. My face is warm, no, it's burning hot and it hurts; I think my nose is bleeding.

She became aware of someone standing over her. A policeman. She stiffened. One knew that the police could be brutal.

But this one helped her, although not too gently, to her feet. He was young, fresh-faced, with disdain like a veil over the youthful freshness.

"For shame," he said, "a lady. Or supposed to be."

Because of my good coat, Hennie thought, he takes me for what he calls a lady.

The toughs were gone, the battle over. Of course, they always fled when the police came. Only a few of the women were left, the bravest. The rest had fled too; one couldn't blame them.

"I've got to arrest the lot of you," the officer said, surveying the poor remainder. "Will you come along decently or will we have to put handcuffs on you?"

His voice was proudly resonant. He played his part; the watchers at the open windows across the street, and the curious passersby for whom the sidewalk was now free and open, were his audience.

For some reason Hennie found herself the spokeswoman.

"We're decent women, so we'll go decently. But why do we have to? What have we done?"

"Disturbed the peace. Brawling on the city streets when you ought to be home tending to your families."

"It's not your business to tell us what we should be doing with our lives, as long as we're not breaking any laws. And we weren't," Hennie said hotly.

The officer looked her up and down. It was apparent that something about her puzzled him. He couldn't place her. She didn't seem to be a worker, not the way she handled the English language. But she wasn't one of those eccentric society women either, one of those who liked to get themselves mixed up in this kind of business, and had to be handled with extreme politeness lest their husbands complain to the commissioner.

"Now listen here, lady," he mocked. "Lady . . . I'd advise you to keep your mouth shut or you'll have another charge against you. Resisting arrest." He caught Hennie's elbow. "I'd advise you further to step into that wagon with the rest of your lot."

Oh, you hero, you upholder of the law against criminals like us!

Olga was coughing, holding a handkerchief to her mouth.

"Are you all right, Olga?"

"I'm so sore where he . . . but you! Your face is turning black and blue! And the blood!"

"The blood's nothing, only a nosebleed. You know, if I'd had a gun, I would have killed that man."

"Less talking there! And step lively."

Two taxis had stopped alongside while the pickets were climbing in. They were crammed with passengers, all laughing, who now got out to watch the affair.

"Well, look at that bunch, will ya?"

"Never saw an uglier crew in all my born days."

"Hey, sister, what you need is a man!"

"That'll cure what ails you!"

Hilarious, they pointed and hooted. Hennie stared back at painted faces, fancy plumes, and soiled silks. Poor, wretched, stupid things, ready for their night's work, victims as much as any of these others who were striking for a decent wage! Except that these, unaware of their shame, were far more wretched. . . .

The patrol wagon drove away to the sound of their tittering malicious laughter.

At the station house, the sergeant behind the high desk looked down on a bedraggled lot. If he felt any pity, he did not show it; if he felt disdain, he did not show that either, as the younger man had. One wondered what he could be feeling, dressed in the authority of good dark blue cloth with a double row of brass buttons. Well, he had his job to do; he had no choice. One by one, they were called before him.

"I'll have to set bail. Two hundred dollars," he said.

From each woman in turn came a gasp.

One ventured, "We're not criminals—"

"Resisting arrest is a crime," the sergeant said. He raised his voice. "Two hundred dollars. If you wish to use the telephone to contact your lawyer, there's one at the desk, and Officer McGuire will assist you."

Olga whispered, "My lawyer. Which one shall I call? The one who handles my real estate investments, or the one who does my trust fund?"

"Or," the sergeant said, "you may use the telephone to notify your families. There are bail bondsmen three doors down on this street."

"What family, what telephone?" Olga whispered again.

"We haven't got a telephone either," Hennie said.

They hadn't needed one, they'd always thought; at this moment, with cold alarm running through her veins, she would have given anything for one. Freddy would be coming home from school and there'd be nobody to let him in. Dan would be in his lab; one could only hope that Freddy would think of going there.

"If we have no telephone," she began, addressing the sergeant, "is there any way somebody will get in touch with our families?"

"Give Officer McGuire the name and address. We can notify the precinct to take care of it. Arraignment is before the magistrate at ten tomorrow morning." A pile of papers, to which he now turned his attention, lay on the high desk before the sergeant. He'd had enough of these troublesome women—a bunch of foreigners, anyway.

"When they're finished with their contacts, take them right back, McGuire."

"Back" was a cell at the end of a corridor. Hennie held Olga's sleeve to make sure they would not be separated. When one cell, holding eight or ten, was filled with strikers, the remaining few went to the next one, which was already partly filled. The iron gate closed and the officer rattled the key, drawing it out with a final click. Final.

For a moment, Hennie stood quite still, watching the dark blue uniform march away. Me, in a cell! Me, Hennie Roth. And farther back, more astonishingly still, Henrietta De Rivera, daughter of Henry and Angelique, granddaughter of—

She came to, and looked around. She was in a gray cement room, fairly large, without a window. There were cots on one side, each with a pillow and mattress; she did not have to look twice to see that they were filthy. Around the other three sides ran a narrow bench. Four buckets in the corners revealed by the stench what they were used for.

It came to her that this was what they called a "holding cell." If you didn't get bail, you had to spend the night here. All of this went through her mind in seconds.

In the next few seconds, her eyes took in the women on the benches: one prostitute, very young and pretty with a dirty lace-flounced dress; one old woman with tumbling gray hair, typical of the homeless who sleep in doorways; and another of indefinite age, respectably clothed, shabby and trembling.

It came to Hennie that this was a scene out of Dickens.

The young one was interested in Hennie's bruises.

"Say! You got beat up! Who done it?"

"We were pickets at the shirtwaist factory."

"You got it easy, then. You'll be out of this dump in no time. A couple of hours."

"Why is that?"

"Because. The high mucky-mucks'll get you out. They always get your kind out." And as Hennie looked perplexed, she explained, "You know, up-town mucky-mucks. Ann Morgan. Mrs. Belmont. Don't you read the papers?"

Now Hennie understood. It was true: Women whose names appeared on the society pages in vivid accounts of banquets and balls were often the same who marched in the suffrage parades and signed the peace petitions; too, often those privileged women came to the support of these other women who made some of the clothes they wore. Hennie had had to remind Dan more than once of that.

"Yes, but it's late," Olga said. "Even if they come, it won't be before morning."

Looking at the cots, Hennie shuddered.

"I asked the officer at the desk to tell Dan to get bail for you, too, Olga."

She tried to recollect what little she knew about bail. Didn't you have to have some surety? Four hundred dollars, she thought. Goodness knew, Dan didn't have money like that at home! They did have more than that in the savings bank, but the bank was closed by this time until tomorrow morning. Again she looked at the cots and shuddered.

Olga had sunk onto the bench next to the middle-aged woman, the only one who looked clean. Hennie looked for a space, although she would have preferred to stand, touching no surface in the room; she had an uncontrollable horror of vermin. Yet it seemed absurd to be standing there alone for what might be many, many hours. She sat down on the other side of the clean little woman, who, after searching her face curiously, struck up a conversation.

"Knocked you around a bit, didn't they? Does it hurt much?"

"A little," Hennie admitted. Her face had begun to throb badly.

"Looks awful. You'll have a shiner. Maybe two."

"I wish I had a mirror."

"I can tell you. You've got a bloody lump on your nose, your left cheek is turning green and blue and is swolled up, like you've got mumps."

"Maybe I could get some ice," Hennie said doubtfully.

The woman laughed. "Who do you think'll give you that? Them, out there? This ain't no hospital. You're lucky they don't punch you another one."

Across from Hennie, the young girl opened her purse.

"Here's a mirror, if you want to look at your mug."

"Maybe I'd better not, since I can't do anything about it. But thanks anyway."

The girl shrugged. Holding the mirror up toward the weak glare of the ceiling bulb, she examined her own painted face. Not more than seventeen, Hennie thought. A doll's face, with dimples.

Olga, who had been sitting with her head in her

hands, raised it and leaned it against the wall. Her closed eyes lay in dark blue hollows.

"Are you all right?" whispered Hennie.

Without opening her eyes, Olga whispered back, "Leah. Little Leah."

"She on strike too?" her neighbor inquired.

Hennie answered for Olga. "Yes. She's not well."

"I see that. I'm in for lifting. A pair of gloves. They caught me this time. Only the second time, though."

Some of the strikers in the next cell began to sing. Starting low at first, they raised their voices a shade and finally burst out singing: of freedom, of bosses, wars, love, and peace. All that energy, that strength, that spirit! Hennie felt none of it now; she was exhausted. The pain in her head was mounting. It was a relief when an officer came pounding down the hall and made them stop singing.

The minutes passed. Two hours must have passed. Her watch had been broken in the scuffle and she could only guess the time. Where was Dan? Suppose they hadn't reached him? How hard would they try, without a telephone? . . . He would be frantic. Would he think of looking for her here? No, of course not.

The minutes passed. It was just as well that she did not know the time, for it would have been unbearable to watch it pass.

After a while a policeman came and unlocked the grating. Everyone except the poor old derelict, who lay asleep in her woolen rags, started up in hope. But it was only some supper.

"Thought you ladies might be wantin' your

evenin' meal. Here's a nice lot of bread for yez and a drink of good cold water."

He put the dishes on the end of the bench, where the stench from the slop buckets rose to hover over the bread. Hennie gagged.

"Not to your likin', missus? You were wantin' turkey, I'll bet, were you not?"

Hennie, choosing to ignore the sarcasm, was about to ask whether any message had come from her husband, when the young girl let out a frightful screech and scrambled up on the opposite bench, raising her soiled lace ruffles.

"A rat! Oh, Jesus, a rat!" Her teeth chattered. "He went behind there—" And she pointed toward one of the slop buckets.

The policeman kicked the bucket aside, splashing some of its contents on the floor. There, indeed, was a hole where the wall met the floor. He threw up his hands.

"Poor thing, come in out of the cold. Better eat your nice dinner, ladies, before he comes back and eats it for you."

Hennie shrank on the bench, drawing her skirts in. For God's sake, where was Dan? What, oh, what could be keeping him?

She waited. Hennie, in a cell. No matter what, even if she had to stay here all night, she mustn't panic. Mustn't. Wouldn't. After a long time she became aware that her teeth were clenched and her hands were balled into fists, thrust into her pockets.

Surely it must be very late by now. The old woman, rousing from sleep, went to squat on a bucket. Olga had scarcely moved, except to stir a little and patiently sigh. The other two women were silent. Like Hennie, they waited. Surely it must be very late . . .

And then she heard Dan's voice. From far down the corridor it rang, and at the sound of it her first tears came. Roughly, she wiped them away and was dry-eyed when he appeared. She flung her arms around him.

"I thought you would never come."

"Wait till we're outside and I'll explain. Paul's here, taking care of things at the desk for you and your friend."

"Olga," Hennie cried, "come, dear. This is Dan and it's all right, you're free. Come along, we'll take you home."

"What have they done to you?"

Dan was aghast, and Paul, who was waiting at the street door, opened his eyes in astonishment.

"Do I look so awful?"

"Yes. I want to take you to a doctor right away."

"No, please, I want to go home. Nothing's broken. I need some ice on it. And a hot bath, and some hot tea. Paul, this is my friend, Olga Zaretkin. My nephew, Paul Werner."

Paul bowed. In his velvet-collared overcoat, with his cheerful young face, he might have come from another continent to stand on this grimy street.

His sleek little auto was at the curb. He covered the women with a lap robe.

"It must be close to zero out, let alone the wind. Where shall I take you?" he asked Olga.

She murmured, "You go down Grand Street, it's left around the corner, then you go—I'll show you."

These were the first words Olga had spoken in

two hours, Hennie realized. How ill she is, she thought, and there is nothing to be done about it.

Nothing to be done either for the three left behind in the jail. Each of them had been there before, each would be there again; the horror was overwhelming.

"What happened," Dan explained, "was that when you didn't come home, I went all over looking for you. I thought maybe you'd gone to the settlement, so I went there. I thought maybe you were at a conference in Freddy's school. I asked everyone in our building who might know. I even went to your mother's; I took Freddy—"

"My mother knows?" Hennie cried.

"She does now. After I left her, she telephoned Paul, who'd just got home on his winter break. He picked her up and they both came to our house, just about the time a cop from the precinct arrived to tell me about you." Dan reached back from the front seat and grasped Hennie's hand. "Don't be afraid about tomorrow. The magistrate will give you a fine and a lecture and you'll go home. Of course, he might not be as lenient a second time."

"This is the house," Olga said abruptly.

They drew up in front of a tenement indistinguishable from the others on the street. The sky, filled with the threat of snow, pressed down on the squat roofs; the street, with the pushcarts taken in, was dead.

"No, wait here," Hennie instructed Paul and Dan, who were prepared to go inside with the women. "I'll just see Olga upstairs and be right back."

She would not say in Olga's hearing that on these silent streets there were people who prowled, who would take perverted pleasure in damaging Paul's treasured auto.

The sewing machines whirred to a halt the instant they walked into the third-floor flat. Four men and women in gray middle age, and three pale boys, stopped work. Seven pairs of eyes stared.

"So what happened to you? The strike again?"

"Let her sit down," Hennie said. "She's about to drop."

Someone moved a pile of woolen pants from a chair.

"So, sit. You want some hot tea?" A woman, evidently the mother of the family, got up. "You look terrible. Frozen."

"I am." Olga removed her hat. "Frozen."

"She's a sick woman." One of the men sighed, and adjusting a seam under the needle, began to work the treadle again. "Very sick."

Olga began to struggle out of her coat.

"Keep it on," Hennie told her. "Let yourself warm up first."

"But I'm also burning. Where's Leah?"

"I sent her for milk," the woman answered.

She brought tea; Olga warmed her hands around the glass and drank. There being no place to sit, Hennie stood. Now she saw that there were two more children, quite young, asleep on another pile of clothes near the window. The light from the kerosene lamps was a sickly yellow; one's eyes must hurt, sewing in such light. Often enough Hennie had been in flats like this, yet somehow never seen one as clearly as now. The stifling air smelled of stale grease and unwashed bodies.

I would lose my sanity if I had to live here, she thought.

Snow had begun to shower against the window, and Paul was waiting. She was preparing to leave when the hall door opened and a little girl came in, carrying a pail and shaking snow off her coat.

"Leah," said Olga, opening her arms.

The child, who had brought a fresh, pure cold into the fetid room, stood staring at her mother.

"Mama! Are you sick again?"

Hennie said quickly, "Mama's all right. She had to come home, but she's all right."

"Yes, I'm all right," Olga repeated, adding, "don't worry, Leah," for the girl's large eyes had opened wide in alarm.

She knelt beside her mother. "Has something happened to you, Mama?"

"I'll tell you later. We mustn't keep my friend waiting, she brought me home. You remember her, my friend Hennie I always talk about?"

Leah looked closely at Hennie. "I remember you. You gave me lemonade once at the settlement house."

Olga looked up at Hennie. Proudly and tenderly the look said, You see, you see . . .

She had not exaggerated. Rather, she had not said enough, Hennie thought, for this was a child you would turn back to look at. Something pulled you toward her, something immediately vibrant and warm. Reddish hair made a tiara of loose curls around her head; each silky cheek held a dimple. Most striking was her look of health, as if she had come from days of milk and sun on a farm. How long would she keep that radiant look?

The child was studying Hennie in return. "You came in the auto," she said.

"Yes, it's my nephew's," Hennie replied, and felt shame, which was absurd for, in the first place, the auto was not hers, and in the second place, why should Paul not own it? He had not stolen it, nor harmed anyone.

All this spun through her mind, repeating a thought that would be with her all her life, wherever there was a juxtaposition of wealth and poverty.

The child went to the window to look out. The man working at the window was amused.

"Look at her! She likes the auto. Maybe you'd like to have one like it, hey, little one?"

Olga shrugged. "Autos! All I ask is enough food to keep up our strength and I'll gladly walk."

Hennie put her hand on Olga's bent shoulder.

"Try to take care of yourself." Foolish, futile counsel! "If there's anything I can do . . ."

Olga shook her head. "For me, nothing. Only for Leah." Her voice was filled with tears.

"I know. I promise."

Yes, there was something about Leah Zaretkin, eight years old. One of the golden ones, Hennie thought; you don't know how to describe what it is, it is just a sort of emanation, a bright glow. Dan has it. Paul has it. . . .

And her heart went out to the child.

Hennie dozed and woke with a painful throbbing in her nose and jaw, which had been pressed into the pillow.

In a chair next to the bed, Dan sat and watched.

He had called the doctor from the drugstore telephone, brought medicine, brought supper on a tray,
renewed the icebags, and warmed her with his enormous pride.

"I thought maybe you'd be angry," she said now.

"Angry? Yes, at the thugs and at the police who
aren't much better than thugs. I'm only thankful
you're not hurt worse." His eyes glowed with admiration. "You'll see, though, it will have been worth
it. Oh, it won't be solved overnight! The employers
will give in a little for the sake of getting work
started again, and there'll be more strikes. But eventually the law will regulate conditions. And it will
be your courage that began it."

It started to snow again. Then came sleet, patter-
ing on the window. Dan pulled the blankets closer
around her shoulders as she slipped back into a half
doze.

My courage, he says. But I'm not brave. I was
scared to death. I'm even more scared now when I
think of it than when it was happening.

Why do I do these things? Because I want to help
and I know it's right. Of course. Yet there's something else . . . I think . . . I know it's that I want
to feel important. I want Dan to praise me. He loves
me . . . but I want him to praise me too.

Suddenly she sprang out of bed into the shock of
cold air and went to the mirror over the bureau.

"What on earth are you doing, Hennie?"

"I want to see how I look." Tilted, the lamp
threw a sallow beam on her face. Ignoring the swollen side, she analyzed herself. It is only expression
that makes my face attractive, she thought, for what
might have been the thousandth time; the features

are too bold, too flawed, the eyebrows too thick. When I smile and my mouth curves, I am at my best. I should remember to do that more often.

"In a day or two you'll be fine. Well, to be truthful, in a couple of weeks you'll be fine. Does it hurt so much?"

"Not much."

"Come back to bed before you freeze. I don't know why you don't fall asleep. The medicine's supposed to make you sleep."

"It's because I can't get that child out of my mind. If you could have seen that vivid little face, Dan, and that miserable room, all grime and gray—"

"I know, I understand. But there's nothing you can do, so you really must try to stop thinking about her."

"You see, I sort of promised Olga that I would take care of Leah."

"What? How can you take care of her? You shouldn't have made such a promise!"

"Those people won't keep her when her mother dies. How can they? They're probably feeding her and Olga for nothing now. I'm sure they expect to be repaid when the strike's over."

"I'll tell you what you can do. You can keep in touch, and when it happens, when the mother goes, you can make arrangements at the orphanage."

Those bleak places. Gloomy, dark red brick. Stingy little windows. Regiments, armies of children, walking two by two. Oh, no doubt they were kind enough in those places, after their fashion . . .

Now came Olga's despairing face, her shivering

hands pulling the collar around her throat, and her despairing cry: What will become of the child?

Can you allow a little girl like her just to go to waste?

Hennie, there are thousands of them.

Yes, but I don't know them all.

Hennie, what can you possibly be thinking of?

I am imagining that I am dying and there is no place for Freddy to go in this jungle of a world.

Freddy. What will he think?

He has the softest heart. She wouldn't interfere with him.

Tell the truth, it is because you haven't had any more children.

If I had a girl, if I had Leah, I would send her to school, dress her up in yellow, in white, in red. I would spoil her in a way I never was.

Dan's warm hand stroked her forehead. "Close your eyes. Try. Let yourself float away."

Hennie's eyes flew open. "We could adopt her. I don't mean legally or anything like that, I mean, just take her."

"Here? Into our family?"

"Why not? We've wanted another child and nothing happens."

"It's late now. Freddy's almost grown."

"It's not too late. You wouldn't say so if I were pregnant."

"Well, but you're not and it's a big step. Your heart is wrung, I understand. But you'd better do a lot more thinking."

"I have thought."

"Well, think some more."

"You don't want me to do it and I should think

you would be the first one to want it, you of all people."

"Ordinarily, yes, but in our case, with Freddy the way he is—"

She cried sharply, "What do you mean, the way he is?"

"Freddy has a long way to go and it may not be easy."

"What can you be saying? There's nothing wrong with Freddy."

"He's complicated. He's different. You know it as well as I do, Hennie, but we're afraid to talk about it."

"I'm not afraid of anything and I don't know what you're saying."

If you don't talk about it, perhaps it will go away.

"He's a sensitive child, of course, I know that, Dan, but does that make him—strange?"

"It makes for a more uncertain future," Dan said quietly.

And she said, hearing the bitterness in her own voice, "You want him to be like Paul."

And so do you.

"I never said that, Hennie." There was a long pause. "It's been quite a day and I'm tired out. I'm going to go see how Paul and your mother are doing."

He opened the door. Quiet, considerate voices came from the parlor.

"Is Mama furious?"

"Not at all. She surprises me. She hasn't said one angry word."

"I would have expected her to blow up."

"Too shocked, I suppose. Paul says the blowup

will come next week, after she's had time to think
about it." Dan hesitated. "I didn't mean to be short
with you, Hennie. I only meant it's a staggering responsibility to take another child, a strange child.
Frankly, I don't want to do it. But if you . . . well,
you ought to be very sure you know what you're
undertaking."

"Oh, I am, I am!"

And it seemed to Hennie, as she lay alone waiting
for sleep and relief to come, that the child's face was
floating, beckoning so sweetly, so brightly there, in
the hazy darkness just beyond the window: I'm
waiting for you, when it's time, when you're ready,
I'm waiting.

Paul was stretched in Dan's easy chair in the parlor.
An amazing day! Wait till he told his friends! Bailing
one's aunt out of jail! Her friend, that other woman,
poor thing, she'd been frail as a blade of grass. God,
it made you sick to see such misery . . . and it was
so like Hennie to take the trouble . . . he remembered the family tales of Hennie's childhood, about
how she rescued sick cats and once brought a lost
little boy home to her house. She'd been lucky today, though, and ought to be more careful; a picket
had lost an eye a while ago in just such a labor
brawl as this one. He'd read about it in the *Times*.

He closed his eyes, feeling half asleep. His grandmother and Freddy were sitting on the sofa talking,
or rather, she was talking and Freddy was listening,
fascinated, with a bowl of uneaten pudding on his
lap.

"After the war," said Angelique, "came the yellow fever epidemic, when my mother died. After that, we came north."

"Tell me about it again."

Angelique was pleased with the boy's attention. "Well, I remember that cannon crashed all over the city. It was thought that cannon fire would kill the germs. They thought night air was poisonous, too, so the windows were kept shut all night. It was so hot, it was terrible. In the morning, when the windows were opened, you could smell burning tar; that, too, was supposed to kill germs."

"Go on," said Freddy.

A romantic. He feeds on these tales, Paul thought.

"My mother told the family she was going to die." Angelique always sat straight, but she could make herself still straighter, and did so whenever the narration required a show of pride, as now.

"From the window of her room, I watched the carts pass, loaded with coffins, and I remember thinking of being dead, jolted through the streets like that, as my mother soon would be. I remember thinking that the people inside the coffins didn't know, and was glad of that.

"We had an old butler, a very old Negro man named Sisyphus; he went outside when she died and tacked the funeral notice, a card with a black border, on a tree at the gate in front of the house. It was raining. When he came inside he told me, 'Going to storm bad. Always a storm after the death of an old woman.' Funny thing, my mother wasn't an old woman at all. The things you remember."

For a moment the grandmother and the boy were

silent, each of them musing into some private distance.

Then Freddy spoke abruptly. "I wish I'd lived then. It seems so sort of brave and beautiful, like a story."

Paul felt a surge of anger toward his grandmother and toward Freddy too. Bravery was what Hennie had endured today, in a righteous cause.

"No, it wasn't, Freddy!" Paul spoke his mind. "It was a time of great wrong in a narrow-minded, backward place. You can be glad you weren't alive then."

"You weren't there, so you don't know," Angelique retorted. "People exaggerate and condemn without knowing. It was a gracious culture. Standards. And we had heroes of the kind you don't see these days. Certainly not around here," she said contemptuously, fanning herself with a handkerchief.

Paul had no taste for futile argument. "Well, it's all theory anyway, since we can't turn time back. You know what the best time of anybody's life is, Freddy?"

"No, when?"

"I'll tell you: now. Yesterday's gone and tomorrow hasn't come, so now is the only time there is. Right?"

"I guess so."

A moody kid, too easily swayed. Paul was irritated and sorry at the same time.

"Would you like to visit me at Yale sometime? You could spend a weekend and see whether you'd like to go there, too, someday. Maybe study science, the things your father works on. Or music, since you play so well, or economics; that's what I'm going to do."

"My father says I'm to go to City College. He says the finest minds in the country go there."

"That's one way I agree with you, Paul," Angelique said quickly. "Dan has the most ridiculous pseudodemocratic ideas, as if there were something evil about a private college."

Paul frowned. She ought to know better than to criticize the boy's father in front of the boy.

"You know what? You've got homework to do. Better go to your room and do it," Paul said.

Freddy got up without protest. An obedient child. It would be better if he were sometimes not so obedient, Paul reflected.

When they were alone, his grandmother turned to him. "Well, and what do you think of this mess today?" And, without waiting for an answer, poured forth her complaint. "I can't for the life of me understand it! My own daughter under arrest! So different from your mother, you wouldn't think they were sisters! This whole household is so foreign to me that I might as well live among Zulus or Hottentots!"

Paul didn't answer.

"Surely you don't approve of what happened today?"

"I understand what she did," Paul said quietly. "And sometimes I'm ashamed that I don't have the same conviction or courage, and maybe never will have."

"Nonsense! You come of a courageous family. You heard what we in the South endured during the war. That's character. It's in the blood. Have you forgotten?"

"I haven't forgotten," Paul said wearily.

And he thought of Freddy. What was to become of the boy, pulled as he was in two directions, whipped daily into a socialist fervor by his parents and at the same time set upon—and enthralled by—his grandmother's aristocratic, romantic pap?

He got up and walked to the window. Families! They bred you, fed you, and loved you, and baffled you so that you got to a point where you didn't know what to think. Even his own household, which was certainly far less contradictory than this one, was confusing. Already he looked forward to being back at college, not because he was unhappy at home—because he wasn't—but because, among his friends, he could say whatever he thought without offending any sensibilities. He turned back to the room.

"The snow's let up, Grandmother. And if they don't need us anymore, let's go. I'll drive you home."

"Very well. Automobiles make me nervous, but I'd better get used to them. I'd better get used to a lot of things, the way it looks."

Hadn't we all, Paul thought, but did not say it.

"I drew a picture, Mama," Leah said. "Want to see?"

Out of her skirt pocket came a creased sheet of copybook paper. Carefully she unfolded it, flattened it with her palms, and presented it to her mother.

"It's a princess. Can you tell?"

"Certainly. You've made such a wonderful crown. Of course, she could even be a queen with that crown, couldn't she?"

"She's too young. She's a princess, waiting for the prince. And her dress is pink. I didn't have the right crayon, but it's sort of pink, anyway."

"It's lovely. You do make lovely pictures."

The mother sat with her chin in her hands, watching the child eat her meager supper: a slice of dried herring, a boiled potato, and some bread. The child ate, nevertheless, with enjoyment; she was hungry. Charity fare, the mother thought, a gift from those others who were still at the machines in the front room. Surely they must know there was no possibility of repayment! It was a gift from the poor to the poorer.

"I wish you would make me a pink dress," Leah said.

Olga trembled. Her child's simple wish, the slight petulance, the direct gaze, all turned a knife in her heart. With what was she to buy cloth? Or how get the use of a sewing machine, since these, here, were in constant use? To say nothing of finding the energy—

"You're shivering, Mama! And it's hot here in front of the stove."

The kitchen was so small that the table and two chairs were almost flush with the coal stove. Thank heaven the place was at least warm; the stench of fish and the sight of the greasy sink you could put up with.

"I said, you're shivering, Mama."

"I'm all right. It just takes me a while to get warm sometimes."

The child looked up sharply, as if to make sure that Olga was telling the truth. Then, seemingly satisfied, she turned back to herself.

"Will you really make me a pink dress?"

Olga said gently, "It seems to me that I should first try to get you a winter coat. Your wrists are sticking out of your sleeves, you've grown so."

"I don't care about that! I want a dress! Hannah's mother made one for her, she wore it today, why can't you ever—" Leah clapped her hand to her mouth, then corrected herself. "I forgot you're sick. When you get better, I mean."

How kind she is, thought Olga. She gives me orders, she demands, and quickly remembering, is kind. Such a little thing, a baby!

"I'll tell you, Leah darling. Pink is a summer color. It would look foolish now. But when summer comes, I'll see that you have a pink dress. I promise."

Dear God, somehow, I don't know how, she'll have it.

"Drink your milk, Leah. You need it."

Even milk was expensive. In Russia, in the poorest village, one could keep a cow. It ate grass that cost nothing and gave you milk in return. Here —Olga stared at the window, which looked almost directly into another window a few feet distant— here there wasn't a blade of grass. It was so dark and grim that the geranium on the windowsill last summer had died for lack of sunlight.

Still, that wasn't fair. America had villages too, and cows and flowers. But they were far from this place. Her gaze returned to the little girl, who, with both hands on the tumbler, was dawdling and dreaming.

"What are you thinking of, Leah, so far away?"

The child smiled, dimpling her cheeks. "I was thinking about that lady, your friend who came in the auto. I wish I could go for a ride in it."

This innocent desire for a trivial pleasure, this total ignorance of what was lying ahead, were enough to make one weep. But it was necessary to be quite calm. And Olga replied evenly,

"That would be fun for you, I suppose."

"Of course it would! She must be rich, that lady. Is she rich, Mama?"

"I don't know. I don't think about things like that. She's a good friend, that's all that counts."

Leah scraped her plate clean and took it to the sink. She dangled a sour, torn dishrag between two fingers, wrinkling her nose with disgust.

"Ugh! Dirty! Everything's dirty in this place, Mama!"

"Shhh, they'll hear you." Anxiously, Olga turned toward the front room. They hadn't heard; they were all bent over the machines, working the pedals, talking and humming.

"You mustn't say such things, Leah. They're such good people, so good to us. They don't have time to keep things cleaner, that's all."

"But our rooms were clean when we lived with Papa," Leah whispered, persisting.

That was true. There'd been two parents working and only one child; it had been easier for Olga than for this crowded family.

"I miss Papa," Leah said.

"I know. Oh, I know."

A silence came between the two of them. The face of the dead young man hovered before the widow's eyes, and perhaps it rose in the child's sight also, for she suddenly wailed,

"Oh, Mama, he'll never come back!"

"No."

"What if you die too? I'm scared . . . you could die too, couldn't you?"

Olga coughed. A fit of coughing strangled and choked her: blood spattered red beads on her hand-kerchief.

"You *are* very sick, Mama! I know you are!"

"Yes, I'm sick." Olga took resolve; one might as well face, at eight, what one would have to face at nine. "It's possible that I could die, Leah, my darling."

"I don't want you to! You can't! I'll have nobody then!"

"It's not up to me, it's not like that. Listen to me, listen carefully. You're a big girl now, in third grade, and you can understand grown-up things. I'm going to write down the name and address of the nice lady who was here. Hennie Roth. I'm going to put it in my box, under my clothes. Remember. And—if anything happens to me, you'll go to her. Or somebody here will be kind enough to go to her for you."

"Why? Why?"

Olga steadied her wavering voice. "Because—she promised me to look after you. She'll take you to live with her, I'm sure. You'll have a good home there."

Leah plunged upon Olga's lap. "But I don't want to live with her! I don't want to live with anybody but you!"

Gently Olga held her away. "Don't come near me, I have to cough again. Darling, they'll be kind to you. I wouldn't want you to go with them if I didn't know that, would I?"

The child put her face on the table and wept.

"Leah. You'll have dresses. Pink, and any other color you want."

The mother sought words; there was so little time in which to prepare the child.

"Toys, too. Things I can't give you. Maybe even a dollhouse."

Out of the muffled, tear-filled mouth came an answer. "I don't want a dollhouse."

"You do. You've talked about it ever since you saw that picture in a book."

The little shoulders shook. . . . Very, very gradually the sobs began to subside. . . . Presently, Leah looked up, wiping her cheeks with the back of her hand.

"And," Olga said, "they would take you out in an auto now and then, I'm sure." She heard herself tempting; her voice was sugared; at the same time, it pleaded. "Just as long as you remember you're a smart girl, Leah. You can make something of yourself. Fight for what you want, for what's right. And you're a good girl, you'll know what's right, I've tried to show you."

The child's dark, intelligent eyes seemed to comprehend something, anyway. Yet she muttered, "Still, I don't want to go there."

"Well, we needn't talk about it anymore just now. Take your dress off and I'll brush your hair."

Warm hair sprang and curled under the mother's

fingers. And Olga, silently, rhythmically brushing that live hair, kept her anguish to herself.

How strange it is that other hands will tend her! When the first grief is over, slowly, slowly, she will become used to those other hands; the memory of mine will dwindle away; I will be a recollected face, a voice half forgotten, a name to be honored: Mother. Dead mother. It's not quite real. Not possible.

Death came even sooner than might have been expected. It is merciful, thought Hennie; her suffering is over.

They had come directly back from the funeral to collect Leah's possessions: a few clothes, a shabby doll, some equally worn books, and a drawing pad with crayons. Now, in the front room, among the sewing machines that had been deserted that morning so that their owners could follow Olga to the Brooklyn cemetery, they stood in the awkward attitude of people who are in a hurry to separate and are not sure how to do it without being abrupt.

Dan and Freddy stood apart in the doorway. Freddy was solemn; he had been scared; this was his first contact with death. Hennie hadn't wanted to bring him, but Dan had insisted that, at eleven, the boy was old enough to know realities; besides, since she was determined to invite a stranger into their family, he ought at least to be familiar with the situation from the beginning. Perhaps that did make sense. Anyway, there they stood observing, Freddy obviously very moved, while Dan was reluctant, polite, and silent.

Hennie opened her purse.

"Who among you collected the money?" she inquired.

One of the men answered that he had, that they had gotten a group to chip in, since certainly they wouldn't have allowed the poor woman to go to potter's field.

"I have enough to cover the cost, with some left over for you people here." It was hard to keep her voice from breaking, and she finished quickly. "You were all so good to her."

The mother of the house grasped Hennie's free hand.

"You're an angel," she said. "An angel."

"No, not I. It's my sister's money, hers and her husband's. When they heard about this they wanted to do something."

"You hear, Leah?" The woman lifted Leah's chin, revealing the full face, swollen, frightened eyes, chapped cheeks, and wet nose. "You're going with nice people. Your mother knew what she was doing. But you won't forget us, will you?" And before the child could answer, she assured Hennie, "She's a good girl, won't be a trouble to you. And smart, she's very smart for her age, you won't be sorry. In a few years she'll go to work. Have you got all your things, Leah? It won't do to keep these people waiting."

Hennie understood that they were anxious, having lost half a day, to get back to work. She took Leah's hand; it clutched hers tightly in return; the child knew enough to grasp a lifeline.

"Well, then," she cried, feigning cheer, "well, then, off we go!"

They took the streetcar home. Leah's worldly goods were in a cardboard box on the floor between Hennie and Dan. Freddy and Leah sat across the aisle. Out of the corner of her eye, while Dan, still silent, read his newspaper, Hennie watched the two.

That dreadful coat, she thought. We'll go shopping tomorrow afternoon. I must get a pretty bedspread. Lucky that we have the little back room. I can fix it up. Yellow will make it sunny. And a shelf for dolls. We'll have to give her some dolls. She'll think she's in fairyland after that place. Look, now, Freddy is telling her something, making her smile a bit. She must be terrified. But Freddy feels for her already.

He understands. He won't be jealous, won't resent her. Gentle Freddy. I saw his face while she was crying so at the grave. That pathetic funeral, just a small band of strangers in a hurry to get it over with. Cold clods flung into the hole, thud on the coffin. Will she remember that? And the sparrows noisy in the trees?

They walked home from the trolley stop. The April day, which earlier had been dismal, now turned lively; clouds and sunshine shifted in turns across the sky. In Washington Square behind iron railings, pools of white and yellow jonquils rippled in a quick wind.

Leah stopped to look. "I never saw so many flowers before," she whispered, and stood still, gazing.

Then came a nursemaid pushing a carriage in which an infant lay surrounded by white frills and taffeta bows. Leah's eyes were astonished. From side to side went her head as if on a swivel, while wonders passed through the square: two gentlemen

wearing striped trousers and silk hats, a barouche
with a coachman in maroon livery, a large old lady
upon whose head there rested a tower of black os-
trich feathers. Wonder upon wonder.

How eager she is! Hennie thought. And strong;
she'll find her way in this new life before very long.
And she urged gently, "Come. We'll go for a long
walk tomorrow. I'll show you the neighborhood and
your new school. Right now we need to get home so
I can make dinner. Are you hungry at all?"

Leah nodded. Of course she was; she was probably always hungry.

"Will you call me Aunt Hennie, dear, and tell me
when you're hungry or whenever you want something?"

The child's eyes filled again. It is the kindness,
Hennie knew at once; it always brings tears, especially on the sort of day this has been. So she spoke
briskly instead.

"Go on, you two. It's getting late."

Leah and Freddy went ahead. The boy chatted.

"Once you learn checkers," they heard him say,
"maybe I'll teach you how to play chess. I'm pretty
good at it."

"I do believe he's happy to have her," Dan said.

"Then do you still think this is a mistake?" Hennie asked.

"Never mind what I think. I have to accept, it's
done."

"Look how the sun glints on her hair! She's a
charming little thing, you have to admit that."

"Oh, she's a charmer all right, and will be. But

you're satisfied, and that's all I care about, God
knows. And I will help you with her, do the best I
can. Don't worry."

Hennie smiled. "I won't."

5

Freddy is in his room after supper, supposedly doing his homework. Twelve math problems await him, and a map on which he is required to outline the major rivers of the world, but he can't think of numbers or rivers tonight. He can think only of what he has seen that afternoon. He lays his head on his arm and grieves.

It was such a good day in the beginning. Walking to school with Bob Fisher, who has never noticed him before and suddenly seems to like him a little; having a piece of apple pie in his lunch box; getting an A-minus on his composition. Finally, and best of all, Mr. Cox asking him to play the piano at Friday's assembly because the music teacher is sick.

So Freddy runs out of school, not even looking for Bob Fisher to walk home together; he has to tell Dad about the piano; he can't wait to see Dad's pleased face. Dad wants him to be a real performer and keeps telling him he could be. He won't mind being interrupted at the lab with news like that.

He runs all the way with his schoolbag bouncing at his leg. He skids around corners, loses his breath,

gets it back, arrives at the door, and rings the bell.
Nobody answers. Dad must be there, though; he
almost always is in the afternoons. Besides, it's dull
weather and the lights are on. Freddy rings again,
harder; it sounds more like a buzzer than a bell,
snarling enough to make you wince. Still no one
answers.

Maybe Dad's taking a nap upstairs? Maybe . . .
he couldn't have died, like Leah's mother, could he?
A pang of fear darts through Freddy's chest and
fades as he ridicules himself. Worrywart. Then he
remembers that he has a key. Of course! It's in his
schoolbag, the inside pocket, along with the house
key they gave him for emergencies after that time
he'd come from school and not found his mother
waiting, the day she'd been arrested. That was the
only time, though. He hadn't liked that, didn't want
her to get mixed up in nasty things like fights and
strikes.

He finds the key and unlocks the door. Dad's not
at the benches. Ceiling lights blaze above the papers,
the scattered plugs and fuses, all the stuff Freddy
doesn't comprehend or care about. So Dad's been
there; he must be upstairs, then.

Freddy walks to the back of the building. He's
about to mount the stairs when he hears voices.
What makes him stop to listen, instead of going
straight up and showing himself? Something . . .
something . . . the sound of laughter, pealing so-
prano laughter. Whose? Not his mother's, he
knows.

Then Dad's voice: "You are the funniest, most
adorable girl . . ."

Freddy is frozen at the foot of the stairs.

Dad's voice: "Oh, stay a while longer, can't you? Come on, we've only begun . . ."

A muffled answer. Giggles. Silence. And sounds. Sounds. He thinks he knows what they mean; he isn't sure, but he's been told things; the big boys talk in the bathrooms at school. Maybe he really does know; yet he doesn't want to; this is his father. His father!

He puts his hands over his ears and stares at the wall. There's a spiderweb left over from last summer hanging in the corner. However did a spider get in here? His mind concentrates, while he understands that he is shutting out the moment. Suddenly he picks up his schoolbag and walks, almost runs, tiptoed this time, to the front door, and lets himself out.

He drags himself home, feeling sick at his stomach. One thing: He has to keep this to himself. He can't tell his father or ask him anything, ever. Ever! He can't say exactly why he feels he can't; he just knows it would be awful. And maybe, after all, there was nothing to it? Maybe he was imagining things? No. No.

The woman, laughing. What right had she to be upstairs in that private room? Suddenly he is furious at the unknown woman.

At home, at supper, his father is no different from the way he is every night, when he comes in and kisses Mama, unfolds his napkin, and starts to talk about whatever is in *The New York Times* that day. But Freddy can hardly look at him. He lets Leah do the talking; he often does that anyway, because Leah is jolly and he likes to listen to her.

His mind touches Leah now. It's been a year since

she came. She doesn't cry anymore, never did cry much, even at first. She's very brave. Looks forward, Mama says, as we all must, not back. Maybe, though, death doesn't hurt as much as betrayal. Leah's lost her mother, but she has beautiful things to remember about her. Beautiful. Soothing. Not ugly, like today.

Freddy raises his head from the desk. I've lost something, he thinks. My father. Not altogether, of course not. But something I'll never get back, just the same.

He'd better not ask me to play for him tonight. He'd better not, that's all.

He sighs and opens the math book.

6

It was a raw night in darkest December, Christmas week, and the twenty-third wedding anniversary of Walter and Florence Werner. The house, which was oppressive by day, especially when the day was cheerful out of doors, was warm and bright with celebration.

In the large, square dining room the company was enclosed as in a velvet box. The walls, paneled in waxed oak, glowed in the light from half a dozen candelabra. Plum-colored draperies of heavy brocatelle covered the windows; a plum-colored Oriental rug covered the floor. Under the ruby glitter of a Bohemian glass chandelier, the table, set for twenty-four, flashed with the white light of silver and diamonds.

At its head, as soon as the tureen of turtle soup had been removed, Walter Werner began to carve an enormous roast. Two young waitresses went around the table to serve. In silver platters, bowls, decanters, pitchers, and repoussé baskets, they bore the food and drink: hothouse asparagus, lobster mousse, creamed oysters, brandied peaches, salads, sauces,

pastry rolls, soufflés, puddings, cakes and cheeses,
grapes and wines.

At the foot of the table sat Florence. Hennie had
an odd thought: The foot becomes the head because
Florence is sitting there. Florence is stately; Walter,
with receding hair and glasses, is not. Besides, to be
fair, the ornaments help Florence. Passementerie
and nine yards of ivory peau de soie sweep the carpet. Fluted lace is gathered low on her white shoulders, and the diamond star gleams on a satin band
around her throat. Florence has authority. She sits
erect, looking taller than she is.

Mama's eyes never leave Florence. She is proud
of this daughter who has regained what Mama once,
so briefly, so gloriously, knew.

Hennie, to her own surprise, was enjoying herself.
It didn't concern her that she was something of an
oddity in this company, a woman "out of step,"
who had actually, however briefly, been arrested by
the police! She could even feel a faint amusement
because of it. Family was family; various members
might go their various ways and still accept each
other.

So she ate and drank, observing her sister's triumph with pleasure. The old secret rivalry between
them had long ago eased away; they were equals,
two married women, two mothers, with the respect
that only marriage and motherhood can bestow.

Apropos of that, it was heartening to see what a
few years of married life had done for Alfie and
Emily. Never would Hennie forget that somber
morning when she had gone with them to City Hall!
It had been, in spite of the love that was palpable
between the two, a depressing experience.

So many dreary scenes had preceded it! Such bitter insults spoken, such bridling pride! Alfie heard it in his home, while Emily heard worse in hers. The two fathers, tied by financial need into their partnership, had arrived at a point where they spoke only what was necessary to each other. Actually they had no reason to be angry at each other, since each had done his utmost to prevent the marriage, to keep his child in the family's community and faith.

Alfie and Emily would not be separated.

She had been crying, and looked quite unbridelike in her plain dark suit. Hennie, in the dingy ladies' room, had encouraged her, sponging her worried cheeks and her eyelids with cold water.

"Do I look too awful, Hennie?"

"Not at all, dear. Besides, the hat brim shades your face very prettily."

"I did so want a white dress and veil and everything! I don't even mind so much not having them, but that my parents wouldn't come today I couldn't have believed!"

The Hugheses had chosen to be out of town. Henry and Angelique, to their credit, had consented to appear, although Angelique's expression as they stood before the marriage clerk had surely not been one to strike joy into the heart. All in all, it had been a sorry start.

Yet here they now sat, having marvelously survived, happy with each other and in the possession of a baby girl, whose arrival had produced between the hostile grandparents a kind of chilly peace. A fragile peace. . . . The world was not going to go out of its way to make things easy for a pair like

Alfie and Emily. Or for the baby either, who would belong—where would she belong?

For a moment Hennie rested a tender gaze upon her brother and his wife, then slid the gaze down the table toward her own children. Freddy and Leah were far down on the other side, so that she could see them only in three-quarter profile.

Freddy seemed to be silent; he missed no nuance, however, and would make his private comments to her later.

Leah's robust laugh rang; she was lively as ever; her face was frank, gay, and bold. After two years, she was completely at home in the household and had become their own daughter—or Hennie's own, anyway. It was a wonder and a blessing that the little girl had been able to recover as she had.

Angelique hadn't seen it quite that way. "She doesn't seem as sad as I expected, a child without a mother," she had observed critically, and then gone on to say, "I do hope she doesn't use Yiddish expressions in front of Freddy. It's a perversion of German, that's all it is."

And Hennie had answered, "Well, I don't know to whom she would speak it, since no one in this house understands it."

"Be that as it may, I still think you are making a terrible mistake."

"Be that as it may," Hennie had told her mother, "I do not think I am."

Only Dan troubled her still.

"Don't you *like* the child, Dan?"

"How can one dislike a child? But she isn't going to be a child forever," he would answer somewhat doubtfully.

So he could still make Hennie feel that she had perhaps been too hasty, not quite sensible in what she had done.

Nevertheless, the girl was thriving. Eager to learn, she had quickly put the slum experience behind her; she did her schoolwork well and filled the house with the schoolgirl chatter of her friends.

She's what I wanted to be and wasn't, Hennie thought.

"You're so quiet, Hennie," Florence said now.

The remark was a reminder to be sociable, to play the expected role of dinner guest.

"Sorry," Hennie said, smiling quickly. "Too much food, I guess."

But she went back to observation. Many separate conversations were taking place. The entire family, even to the least important Werners, were gathered; poor relatives, fading couples related in second or third degree of cousinship, were always invited to such celebrations because "blood is thicker than water." The women had trotted out their small garnets and made-over gowns for the rare excitement. Now, gushing to each other, they praised everything, the food, the flowers, and the house, while Walter and the more affluent men talked business, interest rates, bond yields, puts and calls.

Dan was absorbed with the partner on his left. He had been attentive to her from the start of the meal. They had put him next to a daughter of one of the Werner cousins, a vivacious girl who was evidently having a wonderful time—as was Dan. His laugh had a distinctive timbre; it was the sensual laugh that Hennie recognized. He leaned to the girl, as if they had some very private joke, while she fluttered

toward his attention and bloomed, no doubt mis-
reading that intention.

If only he wouldn't do that! She wished, she
wished he wouldn't! It meant nothing, but how were
other people to know it? He made himself conspicuous; he made Hennie conspicuous; people glanced to
see whether she was angry, feeling sorry for her, the
little wife, the patient little thing. She couldn't very
well say to them, although she would have liked to:
Mind your business, you needn't feel sorry for me,
he really loves me and only me. She must pretend
not to notice. To reveal that she did was to weaken
and shame her all the more. Above all, she must not
let Dan know that she saw or cared.

The funny thing was that Dan hadn't wanted to
come tonight. Of course, he never was enthusiastic
about coming to this house anyway, but on this
night he had a special reason. They were missing a
neighborhood party in their building. It was the
kind of gathering in which he was most at home,
even if—and this was surely a contradiction!—there
were no attractive women there.

"There's life among those people," Dan had
grumbled. "At your sister's house, the only head
that's alive is Paul's. He's the only one who ever has
anything worthwhile to say." And he added, "The
only man in the family I can really talk to, now that
Uncle David's in the home."

Paul was talking quietly to his partner, young
Miss Marian, "Mimi," Mayer. Freckled and fair
and not quite sixteen, she was not destined to be a
beauty, but she was already self-assured, with a definite elegance.

"The Mayers are like family," Florence always

said with a prideful smile, whenever they had to be introduced, forgetting how often she had said it before.

They have the simplicity of great wealth, Hennie reflected, or perhaps not so much great as accustomed and well-worn. She wondered, and then was almost certain, that the families had hopes that Paul and Marian, in time, would— The thought fled. Absurd. One didn't "arrange" marriages in America in the twentieth century.

Paul's thoughts were random. Like Hennie and like Freddy, he was an observer. These dinners, these social games, he often found to be boring, and sometimes, in a way that he could not explain, he even felt a certain sadness in what he saw. For instance, his two grandfathers . . .

His mother's father had little to say; he seldom did. His unfocused eyes, fixed on the opposite wall as he took the fork from his plate to his mouth and back again, were somber. He ate as though his mind were not there at all.

The Werner grandpa, on the other hand, was the master wherever he went, even here in this house that belonged to his son. It was from him that the bounty flowed and would flow on eventually to Paul. And stirring in his seat, he glanced over at the old man's bulky chest, across which a series of gold chains were looped; they couldn't all be watch chains, so what were they? He spoke English with a heavy accent, as though he had arrived in this country just last year; although he had been here since he was younger than Paul was now, he still kept German as the language of his household. Identified with Germany, he went back there every other year.

Paul was sorry that he disliked the man as much as he did.

He didn't care much for the Werner grandmother either, any more than he did for the De Rivera one, and was amused that the two old women—although no one in the family would ever admit it—despised each other, the one because the other was a German upstart and the other because the Sephardic snob had no money. The latter was slender and fashionable, while the German put away enormous amounts of food and showed it. Her pink flesh was stuffed into striped black silk, but she would look more comfortable, Paul thought, wearing an apron and rolling strudel dough.

Still, he thought, they weren't bad people, any of them; really, he had no right . . .

The desserts were being carried in: the walnut cake with mocha icing that was a family tradition on important occasions; ices with raspberries and strawberries from Long Island's hothouses; blue flames spinning on top of a plum pudding. Around and around went the two waitresses, and Paul's eyes followed them; deftly and swiftly they moved, wearing the blank expressions of Oriental dancers, although one was Irish and the other Hungarian.

What could they be thinking? Were they envious, impressed, resigned, or simply hoping not to drop a plate? He often thought about the maids who lived beneath this roof, who had come from God knew where and for what reason, and would go on to God knew where.

The meal had continued for hours; the air was too heavy now with the heat of the candles and human bodies. Gardenias, opening in the warmth, began to

brown at the tips of their creamy petals. At last
Florence stood to signal the end and the party ad-
journed.

Between the double parlors, the sliding doors had
been moved back to make one room that extended
the depth of the house. In the little bustle of finding
seats, Paul came up beside Freddy.

"Is it too awful for you?" he asked.

Freddy's eyes widened with surprise. "Awful?
Why, it's so beautiful! You know I always love it
here."

At the side of the room, next to the fringed
portieres that hid the hall, stood the Christmas tree.
Ten feet tall, it was hung with silver icicles and
crimson balls, and crowned by a gilded cherub.
Freddy stood admiring the shimmer. And then fear
struck him. He had overheard his mother, before
they left home, imploring his father to make no
comment about the tree. Last year Dad had said
something, and you could see that Aunt Florence
had not liked that at all. She had been polite as she
always was—how wonderful to live among people
who were always quiet and not so *emotional* about
things—but she had been very angry. Freddy had
felt it.

"You have no religious belief, Dan, you always
say so, then why should you care?" Aunt Florence
had answered. He remembered it well. "At least we
go regularly to temple services."

"And you don't see the contradiction?" his father
had asked. "Don't see the absurdity of what you're
doing?"

"It's only a symbol of happiness!" Aunt Florence
had insisted. "All America is on holiday, giving

presents, having a good time. Why shouldn't we? It
has no other significance for us."

Then his mother had given his father one of her
"warning" looks, which he did not always heed, but
that time he had, for which Freddy had been thankful. Usually when his father had something to say,
he could not be stopped. He was like a dog with a
bone; you didn't dare take it away from him.

Of course, they should not have a tree. Even Paul
said so, being a far more thoughtful Jew than his
parents were. But the tree was beautiful. . . .

How lucky for Paul to live here! Everything in
this house was perfect.

"How do you like the new portrait?" Grandma
Angelique asked now.

Over the mantel sat Aunt Florence, looking as
royal as the Princess of Wales. The ladies gasped.

"Oh, lovely! Don't you love it, Florence?"

"Well, it's not Boldini, but it's not too bad either,
I must say," Florence responded modestly.

Leah spoke up. "I saw a lady like you in a magazine."

"You did?" said Florence, turning kindly to the
girl.

"Yes, she was wearing a tea gown, somewhere in
Europe. France, I think. It certainly wasn't Russia.
She was drinking from a cup."

The ladies smiled. Hennie's little protégée was
learning fast, though how she knew about tea gowns
was a mystery, since most certainly Hennie never
wore one!

"Leah is interested in fashion," Hennie explained.
"She has done some very fine sketches too."

Hennie wanted to draw Leah out, to show how

far she had come, but the other women had lost interest as they settled themselves around the fireplace.

"We are having the entire house electrified," Florence announced, indicating the gas that flickered in the grate. "They'll be starting work next week. Walter wants to leave the gas fixtures in place, though, in case the electricity should ever fail."

"And you have a telephone too," remarked one of the "poor" cousins, sounding wistful.

"It would certainly be nice to have one," complained Angelique, "instead of having to go to the store every time I want to talk to my daughter. I am trying to talk my husband into it."

Old Mrs. Werner told a joke on herself. "Imagine! When ours was put in, I was afraid to use it the first time. I thought something was going to jump out of the wall on me. But," she added comfortably, "one gets used to modern ways very quickly."

"A time of miracles," another lady said. "Goodness knows what will come next. They say that we shall all go up in flying machines before long."

"Impossible!" another cried scornfully.

They don't read the newspapers, Freddy thought, with his own scorn. The Wright brothers have already stayed up in the air for almost half an hour, don't they know that?

And he looked around for Paul, with whom he liked to talk about such things—although I should be afraid to fly, he thought again, and remembered that Paul had said he would give anything to do it— but Paul had found a chair at the opposite end of the room near the men, and since there was no more room for Freddy there, he was obliged to stay where he was.

The women's talk was dull. But now the conversation turned to something interesting, as it always did when they lowered their voices to whisper and leaned together so that "the boy" would not hear. They were talking about Uncle Alfie and Aunt Emily, just as they had before their baby, Meg, was born.

"He couldn't possibly have continued any longer in the business." Grandma Angelique sighed.

Why was it that whatever she said was trouble, people arguing, one worry after another?

"Given the Hugheses' opposition to their marriage, it's been dreadful."

Gloom, gloom! Her mouth lingered dolefully on the word *dreadful.* Yet, Uncle Alfie and Aunt Emily were sitting together so happily; you could tell by the way his hand lay over hers on the arm of the chair.

"However, it's an ill wind, as they say." Grandma Angelique's tone brightened. "He has always been interested in real estate, you know, and now he has bought, with a couple of partners, of course, a small building near Canal Street."

"Well," said old Mrs. Werner, "that must have been a sacrifice for his wife."

"Alfie has been very good to her," said Angelique, biting the words.

She grew louder; she wanted to be heard at the other end of the room where the men were. But they, drinking brandy, paid no attention.

"Alfie says New York will be bigger than London,

the capital of the world. He is putting everything into property."

She wants my father to hear, Freddy knew.

"Tenements, slum dwellings," Dan always said, whenever Uncle Alfie's ventures were mentioned.

"Your son never went to college, did he?" asked Mrs. Werner.

Freddy knew that Mrs. Werner knew perfectly well that Alfie had not. She was a nasty old woman. Paul said so, and she was his own grandmother.

Angelique answered stiffly, "He was never interested in anything but business. He has a head for it."

"You can do a lot worse than have a head for business," pronounced Walter Werner, who had moved toward the women. "Work hard and do some good on earth, that's all that counts."

"Yes, work hard," repeated his father.

The men brought up their chairs to form a semicircle.

"I myself went to the college of hard knocks," the old man went on. "My son went to Yale. How was he able to go to Yale? Because I first went to the college of hard knocks! My own father was a peddler, you know. He brought me to this country when I was a child. Yes, he was a peddler. I remember it well. I do not hide it, I am proud of it."

His wife, having heard too much about her husband's peddler father, and preferring not to be reminded of these origins, interrupted him.

"Play something for us, Paul."

Paul laughed. "I don't play! I stopped lessons at least ten years ago."

Florence intervened. "We should really hear Freddy play, Mother. He's the gifted one."

Freddy shrank. His horror of being conspicuous was visible in the eyes that he turned toward his mother.

"Yes," Dan said, "he is gifted, more than he knows or will admit to. Why not play the new Mozart, Freddy?"

Still Freddy's eyes implored. Was it only the old, familiar shyness, or was there now, had there been lately, something new? Hennie wondered. Something sullen, even hostile, when he looked at Dan? Especially when Dan asked him to play? But why should that be? Hennie felt impatience; some time or other life ought to stop being so complicated!

She answered the boy in the wordless language that they spoke between themselves: Play, Freddy, your father wants you to. Your father hates to see you so shy. Play.

"Do I have to?" he whispered.

"I'll tell you what," Florence proposed. "While Freddy thinks about it, maybe Mimi will play something. A little German song for Grandmother. 'Röslein auf der Heide,' Mimi?" And with her fine tact that Hennie so admired, she explained for the benefit of Emily, who knew no German, "It means 'Little Rose in the Meadow.' "

Mimi sat down cheerfully and played the simple piece poorly. The contrast to what Freddy could have done was absurd. And Dan looked into space, avoiding his son. The boy's delicacy both angered and hurt him. . . .

But Freddy is like me, Hennie thought, remembering herself as a child. A sickening sense of guilt overcame her, although it was foolish to feel guilt over something she could not help. Still, she thought, at fourteen there's time to change; in the same moment she knew he would not change, and felt for the boy a soft, shielding love quite different from what she would have felt for him if he had been like Paul . . . like Leah . . .

There was applause when Mimi had finished. The girl made a smiling, self-deprecating gesture, as if she were aware of the foolishness of the applause but didn't object to it.

"That was lovely," said Florence.

The girl shook her head. "Oh, I am all thumbs, really stupid at the piano."

"Not as stupid as I am," Paul declared.

Mrs. Mayer shook her finger at Paul. "Now, now, we know all about you, Paul. You were one of the brightest scholars at your school. My nephew goes there now and he told me you left quite a reputation behind you."

One of the cousins asked what school it was.

Walter Werner answered promptly. "Sachs Collegiate Institute. Very fine," with emphasis. He turned to Dan. "You should really consider sending Freddy. He's an unusual boy, one can see that already. His vocabulary is amazing, always has been."

"I wouldn't send him there if I could afford to, which I can't." Dan was in a "mood." "I don't approve of private schools."

There was a moment's pause, until Florence said agreeably, "Oh, I think you must admit, Dan, even if you do teach in a public school—and I'm all in favor of public education—that there still are certain advantages, smaller classes, more personal at-

tention. Even for girls. Our daughters did so well at
Brearley and loved it—"

"To say nothing of the fact," interrupted Grandmother Werner, "that the right young people meet
each other there. The same girls have their coming
out at Sherry's together. They marry each other's
brothers and they go through life together. It's a
beautiful way to live. A community of friends."

The elder Werner smoothed gold chains between
finger and thumb. "Yes, friends. Last winter when
Randolph Guggenheimer gave his dinner at the
Waldorf, I knew every man there. What a spectacle!
Unforgettable. The whole place made into a garden.
Tulips and canaries singing in the bushes. What a
display!"

"A display indeed," Dan muttered.

Paul snickered. Uncle Dan didn't care what he
said.

Florence said hurriedly, "But it was nothing compared with some that you read about. The Four
Hundred giving that party where the whole ground
floor of the hotel was turned into Versailles, and
guests wore costumes trimmed with real jewels. Of
course," she said, prudently lowering her voice, although Emily was still standing on the other side of
the room, "that was for the gentiles. We can only
read about such things."

"And don't you find it disgusting, even to read
about?" asked Dan. He came around from behind
Hennie; his eyes were dark and serious.

"Oh," Walter said, "most of those people, after
all—"

And Paul mentally finished the sentence: Have
earned it fairly, and they do give employment—

But Dan interrupted, "They have earned it, I know. Just like Horatio Alger."

"Stupid books," said Paul. "Foisted on me almost as soon as I learned to read."

His father gave mild rebuke. "My son is super-critical. There is a deal of truth in those simple stories, Paul. They wouldn't be printed or so popular otherwise."

"Oh, there are plenty of popular lies on the printed page," Dan cried out, "look at the Hearst newspapers!"

Freddy cringed. He was so ashamed: his father was too urgent—he sought the word—too emphatic, so that everybody in a room, as in this one now, would turn to look at him.

Hennie worried: He's had too much to drink. His face is bright pink. He can't drink; he hardly ever does, and now he's had wine at dinner and brandy, too, on top of it.

And she tried to meet his eyes but could not; avoiding her appeal, he stood tall above her. He wanted to arouse these men in their black-and-white clothes, in what he called their penguin suits. He despised their suits and them.

"Mark my words, there will have to be a tax on income. It may not be this year, it won't be this year, but some year soon, you may be sure of it."

"A tax on income!" Walter was indignant. "The concept is outrageous. Besides, we are already taxed; men of substance tax themselves voluntarily to give to charity, following their conscience."

"Their conscience?" Dan repeated.

The discussion was now limited to these two men; the rest had withdrawn. As uneasy, silent spectators, they waited for the outcome of the contest. Alfie's amiable forehead contracted in a worried scowl, while Emily, at the window, drew the curtain aside and stared out to the empty black street.

"Certainly by conscience! Fortunes are given away every year. My father—it is possibly not becoming to say so, but my father must forgive me—gives thousands. There's the Children's Aid Society and the Foundling Asylum; there are hospitals, old age homes, settlement houses—" Walter looked toward Hennie. "Your own wife's the one to tell you about settlement houses. Ask her."

"I don't have to ask her. I know, and I'm not impressed. These vast sums are hardly missed by their donors, isn't that so? They're a pittance out of those fortunes." Dan, standing up, leaned forward, resting his hands on the back of his chair. "There are things in this city, I tell you, that would shock you if you heard they were happening in Calcutta or Borneo!"

Mr. and Mrs. Mayer rose abruptly, making a dual murmur. "Good heavens, we've quite lost track of the time . . . so late . . . but such a lovely evening." So they talked their way toward the door, with Florence behind them.

Oh, why, thought Hennie, why must he do this? What he says is true, of course, but not here, not now.

"Last month," Dan said, "it was not in the newspapers, too frightful, I suppose, for the public prints, or perhaps not something that the powers want the public to know."

He lowered his voice. There was an expectant stir and rustle as people shifted in their chairs.

"Last month a family froze to death; they had no money to buy coal or wood. Well, that's hardly news, it happens often enough. This time, though, the mother was ill of pneumonia, and died, and lay dead for a week decaying, while her children, too young or too stunned and frightened to go for help, just lay and waited. It was on the top floor of a half-abandoned building, so no one heard the baby crying. And the baby died . . . and there was evidence that the older children—" Dan swallowed. "Evidence of cannibalism . . . perhaps I shouldn't tell you."

The room became completely still, without a rustle, almost without a breath. Then old Mr. Werner raised himself from his great chair and cried out. His fist shook as he raised it. His voice shook.

"Indeed you should not! This is a disgrace! I've never heard anything like it! In front of these ladies and these young people—your own son! It's disgusting, sir, and I consider it unforgivable!"

"It is only reality," Dan replied evenly. "It is the world they live in. They might as well know what it is."

"Oh, please, Dan," Hennie said softly.

Florence fluttered. "Has anyone tried this marzipan? I always have it when Hennie is coming." She beamed a piteous smile to the room. "Once on Hennie's birthday, she was six or seven, she ate a whole box of it, stole it out of the pantry, it was so funny. Don't you remember, Hennie?" she asked, the smile dying into a wordless plea: Don't spoil everything; can't someone stop this? And she began to cry.

Angelique put her arm around her daughter.

"Don't, don't. It's not worth it. You," she said. "You, Dan, you're not civilized."

Dan made a slight bow. "I'm sorry. It's hard to be civilized when you see the uncivilized things that I've seen. These wretched homes, the dispossessed, five thousand this last year alone—you can't imagine."

"Oh," Florence said, "we can imagine! Why do you suppose we give what we do? Oh, we have always been generous, if not as you say, generous enough."

To Florence, Dan spoke more gently. "Charity's not the whole answer, anyway. What's needed is a radical cleanup of the tenements. Men like Jacob Riis and Lawrence Veiller are still fighting, and so am I, in my small way."

"Still?" said Walter. "In spite of the Tenement House Act? I should think you'd all be satisfied now."

"Oh, it looked good enough on paper! But the old-law houses are still standing—you know that. Rotting away, and the tenants with them."

Walter opened his mouth to speak, closed it, and opened it again.

"It would seem to me you'd do better to use that spare time providing for your son's future. Charity begins at home."

"My son is fine. He's fed, clothed, warm, and loved, which is more than can be said for the children who live in the Montgomery Flats, where I went the other day with Veiller."

Paul drew in his breath, released a little gasp, and looked questioningly at his father. This affair was no longer amusing.

Walter took off his glasses, wiped them, and replaced them.

"What in particular took you there, may I ask?"

"Because the Montgomery is one of the worst in the city. Sure the dumbbell flat's been outlawed since 1901, but that thing was built in 1889! It should be torn down or blown up. You ought to go look at it, stumble up the dark, broken stairs and breathe in the smells! One dirty toilet, out of order, in a cold hall, for six families, when there's supposed to be one for each flat. Nine dollars a month rent on the first floor, eight on the fifth floor. Rent free to the rats, of course."

Dan breathed hard, as if he had been running. "That's the sort of place from which we took that child." He motioned toward Leah. "That beautiful little girl, condemned to filth."

"Very commendable of you. But let's return to the subject of the Montgomery, which you've brought up. I happen to know," Walter said deliberately, "it was built according to current regulations, when the railroad flat was outlawed. It's a dumbbell flat, built to the letter of the law at that time, and modified since according to the new law. There's a window now in every room—"

Dan interrupted. "It's an evil place, Walter, no matter what you say. And worst of all, a firetrap, of which the owners must be perfectly aware."

"The owners are aware of nothing of the sort," said Walter. His pupils, magnified behind the glasses, were black stones.

The Werner cousins got up as a group. There was a general consulting of pocket watches and watches on chains around the ladies' necks. From the outer

hall sounded the flurry of departure: delightful . . .
thanks so much . . . oh, my boots . . . started to
snow, look at that . . . oh, it won't be anything
much, just a few flurries . . . delightful . . .

Walter has cat's eyes, Hennie thought, when he's
furious. I never noticed. I want to get home, get out
of here. When will it end?

The two men still faced each other.

"Why, it's obvious to a child, to anyone who
cared to think about it! The owners don't give a
damn!"

"You know a lot about the owners."

"Well, Veiller has looked it all up. They'll be surprised to see themselves spread over the newspapers
when he has made his report to the legislature.
We're not giving up. We want a new tenement act.
And I'm invited to go along to Albany. Well, I did
do some of the work," Dan added, almost boyishly,
"so I suppose I'm entitled to go." In his enthusiasm,
his wrath seemed to have died.

"So you are going to Albany to make an example
of the Montgomery. Have you any idea who the
owners are?"

"Oh, some sort of a group, a holding corporation.
Veiller knows more about those things than I do."

"Oh, does he? Well, I'll tell you. The major stock-
holders happen to be my father and some of his
friends. We took the property back on default of a
mortgage. Have you anything to say about that?"

Walter was perspiring. He patted his forehead
with a handkerchief. The room was totally silent.

"Well," Dan said. "Well."

And old Mr. Werner repeated, "Well. Yes, well."

"I didn't know," Dan said.

Walter sighed. "I want to believe that. But it does show you what comes of meddling where you don't belong, doesn't it?"

Dan shook his head. "No. I'm a citizen. I care very much what happens in my city, and I do belong."

"Be that as it may, what do you plan to do in this particular situation?"

"What can I do?"

"I think that's pretty obvious. You can go to your people and get them to stop whatever has been started."

"Walter . . . that's impossible. The report is already in the hands of the committee."

"It can be withdrawn."

"Veiller would never do that and I could never ask him to."

"Why not?"

"Because . . . it would be dishonest, against the grain."

"Not against the grain to see the name of Werner smeared in some muckraker's journal? You would do that?"

Dan threw up his hands. "It would not be something I'd enjoy. You can't think it would."

"I don't know what I can or cannot think. All I know is that we have a question here of family, a family to which you happen to belong and to which you owe some loyalty. Talk about principles!"

"Well, if you put it that way—shouldn't principles always, any time, come first, or else they're not really principles?" .

"Sophistry," Walter said with contempt. "Twisting words. It's easy to do that and prove any point you want to prove."

"I'm not twisting. I have never been more straightforward in my life."

"So in your straightforward way you are telling me that you intend to go ahead with this disgrace and be damned to us?"

"I didn't say be damned to you! Don't put words in my mouth! I said the affair is already in the hands of the subcommittee in Albany and I can't call it back."

Freddy's lips quivered. Leah was fascinated. Hennie looked for a place to escape, but there was none; they were trapped.

"Can't or won't?" Walter demanded furiously.

There was a long wait. Hennie heard the blood pounding in her ears.

She could not have known that Paul was thinking: Nothing is as simple as people like my father and Uncle Dan see it. Problems are round. Or many-sided. Polygons. What you see depends upon where you stand.

"Can't call it back or won't?" repeated Walter.

And Dan said very quietly, "Maybe some of both."

"You bastard," Walter replied, also very quietly.

No one moved. For a moment the silence was absolute, until Walter broke it again.

"Look at your wife! Her face is burning! If she weren't as young and healthy as she is, she would be having a stroke because of what you're doing."

Florence began to cry again.

"Stop it, Florence," commanded Angelique. "He

isn't worth it and never was from the beginning. I knew it from the first moment I laid eyes on him."

Hennie cried out, "Mama! How can you? You've no right to say that! No matter what's happening here tonight! How can you?"

Angelique wrung her hands, "Hennie, I'm sorry, I can't help it! God knows my heart aches for you, and now for Florence and Walter, to have this happen here in their home and on their anniversary, this happy night. Oh, dear God, what next?"

Henry had been so silent in his corner that they had forgotten he was there. Now suddenly he shouted.

"Stop it, will you? All of you? Damn fools! It's too much, how much can a man stand?" His face was dark gray. "I'm exhausted! No more, no more!"

"His heart! Look what you've done! Florence, get the brandy!" Walter was distraught. "Lie back, Father, put your head back. Mama is right, Dan, we've put up with you, your attitude, your remarks—you think we don't know your opinion of us all these years? But now to upset this good old man who came here tonight—to my home! for warmth and pleasure, and you—oh, get out! That's the best thing you can do. Get out now and leave us alone. Now."

"You don't mean that, Walter," Hennie cried. "You're not really telling us to leave your house!"

"Not you, Hennie, of course, not you. We can only be sorry for you."

Walter put out his hand, but Dan stepped between Hennie and the hand.

"My wife goes with me, as any wife would, and when I go, I'm not coming back. And neither will you, Hennie. Leah, Freddy, get your coats."

Florence wrung her hands. "Is that true, Hennie? You will stay away from us all because of him?"

Hennie shut her eyes. Black out the room, her son's stricken face, Leah's bewilderment, Dan's stern mouth. She opened her eyes.

"Dan is my husband," she whispered.

"Husband," Florence repeated, making the word an insult.

Dan placed Hennie's cape around her shoulders and, with his hand on her elbow, urged her toward the door.

Walter followed. "If you'll turn from this course, it won't be too late. We can forget what's been said. I'm willing. Just turn—"

But Dan, without answering, had already opened the door and gone down the stoop to the street. Hennie wanted to look back; surely someone would come hurrying to say that what had happened had really not happened! But humiliation kept her from looking. She had to run to keep up with Dan's pounding strides.

In silence, they hurried through the wind toward the avenue to catch the downtown trolley.

This rift would never be made up, not with Florence, anyway. Parents were different; they would come around, but Florence owed allegiance to the Werners, as Hennie did to Dan. When the news came out—oh, she'd read in the papers about these investigations, had seen how the reformer could blacken the names of the most respectable and respected—how scandalizing for the Werners, for Florence! And a wave of purest regret caught in Hennie's throat. Florence was good, she was a sister.

And Paul, she thought. I shall lose him too. You shouldn't have let this happen, Dan.

The snow began to come hard when they climbed into the trolley. Big wet flakes struck the windows and oozed down the pane, blurring the glow of streetlamps. On 23rd Street green lights flashed in the shape of a giant pickle, erected by Heinz. Passengers craned to look at the marvel, which was somehow comical as well as marvelous.

"Look," she said softly to Freddy and Leah, who were both silent. "We're passing the pickle again." But neither responded.

She met Dan's troubled eyes; he, too, had been regarding the boy and girl.

"I'm sorry, Hennie. You're very angry."

"Yes . . . I don't know what I am. Just numb, I guess."

"I had too much brandy."

"I thought so."

"I shan't use it as an excuse, though. I wasn't drunk, I never have been, you know that. But those men at the other end of the room, after dinner, they . . . I couldn't stand them. They were talking about the Boer War and all the money that was made, and investing in diamonds, while I was thinking about what I've been seeing and doing with Veiller, talking to him just this past week. And I was fed up, disgusted and angry, that's all."

He touched Hennie's cheek with his thick woolen glove. "Hennie?"

"I hear you."

"I thought, these are the same men who wrecked the Hague Conference and who make the wars. Out

of their miserable tenements come the poor starve-
lings to fight in their armies."

"Of course you're right. But that's nothing new.
You've been among Walter's people often enough.
And they're really such small fry anyhow, compared with the Morgan crowd or the oil and steel
interests."

"That's so. It was just the way it struck me tonight."

"Tell me honestly, would you have tried to stop
that report to Albany if you had known who owned
the buildings?"

Dan hesitated. "Maybe I would have been
tempted to for your family's sake. I don't know. But
if you had seen that place—I know you've seen
plenty, but this was the very worst. Such filth, not fit
for animals, and, of course, I always think of fire."

*He stood in the poisonous smoke on the ledge un-
der the roof, while the crowd stared up and waited,
hardly believing what they saw. No one else, surely no
one in that house tonight, has so much heart.*

"If it weren't for my teaching salary, Freddy
might be living in a place like that," Dan said.

"I know."

They got down from the trolley and began to
walk through the swirling snow. It beat at their cold
faces and stuck to their lashes. Dan shortened his
steps.

"I'm walking too fast. When you were little, I
used to carry you through the deep snow. Can you
remember that far back, Freddy?"

Yes, Freddy remembered. He remembered everything and would remember tonight too. He thought:
Dad's trying to make amends. And he thought, I

shall never see Paul, now that they have fought. Then he corrected himself: No, Paul will find a way, he always knows how.

Just behind him he felt the presence of his parents as one presence: Mother-Father. One. His mother loved his father; she had been angry at him tonight, and yet now they were walking close together, with their shoulders touching. When he was little, this had angered him, so that he had wished he had no father and there would be just two of them in the house, his mother and he. But that was a long time ago. He wondered about girls, whether they wished their mothers away, and thought of asking Leah, but realized it would be too cruel to ask her.

So this is the way it is and always will be. Mother-Father. If only Dad weren't so loud and frightening

Now he heard his father's voice, very low above the sound of slushing feet.

"Not so angry anymore, Hennie?"

And his mother's soft answer. "I'm sad. I never can be angry with you very long, Dan. You know I can't."

And he heard a swift little sound like kissing, but didn't turn around to see.

7

The mills of the gods grind slowly, and seldom more slowly than in a democratic legislature. They do, though, grind to a finish, more or less: In this case, less. After long, tedious, and acrimonious hearings before investigating committees, nothing was produced in the way of new laws, only a reaffirmation of the need to enforce the existing one.

Owners were castigated for flouting the regulations; as always, outrage and shock were expressed at the wretchedness of the poor in the richest city in the world, and the reformers went home to prepare for another try.

If the newspaper headlines were not as flaming as the coverage of a murder, they were yet flamboyant enough to bring misery into the prominent and respectable homes of people who had never seen their family name in print except to announce a marriage or a death.

Feature writers, especially those of a liberal bent, made full use of the subject.

DISGRACE OF THE CITIES . . . RICH OWNERS RESPONSIBLE FOR CRUEL DEATHS BY FIRE . . .

CRIMINAL   NEGLIGENCE . . . EPIDEMICS . . .
MILLIONS MADE OUT OF HUMAN SUFFERING ran
the headings. In more sober articles, the culprits
were examined and named: builders and mortgage
houses such as Southerland, Van Waters, Werner.

In her white-and-yellow upstairs sitting room,
where Florence, with a sick headache, lay on the
recamier sofa, the Sunday paper, which had brought
on the headache, was scattered on the floor. The
family had gathered to commiserate. Angelique had
come hastening; Alfie and Emily had walked the
few blocks from their apartment in the Dakota.

"I'm glad my parents are in Florida." Walter
sighed. "They'll have the New York papers, of
course, but somehow I think distance softens the
blow."

Alfie assured him cheerfully, "By the time they
get back in March, all this will be yesterday's news.
There'll be somebody else to pick on."

Angelique's white hands trembled from her jet
necklace to the black silk folds of her mourning
skirt.

"Yes, Florence, I'm thankful your father didn't
live to see the end of this. What he did see was
enough! His two daughters estranged and now this,
visited on poor Walter."

"What must people think?" Florence moaned.

"Pull yourself together, Florence," Walter rebuked, and pulled himself together. "The people we
know will hardly believe a handful of sensational
muckrakers. 'Criminal negligence!' " he scoffed.
"They should try owning one of those buildings!
You put in shelves—they knock them down for kin-
dling wood! Washtubs? They store coal in them!

Faucets and pipes? They rip them out to sell at the junk shop. These people come from hovels in Sicily, Russia, County Clare, God only knows where. It will take a century to educate them. I know one thing, though, I'm through. No more mortgages; I'm a banker, not in the real estate business."

Paul surveyed the little group. He had been summoned in on his way back to his room after an afternoon at the skating rink. This was another world. At Aunt Hennie's, the talk yesterday had been triumphant, although Uncle Dan said the law was only a partial victory.

"All these existing buildings should be torn down," he had said, "but of course that could never happen, there's too much money at risk."

"I suppose," Florence remarked now, "there's great rejoicing in my sister's house. They think they have defeated us, humiliated my husband and me."

No one answered. And Florence went on, "Oh, I don't want to make any more trouble than there is already. Mama, I know you have to see Hennie, she's your daughter. Emily, I leave you out, you have to go where your husband goes, and Alfie's a peacemaker, always has been, though surely you must see that there'll be no peace made out of this, Alfie."

"No, I know I haven't been very effective. Though I certainly wish you could all somehow get together."

"Yes, get together," echoed Emily.

The world's too lovely for Alfie, Paul thought, too filled with good things, fine houses and jovial dinners, to be troubled by argument, disturbing one's peace, one's Sunday nap, or even the energy that one must save to get ahead.

"Not your fault! This cleavage is too deep," Florence declared. "And now, after this—it's permanent, I assure you. I will say one thing, though, to Paul. Neither your father nor I have made an issue of this or tried to forbid you, but how can you keep going to that house? We know you go there pretty often, don't think we don't."

"I haven't tried to hide it."

"But isn't it time to take a stand for who you are? You're a grown man!" Her tone was plaintive, much closer to a wail than to a scolding. "To go there and listen to them talk about your own parents—I don't understand it."

"They have never said one word, not one word, about anyone in this house, Mother. I wouldn't go there if they did. They never talk about people, anyway. That's not what they talk about."

Walter was curious. "As long as the subject has been brought up, what do they talk about?"

Paul shrugged. "How can I answer that? All right. The Peace Society. Aunt Hennie goes to Lake Mohonk every summer to the annual conference. She met Baroness von Suttner, after she won the Nobel Peace Prize. And Uncle Dan, well . . ." Paul stifled a mischievous smile. "He talks about electromagnetic waves in space." They wouldn't understand any more than he, Paul, did. "He says someday we will be able to get signals from other planets. In the meantime, he's got ideas for communication at sea."

Angelique rolled her eyes. "Typical!"

"I don't know, Mama," Alfie said earnestly. "You

never know. He might have something there. Look
at Edison."

Angelique reached out and patted her son's hand.
"You're like your father, always making excuses for
people. Never mind, it's a kind trait. And at least
you're a practical man, providing for your little
Margaretta." Angelique liked the sonorousness of
the full name, "Margaretta," never "Meg." "She
doesn't live in a near-slum, as poor Freddy must."

"Oh, yes, I do feel sorry for Freddy," Florence
agreed, "I always have. He seems so—" She sought
the word. "So—remote. And then at other times
overemotional. Of course, I haven't seen him in so
long. Has he changed much, Paul?"

"He's grown," Paul said dryly.

"Well, goodness, I know that! The boy's sixteen,
isn't he? I meant—"

Here she was interrupted by the entrance of a
maid with a tray, which was set down on the table
next to the sofa. Sandwiches, cakes, coffee, tea, and
chocolate diverted them from the subject.

"Have some, Paul," his grandmother said. "You
must be hungry after an afternoon on the ice."

He took a plate. He would have liked to get away
alone, but they would have considered it rude to
walk away from the afternoon ritual.

It was not quite true that they never talked about
people at Aunt Hennie's house. She always asked
what his mother was doing, not, he knew, out of any
sly curiosity, but with regret. And he recalled the
two sisters at Grandpa's funeral, sitting far apart in
the temple, not speaking, and surely feeling the
wounds of not being able to speak.

He wondered again what it was that made people

of the same flesh, born and reared under one roof, so different from each other. Freddy, for instance, born of his parents, was and would be different from either one. So much was troubling that had not been before.

What most disturbed him was that—as his mother had just said, although with different meaning and intent—he was now of an age when he must know himself. Often he thought of that old, old man Uncle David, now slipping gradually into senility in a nursing home. He had never spoken to him very much, having arrived almost at the end of the old man's life, but somehow he had the idea that Uncle David, of all people, might have told him who he was and who he might become.

Uncle Dan was far too extreme, too passionate about his causes and his new world. There was a point beyond which he could not go with Uncle Dan. He knew that Uncle Dan thought men such as his father were evil men, and yet he knew that his father was not an evil man.

Well he remembered the committees meeting long past midnight; after the terrible pogrom in Kishinev, for instance, how Walter Werner had labored! Organizing, raising funds, giving thousands, arguing and pleading, he had exhausted himself. Had not Jacob Schiff, the wise, shrewd mediator, the compassionate philanthropist, bestowed on him the warmest praise? And Baron de Hirsch, the greatest of Jewish benefactors, and Harkness, who was not Jewish, and—

No, his father was simply a rigid man who saw what he called "radicals"—meaning those who would overturn a régime in which people like the

Werners lived—as being troublemakers, destroyers of a decent and improving order.

Moreover, there was truth in that. You didn't have to damn a manufacturer just because he ought to treat his employees more generously. One ought to educate instead. In his father's office Paul had learned how wealth, well used, can build a city; the great towers, rising all over Manhattan, came not out of thin air or out of Uncle Dan's theories; they came from wealth, risk capital, and the results of risk were tangible.

Finished at Yale, and now almost finished with graduate school, Paul would probably spend a year at the London School of Economics, get some international experience, and finally settle into the New York office. He wasn't sure how he felt about it all. But everyone said that his doubts would sort themselves out; with broader knowledge he'd see his way. He hoped they were right.

He knew he was orderly and responsible, essential traits for a banker. Certainly he liked everything to be planned; he would like to know right now what awaited him, whether good or bad.

He would like to know for others' sakes too. Freddy's future was on his mind, for one thing. It was quite true, as had often been said, that Freddy was his little brother; he would like to do "something" for him. Money had always been scarce in the Roth household, and was now, if anything, more scarce since they had Leah to clothe and care for; he couldn't imagine his own parents taking a strange child in like that.

Anyway, he had often discussed with Uncle Dan where Freddy would go to college. Uncle Dan in-

sisted he would go to City College: "At Twenty-
third on Lexington Avenue, where I went; it costs
nothing, and he can walk to it; some of the best
brains in the country have come from there."

Paul had conceded that that was so, but didn't
Uncle Dan have to admit that a change of scene, a
new experience out of the city, might be a fine thing
too? Paul wanted to pay for it. No, not with his
parents' money, for heaven's sake! With Paul's own,
inherited and received when he reached twenty-one.
It was his and he could spend it as he liked. But
Uncle Dan still said no. What stubborn pride! He
wouldn't even accept the gift of a good piano, which
Freddy wanted so badly. Sometimes Paul wondered
how Aunt Hennie put up with him. Still, that wasn't
fair. A man's entitled to a fault or two. And anyway, Aunt Hennie was crazy about Dan. She looked
at him sometimes the way he'd never seen his
mother and father look at each other. It was even
embarrassing. He supposed if there was such a thing
as a perfect marriage, theirs must be.

Still, the whole man-woman thing was a puzzle.
To begin with, there were two different kinds of
women. There were the ones whom in his private
mental shorthand he always saw as "white," probably because their dresses at summer parties at the
shore were airy. You held these girls loosely when
dancing, having been taught that sweaty hands left
stains, and so you barely touched their warm skin
under the cool silk. The tops of their heads beneath
your chin smelled clean and faintly sweet, like tal-
cum powder. You were careful of your speech with
those girls. There was a mystery about them, even
about Mimi Mayer, whom he had known forever,

almost as well as a man might know a sister. And
yet he didn't know her. A distance was kept.

Then there were the Others; in his mind, they
stood written with a capital *O*. These were the town
girls, waitresses for whom you hung about with
your friends, laughing to cover your heart's pounding; after they finished work at midnight, you took
them to the beach behind the rocks. Common girls,
his mother would call them, and maybe his father
would say so too; he wondered whether his father
had done what he did with them. Well, they were
loud, and their speech, the words they used when
you were naked, were not exactly— And yet they
were so sweet, alive and sweet and lovely in the soft
summer night.

He wondered whether everything in life was like
that, with two opposing ways for everything. But
most people seemed so certain of themselves! His
parents in their straight, deep-cut groove; Grandmother Angelique, who was still living in the Con-
federacy; Aunt Emily, for whom the pleasant rituals
of a calm life satisfied all; Uncle Dan, who was per-
petually angry at the world and knew without a
doubt that he was justified; Aunt Hennie, doing her
good works—all so certain.

Perhaps in a few years I will be certain, too, he
told himself, knowing at the same time that it would
not be so, that he would always be divided. It was as
if there were two roads through the world, and he
were walking or trying to walk with one foot on
each road.

Then, being young and hungry after all, he held
out his plate for his mother to fill with little sandwiches and little pink cakes.

8

In the very last row of the hall, concealed from the podium by the dimness behind a pillar, Dan wore a look of total concentration. Concentration? He was enthralled.

"Once it was possible to have short wars, quick, gallant victories for individual heroes. A sort of contest of athletic skills, though bloodier! But now—now, because of all the marvelous new machinery we have invented, because the great powers are so rich, wars will be very long."

The voice dropped softly into a sigh, almost a whisper, distinct in the absolute stillness that, during the last half hour, no cough or shuffle or creak of chair had disturbed.

"And unlike those ancient contests, war now spares no home, no woman or child. Here in our country, during the Civil War not yet half a century behind us, we saw what rampaging armies could do. You know about Sherman burning his way through Georgia. My own parents suffered in Louisiana; it is all as real to me as though I had lived it myself."

Here the hands clasped high; a surprising dazzle

shot from the speck of a diamond in Dan's mother's ring. The pretty gesture was typical: *Look, Dan, such lovely eyes!* when the boy was born, or *Listen, someone's playing the violin in that house,* or on seeing a ragged old man poke in a trash can, *My God, how terrible!*

He felt a lump in his throat, watching her. He had actually sneaked into the meeting; this was her first big speech and, very nervous about it, she had made him promise not to come.

"I'll meet your eyes," she'd told him, "and forget what I was going to say for wondering how well I'm doing—or how badly. After this first time, if I do well and I'm invited again, then you can come."

He hadn't been able to keep the promise and was glad that he hadn't.

So far he had recognized, had expected to recognize, his own words and ideas. Not that there was really anything to call his own. There was hardly anything original to be said at this point about war and peace. It was now merely a question of pounding away at one meeting after the other, of forceful reiteration to arouse, one hoped, an ever-widening public.

But his ears pricked up.

"I recommend to you a book by a Polish businessman—a Polish Jewish businessman, I should say; Ivan Bloch is his name. It's a remarkable book. It's said that the Czar called the 1899 disarmament conference as a result of reading that book."

She's read that! She never told me! I haven't read it myself, I've been meaning to. . . . Dan marveled.

"It has a lot of technical detail about modern

armaments, but he makes it understandable. Firepower is now so devastating that men will burrow into the very earth to escape it! There will be a long, long stalemate. And slaughter beyond imagining. Nations will lose their best young men by the millions. Not thousands anymore. Millions," Hennie repeated with awe. "It will be the suicide of nations."

Again the clasped hands rose; above them the face glowed, the beautiful eyes were enlarged and passionate.

If any single word could describe her, he thought, it might best be *genuine*. Never had there been anything calculated, spurious, or fake, neither in mind nor in body, about Hennie. And while she went on to tell of submarine-torpedo boats and explosive-bearing balloons, his mind went drifting. . . .

Women he had known: How different they were from her! Women one encountered here and there and everywhere, blended in a way suddenly here now blurred into color, pink and white and cream and gloss of hair, the faces all the same, lovely, dull, self-centered, ordinary—None like hers. Not one of them. And now, even as with pride and delight he listened to her eloquence, he thought of the night to come.

"It is always said that we need these enormous armaments for secure defense; the fact is that their existence only breeds more armaments on the other side. It is a dangerous game we're playing, with our alliances and balances and preparations for wars that nobody can win. The Boer War was larger than the Spanish-American, the Russo-Japanese was larger than the Boer. . . . With all this in mind, men and women must speak out to their governments everywhere. It can be done. If we will it, we can."

A kind of music came from her voice. The greatest music is earnest, lofty, and hopeful, he thought, and his eyes filled. Recognizing the rise to a peroration, Dan got up swiftly before he could be observed, and left the hall.

"If I had known you were there it would have been awful," Hennie said.

She was sitting up in bed laughing, enjoying her triumph and his praise. "What are you staring at, Dan? You look so solemn."

"Not solemn. Just looking at you. Asking myself how this happened. You and me, I mean. I am so lucky, Hennie. Sometimes I can't believe it."

Her laugh died. She put her hand on his cheek. "Believe it."

"When you stood there today with all those people listening to you, I was so proud, I can't tell you how proud. And I thought, She's mine, with that bright mind of hers, and all the rest. Oh, Hennie! Do you have to wear that thing?"

"This 'thing' is my Paris nightgown, the last present Florence gave me. I'd better hold on to it, since there won't be any more."

"Well, you can hold on to it, but you can take it off now too. I'll just get up and lock our door."

9

Hennie had an excellent memory for times and places, and so she was quite certain that it was at Alfie's country house, on an unusually mild afternoon of a weekend in early spring, when Alfie first asked Dan about his vacuum tube. They were sitting on the terrace, from which height, above a bank of laurels not yet in bloom, they could just glimpse the four young people, Mimi Mayer and Paul, Leah and Freddy, playing tennis.

"A real family place," Alfie said, "that's what I wanted." A smile of genuine pleasure spread over his face, which was beginning to show chubby folds under the chin. "A place for all of you to visit and enjoy with us. Plenty of room for all."

Once it had been the Werners', but now this would be the house at which the family would assemble: brothers and sisters—except that when Hennie was there, Florence would not be—aunts and uncles, everyone to the farthest twigs on the family tree, would come here to Laurel Hill.

"Not an original name," conceded Alfie, "but

there really are dozens of laurels and you have to admit the name has dignity."

The place itself had dignity; it was a gentleman's farm, in contrast to the arrogant stone piles that the moguls of steel and sugar and coal were scattering around the gentle New Jersey hills. But any impulse toward such grandiosity, even on the comparatively minor scale Alfie could have afforded, would have been thoroughly quelled by his wife. Emily despised whatever was "nouveau." And Alfie had quickly learned what was "nouveau."

Square and white, then, with green shutters and many chimneys, stood Alfie's house. An American flag flew from the pole on the side lawn; every morning Alfie raised it and at every sundown he lowered it. Ample fields ran to a background of sumac and wild cherry thickets; behind these loomed the old woods, dark with maple, oak, and ash, a wildness that could induce a shiver of delightful menace when night fell, so that one could immediately lose three centuries and there, at the fold of the hill, behold an Indian encampment with smoke twisting from the wigwams. A Hiawatha atmosphere.

"This was all farms here in the eighteenth century," Alfie liked to explain. "It's said that Washington's army bivouacked down the road on the way to Trenton. Maybe it's true. The last owners had it in the family for sixty years. A local doctor. He made a few changes, the porch and the porte cochere."

And the iron deer on the front lawn, Hennie added mentally. A homely touch, naive and just right.

Alfie said mischievously, "I know you would have liked me to build something like Beau Jardin, Mama."

"Alfie! Don't you think I know you can't reproduce an antebellum plantation in New Jersey? Oh, something scaled down, maybe, with a veranda and columns. It's so pleasant to have a veranda, and with these lovely views—"

Alfie laughed. "Mama, you'd have liked me to hire someone like Richard Morris Hunt to do a Vanderbilt house with limestone balconies and turrets, or maybe McKim, Mead and White to do a Newport cottage with a hundred rooms." And as Angelique started to protest, "Oh, don't mind me, I'm only teasing."

"Well, you've done wonders. For a man still in his thirties to have accomplished all this!" Angelique spread her arms. "I must say it was very, very smart of you to invest in Kodak. And I want to tell you I have utter confidence in you. Everything you touch turns to gold."

Alfie was embarrassed. "You give me too much credit. The Kodak idea was Walter's." Then, turning to Dan, he said earnestly, "I know, of course, we all know how you feel about Walter, but—"

"And how he feels about me," Dan retorted.

"Yes, it's a pity. Don't think Emily and I haven't tried our best. I don't have to tell you."

"No," said Dan.

"Well, all I wanted to say was—" And Alfie looked puzzled, as if he had forgotten what he wanted to say.

Emily came to his aid. "What you wanted to say

was just that Walter has been helpful to you with advice more than once and that you're grateful."

"Yes, that's what I meant. You know, Dan, it's not as if I didn't see quite clearly that Walter can sometimes be, oh, the way he talks, you know. How shall I say it? What's the word?"

"Pontificates?" suggested Dan.

"Well, yes, perhaps so. But then we all have our small annoying ways. I'm certain I have."

Dan looked amused. "Get to the point, Alfie. What are you trying to tell me?"

Alfie leaned forward. "All right, it's this. Walter knows some people, that is, there's a group that's bought a small company that makes electrical devices. Don't ask me what they are, because I haven't the faintest understanding of those things, but these men are experts. They know what they're doing and I thought—" He fastened his gaze on Dan's eyes. "You've got all these inventions you're always working on. Paul was telling me you've added a room to your lab, is that so?"

"Yes, I needed more space to spread out."

"Making progress, are you?"

"Some." Dan was irritated. As if you could count "progress" like counting the number of bricks that had been laid in a day, when anyone who had the least conception of scientific research knew that for every two steps forward you fell back one, or were perhaps diverted to a completely different avenue.

"Paul mentioned a vacuum tube among other things, but he wasn't very good at explaining it. It's not his field either. He said you felt you were on to something, that you were excited about it."

Dan shrugged. "Paul exaggerated. I'm not ex-

cited because I don't know how it will turn out." He
moved restlessly on the chair. And his eyes, grown
wider, belied his denial. "The question is amplifica-
tion, you see, and with a three-electrode vacuum
tube, you can produce an effect—" He stopped
short. "Wait a minute! You surely haven't got any
damn fool idea of connecting me with some project
of Werner's, have you?"

Alfie cried out in alarm. "Nothing of the sort,
Dan. How can you think I would do that?"

"You mentioned him just now."

"No *project* of Walter's. Only some people I happened to hear about, quite casually, through him.
Quite casually, I assure you. A chance remark. And
it started me thinking. You know how I like to make
connections. And I hope you know I wouldn't put
you in an awkward position, Dan." Alfie was re-
proachful.

"I know you mean well, Alfie. I know that."

Alfie returned to the subject. "Well, as I said, this
is a group with some money and a lot of vision.
We're well into the electrical age, all sorts of possibilities are opening up and they want to get in
early, get in touch with idea men like you, buy up
patents and hold them, waiting for developments.
That sort of thing."

Dan said quietly, "I'm a loner, Alfie. Not that I
don't appreciate your good intentions, but I don't
work well with other people. I just don't."

"But you wouldn't have to work with anybody!
You can stay right where you are, doing what you're
doing. Just patent your inventions, your tube, for
instance, turn it over to these people—with every
legal safeguard, naturally. If something comes of it,

if they can develop a use for anything of yours or they sell it, you'll get your share. If nothing comes of it, you'd be none the worse off."

Alfie wanted to see everyone "set," as he called it. As a result of his generosity, Angelique, since her widowhood, had been occupying a small, sunny apartment uptown near Central Park West. He had hired a maid for her, a motherly Polish girl, who took care of her as though she were helpless, baking hot breads for her breakfast, and ministering to her headaches. Alfie was a dispenser of good things.

"And certainly I could get you a goodwill payment at the start. I would insist on that. Five or six thousand, I'm sure."

"I shouldn't think it would be worth that much," Dan said.

"You never know. I'll bet I could get you the five thousand, enough to buy a nice house."

"I don't want a house. We're comfortable where we are."

Still, Alfie persisted. "Well, you needn't buy a house. Just take the five thousand. It's not to be sneezed at, is it?"

For a moment, Dan made no reply. He examined the backs of his hands, turned them over and smoothed the palms. Then he looked up.

"Alfie, some things are hard to explain. You remember your Uncle David? I don't know whether you know, but long before he began to go downhill, long before he went to the home, he told me a lot of things about himself. Did you know he once perfected a bandage and a wound disinfectant? He never made a cent out of either one. He didn't want to. He gave them away. Some people would say he was a fool, but he didn't think he was, and I don't either. What I'm trying to say is, if anything good results from my fooling around in that lab of mine, if it's something that will make living easier or cleaner and safer, why, I'll give it away. I have enough. I have everything I need."

There was a silence. No one looked at anyone else. Then Alfie stood up.

"All right, Dan. No harm done. I just thought I'd mention it. If you ever change your mind, let me know."

He doesn't understand, none of them does, Hennie thought. Dan might as well have been speaking in Turkish or Chinese.

Dan had not been enthusiastic about this weekend; he hated being drawn away from his projects in the only really free days he had. But Hennie was glad to have come. Reared in the city, she often felt drawn toward country things: the faint green light of reviving leafage and the barely audible buzz of a single bee, awakened by the unexpected warmth of this mid-April. On the other side of the dirt road, at the far end of a chocolate-colored field, a man and a horse could be seen moving slowly and steadily, plowing back and forth in a drowsy rhythm.

She settled back, leaning on a rock ledge, to watch in the other direction. The ball made its low arc across the net; *ping* and *thwack* went the long volleys, as regular as a metronome. They played well. The girls ran gracefully, holding their skirts above their shoe tips with the left hand.

It was remarkable how quickly Leah had learned.

She learned everything quickly. At fifteen, she was as tall as Hennie. She was lively and, Hennie often told her, curious as a monkey. There was even something monkeylike in her snub-nosed face with its round, busy eyes; yet it had a joyousness that made people look again and brought involuntary smiles to their own faces.

"Good shot, Leah!" called Mimi.

Hennie turned toward the clear voice on the other side of the net. A pleasant girl, Mimi, in a quiet way. Everything about her was quiet and of the best, from the crisp cut of her snow-white tennis dress to her spoken French and her manners. She was without hauteur, which was more than could be said of many young women brought up as she had been. Yes, a pleasant young woman. Yet Hennie could not seem to get near to her. Perhaps when Paul and she were married it would be different.

It was plain to see that they would be married. It was a natural evolution; one had long seen it approaching. Mimi was, by now, almost a member of the Werner family.

Now they were crossing the court to change sides, Freddy and Leah against Mimi and Paul. You saw a resemblance and a unity in Mimi and Paul; erect and purposeful, they displayed what an older generation, what snobs, called "breeding." What was it? One wasn't speaking of cattle, after all! And yet there was something. It was as if they knew they would be winners, and not just in tennis. Wistfully, she thought of Florence, who had been born a winner. So long since she had seen Florence . . .

People like Leah and Freddy had to make an ef-

fort. Leah knew that already and did, but very likely
Freddy wasn't even aware of it.

Freddy, the innocent. He walked a few steps behind Leah, who was eager; Freddy was already tired
of the game, Hennie saw, not physically tired so
much as wanting to do something else, to read or
play the piano or perhaps do nothing. But he would
be forced to continue because of the others; in that
way they were good for him; Paul was and always
had been; now Leah was too.

"Hennie! You look half asleep!" Angelique's voice
rang behind her. "I've been taking a walk with Emily and Margaretta, such a darling child, but far too
shy. I wonder they don't see it. You ought to have
been with us, getting some exercise. Why else come
to the country?" Angelique's tone managed to command and criticize at the same time.

"This is the way I like to feel the spring," Hennie
replied patiently. "One gets so little of it in New
York."

"If you lived near the park, you'd get all you
want. I walk there every day. Florence and I often
meet at the Sheep Meadow or the lake. But, of
course, you can't, in your part of the city."

If your husband could provide better, you could.

To that, Hennie made no reply. So many of their
conversations were like this, a kind of fencing,
dodging, and thrusting without ever making a connection. It had been a good thing when Angelique
moved uptown.

Hennie's thoughts ran: I know you look down on
my husband because he isn't what you call successful, but Papa wasn't exactly successful either.

To this her mother would surely reply: That's an

absurd comparison. Your father gave four years of his youth to a war that we lost. He was thirty years old when he came home to the ruin that was left, and then had to go up North to start all over. A cruel discouragement.

But Hennie was beyond anger. This talk of money was contemptible, not to be heeded. Strange that it never bothered her to hear it from Alfie. Still, Alfie never made oblique references to Dan. Alfie's need for acquisition was simply like a child's in a toy shop. He made no excuses, and while you did not approve, you did not resent him either. He was so affable, with his explosive sputtering laugh, so pleased with his comforts, his gifts and hospitality, that you could almost share his pleasure with him.

Hennie moved over. "Sit down, Mama, the rock's quite comfortable."

"No. I'll soil my dress."

Angelique stood erect, shielding her eyes from the quivering light. She looks patrician, Hennie thought, glancing up; her mother's chin line, still firm, made a sharp angle; she held her head high, almost in disdain, Hennie thought, and giggled.

Angelique asked suspiciously, "What are you laughing about?"

"Nothing. I'm only enjoying their game."

Angelique looked back at the court.

"They do go well together," she said.

Hennie almost asked who. It would have been a stupid question.

"Yes, they do."

Angelique smiled slightly. And Hennie, having so often beheld that faraway smile, wondered whether her mother was really seeing the young people on the tennis court below, or seeing Beau Jardin, with the Mississippi curving, in place of the lane to Alfie's new barn. A foolish woman, Dan says of her, who has lived past her time. She means no harm. It is only that her world has died and she has lived on.

Angelique said abruptly, "Marian's parents want her to wait until she's of age, I think. Nothing's actually been promised on either side, but if you ask me, it's been a foregone conclusion ever since Paul finished graduate school. An excellent match for both of them too."

There came another cry from the court, this time from Paul. "Beautiful shot!" He waved his racket in salute. "Beautiful, Leah!"

Hennie glanced at her mother, saying silently, "Do you see?" And was annoyed with herself for always seeming to plead for Leah.

"You spoil that girl," Angelique said.

"Perhaps I do."

What if I do? I do for her what was not done for me. I want her to feel she is wonderful.

"As a matter of fact," Hennie said then, "I don't spoil her. She's very grateful, she takes nothing for granted, believe me. She knows what she has and she loves us."

"She ought to, after what you've done for her."

"You really should approve of her, Mama. She fits your standards far better than I do or ever could. She has beautiful tea party manners. You should see! The neighbor next door has been teaching her."

"What neighbor?"

"The one who's crippled with rheumatism. Leah goes in to help her, dresses her when she needs it, and fixes a little supper sometimes. The woman wants to pay her, but Leah won't hear of it. So the woman gives it to me, to put in the bank for her. She has almost two hundred dollars."

"Well, that's very nice, yes, it is," Angelique conceded. "I can see that she has raised herself out of the ghetto to learn proper ways. Yes, it's very nice. And I must say her speech is excellent."

"Leah's bright. She loves life."

"What is she going to do after high school?"

"I don't know."

Funny, Hennie reflected, there was never any question that my sister or I would "do" anything.

"Freddy is particularly nice to her, I notice," Angelique remarked.

"Why shouldn't he be? Anyway, it's been good for him to have another young person in the house. And she admires him so. She likes his little elegancies. It's fine for his ego, even though he pretends to be amused by it."

"Let us hope it goes no farther than admiration and amusement."

"Mama! I wish you wouldn't talk like that." Hennie got up, frowning. "Why do you, anyway?"

"Do you think I do it to be nasty? No, but a terrible mistake is being made, Hennie, and that's why I have to speak my mind."

"What mistake? Why? Are we the first people to have adopted a child?"

"That's not what I'm talking about now. What's done is done and can't be undone. You know what I'm thinking—that you should let Paul pay for Yale and get Freddy out of the house. Obviously, you can't send Leah away at this point."

"Why on earth would we send her away?"

"You know she has a crush on Freddy, don't you? And that she may turn his head?" Angelique's mouth tightened.

"The girl is fifteen years old."

"Fifteen. Quite so. I wasn't much more than that when I was married. And she's precocious. She knows a lot more than I did when I was her age or than you did, I assure you. Why, look at her! Look at her walk, her figure."

Her breasts, Mama meant. Those full, swelling breasts, not possible to hide even under a loose shirtwaist and a plentifully ruffled camisole, were a bold affront to Angelique, while Hennie was moved to pity by their promise of womanhood, with all of womanhood's capacity for joy and susceptibility to pain. She saw in Leah's body an appeal.

"Hennie, you never see anything." Agitated, Angelique twisted her rings, the round old-fashioned diamonds that had belonged to her own mother and that never left her fingers. "Your eyes are on the stars, or on world peace or woman suffrage or God knows what. You don't see what is happening in your own house. Neither does Dan, not that I'd expect him to."

"They're like brother and sister. It's nasty of you even to have such thoughts, Mama."

"Watch how she looks at him."

"She admires him! It's childish hero worship. And as for that—I can remember how 'sweet' you used to say it was when Mimi and Paul were younger than Freddy is now. They looked so sweet together, you used to say."

"Yes, they did. That was quite different. You can see what's come of it, or very likely will, I hope."

"Oh, it will come if you and Florence have any way to influence it. Men and women—boys and girls—should be able to have friendships without being forced into something else. What you all did with Paul was degrading, shoving them together—"

"Degrading? You're talking of a perfect match. Two fine young people, so suited to each other, two fine families—"

The dialogue had veered from Freddy and Leah to Mimi and Paul, now it veered back.

"But there are other reasons, if not for that one. The education, the social experience he doesn't get at home. Yale, after all, compared with City College. How can you deny it to him?"

"Dan won't hear of it. It's against his principles and I happen to agree with him."

Besides, I don't want Freddy to leave home.

"Principles! Ah, yes, Dan's principles. We know all about those, don't we?"

For a moment, Angelique stood regarding her daughter. A shadow of resignation, surprisingly tender and rather sad, passed unexpectedly across her face.

"Well, I'll say no more. I think I'll go in for a little rest before I dress for dinner."

Hennie followed her mother's straight back across the lawn. The frustrations of family life! People thought they could say anything to you under the guise of love. And you couldn't deny it was love. The righteous, well-meaning fist inside the velvet glove.

* * *

"This is a farm," Alfie liked to say. "We live simply here."

An Oriental rug, color of cream, color of faded roses—a Kirmanshaw, Paul guessed—made a spacious island on the dining room's polished floor. Two lamps of Tiffany glass on the heavy sideboard contributed, with candles and the westering sun, to throwing a gilded light over the embroidered cloth and the Cornish hens on the flowered china plates.

Emily saw Paul looking at the lamps. "Art Nouveau. Do you like them?"

"They're very fine."

"I don't like them much," Alfie said, with good nature. "But Emily loves anything that's an animal or bird or plant."

"You'd love Antonio Gaudí's work, Aunt Emily. Whole buildings, the unfinished cathedral in Barcelona, covered with shells, birds, trees, and animals all carved in stone. You should see them."

"They tell me you'll be going back to Europe soon," Emily said.

"Yes, I expect to have a busy summer." Paul hesitated and then, risking Dan and Hennie's denial for one more time, said to the table at large, "I've been hoping Freddy might come with me. It would be a great experience before he starts at City College."

Dan said, although Paul had not looked toward him, "Hennie and I have already said no, Paul, although we certainly thank you. It's a generous offer."

"A very generous offer," Angelique repeated with a cold glance at Dan. "A rare offer."

"Freddy is my brother," Paul said quietly.

Stupid pride of Dan's! A question of principle, too much luxury, traveling first class on the *Lusitania.* Irrelevant "principles," as if asceticism were a virtue in itself! It was the one side of Dan's character —and Hennie's—that made no sense to Paul. When the world was so replete with beauty! Indeed, it would be wonderful if everyone could have a share; indeed, it would be the Kingdom of God on earth. But until that came, why not enjoy however much of all that beauty fell to one's lot?

"Going over on business?" asked Alfie, taking a second helping of mashed potatoes.

He had better watch his weight, Paul thought, conscious of his own flat stomach. He laid his fork down on the plate, only partly empty.

"Yes, Father's given me quite a few commissions to carry out. He's growing tired of doing business abroad and he wants to break me in. I hope his confidence will be justified."

Alfie was interested. "Where will you be going this time?"

"London first, a short stay in Paris, and then Germany. I'm eager to go." The eagerness welled up in him, a mingling of excitement and apprehension. "I have such a dread feeling that everything's about to explode. This may be my last, or anybody's, last trip to Europe for years."

"What makes you say that?" asked Alfie.

"Well, look what's been happening! The crisis in Morocco last summer . . ."

Alfie apologized. "I'm afraid I don't know much about those things. By the time I get through the financial section, with a few minutes for baseball and maybe"—enjoying the joke on himself—"a quick look at the comics, that's about it! So tell me, what are you expecting?"

"War," Paul said simply.

Dan's voice boomed. "Let them bleed themselves to death over there. We'll stay out of it."

"It won't work that way, Uncle Dan. The whole world will be in it, if it comes."

"Nonsense! The laboring classes everywhere will refuse to fight. Why should a wage earner go to war to save his boss's investments?"

"It's not that simple. When the bands play, people don't think. They wave their little flags and run alongside, like children following the circus parade."

"Such cynicism isn't like you, Paul."

"Realism, Uncle Dan."

Alfie said, "If war does come, I agree with Paul that we'll be in it. Can you imagine what fortunes will be made?"

Dan shot him a look of outrage.

"I meant," Alfie said, "or I didn't mean, that anyone would really want the money that comes from human blood. Who could?"

"Plenty of people," Dan answered. "Jingoes don't talk about that side of war, do they? Jingoes like Theodore Roosevelt. Only 'foolish idealists' hope to eliminate war, he says. 'Cowards and physical weaklings,' he says. Well, I'll stand up to him or any other warrior type when it comes to weakness and cowardice!"

Freddy remarked softly, "There's something to it, all the same." His long fingers played delicately with the stem of a goblet. "What Roosevelt means is, one ought to be ready to die for principles. Some wars have to be fought."

His words astonished everyone. The slight frame, the slight stoop of the shoulders, the way the hair swept back from the fragile blue-veined temples, none of these fit the words.

Dan answered succinctly, "Rubbish."

Alfie thought of something. "Wait a minute, Dan. I should think you'd be a Roosevelt Progressive. Economic democracy and all that."

"True. But I don't trust him on the war issue. So I'm taking Wilson. What about you, Paul?"

"Not sure yet. Roosevelt or Wilson. I fight that out at home, because naturally the family's for Taft."

Dan shook his head. "I'll tell you one thing. If I were young, they wouldn't be able to make me bear arms. I would go to jail first. I would not fight," he said, striking his fist on the table.

"Well, I would," declared Freddy, with equal emphasis. "I would be ready when called. Maybe, if I were needed, I would not even wait to be called."

Leah, who sat across from Freddy, sparkled with admiration. Her round eyes widened, and her lips parted.

Dan shook his head. "Freddy, you may be seventeen, but I tell you, sometimes you talk like a not too bright child."

"Let's hope these are all only words, only something for interesting conversation." Mimi's smile went around the table, making peace.

Emily and Angelique looked their approval of this tact; Mimi had spoken like a hostess of experience, taking charge.

Alfie added heartily, "Have a wonderful time, Paul, and think of us while you're drinking wine on the boulevards. We've never been, Emily and I. How about we set our sights on a trip, Emily? No use waiting till we all need wheelchairs. How about year after next, and no fooling? Meg will be eleven, old enough to enjoy the sights. Let's see, that will be the summer of 1914."

On that note, they all pushed back their chairs and left the dining room.

Not without some difficulty, Alfie had finally gotten a fire started in the parlor.

"The wood's green, that's what's wrong," he apologized as the flames sputtered, sending a waft of bitter smoke into the room. "Open the doors, clear the air," he directed.

French doors led to the terrace. Paul opened them and stepped out into a clear night. The moist winds, a refreshment after rich food and warm rooms, sponged his face. He stood still, letting it blow over him. From the dark woods at the foot of the hill a choir of peepers trilled without cease. There must be dozens—hundreds—of them, hailing the spring, he thought. And a sweet nostalgia surged through him. He wished Mimi had followed him outside to hear them, but she caught cold easily and it was still chilly.

Presently he went back in. The room was now clear of smoke and the fire had taken hold.

Alfie surveyed the comfortable semicircle of sofas and chairs.

"Oh, I'm learning," he said, pleased with the

crackling yellow flame. "I'm learning country ways pretty well, don't you think so, Emily?"

Emily smiled assent.

"I've studied a lot about cows, got three Jerseys in the barn to start with. I'll show you all the new barn tomorrow morning, if you don't sleep too late. I never do. Don't like to miss country life sleeping."

Two red setters settled down next to Alfie. He stroked them, then lit a pipe.

The country gentleman, Paul thought kindly, yet with slight humor, remembering the somewhat irresponsible boy-uncle. Landed gentry. I daresay it's Emily who's responsible for a lot of it. If Alfie didn't have to make money, he would be content just living like this. He should have been born into the British squirearchy. He even looked the part, fresh-faced and ruddy. Some people really did miss being born where they belonged: artists were born into commercial families and radicals were born to aristocrats. I? Where do I belong? Don't know, Paul thought critically. No sense wasting energy trying to figure it out, since I am where I am.

Then something else occurred to him. "Have you made many friends in the neighborhood?"

Emily did not answer. She was doing needlepoint, while Meg, in smocked organdy, took instruction beside her.

Alfie said, "Well, it's only been a year. Far apart as we all are around here, I don't think most people even know we've come yet."

They know you're here, all right, Paul thought. They knew you were coming before you even moved in. The only Jew for twenty miles around, I'll wager.

Meg spoke suddenly. "Yes, they do. They do and they don't like us."

"Why, Meg!" cried Emily, laying her work down. "That's not a nice thing to say. I'm surprised!"

"You always tell me something's not nice to say. You said that when I didn't get into Miss Allerton's Sunday dancing class, and I was upset."

"The class was overfilled." Alfie spoke in haste. "Your mother was right. You shouldn't go around spreading false tales."

"It wasn't false!" Meg was at the edge of tears. "The class wasn't full. I told you so. Janice's mother told her they didn't take me because I'm—we're—Jewish, and Janice wasn't supposed to tell, but she did."

Despite her even tone, Emily was uncomfortably flushed. "I really don't know whether that's true, Meg, and if it is, it's wiser not to talk about it."

Alfie made a deprecating gesture. "I don't for one moment believe it's true. The world's changing, all that nonsense is"—he sought a word—"medieval, that's what it is. You'll be in that dancing class next season, you'll see I'm right."

"Well, they don't like us here either," Meg mumbled.

"That's enough, Meg," commanded Emily, obviously too disturbed by the subject to allow another word.

And Meg, being well brought up, subsided, but not before Paul's sympathetic glance had met hers. The child's more realistic than Alfie is, he thought. And he felt himself to be a good deal older than his cheerful uncle.

A hush of embarrassment fell temporarily upon

the room. Then an auto passed outside, chugging up the hill. Emily put her work down and went to the window.

"Now I wonder who that can be? It's too dark, I can't see."

"It's probably that farmer down by the pond. He's the only one around here who has an auto," Alfie explained. "Of course, the summer people all have them; you need one to get to the New York train."

"The summer people. Exactly. A rich man's toy," Dan said. "Let me tell you, if anything is going to bring about the socialism that you people all dread, it is the automobile. It creates unsurpassed envy."

Leah had been unusually quiet all day. She senses the atmosphere in the house, Paul thought, and knows she is expected to be demure. Now she spoke.

"But, Uncle Dan, suppose they learn to build them cheap enough so everybody can have one? Then that would make life better!"

At home and at ease, Leah's remarks were usually exclamations; her opinions were discoveries.

"Everybody to have one?" Dan countered. "Don't you realize that half the people in this country haven't even seen an auto? And you talk of owning one? Don't talk about things you don't know the first thing about, Leah."

Paul defended the girl.

"She's right, Uncle Dan. It's beginning to happen already. We're not talking about my Stevens Duryea, or a Renault. I know the flivver looks like a buggy without a horse, and it's ugly as a coal stove that needs polishing, but already it will get you where you want to go for only three hundred ninety-five dollars."

"That's still a good deal of money," Dan replied dryly, "a whole lot more than most people can afford. More than I can lay out comfortably, I know that."

He is so irritable tonight, Paul thought, wondering why. There was a subtle atmosphere of dissension in the room.

And Alfie, not usually aware of subtleties, must have felt it, too, because he said briskly, "What we need before we go to bed is some entertainment. How about some of your poetry, Meg?" And he informed the gathering, "Meg has been writing some beautiful poems."

The child's face clouded. "I don't want to."

"Oh, come on," Alfie coaxed. "You're always so shy, Meg. Come on."

The child, in spite of being eight years old and large for her age, shrank on the sofa, becoming smaller and younger. She appealed to her mother.

"Do I have to?"

"Yes, of course, if your father asks you," Emily replied, not looking up from the needlepoint.

Resigned, Meg asked whether she should read or recite from memory.

"Oh, recite!" Alfie told her heartily.

Neither one of them has the least understanding, Hennie thought, and was pierced with memory, seeing herself in the awkward girl, who, standing now with one foot turned in, jutting elbows, and hands folded on her stomach, began to chirp a rhyme about a family of rabbits.

Emily leaned toward Hennie to whisper.

"We're trying to make her more confident. She's too self-conscious, and so sensitive. You know, she cries when we have to go back to the city in September! She worries about her rabbits."

Self-conscious! Why shouldn't she be? She doesn't belong anywhere and you're not helping her, Hennie thought crossly.

In a certain sense, although for different reasons, they reminded her of the way Dan was with Freddy. Oh, not all the time, but often enough! And she hoped Dan wouldn't ask Freddy to play the piano; the tension, when Freddy hesitated, was too painful; if he did finally play, he would go on too long, and it would be excruciating boredom for Alfie and Emily, who did not care about music. Oh, she hoped Dan wouldn't ask!

Fortunately he did not. The clock ticked through desultory conversation; Emily laid the needlepoint away; the evening ended. Alfie opened the door to let the dogs out, so that the scented air flowed in and lured them all outside.

Peepers had ceased. High up, the swaying top of an ancient copper beech etched a pattern against a glitter of stars. Underneath, the earth, rank with leaf mold, lay in dark blue shade.

Mimi was the first to speak. "I'm going in. I'm so fearful of pneumonia since mother's had it."

Then Alfie called to the dogs, and all said good night. Only Leah resisted.

"You can all go in, but I'm going down to the pond to see the light on the water. It's too wonderful to waste time sleeping. Didn't you say so, Uncle Alfie? Who'll come with me? Freddy?"

"It's pitch-dark," Dan grumbled. "You'll break a leg falling over a rock."

Leah laughed. "Don't worry. I'm like a cat. I can see in the dark."

For an instant, Paul's eyes met Dan's frowning ones; then Dan's went blank and Paul looked away. For a moment they stood watching Leah move off down the slope with Freddy following and disappear among the trees. Then they, too, went inside.

On their last night, upstairs in the black walnut guest room, Dan slung his shirt onto the bed, muttering.

"What a nuisance to have to change for dinner! Thank goodness we're going home in the morning. Tell me why one has to change one's clothes to eat . . ." He dropped a collar stud and bent to search for it under the bureau. "Oh, I hate dressing up!"

It was a family joke, the way he fussed about clothes. On the other hand, Freddy had packed carefully for this weekend; he always had liked to dress. He had never been a messy, careless small boy. Hennie could well remember his little striped jacket, his bow ties, and cloth-topped button shoes and how he'd always said he liked the smooth feel of new cloth.

Before the mirror now, she regarded the brooch at the neck of her crackling taffeta waist. It had belonged to her grandmother Miriam and sparkled nicely.

Dan studied her. "You're a good-looking woman, Hennie."

"Am I?"

"I always tell you you are."

Yes, and I always feel and act surprised. I should take it for granted, the way Dan does his looks.

Already in bed, he was stretching; the muscles moved under his milky skin. He didn't age, and she wondered whether he would still look like that when she was a flabby old woman.

"What are you thinking?" she asked, for he was frowning.

"I was thinking that maybe Freddy should go to Europe with Paul after all."

"You can't have changed your mind!"

"Maybe I have."

"Well, we've lived all these years ourselves without seeing Europe."

"True, but you have to admit it's an opportunity for him."

"I don't know what I think about his going, especially with Paul."

"Why especially with Paul? That surprises me."

"You know I adore Paul. He had my heart before I had Freddy, and he still has it, but—he's a sybarite." She hesitated. "A rich man's son, an art collector. I don't know that it would be good for Freddy, giving him expensive tastes."

"He has them already," Dan said darkly. He paused, then seemed to be choosing his words with special care. "I've been thinking, too, maybe Yale would be a good thing for him, after all."

She had been brushing her hair. Now she put the brush down and stared at Dan.

"I can't believe what I'm hearing! Why on earth do you think it would be good for him?"

"Oh, a new environment," Dan said vaguely.

"My God, you sound like my mother!"

"Well, she could possibly be right, once in her life, couldn't she?"

"I can't get over it! You, in agreement with my mother! And you never approved of private education! City College, you said. Free education. It's what you believed in."

"I still believe, but—"

"But what?" demanded Hennie.

"I just think maybe it would be better, that's all."

"I feel as if you'd struck me on the head!" Then she thought of something. "Where will you get the money? You surely won't accept Paul's?"

"What do you think I am? It's Werner money, no matter that Paul says it's his own. No. I'll take Alfie up on that offer he made tonight. That's what I'll do. I'll take a five thousand payment on my vacuum tube, assuming Alfie can do what he said. I've a couple of other things on the fire besides."

"All of a sudden, all of this at one blow! You've been doing a whole lot of thinking, keeping it from me."

"No. I decided everything right now, tonight. I think it would be good for Freddy, that's all," Dan repeated.

"Why? What's wrong with home all of a sudden?"

"If I tell you, you won't like it."

"Tell me. I hope it's not what I think it is. You've been listening to my mother about Leah."

"I haven't spoken one word to your mother! Can you imagine me going to Angelique for advice? I reached my own conclusions."

"About Leah?"

"About Leah."

"Oh, my God! That poor child!"

"Leah is no child, take it from me. I see things in her that you don't and probably can't see."

"What can't I see, in heaven's name?"

"That she's a rascal. Mark my words."

"I haven't the faintest idea what you're talking about! Poor little thing . . . you make me furious. Sometimes you say the most unfounded, unreasonable things."

"Remember, it takes a rascal to recognize another one."

"That's disgusting, Dan. She's a good girl. I know, I'm with her all the time. Besides, since you're so concerned, let me remind you that Freddy's out of the house all day, besides being too busy with his studies anyway to bother about anything else."

"Oh, Hennie, you're an innocent, like your son. You don't see how her eyes say 'come on'?"

"I hadn't noticed," Hennie said coldly.

"You wouldn't notice, my dear. Not you."

"And just what do you mean by that remark?"

"Why, even Emily knows more about people, about sex, than you do."

"Emily? The cool and proper Emily?"

"Don't you believe it. Emily's a lusty woman."

"How do you know?"

"I can tell. I know a thing or two about women. Things their clothes can't hide. You might say I'm gifted that way."

Hennie stared at him. You're hurting me, Dan, she thought. Maybe it's foolish of me, but you hurt me when you talk that way.

"Don't look so wounded! You take everything I say so seriously!"

Dan laughed. Yet there was something rueful in his laughter because, although his lips were curved upward, his eyes were troubled. But he caught her arm, pulled her down to him, and kissed her.

"Don't be annoyed with me. Enough talking. Come to bed."

Dan lies awake. Sleep, immediate and profound, usually follows after love, but tonight his mind is wide-awake, troubled by the abrupt decisions he has just made. For some reason that he does not fully understand, he cannot tell Hennie the whole truth.

Last night also he lay awake, waiting for the sound of footsteps on the stairs. He heard the tall clock on the landing strike the half hour, the hour, and another half hour. Hennie, already asleep, apparently assumed that Leah and Freddy were in their rooms, so he let her sleep and bore the burden of his thoughts alone. Just as well.

An hour and a half to watch the starlight on the pond? No doubt of it, the girl was the aggressor. This was by no means the first time he had seen it. A passionate young thing; her flesh was fragrant, hard in the right places, soft in the right places; her throaty voice had a lilt; she wouldn't need to be courted or coaxed!

On the other hand, though, maybe she would; she was a smart young thing, too, and she'd want a safe marriage, with a ring on her finger, preferably a flawless diamond. She'd find her way in the world,

that much was certain; she was bold and strong.
Not like Hennie.

Little bitch! Suppose she were to get pregnant?

His thoughts go in circles. There is, and has for a
long time, been a gap between himself and his son.
He has vague, hidden fears, of which he is terribly
ashamed, so ashamed that he can't even face himself
with them, let alone Hennie: the fear that his son is
not—quite a man. There are words for this concept,
but he can't frame it even in the silence of his own
mind.

Again his thoughts skim around in circles. If that
is so, ought he not to welcome the girl and be thankful that the boy should show signs of desire?

No. They are far too young. And she *is* a little
bitch. He ought never to have given in to Hennie. . . .

So, he has made the right decision. Best to send
Freddy away to Yale, and let him go abroad with
Paul next summer. Paul will do him good. Maybe
he'll make a man of him. Never mind what Hennie
calls sybaritic! Paul has his feet on the ground. . . .

At the far end of the hall, the "passionate young
thing" lies smiling up at the ceiling. The satin quilt
is glassy smooth under her chin. She puts a hand
out to smooth it. Nice. Nice things in this house.
Not a very smart house, not like some that she sees
in the magazines, but very comfortable. Everything
in it is good. Someday she will have a house like
this, only better, certainly in better taste. Vividly she
recalls the tenement and shudders. Never again!
Never! Of that she is sure.

She sniffs her arm, which smells of the perfumed
soap in the guest bathroom. She loves the feel of her

skin; it is as smooth as the satin cover. She has a good complexion, dark, with a flush of rose under the surface.

She has beautiful breasts, too, round like the ones on statues in the museums, not pear-shaped like so many girls', the kind that will soon droop. She fondles her breasts; it is a wonderful feeling and makes her think of things you're not supposed to think about.

Who says you're not supposed to? Well, everyone. But she thinks about them, and dreams of them often; always there is a thin blond man in the dream, who could or could not be Freddy. She likes thin blond men, romantic, elegant, and refined. Like Freddy. He is so terribly shy, though. Last night at the pond, she made him kiss her; it wasn't a very satisfying kiss, but he'll learn. There was a time when he refused to kiss her at all!

That girl, Mimi, in the other bed, turns in her sleep. It's doubtful that such a proper lady · has Leah's dreams; probably she dreams about tennis or the horse she keeps stabled in the city near the park! Leah laughs.

Sleepy at last, she falls back into her dreams.

So many half dreams in the house!

The child Meg dreads the return to school and the mean girls who lead the class. She's an outsider. It's only here on the farm that she feels safe.

Alfie and Emily curl together in comfortable habit, with their own contentment. They have the ability to pretend that nasty things never really happened, or don't matter.

Freddy, so tired from the day's exertions, drifts too slowly into sleep. They don't ever let you sit still at Alfie's house. Leah, gay Leah, never lets him sit still. She disturbs him. In one way he wants to kiss her, while in another he's not sure, he's a little afraid.

Paul falls asleep with contented recollections of the day, thoughts of work and of his charming Mimi; his life is arranging itself and he can sleep well.

Unbeknownst to Dan, Hennie is also troubled. She wishes for a woman to confide in, and thinks of Florence, who always knew how to solve things, and would be kind. . . . She worries about Freddy; she worries because for some reason, Dan still won't accept Leah as a daughter. Maybe he himself doesn't even know why. Vaguely, she worries about herself and Dan, then scolds herself for doing so. She knows one thing, though: that it's good to be past first youth with all its pains, good to have survived them and to be here with Dan, in spite of all.

So will today's young survive, too, she finally reassures herself, growing drowsy at last.

The planet spins through the silent sky, while on its surface the night-wind rises, soughing through the trees. A cow lows again in the barn. Small wild scurrying creatures squeak in the wood lot.

Under the roof, each sleeper escapes from himself and the others. Yet it is only for the space of the night. For, separate and disparate as they are, they are yet bound. Blood and love and memory, sometimes even hatred, have bound them. They are tied in a hundred secret ways, and will be.

The old house settles and creaks.

10

The sinking sun hung like a red balloon over the Hudson River and the wintry Palisades. From the fourth-floor window Dan looked down onto Riverside Drive, where cars and buses and windblown walkers hurried. He looked without seeing; his thoughts were elsewhere.

"What are you dreaming about? You've been standing there for five minutes."

On the rumpled bed the girl sat pulling on her stockings. She yawned and complained in her whispery little voice, "Oh, I could fall back and not wake up till tomorrow morning!"

"Why don't you? There's no reason why you shouldn't."

"Because I want to ride downtown on the bus with you. That's a whole extra hour to be together."

"It's miserably cold. Besides, you'll have to ride back again alone," he objected, not feeling any need for an extra hour.

"You talk as if you didn't want me!"

"I only meant—"

"Darling, never mind what you meant. I'm coming. Just let me fix my hair."

He glanced at the bedside clock. "Please hurry. I've got to go."

"Don't I know you're due home on the dot for dinner? I'll just be a second."

The comb snapped electricity through her blue-black hair. It was the hair that had lured him in the first place, he reflected now. Seldom did one see hair so black; against the whiteness of skin and the whiteness of the school nurse's uniform the effect had been perfectly brilliant.

She was not beautiful; he had never for a moment thought she was; yet she had caught him and held him all this past year. Each time he'd been with her he'd been sorry afterward, counting the cost of the lies and subterfuges that were an unavoidable part of these Saturday afternoons, and hating the guilt that fevered him when he walked back into his house. Each time he'd told himself that today had been the last. Each time, by the middle of the week, he'd begun to think about Saturday and whether she'd make him wait or be ready in the bed. And each time, leaving her, he'd been ashamed of himself for being unable to keep away.

"There!" she said, giving him her bright, expectant smile, wanting praise. "How do I look?"

"Pretty. That's a nice hat."

She had wound a flamboyant purple turban around her head; it made her look foreign, with those wide cheekbones and dark eye-sockets. She looked mysterious, secretive and tense. Odd, he thought as he followed her downstairs, for she was none of those things. She was lazy, candid, and frankly demanding; she wanted him permanently for her own, even though he had told her a hundred times that that was impossible.

They crossed the Drive to wait in the gusting wind for the bus. When it came, it was almost empty, the flow of traffic being uptown this late in the day. They had the backseat to themselves.

Bernice gasped. "That wind freezes your bones! Let me warm myself, will you?"

She raised his arm to settle around her shoulders, laid her head on his chest, and curved herself into him as if they were in bed. She had no self-consciousness at all, while he, on the other hand, was humiliated by public display. This time, though, there was no one behind them to see the display, so it didn't matter, and he relaxed.

He breathed in her perfume, an Oriental scent, Persian or Indian; it made him think of dancing ankles with bells attached, and of nakedness under veils; no doubt it was intended to. No dooryard daisies for Bernice! All was calculated for arousal. He had to smile at the wiles, so vulgar—and so effective!

"Why are you smiling?" she asked.

"How do you know I am?"

"I can see up out of the corner of my eye. Why are you?"

"I don't know," he lied. "Just feeling good, I guess."

"I'm glad I make you feel good. I do, don't I?"

"You do."

The bus had jolted and lurched across 110th Street and begun its way downtown along Fifth Avenue. Homes of the middle class were replaced by the limestone residences of the rich.

Bernice raised her head. "Beautiful, aren't they?"

"What are?"

"Those houses, silly. On my way back it will be dark, and sometimes I can see a little bit through the curtains. Just enough to give an idea of it. Crystal chandeliers, mostly. Must be wonderful, don't you think?"

"Doesn't tempt me. Quite the opposite."

The bus slowed down, nearing a corner, to pick up a passenger.

"You're such a funny duck, Dan! You don't want anything, do you? Except me."

She reached up and kissed his mouth. Her lips pulled softly and slowly.

Alarmed, he tried to draw away. "Bernice! Not here!"

"Why? You don't know any of these people from Adam."

"It isn't—" He stopped.

The passenger who had just climbed in, who was staring at them in total, absolute astonishment, was Leah.

A chill and a sweat came over him. And with a queer, reflexive movement, he jumped up. He stammered.

"Why, Leah! Here, sit down, let me help—"

The girl was carrying two large dress-boxes. "Thank you, I'll stay in front. I'm only riding six blocks."

She sat with her back to Dan. Her calm, straight back. While his heart pounded. His face must be fire-red. Caught out. With a couple of million people running around in this enormous city. How was it possible?

"Who's that? You look just awful!" At least Bernice had the good sense to whisper.

He frowned furiously. "Not now."

At 87th Street, without a word, Leah got out. He watched her cross the avenue, walking with head up, as if she meant business. A girl, hardly out of childhood. She could destroy him. She had the power.

"Who on earth was that?" Bernice pressed him.

"My daughter. Step-daughter. Adopted daughter. Oh, for God's sake, I don't know what she is! Leah."

"What rotten luck! No wonder you acted so funny! Poor Danny. What's she doing in this part of town?"

"She works after school in a dress shop. Sometimes she has to deliver a last-minute alteration."

"You're afraid she's going to tell?"

"Of course I'm afraid! What do you think? Oh, Christ!"

He bit his lip. He stared out at the dusk and the streetlights, which were just coming on. How to explain this away? The woman lying all over him, her mouth lingering. He was supposed to have been at an electronics exhibit this afternoon too. Ninety-nine chances out of a hundred, Leah would run to Hennie with the story the minute they were alone. She loved Hennie. Hennie was her mother. Oh, Christ!

"I'm sorry, Danny. I really am."

No, you're not, he thought. You'd like nothing better than to have my marriage blow up. You think

I'd marry you. I wouldn't. And you've no right to
feel sorry about that, either, because I told you from
the start, I was honest with you. I don't suppose you
believed me, though. Women always hope.

"I wish I could help you, Danny."

She sounded so piteous that he had to look at her.
She was a good soul after all, a very ordinary soul
who happened to own an extraordinary body that
was bound to get her into trouble. An accident of
fate.

What had just happened now to him, that, too,
was an accident of fate!

"I don't want to talk. I have to think, Bernice,"
he said gently.

"All right. You know what? I'll leave you here
and take the bus home, so you can think by yourself." She stood and rang the bell for exit. "Danny
. . . I'm sure you'll work it out. Just let me know,
will you?"

"Yes, yes I will. Thanks."

He sat and pondered and shook internally all the
way to his stop. Yet, what was there to ponder? It
all depended upon Leah. One chance in a thousand.

At the supper table he pushed food around his plate.
It gagged him. He had to be careful not to let his
eyes meet Leah's. He felt hatred for her. He felt like
an interloper at the table, an embezzler whose books
were to be examined in the morning. He had lost his
dignity, his dual dignity as the head of the house
and the respected teacher at the school. Would she,
could she, possibly spread the tale all around the

school too? Yes, of course she could, and what an entertaining tale it would be!

At the same time he knew that all these thoughts were quite unreasonable; what he was feeling was simply the kind of hatred that comes with owing money to someone and being unable to pay him. What he was feeling was fear, and shame.

His mouth was dry, so that he kept sipping water. No one noticed. They were all talking. He heard fragments: school gossip, neighborhood gossip. The boy downstairs had found Freddy's lost ice skates. The woman upstairs had appendicitis. Then he heard his own name.

Hennie asked, "Was there anything special at the exhibit today, Dan?"

He couldn't look over at her. "No, it wasn't much."

"Really? That's too bad. I remember, last time you said it was marvelous. So many new things."

"It wasn't much," he repeated.

Now his eyes slid toward Leah; he wasn't able to control them. She had a forkful of string beans to manage. She didn't want to see him. And he took another sip of water.

As soon as the dishes had been cleared away, Hennie said she had an errand, a box of old clothes to be taken to the settlement house. For a moment Dan hesitated. Usually he went with her on such errands to carry the heavy box. But to be alone with her right now . . .

"I'll go with you. I have to go to the library before it closes," Freddy said, and asked Dan, "You don't mind?"

"No, go ahead. I'll read the paper."

So he would be here with Leah. Better so. Get it over with. Know where he stood. As if he didn't know already.

As soon as they had left he went to the window and pulled the curtain aside. They crossed the street under the lamplight. His wife. His son. He watched until they were out of sight and stayed there, seeing nothing now except whirling lights and darkness, while in his head another whirling almost cost him his balance.

Go. Get it over with.

He knocked on Leah's door.

"Yes?" she said coldly.

"Leah . . . may I talk to you?"

"I'm doing my homework."

"It won't take long. Please open the door."

She opened it. Her slow gaze went from his face to his feet and back to his burning face. He felt stripped. Sixteen years old, and she was commanding his future, enjoying her command.

"About today," he began. "You're very young, and—"

"Too young to understand, you think?"

"No, I— Well, yes, in a way. It's a question of experience, life experience, you see, and—what I mean to say is, things aren't always what they seem, and this thing today was—"

The girl's round eyes were black as bullets and as fierce. "You're wasting your energy. You know that I know what this 'thing' was. Anybody would."

"Wait. If you'd just let me explain—" And he was struck still by the recollection of what Leah had seen: the purple turban, the lavish body in the tight jacket, the long kiss. What was there to explain?

He said abruptly, desperately, "I love Hennie. Surely you've seen that? This had nothing to do with her. Nothing."

"I love her too," Leah said with scorn.

"I understand that your loyalty is to her, and that's only right."

"But you're afraid I'll tell her."

He didn't answer. Even his legs cringed weakly.

"If I didn't love her so much, I would. It's because I love her that I won't hurt her. Not now. Not ever. So you needn't worry."

"Can I depend on that, Leah?" he begged.

"If I say I won't tell, I won't."

Still he doubted. "Is that truly a promise?"

"I told you, you needn't worry. *I* don't lie."

He could have wept with gratitude. "You're a very good person, Leah. I'll never forget. . . . It's only right for you to know that that woman today was . . . These things are sometimes a sort of accident, nothing that lasts. Not love."

"Then that makes it really disgusting."

Still they stood at the threshold of her room. The word *disgusting* had snapped through the air between them; now it lingered for a moment or two in his ears. At her age she would naturally see it that way; youth makes very harsh judgment.

Still, the judgment was not all wrong. . . .

"It won't happen again, this sort of thing," he murmured.

"That's no business of mine. I have my homework now," she told him.

"Yes, go ahead. And thank you, Leah. You're a good person," he repeated humbly.

Then he went to the parlor, took up the evening

paper, and tried to calm himself with the news. But
the words merely flew past his eyes. Presently he
realized how he was sitting: bent over, huddled,
with every muscle contracted and even his face con-
torted. He straightened them and stood to flex his
arms and rub the hard knot at the back of his neck.

Not worth it, he thought. To risk my darling
Hennie's trust and love! I always truly knew it
wasn't worth it. But the glutton knows what he's
doing to himself and so does the drunkard. And
they keep on doing it.

Some of them do learn, though, and stop, and
stay stopped.

Leah's door opened. He heard her go through the
hall into the kitchen and open the icebox. He heard
the double clink of the milk bottle and the cookie
jar. A child, he'd said of her; yet there was nothing
childish in her compassion for Hennie or her furious
indignation on Hennie's behalf. For these, he
thought now, I thank you, Leah, from my heart.

Something happened to him. At once he recognized it, the old familiar surge of resolve. And he
brushed a hand across his eyes as if to clarify a
vision of himself that had been soiled and dulled. He
knew exactly what he must do, what he wanted with
all his strength to do, and the knowledge cleansed
him.

From the desk he took a sheet of writing paper
and sat down. "Dear Bernice," he began. Clearly,
kindly, and firmly he told her that they had come to
the end. He hastened the pen down the sheet, signed
his name, and sealed the envelope.

Done. Finished with her, the last and final. Finished with them all, so help him God.

11

Dear Hennie and Dan,

We've been here in the country for almost a week. I still have a few days' worth of meetings in London and clients to see, but the Warrens, good old friends that they are, wouldn't hear of me not giving them some time at Featherstone, which is what they call their place.

So here we are, Freddy and I, and it is lovely, there being no season quite as lovely, I think, as an English summer, so fresh and moist.

Freddy and I share a room, since the house is full. There's a fair assortment of guests, cousins, aunts and uncles, one of them a vicar straight out of Oliver Goldsmith. Five or six very young boys and girls (I lose count since they all seem to look alike) and Mr. Warren's nephew Gerald, who, by some good chance, is exactly Freddy's age.

That will soothe my conscience when I return to finish up in London, leaving Freddy here. They've invited him, I suppose, because he'll be company for the nephew, and, of course, he wants to stay. He's "seen" London, the Tower, the palace, Harrods, the changing of the guard—the whole wonderful business. They say about Rome that you can see it in three days or three years, and the same is true of London. Freddy's had two weeks of it, so I'll let him just enjoy this countryside.

Anyway, he's enchanted by everything that's English, I'm afraid! It has been a case of love at first sight. Last night he sat on the side of his bed, pulling his socks off, and then suddenly, just halting as if he were caught in a dream, sat there holding a sock in midair and said to me, "You won't believe me, but I could stay here forever."

I couldn't help but laugh, he looked so stunned. I told him I was glad he was feeling the atmosphere and that that's how you should feel when you travel.

Of course he hasn't met the other England, the unemployed and homeless sleeping on the benches along the Embankment near Westminster, the same sort of scene you can unfortunately find at home. Such things must be seen with the traveler's other eye, after he has satisfied himself with the picturesque.

Speaking of the picturesque, right now there's a flock of sheep ambling down the road, being guided by three busy dogs. I always like to watch the way these clever dogs can maneuver a hundred sheep. It's a scene out of past centuries, timeless, peaceful, and somehow comforting.

Yesterday morning we went riding. Freddy has never been on a horse, as you know, so I was somewhat nervous about taking him along, although they got the gentlest mare in the stables for him. Still, I was nervous. Shouldn't want to get stuck in Europe with a broken arm or leg, and the rest of the summer still to go! But Freddy was game and took instruction very well. There were no mishaps and we are going again tomorrow. There go Freddy and Gerald to the tennis court. I'm supposed to play doubles with them and one of the other houseguests, a man about sixty years old who plays as vigorously as we young ones. He, like Gerald, is a type that's almost uniform here: tall, lean, and fit.

I'll stop now, they're waiting for me, and finish this letter tomorrow and get it off to you. I know you are anxious to hear about your boy.

June 18th, 1912

. . . continuing from yesterday: it's pouring this morning, that English rain you've read about, so that the countryside drips green. Everyone is either sleeping late or reading or writing letters in his room. Freddy is writing in his diary, while I write this.

I really think this trip is wonderful for him. Last night he entertained—no, that's not the right word, I should rather say "enthralled"—everyone by his playing. He wasn't a bit shy, as he usually is, about playing to the group after dinner and even made a nice little speech before starting about how he was going to play an American piece by Edward Mac-Dowell, who studied with César Franck, et cetera. Then, by request, he played some Chopin, perfect fare for a summer night in the country. I've never heard him play so well. It seems to me that he could be a truly great artist, and I don't understand what

holds him back. People were absolutely still. They
have all, older people especially, taken to him, attracted by his modest ways, and, of course, delighted by the way he expresses his feeling for England. Again, I am so glad you agreed to let him
come with me.

On Monday, I go back to London for a few more
appointments, after which Freddy will join me there
and we'll be off to Paris.

All my fondest wishes to you both,
PAUL

June 22nd, 1912

The pages in my travel diary are filling up, which
will please Grandmother Angelique. The book looks
like her, impressive and expensive, with my name in
gold: Frederick Roth.

Here I am in deep country. The house is Elizabethan; they say Cromwell slept here. The lintel in the
bedroom is so low that I bump my head every time I
walk in. Sparrows are racketing in the ivy that covers the house. It's thick and old, must be a hundred
years' growth. I stood at the window a while ago,
watching the dew burn off and a horse and wagon
creep up the hill. Like a scene out of Constable! It
couldn't have looked different in his time, except for
the telegraph poles, which I try not to see. I think I
could stay here and never go home.

Gerald has been taking me all over the countryside, on foot, on horseback and bicycle. He's the
most wonderful companion. I've never known anyone like him and feel that I've always known him.
How can he know so much more, and still be only

my age? He's reading history at Cambridge; what they call "reading" is what we call one's major. He's got so many interests, knows flowers and animals, plays cricket and rides. He got his first pony when he was three years old. What's so appealing is that he's so quiet and unassuming. That's probably the best definition of a true gentleman.

June 26th, 1912

First time in almost a week that I've had time to jot down anything, which I regret because I want to get it all down before I forget things.

I like the manners and the kindliness here. I surely haven't seen much of them in New York, at least where I live! The farm laborer tips his hat to the man on horseback and the man returns the compliment. I often see a carriage full of ladies toiling uphill, while the ladies get out and walk to spare the horses. I like that, too.

We passed a huge estate belonging to Lord Somebody-or-Other. We kept on passing his land; one couldn't see the house, which, Gerald said, is almost a mile from the gates. It has four hundred rooms. In addition, this lord owns fifty thousand acres in Scotland and a winter place in the south of France. All we could glimpse were some yew hedges around the gatehouse and topiary, clipped like crenelated castle towers.

We had a small adventure while we stopped to admire the topiary. A heavyset man on an equally heavy horse came riding up the lane, and prepared to turn into the estate. With his long, grizzly beard, bald head, and ruddy face, he looked like a farmer out of Thomas Hardy, but it turned out he was the brother of the owner.

He greeted Gerald, asked about the family, would have tipped his hat, I'm sure, if he'd been wearing one, and trotted on up the splendid drive toward the house. Maybe it's childish of me, I know Paul thinks it is, but I was really impressed by the fine simplicity of the man. Noblesse oblige, I guess.

June 30th, 1912

I'm staying up late, rethinking the day. I have an impulse to write a poem and have been trying to start a few lines, but nothing happens. Gerald has talent. He's read me some of his poetry and it's rather good, goes straight to the heart. He reads poetry aloud very well, too, and read me some beautiful stuff I'd never heard before. I copied one in particular by A. E. Housman that also went straight to the heart. It's about soldiers, very brave and sad and moving.

> "For the calling bugles hollow,
>   High the screaming fife replies,
>   Gay the files of scarlet follow:
>   Woman bore me. I will rise."

July 1st, 1912

Gerald has a girl. He showed me her picture. She's not as pretty as Leah. He talks about Daphne a lot. He says she's the real thing, not like other girls he's had, but deeply spiritual, a real love.

I can see how a girl would be in love with Gerald.

He's so clean and manly. Last night I had a dream that left me terribly upset. I was in love with Gerald and he was a girl; then suddenly he was himself again. I'm ashamed to write down what we actually did in the dream. Crazy, all mixed up, the way things are in dreams.

It's like the way I sometimes dream about Leah; she's doing things, offering me—like that night by the pond at Uncle Alfie's—and in a way I want to, I want to feel, she's so pretty; yet I don't feel.

July 2nd, 1912

Paul calls me an Anglophile. I can't tell whether he likes it or not. I think he finds me a trifle foolish. Young, wet behind the ears. So be it. I think the world of him all the same, and can't thank him enough.

I wish I could talk more to Paul about these feelings, the way I feel about Leah and Gerald, but I can't. I don't know why, we've always been so close. Maybe it's because he never talks intimately to me, never says anything about Mimi, for instance, even though they'll surely be married. You'd think he'd want to talk about her. But he's reserved, very private. I suppose I am too.

July 3rd, 1912

We saw an owl last night. I'd never heard one, much less seen one. We were sitting out-of-doors on the lawn after dinner when we heard him hoot, and there he was, not twenty feet away, on a low branch, staring at us out of his great yellow eyes.

Afterward, when it grew chilly, we went inside
and they asked me to play again. I played "Eine
Kleine Nacht Musik." This is a group that would
cherish Mozart, rather than music with bravura
flourishes. Mozart is so pure, so subtle, it is music at
its purest. I remember once my father said it very
well, that Mozart is simple as truth is simple, and
then he said something about science and art meeting and being one. Very beautifully put.

I know my father is disappointed in me . . . in
more ways than one, I'm afraid. That's why it has
become so hard, almost impossible, for me to play in
his presence. I have some very uncomfortable
thoughts, certain memories, when he's there . . .
not always, but sometimes. He hopes—or I suppose
by now has given up hope—that I will do what he
wasn't able to do, sit down before a huge audience
and let my soul flow out through my fingers. Then
take my elegant bows. Absurd! I'm good, but I'm
not good enough. And that's almost worse than being no good at all.

                                        July 4th, 1912
Tomorrow is the last day. Then I meet Paul in
London and we leave for Paris. I want to go, yet I
feel sadness at leaving here.

Yesterday we traveled to Glastonbury, Gerald
and I, with two of his friends from Cambridge. We
looked down on the Vale of Avalon, once a sea, they
say, where on the Isle of Avalon, King Arthur was
taken by boat to die. It gives you chills, thinking of
it. The Great Abbey is in ruins, with only the arch
of a tower remaining, and grass growing on the base

of what were once tall towers. It's said that Arthur and Guinevere are buried there. We stood listening to the silence. The only sound was the wind on the hill. It was awesome. I felt the ancient dignity and grace.

It's almost as if I had an English heritage, these old, old villages seem so familiar, with the peaceful fields around them. It's worth fighting a war, if need be, to keep it all like this.

Gerald and I had a long talk all afternoon. We talked about everything: Daphne, Yale, Cambridge, his home and my home. It was hard to describe mine. A good home, surely! But how to describe my parents? He wouldn't like them because he'd sense they didn't approve of him, and I know they wouldn't. Too traditional, they'd say. I can hear them, especially my father, say it. He'd scoff. Too refined, he'd say. He thinks I am, too, I know. Oh, he'd resent everything here, the servants especially.

I asked Gerald whether he thought I should become a medievalist or a classicist. I'm sure I will specialize in history. Gerald says it's too soon to tell, that I should give both a chance before I decide.

This visit has been a great influence on me. I have found a lifelong friend, even though there'll be an ocean between us. I've never had this feeling before, this swift, immediate understanding, as if he were, in some unfathomable way, the other half of myself.

Paris, July 9th, 1912

Dearest Mimi,

We arrived here two days ago and this is the first

chance I've had to write. Father had a list of appointments that began the moment we got off the boat train.

The trip is almost at the halfway mark, and fine as it all has been, I am impatient to get home. I hope you can guess why! I started to miss you on the ship coming over. There were so many little incidents, interesting types, and conversations heard and overheard (you know how curious I always am), that I would have liked to tell about, to hear your comments and opinions, or maybe just have you listen to mine, which you do so well. You're a perfect listener. Yes, I miss you. I suppose that's really what loving is, if you want to put it at its simplest: just being at ease together, wanting to be together.

I happened to speak on the telephone this morning to the wife of one of our clients, a Madame Lamartine, whom you may possibly remember. You met her when you were here with your parents a few years ago. Well, she remembers you!

"And how is *la chère petite* Marian?'" she asked, and called you "a delightful child."

So you see what an impression you make wherever you go! You couldn't have been more than twelve either, as I figure it. She was very pleased when I told her, in absolute confidence, that we were going to be engaged very soon. I hope you don't mind my spilling the beans.

Tomorrow I plan to take a little time off to see something of Paris besides offices and banks. I want to visit some of my favorite places, have lunch at Pré Catalan in the Bois, watch the sidewalk artists in the Place du Tertre and roam through the bookstalls on the Left Bank. Someday, I hope, we'll see all these together.

Right now it will be fun to show it all to Freddy. He's so enthusiastic, such a nice kid. But I must say I am really glad to have gotten him out of England. He pines for it, or at least for that tiny part with which he seems to have fallen in love.

What rot they all talk there! I'm thinking of one night in particular, one wonderful summer night, and the picture those boys made in their white flannels, sprawled out in white wicker chairs, with the white lime blossoms overhead. And what do you think they were talking about, young Gerald and his Cambridge friends, while Freddy took it all in with his mouth hanging open? They were talking about how "the society has gone effete" from too much prosperity, and—believe it or not—too long a peace! It's time for sacrifice, they said; one needs to sacrifice for noble causes; we need new heroes like King Arthur's men. Absolute rot! I only listened, trying to figure them out. The crazy thing is, Freddy has been infected. He talks like an heir to British glory, poor boy. I feel not six years older than he, but sixty. I see war looming in Europe and so do all these bright young men; but while I dread it, they actually welcome it! I'm frightened for them, fantasizing about a lost old world of honor and beauty that never existed except in their imaginations. They're all muddled and don't see themselves.

Of course, it's hard to see oneself. Maybe in some way I'm muddled, too, although naturally I don't think I am! (I have a suspicion that your father, even though I know he likes me, thinks I'm rather a radical, which I am not.)

I don't know why I am writing and rambling so long tonight. The moon is so bright that I could almost do without the lamp. The rue de Rivoli looks silver between the streetlights and the moon. Maybe it's all this light that's keeping me awake, but I don't think so. I'm feeling lonesome, and that's a fact. Lonesome and nostalgic. My mind goes back to those summers when we used to meet on the beach in front of my grandparents' house. Do you know, they used to make me be "nice" to you? Yes, when you were ten years old you really were a nuisance! Then I remember how, suddenly one day when I was the age Freddy is now, getting ready for college, and you were fifteen, how I looked at you— and looked again. You were so lovely! I looked for an excuse to come over that night and help you with your math, do you remember? All in one day, you grew up in my eyes. And in my ears.

"Soft was her voice and low, an excellent thing in woman." Forgive the Shakespeare, please, I couldn't help it because it just fits.

Dearest Mimi, I'll write again very soon.

PAUL

July 18th, 1912

Dearest Mimi,

This has been a long day. I had to wind up all my business, since we leave for Germany next week. But we did conclude the tiring day with festivity, dinner at Maxim's. It really was magnificent. We were guests of one of my father's clients, who brought his wife and three daughters. This is very unusual for the French, who keep their private family life really private; they almost never invite you to their homes, so this was the next best thing.

Freddy said one of the daughters looked like you. Actually, you look much more like an English girl, with your dark blond hair and your freckles—which you hate and I like—so what Freddy saw, I think, was your taste in dress, which is rather French. The girl he meant wore that green-blue shade that you often wear.

I think he liked the girl and was sorry that she didn't pay any attention to his rather timid efforts. Good-looking as he is, girls don't seem to care much about him; his shyness makes him awkward and seem younger.

Incidentally, he keeps asking questions about you; he talks a great deal about love and wants to know how you know when you really are in love. I told him he'll know when it happens and meanwhile not to worry about it.

At this moment he is writing in his diary. The pen goes like mad, spattering ink, as if he can't get things down fast enough. Every now and then he stops and gazes at the sky.

I've just thought of what his parents will think about his aristocratic English sentiments. Far from being unlike his parents, Freddy is their *mirror image!* He romanticizes a past that never was, while they romanticize the future, a kind of socialist utopia, that will also never be.

I'm glad you're practical, Mimi. It's sane, and simplifies living. After these weeks with Freddy, I really need your wholesome common sense. Freddy's nerves are pretty weak. I always have the feeling that at any moment, on impulse, he may do something absolutely drastic. Still, the trip has been a great experience for him and I'm glad I did it.

I've managed to do a little shopping in spare minutes here and there, and I really feel quite proud that I've gotten something to please everyone. I hope so, anyway.

I bought an antique porcelain bowl, Chinese, in that wonderful green-blue that always makes me think of you. I bought it for our house and then I thought, as they wrapped it up, maybe I'm overstepping myself. We aren't officially engaged. What if you change your mind or find someone else? But I don't really believe you will. I trust you absolutely and I know you trust me.

I feel content, glad to be almost on the last leg of the journey, and pleased to have done as well with the business as I have. I think I've dealt successfully with father's clients, and I think I've gotten two or three new ones for us. Father ought to be more than satisfied.

So I feel good tonight. I can't wait to see you again. The thought fills me with a deep, calm joy.

Dearest Mimi, I'll write soon.

PAUL

July 11th, 1912

What words are there for Paris? It, or at least what Paul has shown me so far, seems to be all fountains, flowers, marble and white stone avenues. Splendor.

Still, a part of me remains in England. Foolish, perhaps, after spending so few weeks in a place, to feel so attached to it, but I can't help it. I can still see Gerald waving to me when the little train pulled out of the station on the way to London. My last view, as we rounded a curve, was of lavender thistle in a field, and Gerald in the distance, still waving. It wasn't a real farewell; we are certain that we shall meet again, many times.

Paul is very busy. He took me to a gallery near the hotel, pictures being his first love, and gave me the names of some others I might want to look at, since I shall have to entertain myself here. There were such marvelous things to see, I wish I knew more about art and architecture. I merely admire, whereas Paul knows what he's looking at.

Last night we went to the ballet to see Nijinsky dance in *L'Après-Midi d'un Faune*. It was spectacular. Diaghilev is all the rage here. I wished Leah could have seen it, she's so crazy about the dance. Little Leah! It's astonishing how much she's learned in these few years! I remember—and am ashamed—that I wasn't pleased at all when she was brought into the house, although I pretended I didn't mind, because my mother was set on having her.

Six years ago! It's hard now to remember what it was like before Leah came. She has a way of making you love her, something like the way Paul does, when you think about it, though that seems ridiculous, Paul being so polished while Leah—Leah bounces. That's the best way I can describe her. I guess what they have in common, what I feel, is their enthusiasm. And energy. And curiosity. Paul wants to know about everything. He notices everything. He's interested in what horsepower a new Renault engine has. He stopped a gardener, working on a flower bed in one of the parks, to ask, in his perfect French, about a rose he'd never seen before. Paul gets something out of life every minute.

July 19th, 1912

We had dinner out with a French family. The man is a client of Paul's. We went to Maxim's, but it wasn't a good evening, maybe because I don't speak French and the only one of the three daughters—all of them quite pretty and very fashionable—who spoke some English didn't pay any attention to me. I should have listened to my New Orleans grandmother and learned French. Maybe that would have helped, I don't know.

I wish I had Paul's special skills. I never know what to say. Paul's so sure of himself. He has authority in a very quiet way. Ease. And humor. His eyes—my mother says his eyes are a tropical blue—can twinkle with humor. I wish—

What's wrong with me? The only girl I can really talk to is Leah, and that's because she loves me. I know she really does. Anyway, the dinner was delicious, so it wasn't a total loss.

Paul must be doing a lot of business with these people, because tomorrow we're going on a picnic with them. I'm not looking forward to it.

July 20th, 1912

The countryside around Paris is called the Ile de France, an island. And the place where we picnicked did seem like an island, very peaceful and remote. French picnics aren't like ours, when we spread a blanket on the grass and sit; these people brought a table, chairs, linens, and a real lunch. I must say the French know how to eat! We had chicken and salads and those long loaves of bread, still warm and crisp. Also the best peaches I've ever eaten, big as a baseball and sweet as sugar.

Otherwise, it was the same as last night. One of the girls brought a guitar and played, and then they all talked in French. Paul did try to bring me into the conversation by speaking English to me and the one girl who knew it, but it still didn't work very well, except for a few polite remarks. I'm sure I overheard her whisper to Paul something about "Your cousin's very shy, isn't he?" And I know I am, oh, I'm not always, but I can be.

The best time I had was with the dog. They'd brought their dachshund, called *tekel* in French. He was a young dog, almost a puppy still, and very affectionate. He took my loneliness away. You wouldn't think a dog could do that. I don't know why we never had one. I told Paul when we got back to the hotel that I'd like to buy a *tekel* and bring it home as a surprise for Leah. Paul says wait until we're in Germany and get one there.

I really want to do that. Leah will love it.

München, August 5th, 1912

Dear Parents,

I'll begin with love to you both and ask mother to forgive all the business news that's been in my letters. After all, that's what I'm here for!

So far, I have seen everyone on schedule, have

mailed various documents and contracts to the office in a separate packet and will continue to do so.

Freddy and I have been racing around Germany these last two weeks, as you can tell from the postmarks. This is really the first evening on which I've had time to sit down and write at any length. Father, you really gave me an enormous list of people to see! Not that I'm complaining.

Now we're settled for the next couple of days in München and living well, seeing the gardens and museums and drinking good wine. I realize you may have felt a little uncomfortable with my decision to take Freddy abroad, but I know, too, that you realize he has nothing to do with the family feud.

We are not missing a thing here. Yesterday we went to Schwabing, the artists' section, where I bought two "expressionist" pictures that you will probably not like. They may appreciate in value, in which case I will have bought wisely; if not, I shan't mind, since they are to my taste and will give me a lifetime of pleasure. I also bought a few pieces of Nymphenburg porcelain, much cheaper than at home, naturally. We've seen a good deal in these few days. The Residenz, the Hofgarten, the Frauenkirche, everything you told me not to miss.

Also, we have been invited to dinner by both the Stein brothers at their respective homes. I remembered your instructions about sending flowers the day after, following European etiquette.

Everyone has been most cordial, except for one rather nasty business this afternoon. At the conclusion of my meeting with Herr von Mädler, the conversation, led by him—certainly not by me—got around to the ugly subject of war. It has happened more than once, incidentally, though never as vehemently as this time.

"Surely we Germans don't want war," he told me, "but England is bent upon encircling us. They want to stifle us and keep us from our role as a great world power."

I didn't answer. I could feel only distaste for him, with his monocle and big belly.

"But if it comes to that," he went on, "we shall meet it. Our youth is strong, and war will make it stronger."

There must have been a school near the office where we were, because, looking out of the window, we both saw a column of boys walking. They were about twelve years old, in school uniform, walking in precise formation, and as they passed he said, "War, I say again, if it comes to that, will ennoble those boys."

He was busy biting off the end of a fresh cigar at that moment, so fortunately he was not looking at me. You always tell me that my face is too expressive and betrays whatever I am thinking, and that for business reasons I must try to cultivate an impassive expression.

And then he said, "You Americans will, of course, keep out," and this time gave me a look one could only call sly.

I don't know what sort of answer he expected. I am not in charge of our foreign policy, after all. I said only that one could hope it wouldn't come to that, that the peace movement was strong everywhere.

"Ach," he said, "the peace movement! Radicals, sentimental women, troublemakers, Jews—"

I will give him credit. He blushed, actually blushed, as he remembered.

"Not your kind, of course, Herr Werner, you understand. Of course not. You know the type I mean. The lower classes, Russians, that sort."

I certainly wasn't going to argue with him. I couldn't change his thinking in a hundred hours of argument. I only wanted to get out on the street and breathe some fresh air.

There's a feeling of power in this country that's frightening. It's all mines and steel and energy such as one is never aware of in France, where the emphasis is on pleasure and good living. I saw the Krupp works when we were in Essen, acres and acres of black, threatening industry, storage tanks, railroads, busy as an ant heap or a beehive. I may be wrong, but somehow it made places like Pittsburgh seem small and benign.

At the Belgian frontier, I saw new railroad tracks crossing and recrossing, coming from the heart of Germany and converging there. The Belgians want to be neutral, but it will not work. I know you think I am a pessimist. I don't think I am, only skeptical and cautious. Forgive me, I'm in a bleak mood. After a good dinner, I shall be in a better one. People always are. So good-bye for the present.

Loving regards from

PAUL

P.S. Send my love also to Uncle Alfie and Aunt Emily and little Meg. I have bought her the world's most magnificent doll.

August 8th, 1912

Dear Parents,

You will be happy to know that your son is in fine spirits. I saw the last client an hour ago and am now looking forward to a week of pure vacation before we start for home.

After a lot of research, which made me feel like a detective, I traced the whereabouts of our cousins and reached Joachim Nathansohn on the telephone last night. It was an odd feeling, a thrill. We had a long talk, partly in German and partly in English.

I don't know why we never thought of finding these relatives before, but actually I suppose it's because we've always been in Germany with the Werner grandparents, who wouldn't have been interested in Mother's ancestors.

Anyway, he sounds very nice, this Joachim. He's twenty-two, a graduate of Nürnberg, and a journalist. He works for a large daily and does some independent writing on political subjects. He lives in Stuttgart with his mother. His father died last year. I gather they are well off, since he has traveled all over Europe and speaks of his wanting to see America, especially the West.

How far we've traveled, he and I, from the peddler ancestor in that village that old Uncle David used to tell about!

We figured out that Freddy and Joachim and I share the same great-great-great-grandparents, which makes us fourth cousins. It's strange to think we might have sat next to each other here in a railway car or someplace, without knowing we were related, if Uncle David hadn't kept up some sort of loose correspondence with one generation after the other, all these years.

Joachim suggested that we meet in Bayreuth for some opera, and after that spend a couple of days in the Black Forest at an inn where he always stays. It will be a strange meeting for us both.

Bayreuth, August 11th, 1912

Dear Parents,

What a day! Freddy and I met Joachim in the lobby of our hotel. We had left our names at the desk, so he was directed to us. I don't know what he had been expecting, we didn't ask each other that, although I must remember to ask him; nor am I sure what I was expecting, but he did surprise me. So German! Blond hair, cut hairbrush fashion, bright blue eyes (like my own), but otherwise a thorough Nordic out of the Nibelungen Ring, except that those heroes are always very tall, and Joachim is only average. He kissed us on both cheeks, shook hands, and actually had tears in his eyes. I had a few myself.

We sat across a table and stared at each other, and talked of the family tragedy that all three of us inherited. So long ago! Ancient history. And yet it's not ancient to Great Uncle David, is it? I guess if you lived to be five hundred years old you wouldn't forget those jolly anti-Semitic student riots, or how your mother died. I should have talked more often to Uncle David while there was time. It just struck me that he left that village in a wagon and came to America in a sailing vessel. We got where I am sitting now by train, after crossing the Atlantic in a steamship, a floating palace.

We had a wonderful time, telling what we knew of our families as far back as any of us could remember. Joachim was especially fascinated by what we had to tell about Uncle David, who is the living link. He knew only vaguely about the Civil War and we told about our people's part in it, what they're doing now and so on and so on. He told about his grandfather who had been killed in the Franco-Prussian War, and about a mutual ancestor who had been active in the revolution of 1848. It occurs to me as I write that most of what we had to tell dealt with wars.

Joachim has European cultivation. There is no denying that the education here is more complete than ours, especially in the field of languages. He knows Italian and Spanish, along with French and English. His English improved as the evening wore on, and I think my German did too. We had to speak in English chiefly for Freddy's benefit. The New York public schools certainly do not give training in languages.

Joachim belongs to one of those wandering groups that you see along the roads here, young people who are interested in open-air exercise and exploration. He went with them a few summers ago to Greece.

Interestingly enough, he is a religious Jew, not Orthodox but certainly not as free as our family, either. I don't know how the subject veered onto that, but he did say he had little sympathy with Zionist youth organizations that are also springing up all over Germany. He sees no reason not to be thoroughly German, while at the same time thoroughly Jewish in religious faith. I must say I do agree with him and have no interest in a so-called homeland for the Jews.

We talked almost all night and I'm almost asleep. I'll write probably once more before we leave.

PAUL

August 16th, 1912

Dear Parents,

The Black Forest must be one of the most beautiful places on earth. It's like the pictures in my book of Grimm's Fairy Tales that Fräulein used to read to me when I was six years old.

My room at the inn faces the mountain, which plunges right down to the rear wall of the house, so that when the window is open, I can feel the wind moving in the dark leaves. One can imagine forest voices straight out of Wagner. The myths of gnomes, elves, buried swords, and knight-heroes, all come to life. Yes, it is enchanting and I can see why Grandfather and Grandmother Werner want to keep returning.

We went down to the village to buy Freddy's dachshund. He is determined to bring one home. The village, too, came out of a picture book: the houses have steep roofs and carved balconies like wooden gingerbread. They're cuckoo-clock houses with red geraniums in the window boxes. Cowbells jingled across the fields in back of the main street. Freddy got the puppy and named it Strudel, so now three of us will be traveling home on the ship.

Freddy is delighted. Transportation will certainly be no problem; Strudel fits into my hand and can be carried in a basket on the train in our compartment. Later, on the ship, he will have to live in a kennel on the top deck, though. Freddy was distressed when I told him dogs are not permitted in the staterooms.

I broke off last night and am finishing this letter now; then I'll write no more.

I have to tell you that Joachim truly shocked me last night. We were sitting on the balcony with a group of German men. Freddy had gone inside to read, because they were all speaking German and he was left out, so I was a minority of one. It seems these men all belong to the Pan-Germany League, whose slogan is: *The world belongs to Germany.* They had reams to say about German culture and German blood and German everything else. Every empire has its day. England is going downhill, as did Rome, and now Germany is rising. That's how they were talking. I didn't say a word until they had gone in, and then I remarked to Joachim that they were absurd, that the Kaiser was an idiot with his talk of "my army" and "I am the government."

I told him that the Kaiser was a dangerous man. He really stiffened up. He almost rose on his heels to tell me that "we" don't talk like that about "our" Kaiser; he's the head of state and knows what he's doing. I saw that he was really angry, so I apologized and said I probably should mind my own business, that I understood how he felt (but I don't) and hadn't wanted to offend, et cetera. I wanted to ask him how welcome he thought he was in Prussian circles, and I remembered my Herr von Mädler —"Of course, I don't mean *you,* Herr Werner!"—

but decided it wouldn't be any use. So we parted for
the night with a friendly slap on the back.

Yes, it's a beautiful country, but I'll tell you, I
don't like it. The German myth has corrupted Germans, even decent people like Joachim. All their
endless philosophizing just covers up the truth, that
they want England's colonies and control of the
seas. It's as plain as the nose on your face. And they
will pull the whole world down, themselves in-
cluded, unless something stops them.

So, farewell to Germany and Cousin Joachim.
I'm glad we met and will keep contact, with no hard
feelings, so that our family story may continue for
more generations.

The train leaves early tomorrow and on Friday
we pick up the *Lusitania*. See you soon in New
York. Love,

                                        PAUL

PART TWO

Paul and Anna

1

It was good to be back. There was something astringent, clean, and wholesome in the American atmosphere, in contrast to old, scheming, cynical, luxurious, and sensual Europe. America was more simple and sensible. His judgment might be naive, but if it was, he couldn't help it. At any rate, he was glad to be home, and to be welcomed back by a dear American girl, with her straightforward ways, so different from the arch and subtle charm of the European women.

Mr. Mayer was in his library reading the *Times* when Paul knocked on the door.

"I wonder whether I could have a few minutes, sir? There's something I'd like to ask you."

He had rehearsed this scene, hoping it wouldn't be awkward, and wondering whether he would be stiff and embarrassed. He was none of these.

Mr. Mayer laid the paper on his knees. "I believe I know what it is, Paul. I'll be very pleased if it's what I think it is."

Paul felt the smile spread over his face. "About Marian—Mimi—and myself. We've been—"

"In love," said Mr. Mayer. "And the answer is yes, of course, yes, and God bless you both." The man's eyes were moist. "Only one thing, Paul. I'd like to wait till Marian's birthday in the spring to announce the engagement. We've a tradition in our family. We like our women to be twenty-one before we make things official. Then after that, you can have the wedding as soon as you like. Does that suit you?"

"It will have to, sir," said Paul, who thought it an unreasonable tradition. "After all, it's only a few months away."

"Well, now, let's go find the ladies and open a bottle of champagne."

Mrs. Mayer kissed him and Mimi gave him the first public kiss, with her parents smiling their approval. They made him stay to dinner, during which Mr. Mayer discussed investments, sought Paul's opinion, and gave confidences exactly as if he were already a son of the family.

After dinner, the parents announced that they were going out, leaving Paul and Mimi in the parlor, for the first time really alone together.

Mimi laid her head on Paul's shoulder.

"I'm so happy, darling. Paul, it's going to be wonderful. A whole lifetime! I'm glad we're still so young."

He picked up her hand. The fingers were long and weak; soft pity ran through his veins at the sight and feel of them.

"You must start thinking of a ring, Mimi. Why don't you look in at Tiffany's and see what you like? Then I can order it and be sure to have it on time."

"I'd like you to go with me." She spoke shyly. "I don't know what to look at, how much to spend."

"Spend whatever you like! A ring that you're going to wear for the rest of your life has to be perfect. But you're right, we'll go together."

He drew her closer, resting his cheek on her hair. Such a fine girl she was! A girl to be cherished.

The lamplight glowed. The exquisitely convoluted petals of a solitary white rose in a vase on the desk caught his eye; it was the most extraordinary flower he had ever seen. Under the mantel a small fire crackled gently in the quiet room. A peace of absolute well-being contented him.

One Saturday, Paul came home unexpectedly before noon. A dustcloth lay on his bed, the carpet sweeper was propped against the wall, and the new maid was reading. She had spread open one of his art books on the desk and was engrossed in it, quite unaware that he had come in.

She had a pretty expression of pleasure, clear even in half profile; her lips were parted as if she were about to exclaim. He had naturally noticed— as what man would not?—that the latest housemaid was remarkably attractive; her profusion of dark red hair would catch anyone's attention.

"She's Jewish, you know," his mother had said.

That was unusual. One was accustomed to Catholic peasants, whether Irish or Slavic, but not, for some reason which he had never bothered to examine, to either Jews or Italians. But he had thought no more of her. Maids came and went.

Only Mrs. Monaghan, the cook, was a permanent fixture; young ones got married and vanished.

He stood for a minute now, watching her, until she felt his presence and started.

"Excuse me! I'm sorry, I—"

"That's all right, that's all right, Anna. What are you looking at?"

"This." She faltered.

"Oh, Monet."

A woman in a summer dress sat in a walled and fruited garden. The picture was green and gold; a breeze blew through the fragrant morning air; you felt how cool it was there.

"That's a lovely one, isn't it? You enjoy paintings, Anna?"

"I have never seen any, except in these books."

"Well, this city is filled with museums and galleries. You ought to go. It doesn't cost anything."

"Well, then, I think I will."

There was an instant of silence, during which Paul felt clumsy. Then he asked, "So you like my books, Anna?"

"I look at them every day," she admitted.

"You do? They make you happy, then?"

"Oh, yes! I like to think there are places like that in the world."

The simple statement touched him. "I'll tell you what. You don't have to come in here and rush through the books. Take some to your room. Take your time over them, and any ones you want."

"You wouldn't mind? Oh, thank you."

Her hands were trembling, he saw, when she left with a book in one hand, while the other pushed the carpet sweeper into the hall.

He mentioned the little encounter to his mother.

"A very nice person," she said complacently. "I had my doubts about her working out because she's had no experience, but she's intelligent and learns fast. Goodness knows how long she'll last, though; she has a young man who comes for her on her days off."

Paul wondered who the young man might be, what sort of man would appeal to her. He felt now that he knew something about her, and yet was conscious that this feeling was inappropriate; after all, he had had just five minutes' worth of conversation with the girl!

At breakfast, which Paul and his father took in the dining room while his mother had hers on a tray in bed, his father made weak attempts to be friendly with Anna.

"Well, is it cold enough for you today? They're expecting an early winter, you'd better get your earmuffs out." Or, "Well, did you dance your feet off last night, Anna?"

Paul kept his eyes on his plate. There was something in this jocularity that seemed patronizing, as if, in spite of what his mother had said about her, the girl was not quite intelligent.

He felt uncomfortable. Surely she felt this too? He found himself wishing he might come across her again, if only to make up for his father's foolish manner.

And then, coming home early again one Saturday and finding her in his room with the dustcloth and carpet sweeper, he behaved just as foolishly.

"And how is your young man, Anna? My mother

says you have a very nice young man who comes to see you."

"Oh," she said, "only a friend. It would be too lonesome without some friends."

"It surely would. Do you see him often?"

"Mostly on Sundays. He works most Wednesdays when I'm off."

He knew he was asking too many questions, but curiosity drove him.

"And what do you do on Wednesdays, then?"

"I've been going to the museums since you told me about them. Mostly the art museum on the other side of the park."

How very strange! To have lived in the same house for months with a human being who served you at meals and cared for your possessions, and not to know a thing about that human being, to have found out only accidentally— He interrupted his own thought.

"We never talked until that day last month! Isn't that strange?"

She had a little half smile. "Not when you think about it."

He understood. "Because it's my family's house and you just work in it. That's what you mean, isn't it?"

She nodded.

"Well, that's wrong. People must judge others for themselves, not because of the work they do or the people they know—" He stopped. "I don't make myself clear," he said.

"But I know what you mean."

Her eyes were candid. Of course she knew. He felt the heat of embarrassment.

"I'm hindering your work. Excuse me, Anna."

"No, I'm finished with this room. I have to go downstairs now."

Odd, he thought again. Very odd, the whole business, and poignant. She wants beauty and has likely seen very little of it.

He found, coming home now and then on an early half-day, that he was anticipating her being still at work in his room. They began to have brief conversations; so he learned about her parents— dead in Poland—her brothers in Vienna, and her first months in America.

Then it crossed his mind that perhaps he was waiting for these conversations, looking forward to them. Good Lord, Paul, what can you be thinking of?

He liked to walk through the park on Sundays, crossing to Mimi's house on the East Side. On a certain Sunday between winter and spring, Mimi having gone with her family to visit a relative in the hospital, he took his walk alone.

He walked without aim except to feel the freshness of damp air and the vigor of his stride.

He was full of thoughts. It was funny how the mind was never idle, even when asleep, according to Freud. Just now, he was thinking about justifying his existence.

After what he had learned in Europe, nothing seemed more important than to work against war. He wrote well; perhaps he could write pamphlets for the peace movement. Hennie would know.

His memory of the Civil War tales told by his

grandmother had imbued him with a special horror of bloodshed. Sickened by the trophies hanging on the walls of the Adirondack lodge, and the pathetic head of a slaughtered deer slung over the hood of a car, he had never been able to hunt. War was like that, magnified a million times, and the dead, drooping heads were human. So he would go to the peace meetings and give of himself as was needed. He'd give money, too, and give generously. He thought wryly that Dan wouldn't be able to say he was niggardly.

He had almost reached Fifth Avenue when he saw a woman walking rapidly some yards ahead of him. Her height, for she was tall, and a glimpse of red hair, were familiar, and he sped to catch up with her to make sure.

"Well, Anna! And where are you going?"

"To the museum."

"All by yourself on Sunday?"

"My friend couldn't come today."

"Do you mind if I walk a little way with you, then?"

"No. Please. I mean, yes, walk."

"Well," he began, "have you been enjoying the art books?"

"Oh, yes! I'm sorry, I take too long. I will return them tomorrow."

Poor little soul! He supposed she felt self-conscious, and felt sorry that she did.

"I didn't mean that, Anna! Take as long as you want." Where the next impulse came from, he never knew. "As long as we're walking, maybe you would like to go with me to the Armory Show this afternoon?" And he hurried to explain. "It's a very interesting exhibit of modern paintings, mostly from Europe. You may not like them. But everyone is talking about it and since you like pictures, you should see it."

"Well, I—"

He interrupted. "It's really worth seeing. At least, I thought so."

"You've seen it? Then you won't want to go again."

"On the contrary, that's just why I do want to go again. It's quite marvelous, exciting and new."

Still, the girl hesitated. The blush, which had receded, rose again, flooding her pale skin.

He understood. "If we should meet anyone we— know, I'll say we met by accident, which will be the truth. Come. There's no harm in it, Anna."

They turned toward Lexington Avenue.

"It's at Twenty-fifth Street, a very long walk. We'll take the trolley."

"Can't we walk? I don't mind how far. The air is good. And the sky. So beautiful."

He looked up into the watery blue, which was high and cold above shredding clouds; yet it held a subtle promise of spring and a stronger blue to come. Then he looked down at her, not very far down, for she was almost his height, and caught her upward glance.

"I'm in the house so much. I like to be outside," she said, and added quickly, "not that I mind, it's such a fine house, and I am so glad to be in it."

The little apology made him speak very softly. "Are you enjoying New York? Seeing much of the city on your walks?"

"Oh, yes, I go everywhere. From Grant's Tomb to the Woolworth Building."

"You don't waste any time. They've only just finished the Woolworth Building."

"The tallest office building in the world!" she cried. Her eyes were amazed.

This amazement was both amusing and refreshing. She marveled at passing cars, at a florist's window filled with tulips, and at a huge fawn-colored dog.

"That's an Afghan hound," Paul told her. "Very rare."

At the Armory, she exclaimed over the long line of automobiles, then at the vastness of the hall and the splendor of the fashionables who were inspecting the sculptures and the paintings.

"Look here, Anna. This is a famous American artist, John Sloan. The Realist school. You understand?"

"That he paints what is real? Of course. *Girls Drying Their Hair,*" she read. White laundry flapped in the breeze on the roof of a tenement house. It was sunny on the roof. "Oh," she said, "yes, I know how they feel. Glad to get out of the dark rooms. It's true. I know all about that."

They moved through the hall, on to Van Gogh, Matisse, and Cézanne.

"The Poorhouse on the Hill," Anna said. She spoke so softly that he had to bend to hear her against the background of crowd noise. "The beautiful earth! Round hills. It was flat where I came from in Poland. I should like to see hills someday."

Why did she make him feel so moved by her simple wish? He was suddenly curious. "Come over here, I'd like to show you something."

A small crowd obstructed the view, so that they had to maneuver for places from which to see.

"Marcel Duchamp, a Frenchman. It's called *Nude Descending a Staircase,*" Paul explained.

Behind them, people were laughing.

"Idiotic! Not worth the price of the paint and canvas."

"Not even decent. They should be ashamed of themselves for showing such trash."

"Tell me, Anna, what do you think?" Paul asked.

She hesitated, frowning a little, while he stood watching her.

"Do you hate it or like it, Anna?"

"I don't know. It isn't beautiful exactly, all those lines and squares, but—"

"But what?"

"Well, it's what—what do you say—original? I mean, nobody has ever done anything like this before, I think."

"It's original, all right. And it's called cubism; what you called 'squares' are 'cubes.'"

"Oh, yes, like little boxes. Over and over. But it moves, doesn't it? It's very strange! You look away and then you want to look again, to see her going down the stairs."

"I agree with you. The critics here make fun of it because America isn't ready for it yet. But it will be."

A few days ago he had stood in the same spot with Mimi.

"That," she had declared, "is the most stupid

thing I've ever seen in my life. An ugly scrawl. A child could do it. It's hardly what I call art."

It's only fair to admit, Paul reflected now, that most of the art critics and no less a personage than Theodore Roosevelt shared her opinion.

"I don't even think it's quite—quite moral," Mimi had said, meaning the nudity. He had not answered.

After all, most middle-class houses, when they couldn't afford originals, adorned the walls with brown photographs of the masters: Gainsborough's *Blue Boy*. No, America definitely was not ready for this.

And yet this girl Anna, this uneducated girl, could see, could contemplate and accept the new.

She was still studying the picture. He stood behind her, looking not at the painting but at the back of her head. Her hat, perched high, revealed half a head of thick hair coiled down her neck. How many shades of red there were in that glossy mass! There were tones of russet and copper, and of the fine red grain that runs through mahogany; where a few soft fibers lay free of the coiled mass, the red was touched with gold.

She was saying something. He started.

"I didn't hear you. Pardon."

"I was saying, it's getting late. Perhaps we ought to go," she said quite firmly.

But there was nothing pitiable about her! Why had he thought there was? Because she was slight and young? No, nothing pitiable after all. He was relieved.

"We'll take the trolley," he said.

Ordinarily he would have summoned a hansom

cab. But it would be unwise to drive up to his house with her. He could imagine what would be said if they were seen. It wouldn't do Anna any good! Or, to be honest, himself either!

"You take the trolley. I want to walk," Anna said.

"After all you've walked today? It's uptown and crosstown again."

"I shan't be out of doors until Wednesday, you see."

"Oh, I'll walk with you, then."

She walked rapidly, without flagging. How healthy she was, and strong! The wind came up and it grew cold as the afternoon darkened. Her coat was flimsy, a cheap gray wool, belted around her narrow waist with flair, but surely not warm enough. Paul's own coat was lined with fur.

They walked silently. For some reason he felt irritable. He was annoyed with himself for having weighed Mimi's opinions against this girl's. What difference did it make what a person thought about a painting? It was simply a matter of taste, like preferring chocolate over vanilla.

Anna said, "I forgot the name of that man. The cubist, you said?"

"Duchamp, Marcel Duchamp."

"You know so much about art. Do you paint?"

"Goodness no. I can't draw a straight line. But I try to learn what I can about it. Can't stick with economics all the time."

"Economics is . . . ?"

"Business. Money. Banks."

"Ah, yes, you work in a bank."

"Well, in a way." It was too difficult to describe

what private investment banking was, and of no importance to her anyway.

"I see," she said.

It seemed to him that she had frowned slightly and he thought, I daresay she has the working-class concept of a banker as some sort of ogre who eats the poor.

So his question came quickly. "You think bankers are bad people for lending money and making people pay for it?"

"Oh, no," Anna said. "How else would anything get done? I mean, towers like that," and she waved toward a tall construction that was rising across the park. "Nobody would have enough money by himself to build one of those! He would have to borrow, wouldn't he?"

"Yes," he answered, clearly pleased. "Of course, that's the answer." And he said, "You're a very interesting woman, Anna."

"You think that because you have never talked to anybody like me before." She spoke boldly, with a trace of humor; the shyness of the first hour was gone. "An uneducated immigrant. I am different from the people you know."

"That's so. Very different."

"And I think you and your family very different."

"Do you? How?"

"Well, I have never known Jews like you before. I didn't think you were Jewish until Mrs. Monaghan told me."

"Well, we are, and very proud to be. We are like Jacob Schiff, Americans of Jewish faith."

"Well, so I learned something. Ah, but I get discouraged. Because I think I don't know anything and never will know anything or see anything, when what I want is to see the whole world."

She made a pretty gesture, throwing her hands into the air.

"The whole world? That's a big order. But I'll tell you, Anna, I have a feeling that you're going to have a whole lot more than you think you will. You'll see the world. Europe, wonderful places—"

"Europe? Not Poland again, I can tell you that!"

"Not Poland, but Paris and London and Italy. Lake Maggiore, with castles and islands. The Alps, with snow on their peaks in the middle of the summer. You said you want to see hills."

They had come to the house. It had grown quite dark and windy on the street. Welcome lights shone through the parlor windows, promising warm comfort.

"Anna, it was a nice day."

Under the streetlamp her eyes and her bright hair gleamed. And turning to him with one of the loveliest curving smiles he had ever seen, she thanked him.

"It was a beautiful time. I will think of it, and the Alps with snow, and all the pictures."

Then she turned and went down the steps to the basement, where no light burned. He watched until she had unlocked the door, then tipped his hat and stood looking after her before he, too, turned and went up the steps to the front door.

"When I was a child," said Angelique, "no more than ten or twelve, I used to go visiting her relatives with my grandfather's wife. She was a Creole. Oh,

they thought I didn't understand, but I did! My
mother told me after I was married, about one old
man's slave-children. They looked just like the children he'd had by his wife. Even I could tell they
were brothers. Sylvan Labouisse, that was his
name."

Enjoying the telling, she peered over the coffee
cup to see what effect her tales had had upon her
audience. It was seldom these days, reflected Paul,
that his grandmother found a new audience.

Mimi was properly enthralled.

"Sylvan Labouisse! What a marvelous name!"

Mimi's face, which was not one of those mobile
faces that reveal emotion, now sparkled with curiosity. Paul had wondered fleetingly—not that it mattered practically what Mimi might think, except
that he had hoped she would fit with Hennie enough
so that they would like each other—whether she
would be surprised at the meager flat and the neighborhood. For when had she been in such a neighborhood before, except to pass through without really
seeing it? And she had, after all, met Hennie only in
the very different setting of his parents' and Alfie's
house. Certainly, she looked like a visitor from elsewhere, sitting on the shabby tan sofa. Her feet in
their soft kid boots, and her ruby velvet jacket, were
the only bright objects in the room, except for a wall
of books and Angelique's old silver on the tea table.

"Do you suppose his son knew about his half
brothers?" Mimi asked.

"If he did, he certainly wouldn't talk about it."
Angelique laughed. "Such things were never talked
about. You can't imagine the etiquette of those days!
Talk about court ritual! I remember the first time I

saw Mr. Labouisse I was in absolute awe. He had a
rigid way of holding himself, almost royally, coming
down the parterre in his garden, like Louis the
Fourteenth at Versailles."

Hennie and Paul exchanged glances over the precious worn-out reminiscences. Their eyes smiled
their tolerant affection and amusement.

"Oh, they were courtly, those men; my own father too," Angelique said, impressing Mimi. "All
the men were like that."

"Not Uncle David," Hennie corrected.

Angelique corrected in turn, "Uncle David was
never of the South, you know that."

"What a fascinating family!" Mimi exclaimed.

"Oh, we are a family with a history." Angelique
nodded in appreciation. "I could go on and on
about it. Maybe Paul will bring you to tea at my
apartment, since you are interested in history and
antiques. I have some nice things I could show you,
if you'd like."

"I'd love it," Mimi said. "I really would."

Her courtesy came to the fore. It would have
done so even if the old lady had bored her, Paul
thought, proud of Mimi. There was not the slightest
fault that anyone could have found with her. She
had been simple and friendly. Not effusive, but correct in every way.

They rose to go. Paul laid Mimi's fur cape over
her shoulders.

"It's been perfectly lovely," Mimi said, shaking
hands with both the women. "And the sponge cake,
Mrs. Roth, was the lightest I've ever had."

"Do call me Hennie."

"I wish I had your skill, Hennie. And will you please give my regards to Freddy?"

"By the way, where is he?" Paul asked.

"He's taken Leah to the matinee, Isadora Duncan's dance recital, before he goes back to Yale on the evening train. They already had the tickets. Otherwise, you know they would have been here."

"Mimi and I will have to see Isadora. I hear she's a marvel."

"I haven't seen her. Leah says she's thrilling. But then, Leah finds everything thrilling," Hennie said fondly.

"I tell you again," Angelique complained, "I don't like it."

The sharp tone cut into the affable air of departure. Mimi looked startled.

Hennie responded impatiently. "What is there not to like, Mama? Isadora Duncan?"

"You know quite well what I don't like. He's out with her every spare minute."

"He's not, and you make too much of it, Mama," Hennie answered angrily.

They were standing in the cramped hall with the outer door already open. Mimi was looking away, toward an etching of the Colosseum on the wall, above Hennie's head.

"A good deed," Angelique went on, "an act of kindness, but very unwise all the same. Some things are just not suitable, and I said so from the beginning."

Embarrassment lay like a cloak over everyone's shoulders except the old lady's.

"Well," Paul said, "we really shall have to go. Thank you, Hennie. Thank you, Grandmother. I'm sorry about that," he said as they went down the stairs. "Leah seems to be an unsolved issue between them."

"She's a very smart girl, I thought. And attractive too."

"In a bold way."

"You don't like her, Paul?"

"As a matter of fact, I do. She just isn't my sort of girl."

The words repeated themselves in his ears: my sort of girl. What *is* my sort of girl?

Mimi's new electric car was waiting at the curb. She took the tiller and, with a delicate whir, the little machine slid away down the street.

"Ten miles an hour! It's such fun!" Mimi cried. "My very own car! It's the best present Papa ever gave me."

"I should think so." It was a very costly present, this little shining leather-lined box on wheels. Paul's mother owned one, and so did Uncle Alfie's wife; they were "the thing."

"Do please close the window," Mimi said. "You know how easily I catch cold."

Paul complied, filling the car with the strong scent of the carnation in its crystal vase. He detested the bitter scent of carnations.

"You're grandmother's charming," Mimi remarked as they turned into Fifth Avenue and headed uptown.

"You think so? Sometimes I'm afraid I find she has too much charm."

"What a strange thing to say! I liked her."

"She shouldn't have gotten on the Leah subject. It wasn't the place or time."

"Oh, well, I liked her all the same. She's a lady, a kind of grande dame, don't you think? But tell me about your Aunt Hennie. What was the feud about between her and your parents?"

"Oh, something to do with tenements. Uncle Dan's a reformer. It's a long story, I'll tell you some other time."

He was suddenly tired; the damned carnation was giving him a headache in the close air.

"I'm sorry for your aunt," Mimi said.

"Sorry for Hennie? Because of the feud, you mean?"

"No, because they're obviously so poor. That apartment! It must be awfully hard for her."

He had rarely, if ever, given a thought to Hennie's "poverty" until today. It had never seemed as marked as it had today. And he saw again the sofa, with Mimi's skirts spread, and her pale kid boots resting on the old rug.

"Hennie doesn't mind it," he answered.

"Not mind it! How could she not!"

"She's far too busy," and his mind leapt back to a different picture. "You should have seen her marching on Fifth Avenue with the suffragettes! All of them dressed in white, with their heads up, and so proud." He chuckled. "A sight to behold, I tell you!"

"I've seen the suffragettes. Papa says votes for women won't make a particle of difference."

He let that pass. "This parade wasn't only for women's voting rights. It was against child labor. Hennie's always been active in that. I was proud of her. She's quite a woman, you'll find out."

"I think your grandmother is much better off, isn't she? Better off than Hennie, I mean."

"You think so? Why?"

"Oh, her dress was lovely and she had on very expensive shoes."

"My Uncle Alfie is very generous to his mother," Paul said dryly.

"That's nice. Families ought to be like that. My father sends money to cousins in Germany that he's never even seen, and they're only second cousins too. We're all very warmhearted in my family, so I'm used to it."

That was quite true. The Mayers were solid, good people, part of the fine old German Jewish community, an extended family in itself. You could feel as comfortable in any one of their homes as in your own.

But I don't always feel comfortable in my own, Paul thought. A wry smile tightened his lips. Well, most of the time I do.

"What are you smiling at?" Mimi wanted to know, taking her eyes from the tiller.

"Nothing. Except that I'm happy." He laid his hand over hers on the tiller. "I hope you are."

"Oh, very, very! You know, I've been thinking, I'd like to do nice things for Hennie after we're married. Nothing that could embarrass or offend her, just little presents for her birthday and whenever else it's suitable. I hate to see anyone go in want."

"You're very kind, Mimi."

That, too, was true. She could be depended on for decent goodness; a man knew where he stood with such a woman. And feeling a grateful comfort, he tightened his hold on the hand in the gray kid glove.

* * *

A crazy thing happened to him. He was passing Wanamaker's when he heard two loud feminine voices behind him.

"Oh, look! Oh, I've got to stop a second! Have you ever seen such a hat in all your life? Now tell me, have you ever?"

"Gorgeous! It must cost a fortune, though. It's got to be an import. I'm sure it is. Hats like that are only made in Paris."

He was drawn to look. In the window stood a single hat, displayed like the jewel it was. The model head bore a cascade of red hair. On the silky straw brim lay a wreath of scarlet poppies and gold wheat. It was a hat to be worn by a tall girl at a garden party or a wedding on a ten-acre lawn. Or to tea at the Plaza in the spring. Red hair gleaming under the wide pale brim. He shut his eyes for a moment. Crazy, crazy. He opened his eyes. There it waited, asking to be bought for someone who would adorn it, rather than be adorned by it. Why let it go to waste on some fat woman of fifty or—or some girl who might have the means to buy it, but never the face to go with it?

He had a sudden vision of the cheap coat so smartly wrapped, the drab hat, the curving smile . . .

He had hardly spoken to her since that day, avoiding their little conversations, and staying out of his room when she was working in it. When she served him at table, he was aware of her hands on the platter; a fragrant warmth trembled from her body. He averted his eyes. She must think he was angry at her. . . .

And all this time, remembering these things, he was staring at the hat.

He went inside and bought it. He didn't ask the price until it was wrapped in its big round box and tied with a splendid ribbon. It seemed like an enormous price for a hat, and he supposed it was because of the respectful way the salesgirl handed it over: "Here you are, sir. I hope the lady will enjoy it."

All the way home, clanging uptown on the trolley, the box lay on the seat beside him. Now that he had bought the thing, he was afraid of it. The motorman had to ask him twice for the fare, his thoughts were so far away. His thoughts were terribly troubling. To be truthful about it, they had been troubling for a long time.

But all men had such thoughts! The most happily married man had a wandering eye, everyone knew that. Oh, not like Uncle Dan, he didn't mean that. And that bothered him, too, thinking about Hennie; all these things, questions of loyalty and faithfulness were so painful and perplexing. Yes, every man looked! He'd be a pretty poor specimen if he didn't. And he suspected that women did so, too, surreptitiously, and why shouldn't they? There was no reason to be ashamed of the natural call of the flesh, provided one kept it in decent bounds and didn't wreck one's family.

Yet surely he wouldn't want Mimi or anyone to know his thoughts, or know about the hat. Good God, what had he done? The girl would misunderstand. And he was tempted to leave it on the seat.

Nevertheless, he carried it home. He waited for

her in the hall outside his room, and intercepted her as she climbed the stairs.

"I thought you might like this," he said, extending a stiff arm with the box dangling by its ribbon.

She didn't understand.

"This. A box. A present for you. Open it."

"For me? Why?"

"Because I like you. Because I like to give presents to people I like." The words came more easily now that he had gotten started. "Here, let me," he said as her fingers fumbled. From its crush of tissue paper, he lifted the marvelous hat. "Here! What do you think of it?"

There came that flush again, the redhead's typical flush, so bright on the pale skin.

"Oh! It's the most beautiful!" Her hands flew to her cheeks and fell again. "Thank you, thank you, but I can't, really I can't."

"Why not?"

She raised her eyes. He hadn't noticed before that her golden lashes had dark tips.

"It wouldn't be right."

"Not right . . . yes, I see what you mean. But, Anna, why can't we damn the propriety? Here am I, a man who can afford to buy a beautiful hat, and here you are, a beautiful girl who can't afford a hat —oh, for heaven's sake, give me the pleasure! Wear it next Sunday when your young man comes."

"I shouldn't." The palm of her hand smoothed the delicate crown, around and around.

"Listen here, you love it! He'll love it on you too. It's almost spring, Anna. Celebrate. We're only young once."

He spoke almost roughly. He felt . . . he didn't know how he felt.

"Well, good night," he said abruptly, and swung about and closed his door with a small hard thud.

A dullness came over him. Spring had always been his time, but not this year. The days lengthened; boys played marbles on the street; from open windows came the tinkle of children practicing on the piano; there were ripe wet strawberries on the grocers' stands. Clients came to the office with talk of summer plans for Biarritz, for the Adirondacks or Bar Harbor; their talk was full of sea winds, blue water, and music; still the dullness lay upon him. He sat at his desk with his chin in his hands and five telephone messages to answer, and did not answer them.

"So? Your mind's on the wedding, I suppose?" His father's head appeared at the door, rousing him from his trance.

"What?" It took another second before he registered what his father had said, and he could give the expected smile, the sheepish smile of the man "in love," the bridegroom, butt of a hundred good-natured jokes. "Yes, the wedding."

"Your mother's worried that she's going to lose you forever."

"Lose me?"

"Now that you are going to be married."

"I thought she was delighted."

"Oh, you know she is. She was only teasing because you hardly ever come home to dinner anymore. Or hadn't you realized it? You're almost always at the Mayers'."

"Well, they always ask me to stay."

"The food must be better over there, that's what." His father laid a hand on Paul's arm. "All in fun, all in fun. We're thrilled to see you so happy, wanting to be with Mimi, and, of course, we know we're not losing you. Mimi will be a lovely daughter for us."

He felt dirty. His thoughts were dirty. That was why he avoided their dinner table, except on Wednesday when she was out and Mrs. Monaghan passed the platters. He had never known what obsession was, except for the dictionary definition, which could not begin to describe the horror of it. His inability to control his own thoughts was frightening. He hadn't known that it is possible to think of two things at the same time, to read a headline in a newspaper and, while comprehending it, to see a lovely, thoughtful face under level brows; to sit in a room full of voices or, worse yet, to be alone with Mimi's voice and at the same time to hear, quite distinctly, another one, with a musical foreign accent.

Oh, I want to see the whole world, I want to know everything.

This, then, was obsession. A miserable condition, and when would it end?

He met her in the hall one Saturday morning. He was coming up the stairs while she waited at the top to go down, so it was impossible to avoid her.

"Well," he said, conscious again of that foolish, jocular manner that his father took with her, "well, your young man—did he like the hat?"

"I haven't worn it yet. It's too fine for any place we go."

"Really? Well, make him take you someplace. Out to tea and cake somewhere, when you see him tomorrow."

"Well, maybe. But not tomorrow. He has to work this Sunday."

The words came. He didn't will them; the words just came of themselves.

"Then I'll take you to tea."

"Oh, no! Oh, no! It wouldn't be right."

"Why not?"

She was trying to go past him down the stairs, but he made no room.

"What do you mean, not right? I'd like to sit down somewhere quietly and talk to you. There's nothing wrong with that. Nothing to be ashamed of."

"But still, I don't think—"

"Nobody needs to know, if that's what you're worried about. If anyone sees us, I'll say you're the sister of one of my clients from out of town and I had to be nice to you. Will that do?"

"Well," she said. And there was that entrancing smile again, on the very brink of laughter.

"That settles it, then. Tomorrow."

He took her to the Plaza, where they sat in a corner behind a screen of palms. A waiter brought tea and wheeled a little cart from which they chose cakes.

"You look beautiful, Anna. Especially in that hat."

"My shoes don't go with the hat."

He was puzzled. "Shoes don't go with the hat?"

"They're not fancy enough, but they have to go with my uniform every day. I can't have two pairs, can I? They cost two-fifty."

He glanced down to where her skirt had risen to expose a clumsy high-laced shoe. Anna, following his glance, pulled her skirt down.

"They're all right," Paul said. "Your skirt hides them." And confused, he corrected himself. "Not that they—I meant, they're very nice."

She laughed. "You know they're not!"

And laughing, too, he had a delightful sensation of understanding and of being understood.

"You're the prettiest woman in this whole place, do you know that?"

"How can you say so? Look at that one coming, the one in the yellow dress—"

"Never mind her. She's just another pretty woman, the city is full of them. But you're different. You're alive. Most of these others wear a mask, they're tired of everything, while you're full of wonder."

"Wonder—that means?"

"It means that you love life, you're not bored with it."

"Oh, bored, never!"

"And you've already done so much with your life."

"I? But I've done nothing! Nothing!"

"You've come across the ocean alone, and learned a new language, you're supporting yourself. While I —I've had everything done for me. Given to me. I admire you, Anna."

She made a little gesture of deprecation with her

hands. He saw that he had embarrassed her, and said no more, but sat back and watched her eat the pastries with a child's greedy pleasure.

"Try the raspberry ones," he said, "and these are good, they're called meringues."

The violins began to waltz.

"How I love the sound of violins!" Anna cried.

"You've never gone to a concert or the opera, Anna?"

Foolish question! When, where, or how could she have done so? And when she shook her head, he thought of something.

"I will get you an opera ticket. We all have subscriptions." By "all" he meant, naturally, his own family and Mimi's. "The very next time we have one to spare, I'll see that you get it. It will be a great thing for you, your first time."

There is a limit to the amount of tea one can drink. They came out to the sidewalk and stood for a minute watching the slow procession of Sunday walkers passing the statue of General Sherman. Sunlight glittered on the metal back of the proud horse; it touched the new green leaves in the park; it washed the clouds, and lighted Anna's lovely white face. It was still the middle of the afternoon, and the soft spring day had hours to go.

"We could ride uptown on the el," Paul proposed. "It's not a bad ride."

It was neither luxurious nor scenic, but it was nevertheless a place to sit, something to do, and an excuse to stay a little longer. They walked westward toward Columbus Avenue, climbed the stairs under the black iron gloom, and came out onto the empty platform. Shortly, a train came rumbling down the track.

"The express," Paul said. "We can ride as far as we want. If we like it, we'll just keep going. It will be breezy."

She made no response, but sat where he indicated. On the narrow seat, their shoulders touched; she could have moved away from the contact by leaning toward the window, but did not, and so they started off. When the train lurched around the corner, her whole body from shoulder to knee moved lightly toward his and back again.

The light fragrance that he had noticed before came from her again; not flowery like perfume or scented soap, it was more like the healthy sweetness of grass, or of washed air after rain. He was certain it was the natural fragrance of her hair and skin. Very faintly, he heard her breathing; was he imagining it, or was her breath really quickening as his own was?

The contact silenced him. It silenced them both. He had never been so conscious of the nearness of another human body. Or perhaps it was only the roar that kept her silent? he thought, for it was hard to be heard over the grind of the wheels and the rush of the wind. And in a kind of numbness, almost a trance, he sat without moving, mechanically reading the billboards that ran past: KELLOGG'S CORN FLAKES sprang out at every station.

At the same time he was thinking: What is the matter? Everything that is solid and certain is speeding away, as if the train were careening toward a precipice and there were no way of stopping it.

Grime and pieces of cinder from the locomotive

flew in at the windows and stung their eyes. Anna probed her eye with a handkerchief.

"This is no good," Paul said, "we'll have to go back."

No good. In all the city, in all the sprawling city, no place where two people could sit in peace for any more than an hour at the most.

They came down onto the street. From there it was only a short walk home, where she would go back into the uniform of a maid and the distance would loom between them. He looked about desperately, and suddenly remembered.

"There's an ice-cream parlor up the avenue. We'll go there," he said, not "Would you like to go?"

Still silent, although free of the elevated's roar, they walked together. Her heels clicked twice on the pavement to each step of his until, apologizing, he slackened his pace.

Still without speaking, they sat at the counter on the swiveling stools. Paul ordered two cherry phosphates, and the silence fell again. He read the placards stuck in the curved mahogany frame of the enormous mirror: BANANA SPLIT, CHOCOLATE SUNDAE, VANILLA SHAKE. His eyes traveled down the row and went back to the beginning—BANANA SPLIT—and caught Anna's image reflected in the glass. She had been looking at him.

"Well," he said. "Well. This is somewhat different from the Plaza."

"Yes. But I've never been in such a fancy one."

"Never been in an ice-cream parlor?"

"Oh, yes, downtown on Sundays. But not as fancy as this."

On Sunday. With that fellow, her "young man."

Paul had gotten a glimpse of him once as Anna and he were going in together at the basement door. Anna had murmured both their names, and the fellow had pulled off his cap, a workman's cap, in acknowledgment. A stocky fellow he'd been, with an ordinary face, nothing you would remember, except perhaps that he looked serious. Sober. What sort of man might he be? Did she allow him to kiss her, or— And Paul felt suddenly, terribly, angry.

Anna, having finished, leaned on the counter, tracing with her fingernail the swirls in the marble, white on brown, and when she saw that he was watching her hand, said, smiling, "It's like coffee and cream. Beautiful stone." Her mouth caressed the *beautiful*.

"Marble. The best comes from Italy," he answered, and thought how fresh and moist her mouth was, with her lips parted like that over the strong teeth.

He became aware that he was staring into her face, and she was looking back with widened eyes, as if they were astonished at each other or at themselves. So they held the look. There was a drumming in his head.

Suddenly he was terrified. The sensation he had had in the el of rushing, rushing toward a precipice and being unable to stop, caught at him; his heart pounded, and he stood up.

"We'll go," he said, his voice sounding unnatural in his ears. "Now. It's really late. We'll go."

Mimi would be of age this week and then the machinery that had been held back would be released:

the birthday and simultaneous engagement, then the wedding.

Oh, Mimi, Mimi, how dear you are! But I don't want to marry you, not now, not yet.

When, then?

Oh, I know I must. I will, but just give me a little time.

It's not Anna you want to marry? Anna? How can that be?

I don't know.

What do you mean, "you don't know"? Are you in love with her?

I don't know . . . I think so . . . I can't stop thinking about her.

You know you're in love with her. Why don't you admit it?

All right . . . all right . . . I'll admit it. And so, now what? Tell me that.

He needed so badly to talk to someone. But to whom? Any one of his friends would counsel him not to be a fool. You'll get over it, they'd say, and slap him on the back, make a joke of it, even. Your family's maid, after all! It doesn't mean anything, happens to us all, this sort of thing; in no time you'll be over it. He thought of Uncle Dan, a man to whom you could talk about anything; and then, remembering his way with women, was pretty sure Dan would assume this was the same sort of thing and wouldn't see it as it was. He thought of the old man, Uncle David, who had once been wise and was so no longer. He thought of Hennie, dismissed the thought, came back to it and dismissed it again.

A few days later, a free opera ticket became available because of a family funeral; Paul took it for

Anna. The opera was *Tristan and Isolde.* Would she find Wagner somewhat heavy for a first experience? On the other hand, it was a love story of such poignance . . .

All that afternoon, knowing the timing of the opera as well as he did, he kept imagining her. Now it's the first act, with the ship and the love potion; now the second; now, finally, the soaring, the heartbreaking love-death, and would she be moved by it as he had been and was, every time?

He waited for her on the landing when she came upstairs that evening. He had meant only to ask: Was it what you expected? But the words stopped in his mouth. In the dim light from the wall sconce, she was radiant with happiness and awe. She glowed. She trembled and waited.

So there, in the quiet house, they came together. Quite simply, as if it were the most natural thing in the world—and, of course, it is, he thought, the thought fleeting through a luminous haze, a warmth of desire such as he had never known—they held one another. He kissed her hair, her eyes, and then her mouth. Her arms circled his neck, her fingers moved in his hair. She was soft and firm, strong against him, and so tender . . .

How long they stood so, he could not have said. "Oh, Anna. Sweet, sweet, beautiful." And he thought he said, murmuring into her fragrant neck, her hair, her eyelids, he thought he heard himself say, "I love you."

They could barely stand. For God's sake, pull away . . . pull away before it's too late.

He released her. "Go to your room. Go. My darling."

And he went inside to his own room and lay facedown on the bed until the blood stopped pounding in his ears. Then he took a book, but could not read, turned out the light and could not sleep.

Somehow, he would have to shape the inchoate swirling in his head, to give it a form and words.

"My God, I'll have to talk to someone," he said aloud into the room, that dear space that had been his almost all his life, where now, in a sullen dawn, the Yale banner, his books, and his riding boots emerged like accusing strangers out of the darkness.

He started up. Tomorrow—no, today! It was Mimi's birthday and the family dinner and oh, no, please! Not the announcement . . .

I'll have to see someone. Hennie. I'll see Hennie.

He sat on the sofa with his hands dangling between his knees and his head bent. He had been there for more than an hour in Hennie's parlor.

"Are you horribly shocked?" he asked now.

"Surprised, not shocked," Hennie said hesitantly. "I have always thought it tragic when a person does something he desperately doesn't want to do, out of fear of hurting someone else. I don't mean ordinary things, but something to do with your whole life, what you are and what you want to be."

Paul raised his head. "Mimi's such a fine girl," he said into the vacant air at the dead center of the room.

"One can see that."

"The wedding ring is ready. Before she died, my grandmother Werner gave it to me to have for my

bride. It's awfully old-fashioned, but Mimi's pleased
to take it."

Hennie made no comment.

"All the preparations they've been making! I
didn't realize, I suppose a man never does."

Riding back down Riverside Drive from the
Claremont Inn, Mimi had asked him to come inside
and see the linens.

"I know men don't care about that sort of thing,"
she had appealed, "but it's going to be your home,
too, and everything Mama bought is so beautiful.
Do come up for just a minute."

And he'd gone in to be shown piles of linen, dam-
ask tablecloths, dozens of them, thick enough to last
for generations, with her initials and his entwined in
fine embroidery, permanent as a seal on a document
and regal as a crest.

Mr. Mayer had come in the room and put his
hand on Paul's shoulder, man-to-man, father-to-
son, and remarked on the charming foolishness of
women with all their folderol. But he had been
pleased, all the same, proud to provide these good
things for his daughter.

"She has gotten all the linens ready," Paul said
now, miserably.

"Linens," Hennie said. The innocent noun was
scornful, and Paul knew she was thinking: A ring
and a few yards of expensive cloth. For such trivia
to stand in the way—

He looked down at his helpless hands.

"It's not fair to either Mimi or yourself to go
ahead if you don't care about her," Hennie said at
last.

"I do care about her."

"But not the way you do about the other one."

"Differently."

"Have you told—Anna?"

"Anna." The very name was intimate and alive.

"Have you said anything? Told her you love her and want to marry her?"

"I think I said I love her. But one doesn't have to *say;* one knows."

"Yes, yes." Hennie sighed. "I shall be sorry, whatever you do, since each of them loves you. It's terrible not to be wanted. It makes you feel worthless, not worth living."

He looked up, startled. She was staring at the carpet. Her face had settled into a sort of sadness.

"We always want to measure it out exactly. You give this much, you get this much back."

Her voice was so faint that he had to strain to hear.

" 'Measure,' you said?"

"Yes. That's perfect love, isn't it? Wouldn't it be? But you know that French saying about one who loves and one who is loved? Well, it's true, Paul. It's so unhappy and so unfair, but it's true, believe me."

He was confused. Did she mean his own trouble, or could she be remembering some pain of her own? Surely it couldn't be anything about herself and Dan. . . . Yet one never really knew about other people; it was hard enough to know oneself.

More distressed than ever by these new thoughts, he faltered. "I've said it all, I guess. I'd better go."

"I haven't helped you. I'm sorry."

"It helped to talk about it," he told her, although it hadn't.

"But you need a solution."

He waited. Younger than his own mother, she was yet so motherly, she who fed and nursed other people's children, who had taken a strange child into her home; he longed for her to tell him what to do, to abolish the problem for him, as if he had been a child.

She came to a decision. "I tell you what, Paul," she said rapidly. "I think you should speak to your parents today, before Marian and her family come tonight. Tell them the truth, and then all of you can go on from there together."

"Tell them I'm in love with the maid?" he asked bitterly.

" 'The maid!' Paul, that's not like you. I despise the concept."

"All right. But it's a fact, Hennie. And can you imagine my parents? You, of all people, should be able to imagine what it would be like."

"It would be very, very hard, I grant you."

"I feel as if I were on a bicycle. It has no reverse gear. You can't go backward."

"You can turn it around."

He looked down again at his helpless hands. "I suppose I don't have your courage, Hennie. I never have."

"How do you know? You've never had to test it before now."

Upstairs in his room, he was dressed and ready. He stood before the mirror, talking to himself.

"Father, don't announce, don't say anything tonight. Give me time to explain. I'll talk to you tomorrow. I have to talk to Anna first . . . I don't know what I'm going to say . . . she'll be at the table, serving. Oh, Christ, when Cousin Dora was engaged he got up and made a little speech. He always does. I've got to get downstairs and catch him, before he says anything. I can't wait till tomorrow. Oh, Anna, help me . . ."

But the doorbell had rung. There were voices in the downstairs hall. He could hear happy birthday greetings and Mimi's clear reply.

At the table he sat opposite her, with his father at the head between them. She was dressed in summer blue; a wide collar made a lace frame around her slender face; she was a portrait out of almost any period during the last four centuries, an elegant young woman of refinement and means. A Dutch merchant's daughter. An English squire's sister—by Sir Joshua Reynolds.

He wiped his forehead. The heat and the flower scents, which always bothered him, were sickening; the whole house was filled with flowers, like at a politician's funeral. No, that wasn't fair. The arrangements were really perfect; his mother had a feeling for flowers.

But to escape someplace! On a ship over free water, in free air! To get away from dinner jackets and the cutlery, the mouths smiling, talking, chewing. Panic again.

Mimi looked like a deer. Delicate as a deer, Mimi, with those large, slightly prominent eyes and the long cheeks. Once, in the Adirondacks, he had been persuaded against his will to go hunting. Out of the thicket and dry brown twiggy brush, had come the deer, stepping so daintily. She had raised her head and he had seen her eyes, the wonderful, pathetic

eyes—people always said how pathetic their eyes
were. It was a cliché, but, like all clichés, true—
before she saw him, the enemy, and fled. He could
have shot; there had been time enough, but he
would not, he could not. He had been relieved to be
alone, for the other men would have scorned his
pity.

He shook himself and brought himself back to the
present.

". . . and you know how Paul loves raspberries." That was Mimi's voice, concluding some an-
ecdote. It must have been an amusing one, for there
was laughter, and Paul smiled, supposing that he
was expected to. Mimi's words repeated themselves
in his ears. Already, they were possessive. "Paul
loves raspberries." She remembered everything
about him, that Hardy was his favorite English nov-
elist and that he liked striped ties.

Could he just push himself away from the table,
pleading sudden illness? He imagined himself giving
an awful cry and running from the room.

A platter of vegetables appeared at his left and he
looked down into a mound of beets cut like roses,
surrounded by a moist wreath of orange carrots.
The platter trembled. He looked up to Anna's eyes,
looked not at them but into them; for an instant, a
fraction of an instant, both pairs of eyes spoke, and
properly flickered away.

"We German Jews have always been Republi-
cans." That was his father speaking. "I know some
turned to Wilson because he's an intellectual, and
they're impressed because Brandeis is a close ad-
viser, but I'm not impressed by any of that."

Cordially, Mr. Mayer brought Paul into the conversation. "And what do you think, Paul?"

"I voted for Wilson."

His father raised himself in his chair. "What? You never told me! What made you do that?"

"Because I think if there's any chance of keeping us out of the war that's brewing, Wilson is the man to do it."

"You keep saying there's a war brewing," his father objected. "I don't believe it."

Paul forced himself to speak. "And I'm also hoping he will right some dreadful wrongs. All this strife, the strikes in Paterson and Lawrence, so bitter, so savage."

"You're not turning into a radical, I hope." His father joked, making light of Paul's remarks for the benefit of Mr. Mayer.

"You know I'm not," Paul answered.

"Good. Because one in the family is enough."

Mr. Mayer's eyebrows went up, shaping two sharp black *V*'s, and Walter Werner made a quick explanation.

"Oh, not really in the family! My wife's sister's husband. We don't even see them."

"I see them," Paul said.

"Well, he loves his aunt. That's his privilege and we don't interfere. She's a type, you know. Harmless enough. Marches down Fifth Avenue for every cause, woman suffrage, peace, God knows what all."

The father's half laugh covered his exasperation with his son. He would be thinking: Of all nights, Paul has to make these challenging remarks. What's wrong with him? No tact.

Paul's mother took over, apparently in answer to something Mrs. Mayer had said, and addressed the table at large. Now, she has tact! Paul thought bitterly.

"This silver, you were asking me? Yes, the goblets and the dessert servers that you'll be seeing in a minute were buried in a quarry during the Civil War, the one my mother still calls the War Between the States."

"I loved your mother," Mimi said. "I have an idea she must have hundreds of marvelous stories to tell."

Indeed, Paul thought, hundreds. His heart made a sickening lurch. What had his mother said? The dessert servers? Oh, God, this will be the time for the announcement and the toast, if they're going to do it tonight. Don't, don't, Father, please. God, please don't let him do it. Keep talking, talk about anything, the damned old silver, Wilson, anything.

The dessert was brought in and placed before his mother. It was the walnut cake, the famous family recipe, a celebration cake reserved for great occasions, standing high on the platter, like the crown in the Tower of London. And he felt his heart knocking, actually knocking in his chest.

"Anna," his father said, "will you please call Mrs. Monaghan and Agnes? Ask them to come in and bring the champagne."

Here it came. Too late, too late to do anything.

Mrs. Monaghan brought the champagne bucket, and Agnes carried a tray of fluted glasses. Paul counted. There were glasses for everyone at the table and for the servants too. For her. Anna will raise her glass and drink a toast to Mimi and me.

His father stood up. "I don't need to tell you how happy we all are tonight," he began. "To begin with, it's Marian's birthday." His cheeks were actually dimpled; he was almost chuckling with pleasure and goodwill, in command of everything, as he raised his goblet. "And we all wish her the happiest one, with many, many more. But also"—here his voice rose in emphasis, calling attention to the importance of what was to follow—"also, oh, the Mayers' announcement will appear tomorrow in proper fashion in the *Times*, but I'm sure they will forgive me if, just between ourselves, I make a short premature family announcement. Let's all drink to the joy of this wonderful time in our lives. To Paul, our son, and to Marian, our Mimi, who will soon be our daughter!"

And he kissed Mimi in European fashion, one cheek and then the other. Mimi said something, Paul couldn't hear what; but there was a bubble of laughter, with everyone touching glasses so that they made crystal chimes.

Mrs. Monaghan was saying something like, "Saints preserve us, a wedding in the house!" And kissing Paul, she said, "I knew you when you were sitting in a high chair," then whispered, "Get up and kiss the bride."

Somehow he got up and walked to Mimi and bent to kiss her; the long pearl earrings, like little tassels, brushed his face and he went back to his seat, and his mother's voice sounded above the general murmur and buzz.

"Now I can confess this is what we've all been hoping for since you two were babies."

And more laughter.

"I'll have a second piece of that cake," his father said, flushed with wine and excitement. "Where's that girl?"

His mother rang. She'll be coming in again, Paul thought, looking down at his plate.

It wasn't she, but Agnes, the little kitchen helper who was clumsy and rarely served in the dining room, never when there were guests. Something had gone wrong with Anna, then. He knew it and went cold, so that he shivered and tried to suppress it.

Somehow he got through the evening.

How silent Paul was, they would say, with tolerant affection. He's just in a daze, poor fellow, the typical bridegroom, and will be until the wedding's over.

"What a treasure," his mother said as she moved about the parlor, turning off the lights. "You're a lucky man, Paul. Such a lady! She could dine in a palace and talk to a queen. Such poise for a young girl! Well, breeding tells, it surely tells."

He got up early and left the house without breakfast. On the cleared table in the dining room, the enormous festive flowers still stood in the center: narcissi, crisp and white as a young girl's ignorance, and tulips, richly red, concealing within their cups a scented moisture, fragrant, secret . . . He hurried past the door.

In the office, on his desk, were stacks of papers and correspondence that he had neglected. Get to them, that's the thing, get to work, get the brain whirring, do what has to be done. You have an office. You have clients waiting. You are going to be married.

How was Anna today? Oh, God, Anna, I love you, believe me, I—

In the outer office, telephones rang and typewriters clacked. An automobile horn blew in the street below. He heard the sound of hooves on the pavement.

"Good Lord, what's the matter?" his father cried.

He raised his head. He had been sitting with his head in his hands.

"I—I have suddenly developed the worst ache. My jaw. A tooth that's been bothering me for the last week or two."

"Well, why on earth haven't you had it attended to? Are you sure it's a tooth?"

"Yes. I've been awake most of the night. Probably infected." He stood up. "Maybe I'd better see the dentist right now."

"I should think you should!"

He walked. He had to walk faster and faster, while his reflection moved from one plate glass window to the next. Who is that in the windows? A young man in a good dark suit on his way to important concerns in a bank or a brokerage house or a law court, that's who. A young man rising and fortunate. He passed the statue of Admiral Farragut in Madison Square, past the Garden and the Hippodrome, where he had been taken to the circus when he was a child, and later had taken Freddy. Oh, thoughtless, easy days!

"What am I doing?" he said aloud. "What am I going to do?" And all the time he knew perfectly well what he was going to do, what he had to do. He groaned and despised himself.

It began to rain. He descended into the subway

and took the first train that roared in, whether uptown or downtown didn't matter. For hours he
rode. He watched the white city faces as they passed
in and out. Bloated or wizened, handsome or mis-
shapen, they were all bland, telling nothing; they
were closed doors. He wondered what each might
be hiding, and saw his reflection again, colored red
by warning lights on the track.

When he got out some hours later near home, the
rain had turned to a downpour. He walked rapidly
to get out of the wet, but when he reached the house
he halted: What would he say to her? He wanted to
turn around and walk away again, but instead stood
there for minutes letting the rain beat and soak him,
while he stared at the card left in the area window
for the iceman, on which were marked for checking:
Twenty-five pounds, fifty, seventy-five.

With abrupt resolution he climbed the stoop and
went in. His parents were already at dinner.

"So late, Paul! Good heavens, you're wet through!
Why didn't you take a cab?" And without waiting
for an answer, "What do you think, we've lost our
maid!" his mother said. "Anna left today. Just like
that. Imagine, without more than a minute's notice!
Said she was sick, but I didn't believe it."

Did he imagine that his mother's look was
searching? No. How could it be? Why should it be?

"Too bad," said Walter. "She struck me as a fine
young woman. I hope you got your tooth fixed up."

"What?"

"Your tooth. Was it an abscess?"

"Oh, no. That is, he fixed it, it's better."

"Well, I have another starting tomorrow," his
mother said pointedly, for the benefit of Mrs.

Monaghan, who, Paul knew, didn't like having to wait on the table.

When Mrs. Monaghan had left the dining room, his mother continued, "You know, Paul, I really have a suspicion that the girl had a crush on you. I really think that's why she left."

Crush. A cheap, ugly, mean, stupid word.

"That's ridiculous!" Paul cried, more emphatically than he had intended to.

"Of course it's ridiculous! Nevertheless, it's been known to happen. These girls get ideas. They want to better themselves. And who can blame them?"

Anna gone. Where to? And in what condition? And he thought of the rain, the bleak streets . . . what must she think of him?

He had a wild thought that he should go after her. And he had an absurd, humiliating vision of himself racing and shoving his way through crowds, who turned with curious, gaping mouths to stare as he pushed down avenues and through mean alleys, jolting around corners, searching for her. And after finding her, would he stand before her with nothing to say? Would she, too, stand there silently, despising him, pitying him or pleading with him?

He was netted and trapped. He was a coward, a fool, a victim of rules and expectations and traditions.

Yes, blame everything but yourself, Paul! Will you ever like yourself again?

A wedding is an ancient mystery. The white bride comes slowly, pacing with the stately music, holding her father's arm. He raises the face-veil for a kiss

before he gives her to another man for protection
and care. It is all so solemn, verging on tears.

Only the flower girl in crocus yellow, ten-year-old
Meg, clutching her bouquet, grins up at Paul with
frank enjoyment in being part of the ritual. He gives
her a slight smile in return, and thinks of Freddy,
who was surely thinking of him at this moment, but
would, understandably, not come because his parents had not been invited. And Leah—how that
young one would revel in all this pomp and circum-
stance! As for Hennie, it is just as well she isn't here,
for how would he meet her eyes, knowing what she
now knew? And yet he is sad that she is not here.

The rabbi places Mimi's ice-cold hand in his. In
this place she is "Marian," not "Mimi." The rabbi is
an old man; Paul has known him since childhood;
he has always been an old man, somewhat austere.
He wonders what the rabbi would have said if he
had dared to ask him. He thinks that what they tell
about a drowning man's life passing through his
mind in seconds must be true: He is a child in the
park with Hennie, he is at the Yale commencement,
on the ship with Freddy, at his desk in his father's
office, buying a ring with Marian . . . kissing
Anna.

The music has stopped. Words are being addressed to him and questions asked, to which the
automatic answers *I will* or *I do* come to his lips.
The rabbi's tone is fatherly. He speaks fine, true
words: Trust, family, love, God, faith. The bride's
bouquet trembles in the hands of the maid of honor,
who is wondering when her time will come. The
rabbi talks, changes emphasis, rises to a climax. It
must be almost over. Yes, it is.

The rabbi smiles and nods and the music starts up. He recognizes the recessional, Mendelssohn, with a note of triumph in it. They walk down the aisle. Women have wet eyes, looking at the bride. A photographer stands at the end of the aisle, waiting.

"Smile," he says.

Next is the reception line. Congratulations . . . I knew you before you were born . . . lovely bride . . . so happy . . . hope you . . . health . . . many years . . . thank you . . . thank you.

Then food and dancing; the orchestra lilts and crashes from waltzes to tangos and fox-trots. He dances with the bride, with his mother and her mother and all the bridesmaids, one by one. Creak of taffeta, smell of perfume and perspiration, jingle of bracelets, jangle of talk.

Marian is surrounded and admired. Her ring, her veil, her pearls, all are admired.

He is surprised that he can eat. He keeps on eating: chicken, asparagus, pineapple, wedding cake, all of it, as if starved. His best man teases him about his appetite.

"Getting your strength up, are you?" he says, having known Paul long enough to talk that way.

And it is over, the bouquet thrown, the blue garter revealed, and farewells said. They are alone in the Mayers' Packard town car, alone in the upholstered shell of the passenger compartment. Paul wonders whether the chauffeur is snickering to himself. In the winter the poor devil sits outside wrapped in a fur coat and cap, as if he were going to the North Pole, and it probably feels like the North Pole, Paul thinks.

When Mimi reaches for his hand, he realizes that

he has been too silent, even for a numb, bedazzled bridegroom.

"Well, it was a beautiful wedding," he says, "your mother took care of everything."

"Yes, didn't she? And when we get home our house will be ready; she'll supervise it all. Such marvelous presents, Paul! You haven't even seen most of them yet, you know. Or the decorations, either."

He has been surfeited with description: of carpets and draperies, pillows and puffs, swags, ruching, pleating and tucking, of ecru and café au lait and bois de rose, all of these apparently essential to starting life together.

The car stops at the Plaza, where they will spend the night before the ship sails in the morning. He hadn't wanted the Plaza, but here he is; at least, though, the elevators are right at the registration desk, so he doesn't have to walk past the Palm Court. He hasn't been here since that day and never wants to go again, but will no doubt have to.

The suite is at the end of a long corridor. Their feet make no sound on the patterned carpet. The bellboy unlocks the door and places their luggage on racks; the luggage has the smell of new, expensive leather. Again there are flowers, tall gladioli this time, spread open like rainbow-colored fans on every tabletop. He will put them in the bathroom for the night. And there is more champagne. He has had enough today and Mimi agrees that she doesn't want any either.

Not knowing for the moment what to do, they both walk to the window, to look out upon the park and the city lights.

"I thought the bridesmaids looked lovely, didn't you?" asks Mimi. "And the tables were beautiful."

After theater, he thinks, while riding home, one makes comments about the play.

"It was all wonderful," he says.

They stand there looking at the carriage lanterns and, for some unknown reason, he thinks of fireflies on a summer lawn, of crickets and rustling leaves. He muses about fireflies until it comes to him that this is absurd; they can't just keep standing there.

"Well," he says, "I'll take the other room." And smiling encouragement, departs with his suitcase.

Then he thinks, I hope she understood I only meant to change. But, of course, she must have understood.

When he returns, she is waiting for him, having gotten undressed for the night, although it almost seems as though she has gotten dressed instead, since the negligee flows as voluminously concealing, as opulently lacy as the bridal gown. It is white, but no more so than her timid face, when she averts her gaze, as if she fears what she may find if she were to look at him directly.

She is so young, so frail, so scared. His impulse is to smooth the frilly petals of her collar, kiss her forehead, put her to bed as one puts a child to bed, and then go to sleep himself. Or go out for a walk in the mild, lovely evening. But now, wondering and expectant, she looks at him. Surely she has been told about the wedding night, and she waits.

He moves to her and takes her loosely in his arms. Willingly, she puts her arms around his neck, barely skimming his flesh. Her touch is light as feathers. He lifts and carries her to the bed, as he is

supposed to do. Oh, this is the wedding night, and
his heart isn't pounding; there is nothing in him but
gentleness and sorrow, because there is nothing in
him but gentleness and sorrow.

He lays her down and holds her. She lies there,
rigid and withdrawn, with just their hips and shoulders touching, nothing more. He wants only to
sleep. Gradually she relaxes, and once more puts
her arms around his neck. He holds her closer, but
still there is nothing. Nothing . . .

And he remembers the heat and strength of
Anna, pulling him to her; wanting him as he wanted
her. Her skin had burned. He imagines what it
would be to release her hair, how it would fall in a
dark red cascade, all slippery and alive; he would
bury his face in it and in her round, warm breasts;
he would . . .

Oh, Anna, Anna, he cries silently. And suddenly
now his heart does pound; it pounds so that he can
hardly breathe with the fury of it, and cannot wait.

He reaches up to extinguish the lamp, and he is
able.

2

On a fair summer afternoon, in a dull Serbian town, the Austrian archduke and his archduchess, bowing with regal grace and serenely smiling to the populace from their open barouche, were shot to death.

It was the work of an instant: the gun popped, bystanders screamed in horror, the horses reared, blood gushed on white silk, and all was over—except for the headlines that towered over the world and the four years of war that came after.

"Well," Paul said, "Bismarck always predicted that it would start with some damn fool thing in the Balkans."

For the next two months, the mails and telegraph wires between the capitals were burdened with pleas, propositions, and threats. In their striped trousers and top hats, the diplomats rushed from one foreign office and one chancellery to another, there to bluff and bargain; yet Austria mobilized and Russia mobilized; one by one, the sovereign nations followed, until in the end almost the whole of Europe had been driven into the heart of the storm.

It broke on the second of August. By the first of
September, France had already lost more than one
hundred thousand of her best young men in the anguish of that storm. Photographs reaching the newspapers in America showed dreadful scenes of
soldiers departing by train, with their wives and
mothers running alongside the tracks; of smoke rising from burning houses in Belgium as the Germans
sped through; of fleeing villagers carrying children,
chickens, and bedsteads in farm carts, while their
milk cows stumbled behind them on the teeming
roads.

A terrible fear swept through America: that she,
too, would be dragged in, to be engulfed by this mad
storm. And millions of voices—especially women's
voices—were raised now in a warning cry for peace.

Emotion was so profound that when the first
peace marchers came down Fifth Avenue that August, there was not a sound from the crowd who
watched. To the beat of muffled drums, they came
down the glittering avenue behind the peace flag
with its insignia of the gentle dove; in rank after
rank of quiet women they came, dressed in black
like so many mourning widows, with their feet
softly shuffling on the pavement.

Paul stood with his wife's arm linked in his.

"So awfully sad," she murmured. "So helpless
and sad."

He looked down. Under the fashionable brim of
her hat, known as the "Merry Widow," Mimi's eyes
were wet. She would want to wipe them, for public
emotion embarrassed her, and he gave her his handkerchief. In only a little more than a year of mar-

riage they had evolved so many of these small, intimate signals without words!

He, too, was deeply moved by what they were seeing. This past month had been hard for any thinking person, but for one who knew and loved Europe as he did, it was appalling.

And his mind went back to The Hague in 1907 when his father and he, on business in Amsterdam, had gone over to see what the peace conferees were up to. From tulip time to chrysanthemum time, they had been talking; the white-bearded gentlemen in their frock coats looked out of the windows of the parliament building, where the freshening winds blew from the North Sea through the old copper beeches, and went back again to talking. They were laying down rules as precise as those for a chess tournament: rules about the feeding of prisoners, and the bombardment of civilians (to be permitted or not?), the use of asphixiating gas and dumdum bullets. When they disbanded, the chrysanthemums were beaten down by rain, and gray clouds swam over cold gray skies. In four months, they had made one significant decision: They were to meet again in 1915.

Oh, the damned old men!

Now people were claiming it would all be over by Christmas. Nonsense, Paul thought, remembering the smokestacks and switching yards of Germany.

Then he remembered his cousin Joachim, following the score at the Bayreuth opera, hiking through the Black Forest pines, and lifting a stein to toast his emperor. The true-blue German! No doubt he was already in uniform, to fight for the emperor. Well, God spare him. God spare us all.

Mimi asked, "Do you suppose we'll see Hennie?"

"I'm watching. They all look alike in their black."

Still they marched, the old and the young; a few were pushing baby carriages; all faces were set and solemn.

"Hennie doesn't seem bold enough to do something like this," Mimi remarked.

"That's true, but all her shyness goes when she's in a group. Her conviction carries her. There's Hennie now, there she is!"

"Where? Where?" Mimi stood on tiptoe.

"The third one in from this end, look where I'm pointing . . ."

And there she was, half a head taller than anyone around her, with chin up, stepping smartly.

A smile came to Paul's lips. Good old Hennie! Damn, you couldn't keep her down! Where did she come from? She wasn't like any of the other women in the family. Like her grandmother, old Uncle David said. She'd be a valiant old woman, fighting for causes with her last breath.

"Well, now that we've seen her, let's go home," Mimi said. "If they're all coming to dinner, I want to make sure that Effie does things right."

The new Mrs. Werner was a meticulous housekeeper.

"I was taught," she liked to tell Paul, "never to expect a servant to do anything you can't do yourself."

She knew how to bake, to clean, to serve, and to arrange flowers; she never did or had to do any of these things, except arranging flowers, but she knew how they ought to be done and saw to it that they were done right.

And what was the purpose of all this effort? The comfort of the master of the house, that's what. He had only to ask once for something, an apple before going to bed or a new book that someone had mentioned, and the apple was there on the bedside table every night, while the book would be in the library, beside his chair, on the very next day.

The street was deserted. In this quiet area east of Fifth Avenue, there were few houses whose windows were not covered with gray boards; the owners were away for the summer. A fine dust lay over dry leaves on the trees that lined one side of the street, and a hot wind blew grit into their faces.

"Cross over to the shady side," Paul said, thinking, Next summer she'll positively go to the shore and I'll commute by ferry or go down on weekends.

"You should be on the beach keeping cool in the breeze, Mimi."

"As long as you're in the city working, I'll be here too. Weekends at the shore are good enough."

"You're very unselfish. Don't think I don't appreciate it."

"I'm happy being wherever you are, Paul. Don't you know that?" She squeezed his arm. Her eyes worshiped him.

"I know," he said, patting her hand, thinking, I don't deserve that you should say this to me.

He was at the head of his own table. So the generations march on, he thought wryly, recalling first the Biedermeier table, the red cabbage and sauerbraten at his grandfather's house, and after that, the plum-colored dining room, the dreary, overstuffed opulence of his parents'.

This was a very different room. His mother-in-law's contributions had, after all, not been as dreadful as he had predicted; the brightly flowered linens gave cheer to his own old English mahogany. On the sideboard there gleamed yet another silver tea service, the gift of Grandmother Angelique; they must have grown them on the plantation, he thought humorously. The evening sunshine made a clear pool on the bare parquet floor; it fell over Joachim's wedding present, a magnificent crystal horse that stood on a pedestal in the corner, glistening as if it were drenched. Between the windows hung Paul's prize, a small, radiant Cézanne, a landscape of billowing harvest fields cut into squares by rows of cypress.

To paint like that! What he would give to be able to create like that! In another life, perhaps. In the meanwhile, he would admire it; the sight of it every morning, appearing over the rim of his cup of breakfast coffee, was a pleasure almost physical in its intensity. And he resolved, as soon as he could afford it, to collect more such pleasures.

Dan's forceful voice broke into these musings.

". . . incredible shock that the masses flocked to the colors as they have. I never thought they would, that the workers would forget their common brotherhood."

His face had fallen into folds, the flesh had sagged not two months since, and the lock of hair that always fell across his forehead now lay unheeded, brushing his eyebrows. He had grown visibly older.

"It's been the most brutal disappointment of my life," he finished in a falling tone.

Paul felt like saying that he was tired to death of troubles, the world's and his own, that he just wanted to be free of it all for a while. The inner conflict of this past year had bled him enough. At the office there were other problems, heavy in their way, although not to be compared with his own doubt and guilt, God knew.

To be purely selfish, to feel pure joy again! And catching the inquisitive glance of Leah, who sat next to him, he thought that she must have been looking at him for several moments, and that his face must have shown an expression that had caught her interest.

"This is a wonderful room," she said, drawing them both out of the general conversation. "The amber tone—it's just right. Not too cool for a cold winter night, nor too hot, for instance, for today."

Paul smiled. "You have an artist's eye."

"Not really. Just a good eye for color. And fashion, of course. That's how I got my job."

He was expected to ask her about the job. She had started it a month or two before, after graduation from high school. Actually, though, he was curious; there was something about the girl, he always thought, that reminded him vaguely—different as they were, yet there was something of that same vitality.

And he asked kindly, "Do you like the job as much as you thought you would?"

"Oh, yes! I'm at the bottom of the ladder, of course, but I'm learning. I'm allowed to baste in the fitting room, and I unpack the Paris samples that we copy. I can tell the difference between a Lanvin and a Callot or Redfern. Wonderful, wonderful clothes! They can transform a woman. Except that, sometimes, when I peek into the salon at the customers, and I see some of the old fat ones there, I think, nothing will transform you, madame." And Leah wrinkled in distaste the little nose that Hennie called her monkey nose.

Paul laughed. She was refreshing. The thick hair was caught up with tortoiseshell combs; he was certain there was no rat in her pompadour, the hair was so heavy; then, his eye going to her waist, he was certain there was none of what he called "stuffing"; no mistaking the double swell of the breasts.

Mimi used stuffing, masses of ruffles under her dress.

"We have to stay out," Dan said, waving his fork. "No matter who wins, I tell you it won't matter. The victor will lay down the terms of peace, and what will happen? The loser will harbor vengeance that will only bring about another war. It will go on without end. No. America must stay out."

"Everyone doesn't think so," Freddy said. "I know a lot of last year's seniors who rushed to be commissioned in the British army."

"Besotted fools!" Dan cried angrily.

"No," Freddy argued. "German militarism must be crushed once and for all. H. G. Wells says once Germany's thoroughly beaten, we'll have disarmament and peace throughout the world. That's what he says, and I agree."

"If H. G. Wells said that, then he's an ass."

"I had a letter from Gerald this morning," Freddy continued quietly, drawing it from his breast pocket. "It's an inspiration. 'I have the utmost faith that we are right . . . it is an honor to serve, and we march away in glory.' " He swallowed. His Adam's apple, always prominent, jerked above his collar. "He goes on with details about training. Oh, yes, here. 'I don't want to miss the greatest adventure of our time. I'm confident that I will come back. Most of us will. After all, if by some chance I don't, I can only say *dulce et decorum est pro patria mori.*' " Silently, as if to allow the letter to speak eloquently for itself, Freddy folded and replaced it.

"With all respect to your friend," Dan said, "that is the sheerest poppycock I've heard in a long time. Sweet to die for your country! When is it ever sweet to die for anything, pray tell me? Of course, if you say it in Latin, that makes it mean more, I suppose. A precious lot of idiocy you picked up in England, Freddy, not the least of it, while I'm on the subject, this whole classics business."

Freddy flushed.

"I think," declared Leah, "it's absolutely wonderful that Freddy knows Latin and Greek."

"God knows I have no objection to scholarship! I'm the last person in the world to do that."

Dan was off on one of his tears. This war in Europe is really affecting him, Paul thought.

The heavy atmosphere was becoming unbearable. When was the last time he'd felt light? Lighthearted, light-bodied? All this time, ever since he'd gotten home from Europe, and been engaged and . . . He resolved to get tickets one night this week for the Ziegfeld Follies. Girls with spangles and

feathered hats; long dancing legs; Will Rogers's
jokes. He needed it.

"All right, study your damned languages if you
will, but to spend a lifetime at it, I can't understand!" Dan went on. "Devotion to a dead world,
that's what it is. Why not confront modern problems with your intelligence, instead of hiding from
them?"

"It's not a dead world," Freddy answered. His
face was violently red. "When we talk of the classics, classical architecture, music, anything, we're
talking of something that's pure and basic."

Dan waved his fork again, waving the argument
aside.

"Yes, yes, yes, prattle! Quibbles. It's escapism,
when all is said and done, and that's the way I see
it."

"Freddy is an idealist. He's just like you, you
know," Leah said.

"Like me? I deal with realities, science and social
betterment."

"It's turned toward other ends, that's all," the
girl insisted.

She's grown even more assertive, Paul thought,
since she started to support herself. She sat straight.
Her eyes snapped at Dan.

"I have often thought that myself, about Freddy
and Dan," Paul said, attempting to cut through the
haze of hostility that seemed to be settling over his
table. And he added mischievously, "At least, Dan,
you must be thankful your son's not a banker."

The little remark brought the laugh he had
wanted, even from Hennie, who, understandably
weary, had said nothing during the last exchanges.

Mimi, whose diplomacy could always be depended on, turned her soothing smile upon Dan.

"Paul says you're working on something very interesting. Will you tell us about it?"

"I'm working on a few things. But they're technical, hard to describe. I don't think you'd be interested." Dan spoke reluctantly, yet one sensed that he wanted to be coaxed.

Mimi coaxed. "Oh, but we would be! Just make the language simple, give us a general idea."

"Well, I've been doing things with the Gramme dynamo. It's a generator, but when you reverse it, it becomes a motor. And then I've been working on some ideas about sound signals. Shortwave lengths reflect from solid objects, maybe you know that; and I was thinking about how it could be applied to rescue ships. So many fishing boats go down off Newfoundland, for instance."

"You were right, I don't understand the first thing about it," Mimi said gaily. "Except the part about rescuing ships, that sounds marvelous. What do you think you will be able to do with it?"

"I? Nothing really. I get these ideas, but don't have facilities to make them. I threw that one out to Alfie. Those people he works with have a factory, maybe they can use it. I don't want anything for it. I just want to know whether it's workable, and I'll be happy if it is."

"I don't know why you always say that," Leah challenged. "What's wrong with making some money out of it? Somebody else will, if you don't. I know I intend to make money. I'm not going to stay at this job. I'm going to open my own place one day when I've learned enough."

"You do as you think best with your life," Dan said shortly. "That's your privilege."

"Leah," Hennie intervened, "you've brought your notebook. Show some of the sketches you showed me."

Mimi stood up. "Yes, let's. We'll have our coffee in the parlor and Leah will show us her sketches."

They were mostly pencil sketches, a few of them brightly crayoned, of graceful, attenuated ladies as portrayed in the more expensive, glossy fashion magazines.

"Very nice," Paul murmured, surprised by the deftness and style of the work. "These are copies, I suppose?"

"Most of them, but I design my own too. This is mine." Taking one out of the folder, Leah passed it around. "It's a *robe de style*. I'd make it in blue moiré. I love the rippling pattern of moiré, like water."

"It's lovely," Mimi cried. "Come, Freddy, have a look too." For Freddy stood apart from the viewers' semicircle.

"Oh, he's seen them. I bore him to death with them," Leah said.

Freddy's smile, that of a parent exhibiting a precocious, darling child, said that he was not bored at all.

And Leah continued energetically. "I would have cream-colored lace. It's finer than stark white, I always think."

"Quite right," agreed Mimi, all attention.

"And the ruffles would depend on who was to wear it. Now, for some, I would have double ruffles, elaborate and flounced. For people like—well, like

Aunt Emily, for instance—I would make them much more discreet, maybe one around the back and another halfway down the waist. You have to judge the wearer, the house she lives in, lots of things."

Mimi was amused. "You're a clever girl, and I know exactly what you mean. Now, tell me, how would you trim this dress for me?"

"I would make it go three-quarters of the way." Leah put her head to one side, narrowing her eyes in careful consideration of the subject. "No, I'd go halfway, neither as plain and prim as for Aunt Emily, nor as fancy as for some—some other types."

"Clever," Mimi said again. "So that's how you see me! Tell me honestly now, what do you think of the way I generally look? What improvements would you make?"

"Shall I tell you honestly?" asked Leah.

"Of course, honestly."

"All right, then. You're elegant, you're distinguished as you are. But I should like to see you a trifle more dashing."

"Why, I shall have to be one of your first customers. I predict you'll go far." Mimi clapped her hands prettily. "I say, applause for Madame Leah!"

Dan inquired, "And what would you do for Hennie? What type is she?"

"No type. There's nobody else like her," Leah said very seriously. "She's beautiful, even in that black outfit, as you can see."

It was so; the height and breadth that in her younger years had seemed—at least to her family and to Hennie herself—unfortunate and awkward, were now, at forty, a dignity. She had an uncon-

scious presence; the three parallel lines in her forehead spoke of thoughtfulness and concern, as did
the shadows under her clear leaf-shaped eyes.

She said now, "The truth is, this black is beastly
hot and what I'd love is to get home and take it off.
I want to thank you all, though, for standing in the
heat to support the parade."

When she got up, Dan put his arm around her,
and she made a little gesture almost like a blessing.

"Family . . . you're all and everything."

Not all, though, Paul regretted, thinking of his
mother, who should have been there among them.

When they had gone, Mimi peered into the hall
mirror.

"Paul, do I need to be more dashing, do you
think?"

"You're fine as you are. I wouldn't change a
thing."

"You're very sweet. You always say that."

"Well, and I always mean it."

They settled down in the library, Paul at his desk,
going over the papers that poured in as regularly as
rain, and Mimi with a book. Presently, she looked
up from the book.

"That doesn't seem to be the sort of work Dan
and Hennie would approve of."

"What doesn't?"

"Leah's ambition. Making clothes for rich
women. 'Social parasites' are what Dan calls them,
doesn't he?"

"It's funny . . . Dan likes women to be well-
dressed and, of course, Hennie defends her. Why
not? It's honest labor. Looks to me as though the
girl really has a talent for it too."

"I always wonder what it is about Leah that Dan doesn't like. He can barely hide it. Just barely."

"I suspect he sees that she's got eyes for Freddy, though why she has is a puzzle, frankly. They're as far apart as oil and water."

"That's easy! She's in awe of his refinement and wants to possess it for herself. Besides, he is good-looking—in a frail way. He wouldn't appeal to me in a million years," Mimi finished complacently.

Paul had intended to be absorbed in rows of figures, and was accustomed to stifling his exasperation at interruptions, but something about this conversation, this subject of mysterious attraction, diverted him and he closed the ledger.

"So that's your explanation for her side of the affair. What about his?"

"Oh, I'd guess she's the only girl who's ever pursued him and that's pretty exciting, isn't it? Besides, he's used to her. He feels comfortable with her. Such an innocent, poor Freddy!"

Paul could have said: You amaze me, you're such an innocent yourself. He said, instead, "That's a rather shrewd insight."

"I like Leah, you know. I really do."

"I'm surprised. She's hardly your sort."

"She isn't my 'sort,' as you put it. But she's real. She's strong and honest. I think you could always depend upon her for the truth. She doesn't hide her feelings."

He felt himself flinching, felt a hot twinge down the back of his neck, and returned to the ledger.

"I've really got to buckle down to these."

But it was impossible to buckle down. His mind had gone off into another region, and the figures lay before him in rows of squiggles without meaning; he could scarcely put two and two together. Sighing, he closed the heavy ledger with a small slap.

Then he heard Mimi put her book down and rustle out of her chair. She came to kneel on the floor beside him.

"Paul . . . I can't concentrate. If we do get into the war, will you have to go?"

"We won't be in it."

"Are you sure?"

"Are we ever sure of anything? But I really don't think so. Public sentiment's all against it, as you saw this afternoon."

"But if we should get in, you would have to go, wouldn't you?"

He didn't answer, only looked at her, and saw that her eyes were filmed with tears. She raised her arms to him and put her head on his shoulder; drawing her close, he stroked her back, in a gesture meant to comfort.

His lovely wife! His intelligent, considerate Mimi, who went to the Philharmonic every Friday afternoon with the ladies, who did good works in the temple sisterhood, who respected his parents and his friends, who gave gracious hospitality in his candle-lit dining room and furthered his career, and loved him . . .

How she loved him!

"Don't worry," he said gently. "Go on back to your book and enjoy it."

She stood up. "And you—you work too hard, Paul. You should relax in the evening at least. Shall I get your book from the night table?"

"No, no, I'll get it."

If only she wouldn't be so *good* to him!

This time he sat back in the leather chair by the lamp, half turned away from her. She couldn't tell that he wasn't even turning the pages.

Curious, whenever he saw Leah, how she could lead—in some oblique way—to that other! Little Agnes, one day when he'd gone into the kitchen of his parents' house, had told him that she'd heard from Anna, and that she was married.

Oh, really?

Yes, to the man she'd been keeping company with.

Mrs. Monaghan had shushed the girl. Why? Had he imagined that that sardonic, sharp-tongued old woman had given him a queer look? So he'd said, in his best "dignified employer" manner, that he was happy to hear it and wished Anna the best luck; she was a very fine young woman.

The family had sent her a wedding gift, a clock from Tiffany's. Had he imagined that his mother also had looked queerly at him when she told him?

"She didn't give proper notice, it was quite unforgivable. Your father agrees with me. We treated her very well, she had a good home here. But it's not right to hold a grudge, and she is all alone in the world, poor thing."

So they'd sent a clock, expensive and handsome, no doubt, a mantel clock for a place that probably had no mantel. A timepiece to tell the passing of drab hours. For what else could he provide than drabness, that poor fellow he had seen that day in the areaway with Anna? And she, with all the bright life in her, all the sweetness and heart and— It was wrong, all wrong!

Once, a month or two ago, he'd been crossing the park and seen a woman walking ahead of him, seen a tall, slender back, with a twist of red hair; and he'd felt his heart knock, racing in his chest. He'd speeded his steps to pass her, and, of course, it hadn't been she. She would hardly be living in this neighborhood now.

He guessed he would always be half looking for her, wanting to see her and also dreading to, wherever he went in this vast city. Was it not inevitable, though, that, vast as the city was, by the laws of coincidence they would somehow, someday, somewhere encounter each other?

And what would they say? How would it be to face each other again?

Strange, how his memory faded in and out. Sometimes it was so sharp and clear that he could see the gold wings of her eyebrows; then at other times it almost seemed as though he had imagined the whole business, or as if imagination were embellishing it, keeping alive a thing that had in actuality not been the tender, passionate marvelous thing he thought he remembered.

Oh, but he knew what he remembered!

Dear God, let him be rid of the memory, once and for all!

3

In the Roth household, a truce had at last been called: there was no talk, except when Hennie and Dan were alone together, of the European war. Decent living would have been impossible otherwise.

Freddy's face had blazed with aroused blood, as he enumerated German outrages.

"The most vicious and atrocious criminals since Genghis Khan! Taking hostages, killing children, using poison gas, wrecking the most splendid monuments of Western culture for the pure joy of wrecking! Savages, that's all they are!"

To which his father would retort, "They're no more savages than the others are! They're all the same; can't you recognize propaganda when you read it? Better save all that energy to work for social justice at home, rather than waste it on the Germans."

So a truce had had to be called.

Freddy came and went with the college vacations, carrying books, tennis racquet, and sheet music, while all over Europe young men his age had discarded these for rifles and hand grenades. Clashing in battle, they went on to battle again; each clash was to be a turning point for one side or the other, but there was never a turning point. There were the Marne, and Ypres, and Neuve-Chapelle . . . At Neuve-Chapelle, the British, taking the offensive, met disaster. Hundreds of thousands perished under German fire. Those who survived went on to battle again. . . .

When Freddy came home for the midwinter recess, a letter with a British postmark had just arrived and was waiting for him. He went into his room to read it. The supper was already on the table. From where she sat, Hennie could see down the hall to his room at the end. Something about the finality of his shut door disturbed her, and she got up to knock at it.

"Freddy, we're waiting. The dinner will get cold."

He didn't answer.

"Freddy! Don't you hear me?"

Then the door crashed open and he came out with reddened eyes and choking voice.

"They've killed him! The goddamned Huns have killed him!"

The sight of his grief—they had never seen him weep—was in itself more awful than the fact of that other boy's death. Hennie, appalled, felt herself retreating from the sight of her son's grief.

He waved the letter. "It's Gerald's mother. She says in his last letter he told them not to worry about him; he was well, in fine spirits. Yes, he would say that . . . she writes that his commanding officer says he died bravely. At Neuve-Chapelle, it was."

Freddy sat down with his head in his hands. Hennie looked over at Dan; his answering look said silently, I don't know what to say. Perhaps nothing is best. So the parents stood without words, but Leah laid her hand on Freddy's head, caressing it softly, also without words.

After a moment or two, he spoke.

"I'm sorry to make a fuss. But we were awfully close in that short time, he and I. He was so wonderful. And this is such a waste."

Dan sighed. "Yes, all of it. A waste."

"Do you still deny that they're savages?" Freddy cried out. "Have you read their 'Hymn of Hate' against England? And Kipling's answer, 'What stands if Freedom fall?' Can you still say they're all the same?"

"You've lost your friend . . . it's a terrible thing," Dan said quietly. "But come with us. Drink a cup of tea, if nothing else. Talk to us."

They went back to the kitchen table and Hennie served the meal. Freddy could not even swallow tea. The whites of his eyes were bloodshot; his voice quivered, going up almost as high as it had when he was fourteen and it was changing.

"But he was ready for sacrifice. I have to remind myself of that," he said.

Dan cried, "Sacrifice for what?" throwing up his hands. "Of all the sentimental, revolting hogwash! Mental garbage. . . . Have you ever seen blood, a man wounded or bleeding to death? I saw a workman once, fallen from a scaffold, with his guts spilled out: slimy gray guts. Christ!" he said.

Freddy spoke stiffly. "There are those, not unintelligent, who would disagree with you."

"Yes, I know about the fools who've gone off to

enlist in the British army. You've told us about
them, and you think they have my respect? No, they
have my disgust. Imbeciles, poor children, still wet
behind the ears! Give them drums, brass buttons,
some bad poetry, and off they go, while"—here
Dan's glance fell on Leah, then quickly skimmed
away—"while a bunch of equally stupid females
clap and sigh over the brass buttons, and watch
them march away to be slaughtered."

"There's no talking to you," Freddy said. "We
might as well be speaking in Bulgarian or Urdu.
Maybe I'd better leave the table. I can't eat anything
anyway, and whatever I say offends you."

At once Dan's tone softened. "Sit down, Freddy.
Sit down. All right, I know I get emotional. I'm too
noisy, I'll admit. But I have strong feelings and,
especially in these times, they're hard to control."

"Freddy has strong feelings too," Leah remarked.
"Gerald was his friend."

"I understand that." Dan reached out to touch
his son's arm. "I'm terribly sorry you've lost your
friend. God knows I'm sorry that any young man
should die. It's just that I view it as tragedy, and
can't see glory in it. Especially when men on every
side are making fortunes out of the horror."

Hennie served the bread pudding and cleared the
table. Quaking inwardly, she had to keep moving,
and refused Leah's help. Her thoughts were confused and fearful. It was spring; by this time each
year Freddy had already found a summer job; but,
so far now, he had said nothing about work. She
had not dared—why had she not dared? she asked
herself—to question him.

He had grown away, which was proper and to be

expected, especially in view of that subtle secret aversion that, in spite of Dan's love, had long existed between him and Freddy. Mysterious and always painful it was to Hennie, but in the end accepted; now they were simply growing farther apart. Farther from me, too, she thought, and although I tell myself that it is natural and wholesome for his attachment to me to loosen, why is it that I—and Dan as well—can still talk to Paul and reach him?

When they were undressing for bed, she asked Dan, "Do you suppose he would go to Canada or do anything crazy like that?"

"He has another year of college. That's a comfort."

"And then graduate school. He's been saving money toward it, so he wouldn't, would he?"

Dan didn't answer.

Leah was singing in her room across the hall. Smiling, Freddy put down the Greek text to listen. She was singing an aria from *Aida* and was only slightly out of tune. He thought of the festive day during Christmas vacation when he had taken her to hear it, and of how entranced she had been. He had really wanted to take her someplace again during this vacation week, but midterm exams were coming up and he needed every minute for study.

Closing his eyes, he lay back in the armchair. Concentration on Greek print strained them, no matter what anyone said. Yet his skill with the wonderful ancient language thrilled him. He was learning to enter the ancient world; he could actually see it and feel it, all bronze, purple, and sunstruck; he could touch the hot stone of its great barbaric temples and hear the voices of its keen philosophers. And he smiled again, this time recalling all those discussions he'd had with Gerald about Cambridge and about whether to stay with the classics or become a medievalist. He missed those long discussions, missed Gerald with pain of loss and joy of remembrance. Often he would ask himself what Gerald would think: about a book, a person, or an event. He wondered now what Gerald would think of his little Leah, who was so un-English in her blunt, lively ways.

She was bustling around in her room, bumping and knocking. Then suddenly there came a dreadful crash and an exclamation: "Damn!"

Freddy jumped up. Through the half-open door he saw her kneeling on the floor next to an overturned bureau drawer, the contents of which were strewn around her. She was laughing.

"What an idiot! It was stuck and I pulled it out too far!"

"Let me help you." He began to pick things up; then, seeing what it was that he had in his hand, he dropped it. "Well, perhaps you'd better—" he started to say, but was interrupted by more laughter.

"Maybe I'd better, if a pair of silk bloomers can make you blush! Go look at yourself!"

Instead, he looked at her. She had on a robe, a bathrobe, he supposed, but unlike any he'd ever seen, that is, unlike his mother's or grandmother's. It was light blue, with blue feathery stuff at the collar and hem; when she leaned forward, getting up off her knees, it gaped open on top. Her breasts swung heavily under the silk.

"What are you staring at, Freddy?"

"What you've got on. Those feathers," he said awkwardly.

"It's marabou, and awfully expensive. My boss let me have it because somebody burned a hole in the back with the pressing iron. You like it?"

"It's beautiful."

He stood and watched her. She moved quickly, scooping the clothes back into the drawer. When she was finished, he picked up the drawer and replaced it in the chest.

"What are you going to do now?" she asked.

"Study some more, I guess."

"Haven't you studied enough? You haven't done another thing all week."

"I know, but I have to."

"Take a few minutes off. I feel like having some tea and a piece of cake. I'm bored."

"You could have gone to the theater with the folks. They'd have gotten a ticket for you."

"But I would rather be here with you."

He saw that she wasn't teasing him this time, as she so often did. When was it that she had begun to tease him? He didn't know exactly; it had happened so gradually. He knew only that she wasn't the same Leah as the one who had grown up with him.

"I'll fix a tray and bring it to your room. It's nicer than having it in the kitchen."

He waited for her, feeling a new kind of excitement. And when had that begun? Had he been feeling it, or had it just come now, when she had purposely let him see her breasts?

She plunked the tray on the desk, sweeping the books aside. Noisy and swift in everything she did, she fascinated him. It's because she's so unlike me, he thought; I wish I were as sturdy and sure of myself as she is.

They ate without talking much, she because she was hungry, and he because these thoughts were swirling in his head. When they were finished, he heard himself sigh.

"What's the matter, Freddy? You sighed."

"Sometimes I do."

"What is it? Aren't you happy?"

"Sometimes yes and sometimes no."

"Well, that's only natural, isn't it?" She licked icing from her lips and brushed crumbs from her lap. "One can't be happy all the time. Although *you* should be, if anybody should. You've got everything."

"I?" he repeated in astonishment.

"Yes. To begin with, you're handsome. No, don't wave me away. You are, and you must see it. You're smart and educated and elegant. I wish I could have your elegance, but I never will."

He shook his head. "Funny, I was thinking that I'd like to be like you."

"I don't believe it! In what way, for goodness' sake?"

"You're so confident."

Leah persisted. "You've got parents, a home that's really yours. Don't you know what that's worth?"

There was such confusion in him! The tension of being with her in his own intimate room, his strange inner stirrings, mixed with a wistful melancholy—all was confusion.

"I do know," he answered finally. And without planning to say it, he added, "But things aren't usually what they seem."

A touch of irony twisted Leah's lips just long enough for him to recognize it.

"A trite remark," he apologized.

"That's not why I smiled. I was remembering a time when your father told me the same thing. And for an instant you looked like him."

"You don't think I look like him, for God's sake!"

"You don't, not very much. But would it be so awful if you did?"

The conversation was leading toward something. It was as if each of them were vaguely, hesitantly, feeling his and her way toward some confession, some lifting of a mental burden. . . .

He said slowly, "I've never understood how I really feel about my father. I've wanted to love him, but—there was a time I hated him, Leah."

"Why? What had he done to you?"

"Nothing directly to me. Something happened that a child shouldn't know, that's all. I was very young. I've never told anyone."

"You might feel better if you did," Leah said gently.

He bent his head. Things were swirling again. Then he felt her hand on his head.

"I think I know what it was. You found him with, or you found out about, a woman."

When, startled, he looked up, he saw comprehension. "I've often wondered how much you knew about him," she said.

Her hand moved to his shoulder and lay there. He was sure he could feel the warmth of it through his sleeve; he was sure he could trust in anything she might tell him.

"I was riding on a bus a couple of years ago, and he was there with a woman. They were—well, she was kissing him. It was—"

"Go on," he said.

"Your mother thought he'd been working or something. He was scared to death that I'd tell her."

"And you never did."

"Can you think I would? She never knew. She never will. I could swear that he doesn't do that kind of thing anymore, though."

"How do you know?"

"We had a long talk afterward, he and I."

A composite picture took shape in the air. His father is kissing a woman, a cheap type with a painted face; he is waving his arms on top of a burning house; he is giving a speech, and the audience is respectful before his dark suit and his dignity; he withers in guilt before Leah's tongue—

"With me it was what I heard," he said. "It was in the room over the lab. I didn't see, I didn't have to see. I ran all the way home. For a long time I couldn't even look at him."

"Poor child!" Her breath was fragrant with lemon as she leaned to him. "You kept it inside of you all these years!"

"Whom was I going to tell?"

"You could have told Paul. You're so close to him."

"It would have seemed like shaming my mother to let anyone know, even Paul."

"But you don't mind telling me now."

"No," he said, marveling. "Not at all. Suddenly, not at all."

"And you *are* relieved."

"Yes, strangely enough I am. You've taken the weight away."

"It's not strange, Freddy. Don't you know that we're special people, you and I? Haven't you felt it all this past year?" The words drifted away into the still air.

They rose to stand only inches apart. He thought: It's said that lovers see each other's reflection in their eyes. For an instant, then, he caught his own image in two jet circles, and saw nothing more as her arms drew him in. A crazy joy sprang up in him, while his heart drummed.

"I love you, Leah. . . ."

Her mouth drew him; it wanted him; it was sweet; he had never known such sweetness. He had no idea how long the kiss lasted. The alarm clock ticked; silk rustled in his ears. Her mouth still held him.

When her lips released his, he had been gently propelled toward the bed. In a dream and a dazzle, he heard her whisper:

"Now, Freddy, now."

The heat, the roundness, the whole secret softness —these were his to take! He hadn't asked, heaven knew he wouldn't have dared to think of asking, and yet here she was giving it all!

His nerves stretched, quivering. He wanted her, and still, suddenly, he feared. Kissing was one thing, but this—from this he held back. Why?

"Not until we're married," he heard himself say.

"Freddy . . . I'm not afraid."

"Darling Leah, I can't do that to you."

With her silence she questioned him.

"I should want you to remember all your life that you were a proper bride."

There was truth enough in that, the truth of a decent young man who wouldn't "take advantage." But at the same time he was afraid for himself, because it ought to be harder for him to resist and it wasn't. Again: Why?

"I understand," she said. Two charming dimples accompanied her smile. "You're very good to me, Freddy . . . and you really love me enough to marry me. You really do."

"Maybe I always have and wasn't old enough to know it."

He kissed her forehead. Her head came just to his shoulder. Just nineteen she was, and his own for life. He felt tender, he felt responsible and older than his twenty-one years, as if youth and dependency had dropped away. The smallness of her, and the way she clung to him, fitting into his shoulder, made him feel his own size and strength as he had never felt them before. How fast it had happened! An hour ago his exams had been at the top of his mind; he'd been a schoolboy, Yale or no Yale; and now he was a man, with a woman to care for.

There'd be a whole new life with her; it would take getting used to, but it would be beautiful, and that odd fear of a few minutes ago would be nothing.

Leah looked up in alarm. "Your parents—"

"We won't tell them yet," he said quickly. "I have to graduate first. Time enough then."

"But your father won't like me anymore then. He was never happy about me in the first place, a stranger in his house. And after my seeing him that day—"

He put his hand over her mouth. "Darling, it's not worth your words. He can have his life as he wants it, and we can have ours."

They heard a fumbling at the front door.

"They're home!"

Leah lifted her long skirt and ran. Blue marabou flew across the hall and vanished. He closed his door, and went back to his books.

Blue marabou and black eyes danced on the pages. Oh, how bright and funny she was! And she thought she wasn't "elegant"! He had to laugh out loud. She was the dearest thing! And when their time came, surely it would be splendid, because it would be their right time, and he would be ready for it.

He couldn't believe his luck.

4

Carrie Chapman Catt had founded the Women's Peace Party at Washington in January 1915; shortly afterward the New York branch was formed. Hennie promptly joined and was elected an officer. She was full of proud enthusiasm.

"If women had the vote all over the world, you'd hear a different story," she liked to say. "We wouldn't vote money for guns, I guarantee. Women are different, we're not enthralled by power and force. Not," she would add, "that all men are, either. Certainly not men like my husband."

She went to all the meetings, spoke at many, and was complimented on her eloquence. She made posters and went about the city placing them in store windows or wherever anyone would accept them. All this activity gave her a good feeling that, in her own small way, she was building peace. Brick after patient brick, she told herself, but we are building.

Late one Saturday afternoon she came home from a meeting at which she had spoken, she knew, unusually well—setting forth a plan for extensive publicity in the popular magazines.

She was euphoric as she took a long walk home, bypassing the bus. It was a tender late afternoon, still very cool. The western sky was overlaid with coral fire. On a street corner she stopped to buy tulips from a vendor. Pink and white, with satin sheen, they were a rare extravagance, but it was spring, she argued, and there ought to be some celebration of it.

When she unlocked the apartment door, she was surprised to find Freddy in the kitchen with Dan, who, still in his topcoat, had apparently just come in. Freddy, kneeling, was filling Strudel's bowl.

"But how nice! We didn't expect you this weekend. You didn't say—"

"I know. I started at the crack of dawn. How are you, Mother?"

"Oh, fine! I'm late, I just got out of a meeting. I suppose you're starved. But I only have to warm dinner. I made it all this morning."

"Don't make any for me or for Leah. She and I—"

"Leah!" Dan interrupted. "You give with one hand and take away with the other. Have you come home to be with her or to give your parents a few hours?"

"To be with her," Freddy said quietly.

Hennie's heart sank. Not again. Don't let them quarrel again.

The muscles were tight in Dan's neck as he stared at Freddy.

"Did I really hear that? If I did hear it correctly, I don't understand it."

Freddy's hand had been caressing the dog, sliding over its long brown back while it ate. He looked up, then rose from his knees and said, "I love her."

Dan sat down. And Hennie, with coat and hat still on, stood looking from one to the other, then, for some idiotic reason, at the clock, on which the long black minute hand jerked through half a minute before anyone spoke another word.

Dan said roughly, "You don't know what you're talking about."

"I think I do. And I beg you, don't say anything that I won't want to remember."

"What the hell *are* you talking about, then? Do you mind telling us?"

Hennie pressed her hand to her heart. Under the woolen coat she could feel it pounding.

"I'm talking about Leah, whom I love. I asked you not to say anything I won't want to remember."

Dan softened his voice as if, Hennie thought, he had sensed something in Freddy that warned him really seriously to guard his anger.

"I'm not going to say anything evil, Freddy. You ought to know me better than that. Leah's fine. Haven't I been good to her? Raised her here in this house? I'm only telling you that you're too inexperienced to be talking about love, that's all."

"You weren't that much older when you fell in love with Mother."

"As a matter of fact, I was. Twenty-four when I met her, as against your twenty-one. So you're very young, you see, and—no offense intended—even younger than your age, too, in some ways. You lack judgment, Freddy."

"That's not what my professors tell me."

"I daresay you and they haven't talked much about women, or they'd tell you, too, there's a lot you don't understand yet."

"I only understand that I love Leah and she loves me."

"You don't see that she's not for you? You have almost nothing in common! You're at Yale, planning a doctorate; she works in a dress shop. She's ambitious and a striver; she—"

"You astound me! You, the thoroughgoing democrat, to say anything as snobbish as that!"

"I don't mean it to be snobbish at all. I mean it only to say that you're different, and will grow more so with time. Love between you makes no sense, no practical sense at all. The sooner you put it out of your head, the better it will be for you, and for Leah too." Dan's voice rose in emphasis. "She's a manhunter, Freddy."

"Don't, Dad. You don't know what you're saying."

"Oh, but I do! There are things that experience teaches, a man of experience can feel."

A man of experience . . . Hennie felt a weighty sigh. As always. Always.

Freddy did not reply. He bent and picked up the dog, set it on his lap, and held it close, sheltering the little sleek thing that rested its chin on his arm while he stroked the loose, wrinkled flesh under its chin.

At last he took a deep breath and spoke.

"I'm sorry you think that way," he said slowly. "Because we were married just this noon."

The words seemed to come from far away. Hennie's mind accepted them doubtfully.

"You were married?" she repeated.

"Yes. At City Hall." And Freddy swallowed hard, bobbing that vulnerable, always pathetic Adam's apple. "Don't be angry . . . don't spoil things. Please. It's our wedding day."

He looked like a scolded child, limp and defiant. Hennie's hand went to her mouth again to stop her trembling lips, and she held it there for a moment before she could speak.

"Why didn't you tell us?" She could hear the wail in her voice.

"You would have argued us out of it, or tried to. So it was just easier this way."

Dan cleared his throat. "Not to mention a little matter of honor," he said. He pounded his knees with his fists. "I call it a sneaky way of repaying your mother and me for the trust of a lifetime. I don't know what you call it, but I call it sneaky and foul."

"We didn't mean it to be. If you'll let me explain—"

"Yes, do. I'd really like to know how you came to make what, I promise you, will turn out to be one of the damnedest mistakes you'll ever make if you live to be a hundred. To saddle yourself before you've even got two feet on the ground—Jesus Christ, I've never seen anything more stupid! Damned if I have."

"I ask you," Freddy pleaded, "to keep it for some other time. Can you leave us a happy memory of today? Because this is a day we'll remember all our lives."

" 'Happy memory.' 'Happy pair,' isn't that the phrase? Where, by the way, is the other half of this happy pair?"

"Leah ran out to get gloves; she lost hers in the cab. Here she is. I hear her now."

Breathless and pink from running up the stairs, Leah appeared in the doorway. Seeing Dan and Hennie in a frozen tableau, she stopped short.

"Well! I see you've heard our news."

And she stood respectfully, waiting for a sign, and yet with an air of assurance, as if to say: We have done what we wanted and are not afraid.

All that ran instantly through Hennie's mind as her eyes swept over Leah: the smart lavender suit, a new one, naturally; the slender ankles in silk stockings, the lace jabot, the waist-length pearls, knotted and worn with dash as if they were Orièntals; the pert feather standing straight on the brim of the lavender hat. So Leah smiled and waited.

"Aren't you going to wish us joy?" She appealed at last to Hennie, ignoring Dan.

A second thought then flashed through Hennie's mind. That fear, so many times examined and denied, that her son would find his way to the war, that fear she had never been able to put to rest— that was over now! Married, he was safe! Leah and he would stay on here together. He'd finish his schooling and go to work; they'd have a baby. This marriage would prove to be a good thing, after all, another knot in the cord that bound them as a family. Yes, it was! Dan would get used to it. Swiftly her thoughts ran, coalescing with her quick optimism, her usual adaptability. And she took Leah into her arms.

"Of course we wish you joy! Yes, yes. I'm disappointed that you've done it this way, but I wish you joy!"

"Married on Saturday, too, and at City Hall," Dan said furiously. "That part doesn't bother me, but you know how your mother feels. You could have had a rabbi, at least, and waited till the Sabbath was over. You didn't have to add insult to injury."

Leah said quickly, "I know. I feel that way about it, too, and we will have a religious ceremony later. But today, there just wasn't enough time. . . ."

Dan jumped on that.

"What do you mean, not enough time?"

Leah turned to Freddy. "You haven't told them?"

"No, I was—" He still held the little wriggling dog, pressing it to him as if it were a protective garment. "No, I—"

Leah interrupted. "He dreads telling you. Freddy has enlisted in the British army. He only has a week. That's why we had to be married in a hurry."

The beaded fringe on the lamp shade in the parlor danced in front of Hennie's eyes. Her strength ebbed out, and she sank down onto a kitchen chair. In a whirl of vertigo, she saw Dan's open mouth, dark as a cave; his face was dark, the room was dark, and it whirled. She put her head down on the table.

A hand was laid on her head and she heard Freddy's voice above her.

"Don't cry, Mother. It's something I had to do. You always say people have to act on their principles, or else their principles are worthless."

She gave a long sigh.

"It's sad that our principles aren't the same, but that's how it is, and all I ask is that you respect mine as I have always respected yours."

Her son's large warm hand cupped her head. It was the hand she had taught to guide a spoon, that had gripped hers on the first day of school, that had charmed her as it rippled over the keyboard.

She opened her eyes and raised her head. The commonplace, familiar room with its four occupants, who had taken so many hundreds of meals here at this table, in front of this stove, assumed now a poignant gravity and would be remembered exactly as it was, with the red gingham curtains and the iron soup pot; with Freddy's white, beseeching face and Dan in his shirt-sleeves, caught between fury and sorrow, grown ten years older; with Leah, composed in her new status and stronger than any of them.

"Oh, Freddy, what have you done?" Hennie cried.

One wrings one's hands. That's what they say in books, and it's true. One clasps them and wrings them.

"Oh, Freddy, what have you done?"

"Mother, I've done right. This war is the last one. After this will come peace and freedom for all the world. I know I've done right."

With this new outrage, Dan jumped to his feet. "You've quit college! Thrown your education away! You couldn't have waited a year before going off to play the hero?"

"I'll make up the year when I come back. That's no problem."

Dan turned on Leah.

"And you—is it you who's behind this? You who encouraged this—this fool, who's throwing himself

away, throwing his life out the window?" His voice
roughened and broke.

"No, Dan, that isn't fair!" Hennie cried, before
Leah could answer. "You know how Freddy's felt
about the war since it began. It's not fair to blame
Leah for his wild ideas."

"All right, I'll take it back. Christ, I don't know
what I'm saying!" Dan pounded his head. "I'm trying to find out whether I'm asleep and having a
nightmare . . . I guess I'm awake."

Leah said softly, "You don't agree with Freddy's
point of view, but I should think you might be
proud of his courage, all the same."

Hennie looked at her son. He didn't age. She saw
the child standing there, the slight fair child with
the lake-blue eyes. Going off now, perhaps to die,
and for nothing. She had given all her energy, since
long before this war had begun, since she had been
an adult and old enough to think about such things,
to opposite tenets. Through the force of her conviction she had even sometimes converted strangers;
but she—and Dan too—had failed with their son,
leaving on him no mark of those convictions.

"I don't know what to say," she whispered, and
began to cry.

Dan put his arms around her.

"Look what you've done to your mother," he
shouted. "And you, Leah, what you've done to this
woman who rescued you, fought for you, gave you
her heart and soul! God damn it, you ought to be
cringing in shame, both of you!"

"No, Dan, don't," Hennie protested. "We can't
undo. We have to think, have to go forward. Can't
undo."

"If you don't want me to come back here," Leah said, "I have some friends where I work. I can live with them after Freddy goes."

How far she's come, the little waif! Trudging in the January wind with her mother, I promised to care for her and I have. Now she's my daughter, who loves my son, and will send him away after they've had a week together. Crazy. The whole thing is crazy.

Hennie got up and took Leah in her arms again. "Do whatever you want. This is your home, if you want it. Surely you know that."

Suddenly Leah's voice filled with tears. "Whatever Freddy says. And if Dan wants me, I'll stay."

"I would feel better if I could know she was here with you," Freddy said.

"You're my son's wife," Dan told Leah stiffly. "And as such, you're welcome here. So it's settled." Then his voice broke. "As much as it can be."

"We're going away for a few days," Freddy said. "Uncle Alfie's offered to let us stay at Laurel Hill. They're not using it this week."

"You mean to tell me Alfie knew about this?" Dan demanded.

"Only this morning. Paul asked him whether we could come. Paul's going to drive us there."

"Paul knew about it? All this thing was done behind our backs? Everyone knew but your father and mother?"

"Only this morning. Don't be angry at them, it's not their fault. I made them promise not to tell and —and it wouldn't have mattered, because we'd have done it anyway, and Paul knew that. Alfie knew it too."

"So," Dan said. "So."

And again that solemn silence fell; like a gray pall it lay over the little kitchen and the four who stood now in a circle, as people stand who wait for a way to break the circle, to say the final words and depart.

Leah spoke first. "It's half past four. We told Paul we'd be waiting downstairs."

The dachshund whimpered and she picked him up.

"He'll miss me. But I'll be back, Strudel. You'll take care of him, Hennie?"

"Of course."

Freddy picked up the bags.

"We'll be back on Friday, so we'll say good-bye then. We won't say it now."

Dan opened the door. "No. Just—just be well," he said.

When he closed the door, he laid his forehead against it. Hennie watched the quivering of his shoulders and heard the footsteps going down the stairs; she heard the noise of a motor starting up in the street, before the grave silence surged back.

"It won't last," Dan said. Numb and rigid, they had been awake, talking in bed through most of the night. "He'll never satisfy her."

"In what way?"

"She's too strong for him. She'll tug him and push him till he falls."

"Leah's a good girl."

It was the thousandth time she had said it and she was tired of saying it. Anyway, the marriage wasn't the uppermost thing. Freddy in uniform was what Hennie saw, kind, gentle Freddy with a gun. And she saw those terrible photographs of the trenches, devastated as a moonscape; no, far worse, for though the moon might be pitted and without trees, surely it was not stained with blood. What was the marriage compared with that?

Dan spoke bitterly into the dark. "She can wrap him around her little finger, and she will. Mark my words."

"They love each other, Dan, and must have for a long, long time. You were right when you said it. I didn't see it."

"There are many things you don't see. I always tell you that."

She thought, And now my mother will be able, too, to say "I told you so." And I shall answer, "You thought I was all wrong to marry Dan, too, didn't you?" No, bless you, Leah and Freddy; may he come home safely and may you be good to one another. I have faith that you will. It's strange, she thought, the mother of the boy is always said to believe that no girl's good enough for him, but I don't feel that way; I do believe that Leah will be good for him; her strength will be good for him.

She sighed. "Let us only hope they'll be as happy as we've been," and moved closer to Dan.

He drew her head to his shoulder. "Yes. But the goddamned war—"

"Darling, there's nothing we can do now. Except hope, that's all we can do. And keep the peace of this house. . . . Poor little Leah! Poor girl! What a way to begin a marriage!"

She thought: And our marriage didn't begin so auspiciously, either.

"Poor Leah, nothing. Poor Hennie," Dan grumbled.

"Not poor, as long as I have you. Hold me, Dan, I'm so tired. I think I can fall asleep now."

At Laurel Hill the peepers were loud in proclamation of spring. Wrapped in sweaters against the cool night, Paul, Freddy, and Leah sat on the terrace after a late supper.

"Listen to their music! What a wonderful night!" Leah exclaimed. "It's a pity Mimi won't come out."

"It's too chilly for her," Paul said. "She's too susceptible to colds." He stood up. "I'm going in too. And we're driving back to the city first thing in the morning. We'll be very quiet and not wake you."

"You needn't leave because of us," Freddy said.

"It's your honeymoon. You surely don't need our company."

"This house is enormous," Leah assured him. "We can rattle around in it without even seeing each other unless we want to."

She got up and walked to the edge of the terrace. "Look at the stars! The glitter's not cold at all. It seems to burn. Look!" she cried suddenly. "What's that?"

Above the hill and between the trees, the sky, in the splitting of a second, had erupted in a dazzle of fire.

"It's a meteor shower!" exclaimed Freddy.

The three ran down to the wall. The light burst; it raced like rain. Awed into silence, they stood before the spectacle of such miraculous power. And in a few more seconds it was over.

"What was it?" Leah cried. "What was it?"

"Nothing to be afraid of."

In the half-light, Paul could see Freddy's smile and his protective arm around the girl.

"They're balls of ice," Freddy told her. "They go zipping through the universe a hundred times faster than a bullet."

"I've never heard of anything like that! And you always say you don't know anything about science."

"I don't, really. I've just picked up a little stuff here and there because of my father. He used to take me out on the fire escape and show me the stars. A little of it stuck in my head, that's all."

Leah stretched her hand out from the shadow.

"Light from a star a million miles away, and it lies on my finger," adding, "We really don't know anything, do we?"

Stars, stars, lovers and stars! Paul thought. Vaguely he remembered some poem written by an ancient Roman about love and stars and eternity, how after centuries lovers would look at the stars as the poet was doing. He turned away and went back into the house; they did not even know that he had gone.

What had Leah said? That we don't know anything? No, surely we don't, or not very much, when all's said and done. Paul hadn't expected sensitivity in Leah; she'd seemed too clever and too worldly, but that only proved one must be careful of making judgments. Still, he suspected, she didn't have an awful lot of softness! Maybe she'd be a balance for Freddy, who had too much of it.

Good Lord! What had possessed him? Poor boy, going off to war when he needn't go! Was it because of that fellow Gerald, a compulsion to match his heroism? Or to show his father—of whose bravery at that long-ago fire he must have heard uncountable times—that he also could be brave? Perhaps some unconscious need to prove his own masculinity to himself? It was all too complicated; some of those psychology fellows in Vienna would have more understanding of it. Or maybe they wouldn't. One thing was sure, though; Freddy was a romantic, and God alone knew what it would bring him if he survived. He might end up exploring Arabia or, more likely, end up teaching the classics in some conservative private school, feeling sorry for himself for having been born a century too late.

And Leah—what had possessed her? Drama, perhaps? He'd be quite stunning in uniform with that angelic blond head in a military cap. It was said that uniforms were aphrodisiacs for women.

No, that was cruel, she was too intelligent for that. She wanted him, that's all. She loved him, or thought she did, which was the same thing—and had taken him while she could. There were millions of women like her, poor young things. If one could only know what lay ahead for them all! And for us all . . .

More than a hundred Americans lost on the *Lusitania* just a week ago. And he remembered dancing on that floating pleasure palace, eating caviar while the music played at dinner; or reading on deck, looking up from the book to watch the wake cut through the gray Atlantic as they sped. Now it lay at the cold, still bottom of the sea. Wilson says he won't be stampeded into war, but one wonders.

Still, we may keep out . . .

He trod the stairs softly to the bedroom, past Alfie's hideous still lifes of rotund fruit and dead birds, with their piteous open dead eyes and their broken wings. Mimi was already asleep; her needlepoint, a tidy wreath of muted flowers on a tan background, had fallen to the floor next to the bed, and he picked it up.

Vaguely restless, he walked to the window and looked out. A shaft of light from a lamp in the parlor below fell onto the lawn, where he could see two figures making a single shadow, so close was their embrace. When they broke apart to walk back to the house, he drew away from the window. In the depths of his body, he felt a surge of longing—powerful, and unfulfilled—as though their sexual passion had been contagious.

He undressed and went to the bed. His wife's face was calm in sleep; beside it lay her hand; the gold band, symbolic of her union with him, gleamed on her delicate finger. Even her fingers are refined, he thought.

He lay down. He made himself think about the client with whom he was to confer about a very important matter in the morning. His mind clicked carefully from point to point, clarifying his plan of procedure. After a while he was able to fall asleep.

PART THREE

Freddy and Leah

1

There was something about pregnancy, thought Hennie, that softened angers and resentments; one could watch them melt, like hot water softening a block of ice.

Angelique's first contempt for the marriage seemed to be forgotten at once as soon as Leah's condition could no longer be hidden from her; she became all sympathy. She bought sheets and embroidered gowns for the layette. She began to knit. Some basic instinct for survival of the race? Hennie wondered. Or else her mother was simply mellowing with age?

As for Dan, once his first rage had, out of sheer exhaustion, come under control, he had reluctantly adjusted himself to Leah's new position in the household.

The winter was severe. By the fifth month, Leah had stopped going to work, not because her condition was yet visible, but because by the sixth month streets were coated with ice. Now, in the seventh month, with her needlework on her lap and the little dog lying where the soft folds of her skirt touched the floor, she was a Renaissance portrait; her lively face wore a changed and peaceful expression; her hair was simply combed in the "madonna" style just recently made fashionable by Lady Diana Manners, Hennie thought, with affectionate amusement.

Leah, wearing a silver-gray blouse cut loose enough to fit her present state, explained, "It's from Poiret, last year's, and it has a spot, so they gave it to me. Look at the handwork! Only the French do work like this."

"You've got good taste, my dear. Expensive, too," added Angelique.

Hennie agreed and Leah looked up quickly.

"If you're worried about Freddy and me, don't be. I know he'll never make money. He's a scholar, a teacher like his father. I should like him to teach in a fine private school. Not a public, he'd hate that. And I'll make plenty of money for us. One of the seamstresses—she's a Russian Jew like me, except she's actually from Russia—has worked in Paris, she's very clever and wants to open a place with me. We know now what's wanted and how to do it. What we need is capital to start."

Hennie regarded the girl thoughtfully. She had learned a good deal since she'd gone to work. Even her English had a slight, attractive lilt, acquired no doubt from the Irishwoman who owned the establishment. And remembering Leah's militant mother, that plainspoken radical, Hennie marveled at the world's inconsistencies.

"You know, I think I saw your sister buying dresses at my place a while ago. She looked very well, very smart. I haven't mentioned it because I thought maybe I shouldn't, but then," Leah said, "maybe you'd like to know?"

"You wouldn't remember her."

"Oh, yes! I remember everything, even about that night, the last time I saw her. I can even tell you what she was wearing."

So could Hennie. In 1908 it had happened; eight years of grieving estrangement had gone by. Almost one eighth of the biblical life span! Too long to be undone, though; far too long. On both sides the resentment and the sense of injustice had hardened. It was accepted now, even by Alfie and Paul, that this was the way it would be. And Hennie could only mourn in silence.

But Angelique, from time to time, would lament: "It is the heaviest burden of my life, to see my daughters estranged from one another."

"I was thinking," Leah said abruptly, "that maybe Uncle Alfie would lend me the money to get started. Do you think he would? He's so generous." Then she paused. Her face hardened as she added, "Besides, unlike Dan, he happens to be fond of me."

"Oh," Hennie said, "I can't answer about the money, but about Dan, I'm sure he's fond of you, why should you think—"

Leah gave a dry laugh. "Fond of me! Hennie, I'm not afraid of the truth, so why should you be? He never wanted me here, and we both know it."

For a moment Hennie was silenced. The remark was so bitter, so unlike Leah! And she answered, stumbling a little, "It wasn't that he didn't like you, it was only that in the beginning he couldn't get used to having another child in the house. There'd been just the three of us."

Leah had such an odd expression! Had she, then, been so hurt that the wound was still not healed?

"It was nothing more than that, Leah dear, believe me. Not everyone wants to adopt a child. But he came to care for you—he's especially good to you now, isn't he? So I think you're reading too much into it. I really do."

"I'm not reading too much into it, Hennie."

This was a queer conversation. Leah looked, with her brows drawn together, why, she looked positively angry! Her lips were pinched and she had turned away as if she were holding something inside that she wasn't willing to release. Hennie felt bound to pursue the subject.

"I think you are," she said calmly. "I think it's you who don't like Dan. It's not fair of you not to like him, Leah. Or not to tell me why."

"Don't worry about it," Leah retorted. "I know what I know, I feel what I feel. But we're living here peacefully, aren't we? So what does it matter?"

It matters, Hennie thought. You're making me upset, suspicious. What did you mean by "I know what I know"?

"Are you trying to tell me something about my husband?" she asked.

Leah's face melted, making her look like herself again. "Oh, Hennie, no!" she cried. "I didn't mean —of course not! I shouldn't even have mentioned those old, childish feelings. I'm sorry I dragged them out of the closet, I really am."

There's something else, Hennie thought still. Or is it my old fear coming up to the surface, my old, foolish fears about Dan, so that at the first hint of anything secret or hidden, that's what I think about?

Yes, yes, of course it is! Absurd! And as for Leah, the girl is tense, worried to death about her own husband. Poor young thing!

All of us are living in terror, day after day, because of Freddy.

"Read Freddy's last letter aloud again, do," she said.

A sheaf of them lay on the table; Leah was in the habit of reading them aloud, skipping and, naturally, concealing intimacies. What was left were banalities, at least to Hennie's worried ears. Now that the letters came no longer from England but from France, all that mattered was that they should keep coming to prove that he was alive.

"I'm in good spirits," he wrote (shades of Gerald! Were they taught somewhere to say that?), "and very optimistic." (How can anyone be optimistic with all those thousands dead? He must not yet be in the front lines.) "It's a wonderful feeling to be part of this gallant army. The men are a staunch and plucky lot."

"He sounds so British; we don't even use those words," Dan had remarked wonderingly.

Now Leah's voice quavered, pulling Hennie's attention back to the moment.

"Listen, Hennie. He says: 'We underwent our first fire. It was pretty frightening, the noise alone could terrify you if you let it, but we got through all right and we're all safe. I'm glad I'm not a coward.' "

Hennie bent her head over the stitches. No comment. A thick, silent snow had been falling all day out of the dark sky; now suddenly a veering storm-

wind sent a spurt of sleet crackling on the window-
panes. Cruel to be outdoors in weather on a day like
this! Cruel to be in a hole in the ground, waiting and
waiting.

Her eyes were dry; her mouth was dry with fear.
The world was mad.

Here in this country, Wilson talked peace and yet
supported the buildup of a mighty navy. In Congress they said that only preparedness could preserve neutrality. To arm was the best way to keep
out of war. Madness!

The War Department had organized a training
camp for volunteers at Plattsburgh.

"Paul's going," Angelique had informed her. "As
an officer, of course."

And when Hennie had expressed her shock, along
with surprise that Paul hadn't told her himself, Angelique had explained, "It's not that he's for war;
it's that he wants for his own good to have some
training, if it should come. He'll get around to telling you. I suppose he hesitates because of the way
you feel about it." And then she'd said, "Florence
has gotten active in the Special Relief Society.
They're all for preparedness, as you know."

When Hennie hadn't answered, Angelique had
added, "It's a woman's counter-action to your
group."

Hennie said aloud now, startling Leah, "They'll
drag the whole world down, that's what they'll do."

Leah was puzzled. "Who will?"

"I was only thinking aloud. The preparedness
people, I meant. They're growing louder and louder
by the minute. Haven't you noticed how we 'pacifists' are being attacked now in the papers?"

"Hennie . . . Freddy's over there. How can one be a pacifist? He may need our help before it's over."

Again Hennie had no answer.

Leah's boy was born on a sunny morning during a February thaw. Icicles dripped on the windowsill in the room where the baby lay in his bassinet, a magnificent affair, draped in embroidered white organdy and blue satin bows. Mimi had brought it when the baby was two hours old.

"From Paul and me, with all our love," she had said. She had stood for a time bent over the baby, with a wistful expression, then straightened up, straightening her face as well, lest it reveal too much.

"Take care of yourself, Leah. Rest and don't catch cold," she had counseled before she left.

But Leah, to Hennie's dismay, had gotten out of bed on the third day, and now, flat of stomach and nicely dressed in a flowered wrapper, sat in a chair by the bassinet.

"It's my peasant blood," she proclaimed. "I can't lie in bed when I feel this good. As soon as I can stop nursing, I'm going back to work, since you said you'll take care of him, Hennie."

Indeed she would take care of him! The boy was already the household king.

"Look at him, he's smiling," Dan said.

"Gas," Leah told him. "Only gas."

"He looks like you, Dan," said Alfie, who had come with Emily and Meg to see the new arrival.

Really he looked like no one, except that he did

have Dan's black hair and plenty of it. His eyes were large, he had a sharp little nose, and his chin was strong: a handsome baby.

"What are you going to name him?" Meg wanted to know.

"Henry, after my father. And we'll call him Hank. I like that, it's a good thing to call a boy. Of course, my father's real name was Herschel," Leah said.

"Then why not call him Herschel?" Meg asked.

"Oh, because it's not American. It wouldn't be fair to give him a name like that, when other boys in school will be called Bob and Ed. Would you like to hold him when he wakes up?"

"Oh, yes!"

Leah had a nice way with children, Hennie saw.

And Leah went on, happy with the boy's being the object of attention, for after all, Hennie thought, it's hard to have no one of your own family to praise and marvel over your baby.

"His Hebrew name is my father's too: Avram. My father was named after his grandfather and so it goes, way way back."

Meg was interested. "What is a Hebrew name?"

Hennie answered promptly, "All Jews have a Hebrew name, because we are originally from Israel. We are *Israel,* one people, that's what it means. Your father has a Hebrew name, 'Jochanan.' "

"Why didn't you ever tell me about it?" Meg asked Alfie.

He blushed and glanced at Emily; there was something almost guilty and ashamed in his quick glance.

"It never came up. It wasn't that important."

Alfie's blush mounted; even his earlobes flamed. He coughed.

And Hennie was instantly sorry for him. If he wanted to send his daughter to an Episcopal academy, that was his business, wasn't it? She didn't know what had made her do that to Alfie, unless it was some need to reprimand him, along with her feeling that his child oughtn't to be kept in the dark about the family, deceived, or confused. Still, it was none of her business.

Meg, however, was making it her own business. She accused.

"You always hide things about yourself. You never want me to know about anything Jewish. I almost think you don't like being Jewish."

Sharply, Emily intervened. "That's an insulting thing to say to your father! I think you owe him an apology for that."

She didn't insult him, Hennie thought; she only made an honest observation.

Emily was breathless, embarrassed before the others in the room. "Really, I don't know what to make of children these days. They think nothing at all of insulting their parents. In my time, we wouldn't have dared."

Hennie thought again, She's not a child, she's thirteen, a very sensitive thirteen with a good mind, and you can't fool her, don't you both see that?

"As close to his family as your father is," Emily reproached, and glanced about. "I really expect you to apologize, Margaretta."

The two faced each other as if they were preparing for battle. Alfie frowned and examined a bunch of keys, removing himself from humiliation. Leah was busy folding a pile of diapers. Dan and Hennie glanced at each other and glanced away.

Then Meg spoke. "All right, I'm sorry. I didn't mean to be nasty. It's just that I do wish you would talk to me about things." Her tone was level and quiet; yet Hennie heard a new and unfamiliar firmness in it. "At school," she said, speaking not to anyone individually but to the listeners at large, "at school, Episcopal or not, I am called Jewish, while the Levy girls in the next apartment tell me I am not. It seems as if nobody wants me, doesn't it? I'm neither here nor there. It's fine for all of you. Everyone in this room knows what he is except me," she concluded.

"Now, now," said Alfie.

"And there's another thing. You always say that everyone's the same and it's wrong to be prejudiced, Mother, but you don't say anything when your friends tell mean jokes about Jews—"

"That's preposterous, Meg! And you know it is!"

"No, I don't. I heard that Mrs. Leghorn when you were playing bridge."

"Eavesdropping?"

"I wasn't. I was getting the dictionary from the shelf in the next room and I heard her say—"

Emily flared. "Never mind repeating what an ignorant woman said! We don't want to hear it. That's enough, Meg. Enough."

At this, Alfie spoke. "You're oversensitive, Meg," he told her, not unkindly. "Always have been. You need to grow out of it, not think so much about yourself. Just do your schoolwork, you're a good student, forge ahead and pay less attention to what people say. You'll get along better. That's always been my way and that's my best advice."

Hennie was outraged. Fools! A perplexed and lonely human being stands before you asking for truthful help, and you don't even see her loneliness. Yes, you're a fool, Alfie, and so are you, Emily, for all your gentle and genteel ways.

Meg had walked over to the bassinet. She was pretending to look at the baby, Hennie knew; she only wanted to turn away from them all. Her narrow back in the somber school uniform was rigid. No doubt she was controlling tears, preserving her dignity. Hennie knew all about that.

Alfie followed her to the bassinet. "Let's talk of happy things." He waved his hand in dismissal of life's little worries. "I've brought a present for this fine fellow, Leah."

"Aunt Emily's had it sent!" Leah cried. "The most beautiful quilt. It's so good of you."

"No, this is something else." Alfie reached into his pocket. A check for you, Dan. You earned it. It's only a couple of hundred dollars, but I thought you might want to start a bank account for the boy."

"You surprise me. What's it for?"

"You remember one of those diagrams you handed me last year? Something to do with—what was that word? A *coheard*—"

"Coherer. It's a detector. When you apply voltage to the tube—"

"Never mind. I wouldn't understand. Whatever it is, these people of mine are interested. They haven't done anything with your stuff yet, but somebody happened to ask whether I'd seen you lately and I said yes, and mentioned the baby, and they said, well, send this over. He deserves it, even if it turns out we can't do anything with his stuff."

"That's very decent, overly generous. I'll take it for the baby, because it does at least cover what I laid out to have my diagrams printed. Thanks, Alfie."

"They're very interested in your work, Dan. And the more I see of them, the more I see this is a growing concern. They've moved, taken four floors just off Canal Street. They're big business and no mistake. I know what I'm talking about." And Alfie jingled coins in his English-tweed jacket pocket.

"You generally do, Alfie."

"What do you hear from Freddy?"

"Not very much. Often, that is, but he doesn't say anything. The mail's all censored, naturally."

"You ought to be very proud of him, Dan." Alfie's voice was lowered in respect.

"Proud? He's a goddamned fool!"

"Oh!" gasped Emily. "How can you say such a thing? It's young men like him who will save us all! I just wish we had such a son," she added, looking almost indignantly at the retreating back of Meg, who had followed Hennie into the kitchen.

"They only say that because they have no son, Aunt Hennie," Meg whispered.

A lump filled Hennie's throat. "You think so, Meg?"

"Oh, yes. I saw the movie *Birth of a Nation*. It was horrible, the young men wounded and suffering so—" The girl clapped her hands to her mouth. "Oh, I'm sorry! It's stupid of me to talk that way to you."

Awkward as always, with her pink pointed

elbows akimbo, her prominent little stomach, and her kind, concerned face, she touched Hennie's heart. Thirteen was a difficult age at best. And Hennie felt tight kinship.

"That's all right. You're a lovely girl, Meg. You understand."

In the middle of winter, in 1917, the German government warned of the start of unrestricted attack by submarines; not long afterward the threat was carried out. Unarmed American merchant vessels and their defenseless crews were torpedoed to the bottom of the sea. Harmless fishing schooners, too, went down, and German submarines were sighted off the Long Island shore. In despair, Hennie and Dan looked at one another over the top of the morning newspaper.

"Times that try men's souls," Dan said.

He kept up the old arguments with Paul whenever they were together, which was no longer as often as it had been years before.

"We must keep ourselves peaceful, an example to the rest of the world, in spite of all," he insisted.

Paul was not so sure.

"I find I'm not very sure of anything anymore," he said, which remark might have seemed, to the ordinary hearer, either banal or enigmatic; for Hennie, who knew rather a good deal about Paul, the words were neither.

However, she had her own heartache: sometimes it seemed that she, with Dan, stood almost alone against the onrush of war. One by one now, the old idols fell and went over to the other side. Samuel

Gompers promised the support of the unions should the nation go to war. Even the Carnegie Endowment for International Peace caught the war fever, and Carrie Chapman Catt, the suffragist, Hennie's earliest heroine, pledged the women of her organization to help the war effort if need should come. So Hennie mourned, and mourning, marveled that the world around them could be in such high spirits.

Getting and spending were everywhere: theaters were filled; on Fifth Avenue, carriages were being outnumbered by Pierce-Arrows, chauffeur-driven; new shops were opening to meet the new need for glittering luxury, from platinum watches to silk shirts. The city was lively. Fashionable couples went tea-dancing at the Plaza. Women bobbed their hair à la Irene Castle, and did the tango wearing egrets on their little satin hats.

"They're making fortunes already," Dan said gloomily.

The Allies needed everything, as well as credit with which to buy: grain, tools, medicines, ammunition, cloth, steel, coal, iron, leather, wire, powdered milk—they needed everything. The securities and commodities markets boomed; factory orders soared; railroads were jammed and warehouses crammed; real estate tripled in value and everyone, from lawyers to shippers, felt the zest of expansion. A whole new crop of millionaires was born.

One evening, Alfie rang the doorbell. Leah had just come in from work. In the kitchen, Hennie was spooning cereal into the demanding mouth of young

Hank, who, in shirt and diaper, was happily perched on his grandfather's lap.

"Have I surprised you? I couldn't wait till tomorrow. I had to phone Emily and tell her I'd be late for dinner, because I've got such news for you."

Alfie's smile was so bright, like laughter contained, that Hennie could only think he had news of Freddy, that Freddy was coming home, or perhaps was already hiding behind the door.

"Is it Freddy? He's coming home?"

"No, no, nothing like that, I'm afraid. But very, very good all the same."

Alfie looked around for a place to put his derby, and since there was none in the crowded kitchen, where every surface was covered with something that belonged to Hank—bottles, bibs, or a ragged cloth animal—he held it on his lap.

"You remember, quite a while ago, oh, I should guess it's three years now, when you gave me a plan for a radio direction-finder?"

Dan corrected him. "Not for the finder, just for a little part of it, a tube."

"Well, whatever it was—I've told you I never can understand this technical stuff of yours—but anyway . . ." Alfie paused, relishing what he had come to say, building it up to a crescendo. "Well, it's been sold! Finn and Weber Electroparts, that's the subsidiary company, is putting it into production! And it's going to be a howling success, Dan. It will make you rich, Dan, and it will make me richer. It's a regular windfall! I wouldn't have believed it was true, if I hadn't got this check in my hand. Look," he said. "Take a look at that."

Dan took the check over the baby's head. Puzzled, he turned it over to see the back of it.

"I don't understand this, Alfie."

Alfie wore his familiar dimpled smile, one that almost made his cheeks burst.

"Why, it's easy! Just read: what does it say?"

"It says, 'Pay to the order of Daniel Roth—twenty thousand dollars.' "

"What?" cried Hennie, dropping the spoon.

"Twenty thousand dollars!" Leah repeated.

Alfie tipped the chair on two legs. He relaxed, pleased and proprietary, as if he had given a beautiful, unexpected toy to a child and was now sitting back to enjoy the child's rapture.

"I don't understand," Dan said again, frowning.

"Well, Dan, it's just your first share of the sale price, that's all. I took stock in your name, you see, as well as my own, fifteen shares for each of us, yours because the invention's yours, and mine for making the contact." Alfie's eyes narrowed, giving his face a canny expression. "You've got to know how to handle these things. Of course, I had my lawyers' advice all the way through. We've arranged to take a greater share of the profits as dividends in the form of stock. That helps with taxes, naturally. . . . You look perplexed."

"I am perplexed."

"Well, never mind. We'll sit down quietly one evening, you and I—no, what am I saying? I'm so stirred up, I'm not thinking straight. Not one evening, but one day. I want you to meet my lawyer at his office. He's first-rate, and he'll lay the whole thing out clearly for you, advise you on investing, too, because"—and here Alfie chuckled—"you'll be getting a whole lot more of these nice checks, my friend, and you'll want to handle them wisely, make them grow."

"All that money for this little tube! A gadget," Dan said. "It doesn't make sense."

"Oh, it makes plenty of sense! That little gadget is worth a gold mine in the right hands, as you see."

"Whose hands? Who wants it?"

"The War Department, Dan, that's who wants it! You've got a government contract! And it'll go on forever, all through the war that's coming, sure as shooting, and after that, too, because, as Larry Finn explained it roughly, it's being used for radio direction-finding, which is only in its infancy. Right now, though, they can already keep track of an enemy ship, when they have two or more transmissions and—"

Dan raised his hand. "The War Department. I don't sell the work of my brain to the War Department, Alfie. You should know that."

Alfie stared. "Are you crazy? You don't sell—"

"No, I don't. If, as you say, this thing is to be used to find ships at sea, that means sending human beings to their death at the bottom of the sea. And you think I want that kind of money?"

"Dan, you are crazy, crazy as a loon. War isn't a game. It's survival. People get killed. My God, your own son's over there fighting and you—"

"Leave my son out of this discussion, please."

"You keep interrupting me! What I'm trying to say is, trade goes on during wars, the same as any other time. And why shouldn't it? A man's entitled to the fruits of his labors. Why shouldn't you be paid by the War Department or anybody else who can make use of the thing you invented?"

"For the same reason that a man shouldn't get rich by owning firetrap tenements. You've always known how I feel about tenements—"

"I never owned any tenements."

"I didn't say you did. I said all those things are related: munitions, tenements, they're all exploitation, and I want no part of any of them. That's why I can't accept this."

The room was hot. Or maybe it was only Hennie's pounding blood. These two men, both decent, but so different, and yet in their differing ways fond of one another, were now squared off like fighters in a ring. Her brother, red-faced, clutched his hat; Dan, red-faced, hugged the boy who, sucking on a piece of zwieback, was half asleep.

All that wealth! she thought then. It was unreal. And she glanced at Leah, whose round eyes darted in fascination, observing everyone quite as though she were at a play.

"I thank you," Dan said. "You've meant to do something wonderful for me, I understand that, and I appreciate it. But you have to understand, too, that I can't accept it." And he reached the check out to Alfie.

"I'm not going to take it back," Alfie said.

"Then I shall just have to tear it up if you won't."

Alfie wiped the perspiration from his forehead. He clasped his knees and leaned forward, as if by coming closer to Dan, he could somehow reach him with reason.

"Dan, it's done and it can't be undone. The deal's made, the stock's issued in your name, everything's rolling, and I can't unroll it even if I want to. Why not take it for Hennie, since you feel this way about it? Just sign it over to Hennie, and that will be that."

Dan shook his head. "I don't mean to sound holy, Alfie, but Hennie's my wife. We're married. We're one." And he laid his hand on hers.

She felt the pressure of his hand. She felt strong and proud.

"I agree with Dan," she said clearly. "I don't want to make money out of war. Oh, don't be angry with us, Alfie! We love you . . . you have to do what you think is right for you, and we have to do what we think is right for us."

Alfie stood up. "You're a fool, Dan. My sister I won't criticize; after all, she's a woman, and can't be expected to know much about the world. But you should know that a day may come when, God forbid, you get sick, and the day surely will come when you're too old to work. Then you'll regret this. Here's wealth being poured into your hands. Freedom from worry."

"We'll manage, Alfie. We always have. We don't need more money."

Hennie saw her brother's eyes move around the little kitchen and, through the open door, into the simple parlor. The movement was, no doubt, only an unconscious reflex for him, who must shudder inwardly at the thought of having to live in a cramped and mediocre place like this.

"Twenty thousand dollars, Dan! Doesn't it stagger you?" Alfie pleaded.

"Have you forgotten that night in the country a couple of years ago, when I told you I'd be glad to give away anything I made if it would make life better on this earth? I don't want wealth. I wouldn't even know what to do with it."

"Think again, Dan. This is only the first payment. Twenty thousand a year, and more, into the foreseeable future. This firm's going places and they're very interested in your work—"

"Sorry to interrupt you again," Dan said. A shadow of exasperation crossed his mouth. "The answer is still no and always will be. Will you take the check?"

It lay on the table, crisp yellow paper with neat black letters. Leah picked it up to examine it and put it back.

"I'm shocked," Alfie said, looking from one to the other. "Shocked. Nobody who didn't hear this with his own ears would believe it. For all your knowledge, and I've sometimes been in awe of your knowledge, Dan, you're a fool. Naive. You don't even know which end is up."

"Take the check back, Alfie?" Dan spoke gently.

Alfie grabbed it. "Yes, by God, I will! I certainly will!"

"Don't be angry, Alfie," Hennie said again as he went to the door.

"Angry? No, just flabbergasted and sorry for the lot of you." He took one last look around the room. "Okay, then. That's the way it is. Good night, Hennie." He kissed his sister and went out.

"I suppose you think I'm crazy, too, don't you?" Dan asked Leah.

She answered frankly, "Yes, I do. You asked me, so I tell you."

Dan smiled. "Well, that's all right. I thought you would think so."

"I feel sorry for Alfie," Hennie said. "He looked so crestfallen."

"I know." Dan got up. "Take Hank, somebody, he's asleep. He's a good sort, Alfie. I can't help but like him, even though I think sometimes I'd get more understanding from an Eskimo."

On a brisk April day, the wind tossed the budding cherry blossoms around the tidal basin, while at the Capitol, Woodrow Wilson spoke before the Houses of Congress in joint session.

"Neutrality is no longer feasible, nor desirable, when the peace of the world is involved," he said. ". . . It is a fearful thing to lead this great peaceful people into war . . . we shall fight for the things which we have always carried nearest our hearts, for democracy . . . for the rights and liberties of small nations." And, in solemn tones, he concluded that "the day has come when America is privileged to spend her blood and her might for the principles that gave her birth and happiness. . . . God helping her, she can do no other."

On April 6, America entered the war.

All that day, Hennie walked. It seemed to her, as she went through the familiar streets, past the little shops, that they were now threatened by a terrible, great cold. A new ice age loomed, creeping nearer hour by hour to crush them all: the children in the schoolyards, the fat grocer, the old woman carrying a sick cat in a basket, all of them, all of us.

Her mind traveled back through the years to

peaceful, hopeful meeting places here in the city and at Lake Mohonk, where the teachers and the Quakers met beneath drowsy summer leafage to speak about a better world, and were so full of confidence. That was past and over.

She came, in her drifting, to the avenue on which Uncle David now spent his days at the home. It had been months since she had paid a visit to him, so busy had she been with the daily affairs that make up a life: the care of the household and the little boy, the now futile effort for peace, and most of all, the heartache, so often buried for Dan's and Leah's sakes, over Freddy. Guilt about this neglect, as well as a sudden, unreasoned wish to talk to the old man, a memory of those years when he had been the most trusted person in her life, directed her to the entrance of the dingy building.

"He's reading in his room," the attendant told her at the desk. "He spends a lot of time reading."

A book lay on the table by the chair where Uncle David was sitting. It was unopened; he had not been reading. He had only been staring out of the window, from which there was nothing to be seen except grim gray rooftops.

When, with a gleam of interest, he asked her what was happening in the world, she told him the truth: that we had gone to war.

"Yes, yes, war," he said with a vague smile. "I was there—with the men in blue, did you know that? Have I ever shown you my picture?"

At the side of his bed stood that ancient brown photograph of himself in uniform, posed in front of an army tent somewhere in Tennessee.

"Have you ever seen it?" The smile was proud.

"Yes, Uncle David, I've seen it."

Foolishly she had hoped for some return of comprehension, so that she might talk to him about Freddy and tell him of her despair over the war; she had hoped to receive from him some of the comfort and strength he had given her long ago. But she was years too late.

"The men in blue." He began to quaver a few bars of a marching song, then stopped in confusion and closed his eyes.

"You're tired, Uncle David."

"Yes, it's past midnight and you should be home. What are you doing here? Go home."

So she fled down into the sad, bright afternoon and walked away.

Paul came a few days later to say good-bye.

"I've enlisted, got my commission. Conscription's coming, so there's no use waiting."

Hennie wondered how a man really felt, what he might be ashamed to say about the hell he was to enter. And she remembered Freddy, sitting in that same chair, talking of glory and honor and sacrifice, with the glow of faith. Paul's quiet features, on the other hand, were unreadable.

"Your father, with his connections, could surely get you a job with the War Department in Washington, couldn't he?" she suggested, and, when Paul's eyebrows were raised, added quickly, "I know you're thinking there's no honor in a thing like that, but is it more honorable to take up a gun and kill?"

"I'm a conformist. I simply do what has to be done. I've never used a gun, but I know I will be expected to learn how." And he said thoughtfully, "God knows I'm not going with any of Freddy's spirit. I'm just going. . . . What do you hear from Freddy?"

"Not what we heard in the beginning, I can tell you. He's seen dead Germans, he says, and 'they look like us.' I suppose it hit him hard; they weren't devils or subhuman, after all. But his latest letters are just forms, postcards, actually, where they cross out what doesn't apply: I am sick in the hospital, I am wounded, I am well. So he's in the front lines, and that's all we know."

Paul was silent.

"To think the baby's walking and Freddy hasn't even seen him!" Hennie cried, for perhaps the hundredth time.

"May I see him?" asked Paul.

"He's asleep, but he sleeps like a log. We can go in and look."

The child lay on his stomach with his face turned into a little pillow and his dark hair tumbled. Animals surrounded him in the crib: a teddy bear, a pink rabbit, a white dog, and a lamb with a bow and a bell.

Paul stood for a long minute looking. Then, following Hennie back to the parlor, he said, "I wish I had one. I suppose going away like this makes you want one more than you ever thought you would."

They've been married four years, Hennie thought. Not since that day just before the wedding, when Paul had come to her in his despair and wild with pain—a bitter day, she recalled, with the cold rain flying—not since then had there been any mention between them of his marriage.

She ventured it now. "Paul, tell me, is everything all right between you and Marian? Do you mind my asking?"

"It's all right. She's a good girl, Mimi."

Hardly a full answer! And Hennie went on, "Oh, yes. Dependable. Responsible. She'll never upset things, make you worry or doubt."

"No, not Mimi."

Now something drove Hennie—some queer, sudden need to reveal her own self—to the edge of caution. "It must be a wonderful feeling to be so safe with someone."

"Well, you know all about that, I'm sure."

This answer pulled her immediately back from the edge to firmer ground. What had she been thinking of! To reveal her foolish fears about her own husband, to betray the close and lovely life that was theirs, to admit even for an instant that it was less than perfect. . . .

She said quickly, "Of course. I was thinking about you."

And indeed she was. Paul deserved the best. The beginning of that marriage had been so wrong. One could only hope that time had made a difference.

"I don't mean to pry," she said, wanting through the tenderness of her tone to draw him toward her, so that he might speak out. But he did not answer. She could not even catch his eye. Worried now, she went further, pushing at his reluctance. After all, she had helped to bring him up! She could feel almost a mother's rights.

"That other—Anna?"

He looked up sharply at that. "What about her?"

"I meant only—you've never heard anything of her?"

"No. Why should I?"

"I don't know." Flustered now, Hennie made apology. "I meant nothing. Of course you wouldn't have heard. Forgive me."

"That's all right."

Clearly he didn't want to talk about private things, any more than she herself did. And for the first time that she could recall, she felt clumsy in Paul's presence. So she sought for something to say and, seeking it, said the first thing that came into her head.

"I suppose Alfie's told you about Dan's turning down a fortune, a big War Department order?"

"Yes, he thinks Dan's very foolish."

"And do you too?"

"I don't know, Hennie. I suppose you have to do what your conscience compels. All I know is, the Allies are hard-pressed. Frankly, I haven't wanted to see the Germans win, and so our firm from the very beginning has been financing Allied purchases on a large scale. Is that bad? War is bad, but we're in it, and they have to buy supplies, so we make money." He brightened and laughed. "All I do know is, my father's old relatives had better stop speaking German on the streets, if they know what's good for them."

"It's not their fault. I'm sorry for them," Hennie said. "Sorry for everyone. For Marian, and for your mother, seeing you go off like this. I think of your mother so much, Paul."

He was still for a moment. Then he said, "None of it makes any sense, not quarrels nor wars. . . ."

But they'll be all right, those two. They do what's expected of them. Mimi's very much like my mother in many ways. I guess that's why they get along so well."

"I'm glad they do," Hennie told him, meaning it.

Paul stood up. "Tell me, would you like to see the farewell parade? I'll be in it, on the thirtieth. The Twenty-seventh Division will be marching away. You can stand anywhere and get a look. You might even see me! Think of that!" he said, mocking himself.

"I'd rather see you almost anywhere else, but yes, I'll come. God bless you, Paul," Hennie said as he kissed her.

At the top of the stairs, she stood and watched him running down. She had an uncanny feeling that she would never see him again. Strange, she thought, swallowing tears, I didn't feel like that when Freddy went. I know I'll see Freddy again. I know it.

The 27th Division swung down Fifth Avenue under the August sun. Flags draped the windows and fluttered on sticks in the hands of the thousands who watched. Thousands of legs, wrapped in puttees, moved in time to "Stars and Stripes Forever" and "The Battle Hymn of the Republic." With guns slung over left shoulders and heads up, they went briskly, while the drums beat, the reverberating brasses clashed, and the cavalry pranced ahead. The crowds joined in: "Over there, over there . . . the Yanks are coming, the Yanks are coming . . . and we won't get back till it's over, over there."

Hennie didn't catch sight of Paul, but she knew
he must have passed her, so she said her silent farewell to him and the 27th as they marched out of
sight down the sparkling avenue. Then, among the
dispersing crowd, all whistling cheerfully, all
thrilled by the might, the pomp, and the circum-
stance, she walked home, solitary and quite unable
to sing.

2

The country settled down for the long, long haul. Factories not essential to the war effort were ordered shut to save coal. Daylight saving, wheatless Mondays, meatless Tuesdays, and days without gas all followed. Every blank wall was plastered with posters: ASK HIS MOTHER HOW MANY BONDS YOU SHOULD BUY.

Hennie and Dan bought no bonds. They gave instead, more generously than they could afford, to the Red Cross, and even went to see President Wilson in top hat and tails march down Fifth Avenue as head of the Red Cross Fund Drive.

"Contributing for bullets is one thing," Dan said grimly. "Helping the wounded in the hospitals is another."

This he dared say only to a very few intimates who shared his beliefs. Otherwise, silence was the only prudent course. One didn't dare say that there might be such a creature as a "good German." The German was the "barbarous Hun," vilified in the movies and the newspapers. Down the street from the Roth's own house, meeting their sight as soon as they came out of their front door, was another enormous poster, this one of a powerful hand dripping blood: THE HUN, HIS MARK, it read; BLOT IT OUT WITH LIBERTY BONDS. The garrulous butcher, Schultz, who had provided chops and roasts to the neighborhood for the last thirty years, now called himself a Swede and changed his name to Svensen, even as the royal Battenbergs in England had become Mountbatten.

Yes, the world has gone mad, Hennie thought again.

Everything fell apart in less than a day. It would seem to her later that it began with the death of poor Strudel.

Hank was in the stroller with a bag of groceries at his feet; the dog trotted on his short legs at Hennie's side as they finished their daily errands. On the way back, a few blocks from the house, a cat came sauntering out of an areaway to confront Strudel, who, quite naturally furious at this temerity, pulled at the leash to go after it. He planted his feet, he yapped, he barked. The cat jumped up on a railing, arching its back, and hissed.

"No, Strudel, no, come along . . . Strudel!" Hennie commanded, pulling the leash until he was forced to give in and turn his face toward home.

But attention had been attracted. Four or five youths, of the sort that Hennie would characterize as "louts," had been loitering at the curb.

" 'Strudel! Strudel!' " one mocked. "What kind of a name is that?"

Hennie, ignoring the question, pushed the stroller ahead.

Four of the louts planted themselves in front of the stroller to block her.

One challenged: "I said, lady, what kind of a name is that?"

"A dog's name," she replied. "Let me pass, please."

One of the louts grabbed the leash. "It's a German name, a Kraut name. What are you doing with a Kraut dog? You ought to be ashamed of yourself, lady," he said, showing his bad teeth.

"Let go of that leash at once," she said sharply.

The fellow jerked it, and Strudel let out a yelp of pain.

Hennie grappled with him. "Let go, I said. This is my dog. Leave it alone!"

"Now, now, lady. Take it easy! We know it's your dog, but an American shouldn't have a lousy Kraut dog. What do you say, guys?"

"No. An American should have an American dog!"

They pulled the leash from Hennie's hands; her other hand was needed to hold the stroller. She looked around for help. The street was empty.

They raised the leash, so that Strudel dangled, choking in midair.

Hennie screamed. "You'll kill him! For God's sake, what are you doing? You're killing him!"

"You think so, lady? Now ain't that too bad. Listen to that, guys! We're killing him!"

Now, from the rear of the threatening group, another came forward, holding a baseball bat. And with sudden clarity, in the shock of total terror,

Hennie saw what these subhuman brutes were really going to do. . . . Should she not abandon the dog and flee with the child? But they barred her way. They wanted her to see what they were going to do.

She pleaded then. "Come on, I haven't done anything to you! You see I'm here with a baby. Please. Let me have my dog and go home. Please."

"You want your dog?"

Strudel was wriggling, tortured and gasping for air. The fellow who had been holding him now dropped him—or smashed him, rather, to the pavement; the one with the bat raised it over his head and brought it down—

One cry sounded. Such agony Hennie had never heard in her life or could have imagined. . . .

"There's your lousy Kraut dog! Here, take him and go home. Go home!" For Hennie stood frozen. "Go on! What are you waiting for? You said you wanted to go home!"

She sank on her knees before the mess of oozing brain, crushed bone, and bloody flesh; only the little brown rear end, intact, still twitched.

"Oh, oh, oh," she moaned.

And wept. And heard feet go pounding away down the street.

Hank began to wail, making, with Hennie's moans, the only sounds in the fallen silence.

Then two women came running out of the house. "Jesus!" one said, and covered her eyes. A man walked past and turned away. Someone else came and put a hand on Hennie's shoulder.

"Get up, missus," the voice said kindly. "There's nothing you can do. . . . It's a disgrace."

Where had all these people been when she needed them?

"What can I do for him?" She wept. "He's in pain. Poor thing, poor brown Strudel . . . I have to take the baby home . . . but I can't go away and leave him lying here." She turned her helpless weeping face to the sky.

A minute later a policeman appeared.

"Look, look," she cried. "Oh, my God, what a world!"

The policeman shook his head. "Yes. It's a tough world, missus."

"Can we—can somebody carry him? Is there a veterinary, an animal hospital?"

"Missus." The man was very patient. "Missus. The dog is dead. Best get up and go home."

Indeed, the twitching had stopped. The un-smashed half of Strudel that was still recognizable lay quiet; two round neat paws and a long slender tail lay on the sidewalk in the middle of a spreading wet stain.

The policeman knelt down. "Here, you want the collar and leash? I'll take care of the rest. Get rid of this."

She shook her head numbly, but he pressed the green leather collar, after wiping it with his own handkerchief, into her hand.

"Go home. Take the little boy home."

She bent to comfort Hank. How much had the baby understood? One would never know what memory might have been printed on his brain.

Dan was home early, and she was thankful. Her legs trembled; she was so weak that she could hardly lift the child out of the stroller. When, with a few choked words, she told Dan what had happened, he took Hank from her and made her lie down; he himself would give the news to Leah; she must just rest. His face was dark with rage.

All night she lay in his arms to be comforted.

"You must think, my darling, that this is a disease, an epidemic. Thousands of men are dying as brutally as the poor little dog died."

"I know, but I haven't had to see them," she whispered.

"You'd make a poor soldier, dear Hennie."

Then, with thoughts of their son in both their minds, they said no more. And Dan made tender love to her, and she thought, You are everything; you make everything whole; without you, it is all fragments and shards, all broken.

After Hank's nap the next afternoon, Dan took him out. Hank was the only lure that could keep him away from the loaded workbenches in his lab. He was a vigorous little boy, friendly even to strangers, who, amused by his hearty greeting, often stopped to talk to him. He loved to let Dan throw him up into the air and catch him; quite simply, he loved Dan more than anyone. And Dan returned his love, with none of the hovering, worrisome fretfulness he had shown to Freddy.

Hennie stood at the window, smiling, and watched them go down the street for as long as she could see them. These were the joys of life that evened the scale.

When she had prepared the vegetables for supper, she thought about what to do next. For a long time, she hadn't gone to the settlement house, now that she had Hank to care for, and she missed it, but it was more important to care for the child so that Leah might support herself and prepare for a vocation.

Some of Leah's handiwork lay now on a chair in the parlor. Often she brought work home to earn something extra: nothing too complicated, only a hem, perhaps, to be finished with careful, tiny stitches, or a lace collar to be attached. An evening jacket of lime-colored brocade was on her sewing basket now, and Hennie picked it up to stroke the crisp, thick silk, admiring it without having any wish to own it. She straightened it out, lest it wrinkle. Leah was not the most tidy young woman!

Hank's toys were strewn on Dan's big chair. She put them back on the toy shelf, then thought of something else that she had long put off; Dan's hall closet, filled with the accumulation of years, was a space that could no doubt be better organized to make room for some of the toys.

She got a step stool and began with the top shelf, on which there were half a dozen grocery cartons stacked with papers. The dust flew as she lifted them down. Where to begin? Old miser, she thought, he never throws anything away! Receipted bills, twelve years old, check stubs, a department store's advertisement for a child's roller skates from —can you believe it? she laughed—from Freddy's time!

Her eyes caught something as she rummaged, and held there; a sheet of bright pink letter paper turned up among the nondescript rubbish.

"Darling Dan," she read.

Something happened: It was the startled thump
of her heart.

In the upper right-hand corner was a date: three
years ago.

She closed her eyes. Put it back on the top shelf.
It's not yours. It must be from one of his pupils, a
child. Don't be stupid; of course it isn't. Put it back!
Don't look for trouble. You don't want to know.
You've no right. It's not yours.

She fled with it to the sofa. Now her heart really
raced; it skipped and staggered; she heard its frantic
pulse in her ears. Her eyes flew down the page.

"Darling Dan, for in my heart, even though your
letter broke it, you will always be my darling . . .
you told me this year was the best year in your life,
you told me a hundred times, and now you write
that we can't go on together . . . you told me
you've never known a woman like me . . . I know
you've had *many,* not being happy with your wife
. . . I'm broken up, I'm getting a job upstate where
I won't have to see you every day at work . . . I
understand you can't get a divorce, I know you said
you wished you could, but these women hang on so
and make a scandal . . . I would never make a
scandal . . . why couldn't we have gone on as we
were on our beautiful Saturdays . . . I don't understand why . . ."

Hennie went mad. The first thing at hand was the
glass dome containing the violets in a paper frill that
had been her wedding bouquet, and that Florence
had had pressed for her. She smashed it. She hurled
it against the wall so that it scattered and flew.
Wicked pointed splinters fell over the teddy bear.

She sobbed and went to clean them up, weeping and strangling.

She beat the wall with her fists. She went to the mirror and scratched her wild face, tearing one cheek so that two beads of blood seeped out.

"I'm going insane," she said aloud.

The mirrored face begged for pity. "Insane," said the mirrored mouth.

She rushed back to the scattered letters and scooped them up. Words jumped on the page. "I understand you can't get a divorce. I know you said you wished you could . . . I know you've had many, not being happy with your wife . . ."

"I don't believe it," she said loudly and clearly.

You do believe it. If you hadn't been pregnant, he wouldn't have married you; he can't keep away from women. You told yourself it was ridiculous to be jealous, that you were a fool to imagine things that weren't there.

But they were there.

Cold seeped into the apartment. Outside, the day was bright and looked warm, yet the cold seemed to be coming from the poles to freeze her blood. She got a coat from the closet and, huddling in it, lay down on the floor.

"I ought to die," she said.

For a long time she lay with her head on her arms, listening as the silence thrummed. Then the telephone rang, and automatically she got up to answer it. The world collapsed, but one answered the telephone.

"I was wondering," said Angelique, "whether you and Dan might want to come to dinner tonight.

I have a beautiful roast and the girl baked a cake . . ."

Tears clouded Hennie's eyes, so that the walls swam before her; nevertheless, she steadied her voice.

"Thanks, Mama, another time. Our dinner's all prepared."

"Well, leave it to Leah! You never get out of that house, it seems to me, stuck in with the baby."

"I don't mind it, Mama. You know that. Maybe later in the week."

Angelique was prepared for a chat. "I'm invited to Alfie's next week, did I tell you? It's Meg's school vacation and they're spending it in the country. You know, she's growing up to be such a sweet girl, but I worry about her, she's so awfully confused. All that business about religion and the family—"

"Mama," Hennie cried, "I have to go, there's a delivery man—"

"Are you all right, Hennie? You don't sound right."

"I'm fine, I'm coming down with a cold, the doorbell's ringing."

She hung up. She needed to scream. But the neighbors would hear and call the police. If only she could go somewhere and scream! She could feel the screams tearing her throat until it hurt. Clenching her fists, she beat her head; then she pounded her tight shut mouth with a fist.

Oh, God, oh, God, what have You done to me?

She thought of going to Uncle David. So, you were right, Uncle David. I used to think, when Dan flirted, that that was all, only a trivial embarrassment that I could endure, and I thought you had been wrong, but no, you were right. You said there are men who can't be satisfied with one woman. Oh, I heard you, but I didn't want to hear you, and now I have to. . . .

Uncle David is senile. You can't go to him. You can't go to anyone.

She went numb. An organ-grinder on the street below began to play a tarantella: a wedding dance, merry peasants with whirling skirts. When she went to the window to slam it down, the man was bowing and holding his cap out, while his sad little monkey, in a red suit and cap, did the same. Oh, poor creature! But she had no room for anybody else's pain.

Suddenly she was calm and worn out. Her mind clicked: Pull your thoughts together.

Would it have been better if, back then, she had told him to go, setting him free with the letter she had written and not mailed? A gallant gesture, she thought, mocking herself now; it was only half meant and she had known it when she wrote it.

What would I have done if he had abandoned me?

Her mind stopped clicking; she put her face in her hands, rolled in the sofa pillows, and cried and cried.

The key turned in the front door.

"We had a fine walk," Dan said cheerfully. "This fellow attracts attention wherever he goes. Have you ever noticed that the parents of a boy show him off more than people do with girls? Really stupid of them—why, what's the matter, for God's sake, what's the matter?"

"Nothing to do with Freddy," she said coldly, while her heart resumed its pounding. "I have something to talk to you about."

Dan stared at her.

"Take the child in for his nap," she commanded him. "And close his door."

In utmost alarm, Dan obeyed. When he came out, she was standing in the center of the room with the pink letter in her hand.

"Take it. It's yours."

He glanced at it. His face blanched; he sat down on the sofa.

"Oh, my God," he said.

"Yes. Oh, my God. I was cleaning the closet, not snooping. I never snoop. I had no reason to, or so I thought."

She couldn't read his face. His color went faintly green. Green-white, like death.

"Do you want a divorce?" she asked in that same cold, thin voice, holding her head high.

"Are you crazy?" he implored.

"Well, you apparently told this—this *person* that you did."

He clasped his hands before him. "Oh, Hennie, Hennie, how can I ever explain this, or make any sense out of it for you? I'll tell you. Yes, I had an affair with her. I was stupid. . . . You must understand, a man lies to women like her. I never meant one word of anything she claims I said . . . or I did say. Not one word."

"You tell me you lied to her, but what you are telling me now is the truth. How can I know it wasn't the other way? Do you lie to all your women, or only to me? Which is it? How am I to know?"

Dan flung out his hands, palms up. "Believe me!"

"I always believed you, fool that I was."

"Believe me now. I never loved anyone but you. Yes, you. Why do you think I married you if I didn't love you?"

"Because in the circumstances you had to, that's why. It was a matter of conscience. You might well have married Lucy Marston otherwise. How well I remember her!"

"Lucy! She wasn't worth your little finger, Hennie, not one of them ever was. Not your finger," Dan repeated. His voice was full of tears. "It's true that I've been driven a little out of my mind for a couple of months now and then. But it was always sex, and nothing else. It never lasts. I know all the time that it won't." He paused and frowned. "I never intend it to."

He was in pain and she stood there tall above him, inflicting more.

"You tricked them, too, as well as me, then. You promise love and haven't any intention of keeping your promise. You're an honorable man, you are."

"I'm ashamed, Hennie. I've done things I'm ashamed of. But I never tricked anyone. I told the truth, that I had a wife and would never leave her."

"Only that you were unhappy with her."

He groaned. "It was a way of talking, that's all."

"Oh, I see. Tell me, what made you finally get rid of this one?"

Dan answered, very low. "I realized that I had to put a stop to that sort of thing, that I had to grow up—too late—that I might hurt you terribly, the last thing in the world that I wanted to do."

"To think," she said, "if you weren't so sloppy

and had thrown this away, as most normal people would have done, I wouldn't ever have known, would I?"

"Hennie, please come here, take my hand. I swear to you, it was nothing. Nothing that meant anything. I would give ten years of my life to undo it."

"Don't touch me. Uncle David warned me from the first. Oh, God, he warned me! Why didn't I listen to him?"

"Uncle David said—"

"Yes, he told me you couldn't be faithful, that some men can't be, and you were one of them."

And, her glance falling upon the ivy that erupted and flowed in gleaming, moist cascades from the bowl on the windowsill, she thought: That was my trust, as healthy and strong as that ivy, and it's gone, ripped out by the roots and thrown away.

"Oh, the bitch!" she cried. "If there weren't laws against murder, I'd kill her! I'd find where she lives and I'd wait for her one night, I'd get my hands on her and, oh, God, how I would love to kill her!" She fell onto a chair and laid her head back: "Why don't I want to kill you? Because I love you? Oh, no! It's only because I feel . . . I feel you're not worth killing, any of you men. You're like dogs, running after every bitch in heat. Last year at Alfie's place, how those dogs drove us crazy trying to get in at the setter, snarling and fighting; they almost broke the screen door down. That's how men are."

"You flatter us," Dan said gently and ruefully.

"It's the truth, isn't it?"

"Not quite. Maybe a little."

"Tell me, how many have you really had all these years? Can you count how many?"

"I never loved anyone but you, Hennie."

· "Don't quibble and dodge. I asked how many you *had,* not *loved,* since you married me. How many times you've been unfaithful."

"Unfaithful? What is unfaithful?"

"Quibbling again?"

"No. Have I in any way failed you? In our daily life, in all the years, have I ever been anything but good to you?"

This evasion enraged her.

"Answer me!" she demanded fiercely. "I want an answer!"

There was a dreadful stillness in the room. It tingled, waiting to be broken, while they stared at one another.

I'm looking at you and I don't recognize you, she thought.

Then, somewhere below, a whistle sounded, the short summons a boy makes when he puts two fingers in his mouth. She started, and spoke again.

"So I was not a suspicious fool, after all. I berated myself and was ashamed of myself, while all the time I was right. What an actor you are! Without heart or decency, to come home and make love to me, to keep telling me you loved me, when all the time you were saying the same things to God knows who else and how many—"

"Oh, not how many, Hennie, and it wasn't the same, ever!" Dan beat his head, and put a hand over his eyes.

"I've been a second-rate woman, an unwanted woman. How you have shamed me! You and your women, lying in bed together, laughing at me and pitying me."

"No, no! I never talked about you. I—"

The key turned in the lock.

"They let me off early," Leah announced. And glancing from one to the other, she opened her mouth again as if beginning to ask: What's the matter?

"Don't worry, it's nothing about Freddy," Hennie told her at once.

"Hank's still having a nap," Dan said.

"I'll cook dinner," Leah said quickly, rising to what she saw was a situation. "I never get a chance to."

Hennie responded, "Not for me. I don't feel well. I'm going to bed." And when Leah had gone into the kitchen, she said to Dan, "You can make up the bed on the sofa in here. It's comfortable enough."

Much later, when he came into the bedroom, she pretended to be asleep. When he whispered, she did not answer. When he reached for her hand, she slid it away beneath the quilt. Frozen, she lay and waited for him to tiptoe out. Then, alone in the silent room, she wept and shook, muffling her sobs in the blankets.

It seemed to Hennie now that a fog had wrapped her, stifling, clinging and damp. Her breath came hard; her legs and arms moved as if they were weighted.

Leah's presence was a fortunate barrier to another long confrontation with Dan. To Leah's enormous credit, she kept up a pretense that nothing was wrong in the house, going about her busy routine as always.

But on the first Sunday, after Leah had taken the boy and gone out, Dan came to where Hennie sat at the bedroom window. She had been looking over toward the avenue.

"You sit there," Dan said not unkindly, "as if you were waiting to die. Your face is like stone. Or is it that you are waiting for me to die?" And he laid his hand on her head.

She jerked away, crying out, "Don't do that! Don't do that!"

He drew his hand back as though she had burned it. "I'm sorry."

Even in pain, his face was handsome. The shadows beneath them only made his eyes more luminous.

"I've lost something," he murmured. "Tell me, Hennie, shall I find it again?"

"You've lost," she answered, "but not nearly what I have. How could I have been the way I was? How could I have believed in the truth of Romeo and Juliet? And yet it's true, isn't it sometimes true, that a man and woman can go through life and never lie to each other? I don't know. I can't think anymore."

"Can't you forgive? If a person goes temporarily crazy, can't he be forgiven?" Dan's voice was low and hoarse. "Will you? Can't you, Hennie?"

"I told you I could forgive a love affair. It would be hard, but I believe I could. What I can't forget is what you said about wanting to divorce me."

"But I've told you how it was. And my God, I would cut off my foot to undo it."

"I was ignorant," she said, still staring out of the window at the people, all walking so fast on their way to church, or to an amusement park, or to visit the sick—all bustling along and full of life, as if it mattered.

"I was ignorant," she repeated, "I knew nothing at all about real people."

"And you still know nothing about them," Dan corrected quietly.

She turned to him, blazing. "How can you dare to say that to me after this? How can you dare?"

"Because to you there's only black or white. Good people, good ways to do things, and bad people, bad ways. You love or you condemn."

"Have you actually got nerve enough to be scolding me?"

"I'm not scolding. I'm only asking you to allow me the mistakes that I regret and haven't repeated for the last three years. And that I won't repeat. I swear I won't."

"Mistakes! Telling a—a trollop that you're unhappy with me, so that she can gloat over me while she sleeps with my husband—"

"We come back full circle. I don't know how else to explain it to you. I was caught . . ." He shook his head. "Give it a chance, Hennie, please? Lie down and rest. Sleep. Maybe it will heal the pain," he said as he went out and closed the door.

It did not get better. And one evening it became unbearable. She stood with her hat in her hand before the hall mirror and stared at herself.

Oh, she was awful! In these few days, two lines

had formed from her nose to the corners of her grim, pinched lips. She put on her hat, clapping it any which way over her untidy hair. Why? Simply because one did not leave the house without wearing a hat.

"Where are you going?" Dan asked, putting the newspaper down.

"Out," she replied.

The street sloped. Two blocks up, at the place where the slope became steep, the omnibus rounded the corner and took on speed downhill. The last one passed every evening at nine o'clock. Now she stood at the curb and waited for the whine and wheeze of its approach, and the blazing yellow eyes coming out of the darkness.

She thought: In one instant, so fast as to be painless, it would be over. This heaviness in the chest was so grievous a weight that to speak of heartbreak was no longer an exaggeration or sentimental figure of speech, but an absolute reality. Something was giving way, something breaking within her, and she did not want to live.

Dan came up behind her.

"If you do anything to harm yourself," he said very quietly, "I swear to you I will do it to myself too. And Freddy will come home to find both parents gone. And that little boy upstairs will have no grandparents."

The bus was already grinding down the street when she followed him slowly back into the house. She thought wearily: I suppose I wouldn't have done it anyway. At the last minute, I wouldn't have been brave enough.

* * *

Something began to firm within her, something hard and sore. It was the knowledge that she could do without him.

During these past weeks he had begun to eat his meals out and come home late. In the evenings she would sometimes sit in the kitchen with Leah, drinking the good coffee that Leah had freshly ground. Mercifully, throughout the first dreadful week or more, Leah asked no questions, nor did she even glance into Hennie's face. Only when Hennie was ready to give sign did she admit her fears.

"Of course you see that something terrible has happened," Hennie began, in a voice filled with tears. She stirred the coffee and stared into the cup. "I owe it to you to say something about it, I know. But it's hard, very hard—"

"Don't, then, unless you want to."

"It's not fair to you, you're part of this family." Hennie struggled, repeating, "I owe it to you."

Leah shook her head. "No, when it comes to owing, that's all on my side. You've given me everything, you've been my mother, you've taught me." Her light, cool fingertips touched Hennie's hand. "I would do anything in the world for you, don't you know that?"

The words and the tender gesture moved Hennie's heart; this was the daughter she had wanted. And, unable to speak, she nodded.

"Has Dan—may I ask—has Dan hurt you so?"

The silence ticked; it is my own blood pulsing in my ears, Hennie thought. To speak, to pour out all the grief and anger, the injustice, cruelty, shame . . . to rid oneself of their weight . . . She trembled. No! That's disgraceful, Hennie! Where's your courage? And she raised her head, not ashamed that Leah could see her wet eyes.

"As you say, I'm your mother. Mothers don't burden their children, they strengthen them. So let it be."

"You forget, I'm not a child anymore," Leah rebuked her gently.

"You're young! You have everything in the world to look forward to. When Freddy comes home . . ." Hennie swallowed hard on the name. "When he comes home you'll have such joy together! And he'll be kind to you, loyal to you. That's why I want you to have only good thoughts now."

"All the same, I might be able to help you if you'd let me."

"Dear girl, thank you. But help must come from inside. You know that from your own life. I'll get used to—to what's happened. I lived with certain fears . . . I stifled them, and now they've come true, that's all. So I'll live with that too."

Leah looked thoughtful. She opened her mouth as if to say something, and closed it.

"I'm sorry to be so mysterious," Hennie said.

"That's all right. But if you ever want to ask me anything, I'll listen. I might understand more than you think."

Long after Leah had gone to her room, Hennie remained at the table, comforting her hands on the hot cup and staring into the gray air. What might Leah understand? Did she possibly know something else about Dan? Well, there was nothing to be done about it if she did. I don't really care, Hennie thought; she's my own girl. The question is: What's

to be done about myself? Her mind drifted from
weary blankness to sharp focus and back again to a
blank.

Then she heard Dan come in. He stood in the
doorway behind her waiting for acknowledgment,
but she would not notice him. She felt him draw
closer, his presence seeming to warm the circle of
air in which she sat and he stood. Without looking
up, she knew the way his tie must be loosened, how
he complained because teachers had to wear ties!
She knew the crisping of the hair at the back of his
collar when he needed a haircut, knew the feel of it
in her fingers, and knew the feel of his fingers on
every part of her body.

Something struck at the pit of her stomach, giving a terrible blow.

"It's in my gut," she whispered.

Gut was Uncle David's word, one she had never
used.

"What? What did you say?"

"Deep inside." Hennie began to speak rapidly.
"Out there, down the street, you know where
they're building? I watched those men on the beams
with their hammers, or whatever those things are.
Ten stories above the street they work, on a narrow
piece of steel, with nothing to hold to. I think, I'm
amazed: How can they do it? It would be impossible
for me. And what you expect of me is impossible
too."

"I don't expect much. Just that after all these
years you might try to remember—"

"I remember all too well! Don't you see that's the
trouble? Oh, it's so sad. Everything is so sad. I had
so much love and tenderness to give you, Dan."

"You did, and you gave it."

She could hear that he was very tired.

"But I should have been stronger. And wiser. Because one is always alone."

For the first time she looked up at him. When he was old, he would still be strong. His hair would be thick and white. People would talk of how handsome he must have been when he was young.

"I must understand, I do understand," she repeated, "that one is really alone."

"That's not true. If you can't think that way of me just now, think at least of your son."

"I can't. He's a grown man. He'll have his own life when he comes back. If he comes back. I can't do anything about that either."

"Hennie, won't you try, really try, not to be angry at me?"

"It's not anger. I wish it were only anger. It's far, far deeper." She threw up her hands. "I can't describe it. I want to go away."

"Go away? Where to?"

"Out of here. I can't live with you anymore. These conversations don't do any good. They go nowhere. The atmosphere here is bad and the child is bound to feel it. I want to go."

Dan whispered, "If anyone's to leave, I will."

"All right, then. Let it be you."

"You don't mean it, Hennie. You can't mean it."

"I do. You and I can't stay here together."

She wanted to go down so far that there could be no more coming back up. She had no will for anything, wanted only to be left alone.

"Hennie, you can't mean it?"

"Yes. Go away, Dan. Go away."

3

It seems to Paul that he has been here forever, as if years must have passed since the blizzard winds and icy mud of the winter, yet it is only the following summer. At any rate, it is hot, except now in the hour before dawn, when it can be so shiveringly cold before the day's heat starts to blister.

Officers and men are at stand-to on the fire step with weapons ready. A little less than half a mile away, in the German front-line trenches, men are doing the same, each side waiting to detect the smallest movement on the other side. When first light comes, a blurry penciled line on the horizon, all will step down and no head will show itself over the embankment.

If there should be no long bombardment or no attack today, they will get some sleep. All through the night they have labored; patrolling, raiding, and repairing wire in no-man's-land; digging trench extensions, shoring up the ever-crumbling earth walls of the trenches, scurrying like ants or moles through this underground world to bring up ammunition, timber, sandbags, mail, and food from the rear.

At least this had been a "peaceful" night without bombardment, when the red sky burns and rockets flare, as on some Fourth of July gone deadly mad and magnified a thousand times over.

Hugging his shoulders against the chill, Paul has a moment of recall: the fresh shock of dawn when he rose to go fishing on a silent lake, or in an Adirondack stream crowded with trout, where the shoals flicker in the mottled shade . . .

The recall is gone. Silence here is only an exhausted pause before the air will shake again with hellish noise. There are no words for what has happened yesterday and all the days before.

He begins to think of all he has to do today. He'll check the men's cleaning of their weapons. He'll send back to the reserve trench for supplies. He'll write letters of condolence. A first lieutenant should be not only literate but literary, he thinks ironically; these letters are a dread to write. Dear Mother, your son died—how? (Died screaming your name, weeping out of his blinded eyes.) What is he supposed to say? They want to know something! Dear Newlywed Wife, your husband died—(He never knew what struck him, blown into a thousand pieces, maybe more, and lies shredded over the mud.)

A mist is rising in little white puffballs over the dark land. Soon it will be light enough to reveal the distant hill behind the German lines. There is no leaf nor blade of grass; it is as though the very concept of green has been forgotten.

At Belleau Wood it took a week to beat the Germans and cost fifty-five men out of every hundred, so it is rumored. Paul's own platoon is filled now with replacements. He himself is relatively new,

having come to replace a previous first lieutenant,
lost just before Belleau Wood. Next week or tomorrow there may very well have to be a replacement
for him.

There is nothing happening on the German front,
so perhaps it really will be a quiet day. Now comes
the first pink light, and at the same moment, two
birds fly overhead, calling; their cries are pure and
clear as that first light.

The men step down, splashing into calf-high water at the bottom of the trench; dispersing in groups
of two and three, they come forward for the breakfast that has been brought up from the rear.

"Sir?"

It's Koslinski, the sergeant.

"Sir, shouldn't we bring up another pump? We'll
soon be up to our asses in water."

The tone is respectful, yet there is something
mocking in it; the eye contact is bold. He is thinking
—saying, really—that Paul ought to have thought
about the pump. As a matter of fact, Paul has, and
has been about to order it as soon as the men finish
eating. Koslinski merely wants to embarrass him.

Koslinski doesn't like Paul. Paul knows that he
and a couple of others have "sized him up"; they
think he's finicky, superior, and probably not dependable. Paul is puzzled by this, because he has
always thought himself to be a democratic, friendly
type; nevertheless, there must be something about
him that offends men like Koslinski, and he is sorry
about it, but can't worry about it, either.

It's almost impossible to keep the trenches dry.
You can get used to standing in water, but you can't
get used to the rats that come with it, big black rats

that feed on dead flesh, on the corpses that tumble down from the parapet, and on the parts of bodies that float. Paul shudders, declining breakfast. It's the thought of the rats that has made his stomach heave.

"Sir?"

Paul turns at the whisper.

"Sir? What do you think? Will they attack to-day?"

It is McCarthy, just arrived this week. He's very young, about nineteen and looks younger as he frowns up at the rectangular strip of sky, which would be what you would see if you were lying at the bottom of a grave.

"Maybe not today," Paul answers, understanding that McCarthy knows that he can't know.

He heaves aside a sandbag that has fallen from the parapet.

"You could be bringing more bags," he says, giving the boy something to do.

The trenches are continually being constructed and repaired. You'd think, Paul says to himself, we were building a house. The master builder, he thinks, irony being a kind of weapon for self-defense.

Some of the men are still asleep. Rumpled and filthy, they lie cramped or sprawled in temporary escape. Others, awake, are bare-chested; they have pulled off their shirts to pick lice out of the seams. They're of any age from eighteen to maybe twenty-five, he guesses; they seem like children compared with his twenty-nine. One of them, named Drummond, was a salesman in a Madison Avenue haberdashery; it is very possible, they both think, that

Paul and he may have met in that other life. Paul touches the man's shoulder.

"You got a bunch of mail yesterday, didn't you?" he says. "Everything good at home?"

Pleased, Drummond tells him. "The twins were three last month. My wife sent pictures of their birthday, blowing out the candles."

"Fourth birthday, you'll be there," Paul says cheerfully. It's one of his responsibilities to be hopeful for his men.

Now, for a while, there is nothing to do but wait. He goes below to the officers' dugout and sits down, leaning his head against a timber prop, and closes his eyes. He should write home, hasn't written in a week; they mustn't be made to worry any more than they already do, but he is suddenly too weary to think of doing it now.

Marian—here in this place he thinks of her as Marian, not Mimi, a name too lighthearted for this place—writes to him every day. Her letters come in packets and he thinks of them as medicine, as tonic. She writes descriptively, so that he can see the flags flying over the marquees at Fifth Avenue department stores; he sees his parents at dinner and the circle of light making a pink stain on the plum-colored rug; he hears the crickets on Uncle Alfie's porch; he sees Marian's pen moving over the fine-grained paper, Crane's best, light gray with her monogram in dark blue: *M-M-W,* with the larger *W* in the middle, as is proper.

She sends snapshots of herself with his parents, or again at Uncle Alfie's; Alfie is holding a cigar, a Cuban, the best, of course. Paul chuckles. There's Meg in tight braids, poker-faced. She sends a snap of Hennie, standing in a city doorway, probably the settlement house; of Uncle David, to whom she has brought a box of goodies, at the home; of herself in Red Cross uniform; of herself, taken by an itinerant photographer on the street; she is standing in bright sunshine and he has caught her at her best, better than in many a portrait photograph; she's wearing a summer suit he thinks he recognizes, a cream-colored linen, worn with a pale straw hat. She is smiling, and is so slim and elegant and feminine and gentle. . . . "All my love," she has written at the bottom.

She is never effusive, she never overburdens him in her letters with her fears for his safety, as so many women do to their men here, or with laments about loneliness.

"I am thinking of the hour when you come home," she writes, "and of your being here when I wake up the next morning, and of the beautiful days we'll have together after that."

She is always cheerful; she has style. From this distance he can see her more clearly than ever; he is a lucky man and he knows it, when he listens to other men talking, sometimes about their wives and sometimes about their women who are not their wives.

He knows he has the average desires of any young, healthy man. Yet, on leaves, he has almost never been tempted by the prostitutes who sit around the bars in Paris. He wants a woman—oh, yes, he wants and he needs one! but not their kind.

One he wanted so badly, it was like fire. . . . He winces at the image of the name that now forms behind his eyelids: Anna. It's a long time since he has thought about her. He conjures her up now, wearing a velvet dress, which is certainly strange, since surely she never owned one. In thin, cool silk, then, blue-green as the August sea? No, not blue-green; that's Mimi's color. What about white? It would be like snow against that bright hair. And he remembers the floating dresses that women wear in quiet rooms a million miles away from here. She stands near a tall window with a book in her hand; he has surprised her and she smiles in delight; she puts the book down and comes to him, all warm, desirous, eager . . .

She's a married woman. She married the sober young man in the cap and jacket, don't you remember? The somber, overworked young man. He had no gaiety, poor fellow, not enough to fit Anna. . . .

Oh, how can you make such judgments after a minute's encounter? You want to think he's all wrong for her.

But she didn't love him: she married him without loving. There's no doubt of that.

He wondered how many men or women, if you could get the truth out of them, would admit that they married without love. His parents? How can one tell? They almost always are agreeable to each other, considerate and attentive, but is that love? He can't be sure.

Aunt Hennie and Uncle Dan, now—of them one can be sure. It's in her eyes when she looks at him, in his voice when he boasts of her, in the very air around them. Yes—and in spite of Dan's idiotic flirting—yes, there's love there, without a doubt.

He breaks off, sits up straight, and opens his eyes. Fantasizing again! Well, it's to be expected, isn't it, living from minute to minute as we do? Every man overseas, even the generals safe in some château fifteen kilometers to the rear, with sixteenth-century boiserie and topiary gardens, must have their fantasies, which would evaporate as soon as they got home again.

Mine will, anyway, Paul thinks, because they're foolish. They were never meant to be.

Or else they would have been, wouldn't they? Isn't that so?

What is meant to be, what exists and waits for him, is his library at home, with his mosaic of books from ceiling to floor, with the fireplace and the glorious Matisse, a field of white and yellow butterflies, hanging above it. And the dining room table set for late breakfast on a Sunday morning, with Marian sitting across from him, wearing the marabou negligee. She butters a piece of toast for him and speaks in her pleasing voice; past her shoulder he can look out toward Central Park; maybe it's a fall day and they'll get dressed later for a walk under the drifting leaves. These are real, these are what wait for him.

And he thinks too: a child will be real. A son. Two or three sons. To think that Freddy has one, a boy he's never seen! Suddenly he wants one badly, so badly . . . They'll wear sailor suits, they'll have merry faces; he'll take them to the park, buy toy sailboats, fine big ones with mahogany hulls, and they'll sail them on the pond and he'll stop thinking about Anna; he'll be husband and father—

Crash! Oh, Jesus Christ, here it is again!

A roar like an express train passing through, and then the crash, ten locomotives colliding, Vesuvius erupting, a 150-mile-an-hour hurricane smashing

through a town. The men dive for the dugouts. Paul
can go below to his own dugout command, but he
wants to stay above. It could be a light shelling,
soon over. Maybe.

Crash! Another, a close one, and he is knocked to
the ground by the impact; it was really close, that
one, doesn't do your eardrums any good! And he
remembers the time a few months back when he was
terrified that he'd been deafened, actually was deaf
for hours afterward. He makes himself small on the
ground, flattening shoulder and hip against the wall,
hugging the earth, wanting to crawl into it. Now
come some small ones; these whistle before they
crash; they're coming in low. Mechanically he
counts: ten, twenty, thirty seconds and a roar—
that's a big one—crash! and silence. Ten, twenty,
thirty seconds, a roar, another big one—crash! and
silence. Ten, twenty—it's getting heavier and
louder, they're coming faster and closer.

He crawls to a dugout and huddles again. The
. . . he . . . Fritz is preparing an attack. No
doubt of it. Mentally, Paul counts, trying to remember how many grenades he ordered from the quar-
termaster in case, God forbid they should get that
close. Must keep them at least forty yards back.
And he has a picture of them coming, sees their
pointed helmets near, nearer, until their faces appear, mad with hate and fear, as human and as in-
human as our own must be. He's been hand to hand
only once and doesn't want to think about it,
doesn't want to remember himself using a bayonet;
never thought he could; he had to and he did.

The terrible thud and roar, the whine and thunder, go on. From where he lies, he can see McCar-

thy vomiting. Saliva collects in Paul's mouth at the sight. This shelling is to soften us up, then they'll be coming, he thinks again, and hopes that their own machine gunners behind them won't aim short and get them instead. It's happened, God knows it has. In spite of the incessant pounding, he tries to think, then tells himself there's really nothing to think about, nothing for him to do but wait for the jangle of the field telephone with orders. So far, none.

Then he does think: This shelling's bound to knock out that jungle of barbed wire we've laid down ahead. They will get close enough, they will.

He jumps up to the periscope. It's foolhardy, but he has to see what's going on. Far in the distance he sees explosions, our shells cutting the German wire. So, then, the offensive that's been rumored, along with a hundred rumors that haven't come true, is true. Tomorrow, probably. His heart pounds. He's gone over the top once before, the time he got to use the bayonet. Leading the men, that's his job; he's left some good men on the field, dead or better off if they were dead. He came through untouched, with them falling behind him. He won't be that lucky again. Not possible.

Far off now, he sees a tree explode. It rises, splits, falls apart, and sinks. It's like a slow-motion moving picture. Queer.

One of the men is sobbing. Koslinski curses him. It's Daniels, a good man, but he's reached his limit, standing up and banging his head against the stony wall. Paul puts both hands on Daniels's shoulders.

"Take it easy. Lie down again and plug up your ears with your fingers, it'll help." His own ears are almost bursting.

"The noise," Daniels gasps.

"I know. Stick your fingers in your ears. Do it! Close your eyes. Come on, now," he says quietly and firmly between explosions; too much sympathy won't help the man and besides, Paul has none to spare. "You're in for the duration. We all are. You can stand it. I know you can."

Daniels lies down in the dugout, crying softly.

How long? Two hours now. Three. It may last all day. This fearful, god-awful noise may last all day. It lasted four days once. Last month, that was. Four days of this. Your head splits.

There's another sound. They've brought new heavy artillery, in the rear. That means, surely, we attack. Maybe not even tomorrow. Later today?

He can't contain himself. Again he jumps up and goes to the periscope. He sees—does he really? He sees . . . a thin gray line, thin as a wave at low tide. No. Yes. It is. They're climbing out of the trenches. They're coming.

"Up! Up!" he cries, and the men leap to the fire steps.

Where are his orders? The telephone jangles, he races and picks it up, but the roar is in his ears, all he can hear is a crackle, and has to guess what he's being told, has to think for himself. What's there to think about, though? Only fire! Fire! He knows when they get near enough, so it will count. He knows.

Now another roar, entirely different, with a buzzing in it. He looks up; three aeroplanes move across his narrow segment of sky. Three. But there may be more.

He looks back into the periscope and sees explosions all along the German line, attacks from the air. Then he catches sight of one machine swooping low, and flame bursts all along the line. They're firing machine guns from the air. Incredible!

It looks as though they're cutting Fritz down. But you can't depend on aeroplanes. It worked this time; that doesn't mean it will work again. Fritz was not really ready this time, that's all. He'll be back tomorrow, better prepared.

Suddenly he realizes that the shelling has stopped. It has been more than thirty seconds, surely. He counts. Thirty, forty, fifty. He waits. The men look up questioning, doubtful, hopeful. Two minutes, and three. Yes, they've stopped. Tomorrow, then. But respite for today.

Silence. A relative silence. Always there is the rumble of distant guns somewhere. It's said they can be heard across the Channel. They're in the north now, in the British sector. But here there is vast relief. The men stretch. They look green.

"Well, we're still here," Paul says. "Maybe we should try to catch some sleep while we can. Daniels, you stand sentry. You'll be relieved before mess."

Now at last he goes below and stretches out to sleep, with his hands behind his head. His whole body still feels vibration in the air, and sleep can't come.

His thoughts move restlessly like water, without form.

He can still hear the far-off pounding in the north. A few hours' journey by rail, if this were a normal day, and he would be in Germany. In a street of gables, clock-towers, and medieval cobble-

stones, he'd meet his cousins, men of his blood, even
though three generations removed. Three are not so
many.

In the town garden, walking under the lamps after a night of beer and sauerbraten, their footsteps
had rung. He remembered the day they bought
Freddy's dachshund. The gate's creak set a dozen of
the foolish little creatures barking with the ferocity
of lions. At the railroad station, Joachim had put his
arms around him.

"Auf wiedersehen"—not *adieu*—*"auf wiedersehen,* till we meet again," he said, in his careful
English.

Meet again! Now he was in the uniform of his
Vaterland. Strange, this fierce conviction, being
ready to die for that one-armed tyrant Wilhelm. Especially when the tyrant and all his kind despised
you.

But things are changing rapidly, Joachim had argued. Germany was the most civilized country in
the world. His will be a grand career; nothing stands
in the way. His sister has just married into a prominent German family, of Jewish faith, of course, but
German through and through. The future couldn't
shine more brightly for the family.

"Sir!"

Paul starts; he must have fallen asleep, after all.
Koslinski is standing with a tin plate in his hand.

"Thought you might want some of this. It's stew.
McCarthy got six cans in the mail. It's heated up."

"Tell him I thank him," Paul said. "And thank
you. Put it here. And oh, Koslinski, relieve Daniels.
I fell asleep."

"I've already done it, sir." The eyes, buried between jutting cheeks and forehead, are scornful.

"Thank you."

Paul sniffs the stew. It's good and hot, though it's mostly potatoes and carrots. Well, what did you expect out of a can? But awfully good. Koslinski really does despise me. . . . That pounding up north has stopped. With a piece of bread that he'd stuck in his pocket, he sops up the gravy. It's gotten very quiet. Except—he hears something. It sounds like a wail.

He goes up the steps, carrying the empty tin.

"Do I hear crying? Wailing?"

"Yessir. It's been going on for an hour. Must be some poor bugger caught on the wire," someone answers.

"Or beyond," says Koslinski, correcting. "It's farther out."

It's a thin sound. Suddenly it rises, grows stronger, and ends in a squeal.

Daniels makes a grimace. "Sounds like a pig slaughter," he says, shuddering.

He's from a farm in upstate New York. An unfortunate simile, Paul thinks.

It's growing louder and it's awful. Paul sits down. One must simply shut one's ears; this is another sound of war, that's all. But he wonders why the medics haven't gone for him, and says so.

"I think they tried, sir," Drummond answers. "Over from section forty-two, it looked like. I took a look-see through the periscope. He's too far out and covered by German guns over to the right."

"I'll take a look myself," Paul says.

He doesn't know why he wants to. Morbid curiosity? The light is going fast, so he adjusts the sight.

Yes, yes, far out past the wire jungle, now half blown away by the day's shelling, he can make out a shape, a darker gray lump against the fading gray day. The fellow must have crawled out of a shell hole. A sapper, probably, gone far ahead of the line. The shape moves, humping and thrashing. For an instant, something is flung up, an arm or a leg, one can't tell which.

Paul gets down. God, one ought to be allowed to shoot! We're more merciful to a wounded horse. Not that I'd like to be the one to do it. Still, I'd want someone to do it for me. No one would, though. God! The terror he must feel if he's still conscious, and he must be, thrashing about like that.

Paul drinks hot coffee. His men are talking among themselves, talking very low as if the Germans were next door. You got used to talking very low, when there was quiet. Voices carry at night. He catches some of what they're saying, something about getting laid by a widow with five kids. They're laughing. Good! It will take their minds off tomorrow for a little while.

The cries grow louder. Then there's a scream so terrible that the men stop talking and look at each other.

"He'll die soon, probably," McCarthy says bleakly.

He doesn't. Darkness falls, the men stand to and stand down, and still the screaming goes on. It's getting worse. It's intolerable.

Something jumps in Paul. My nerves can't stand the screams, he says to himself. I'm going for him.

He springs up and says it out loud: "I'm going for him."

The men stare at him. They are not sure they've heard correctly.

"It's almost dark!" he exclaims, "And I've got fixed in my mind where he is."

"Sir," says Koslinski, "it's suicide."

"No. I'll take a wire cutter, may not even need it, the way they've shelled."

The men can't believe he means what he says.

"He's too far out."

"Sir . . . there's no point risking yourself."

"If the medics could reach him, they would, sir."

"Wait until dark when the wiring party goes out for repairs, at least," Drummond suggests.

"That's hours away. He may be dead by then," Paul answers.

"It's suicide," Koslinski repeats. "Why do you want to do that?"

If he tells them that he can't stand the man's cries, they'll think he's crazy. And maybe he is at this point, although he doesn't think so.

"I'm going."

He climbs to the fire step and looks over the top. The sky is white and it's barely light enough, if one strains, to see motion on the field.

"It's crazy," Koslinski says, meaning *you're crazy*, but that's not something a man says to his commanding officer.

Paul scans the field. If he crawls, staying low, from hollow to hollow, flattening himself, they may not see him (that's stupid; of course they will). But still, if they do, he's too far away to hit with a grenade, and bullets will pass above him. Wriggle like a snake. And wriggle back like a snake, too, carrying the man?

"Don't go, sir," says young McCarthy. "Don't do it."

The screams have turned into a bellow, the most hideous, agonizing lament under the heavens. If I live to a thousand, I'll never forget it, Paul thinks, and swings himself up over the top and plunges, gets down on all fours, and starts to crawl.

A snaggled end of barbed wire tears his hand. He shuts his eyes to protect them. He should have thought of heavier gloves. It is slow and painful, cutting wire. He thought he saw exactly where the wire barricade was destroyed, but he hasn't got it right and he has to do a lot of cutting. Yet he is making a path, shoving the ends aside. He'll be able to find it on the way back, he hopes.

So far, no one has seen him. He calculates that he's been out about fifteen minutes. The terrible bellowing comes closer. This crawling position, keeping head down, is exhausting. His knees are torn, his hand is bleeding, and the back of his neck is a tormenting ache, but he mustn't raise his head, must not. He lies down for a minute to rest, smearing his cheek with damp earth. It occurs to him that it would be prudent to turn back, but he takes another breath and starts on ahead.

Then he falls into a shell hole, landing on something soft, and eases out with a shudder, not wanting to think that the softness was a body, which he knows it must have been. A dead body, better off than the one who is still screaming. He imagines he can make out the words "please . . . oh, please," but probably it is just a long drawn out *e-e-e-e*. He keeps crawling.

He's there. He's reached it. The shape is humped

and now not moving, but still crying out. Somehow he wriggles himself beneath it, laying it over his prone back, with the arms drawn around his neck. It's heavy, so its weight will keep it from rolling off. And he turns around. The way back will take much, much longer, of course.

It dawns on him that the men were right, that he really is crazy to do what he's doing. But if this man who lies on his back goes on living because of him? "He who saves one life saves the whole world." He remembers that from religious school. Hennie liked to quote it.

The man is hot and breathing heavily, snorting in Paul's ears. The weight falls off; he wriggles it on again and they proceed. He stops with no breath left, and raises his head an instant to see how much farther it is.

At once there's machine-gun fire. It passes over him and the earth spurts just ahead of him. They've seen his path. He stops and waits. They may think they've hit him if he waits without moving. He counts off seconds, and when he's counted two minutes, starts crawling again. The guns rattle and the earth explodes. He's in their sights; he's in the center of a circle of explosions. Now, even if he stops moving, they know where he is; he has only a thousand-to-one chance of getting back, so he might as well keep going.

The rattle, whine, and thud seem now to come from everywhere, which is impossible; it only seems that way, as if he's at the center of a circle, and from 360 degrees around him they are aiming bullets. He keeps crawling. Suddenly he is so certain of being hit that he is no longer panicked; it's the end for him, no doubt about it, and he's numb, calm, as if it had already happened. So he goes on, inch after inch. . . .

The crown of his head strikes something plump and firm: sandbags. Sandbags! He can't believe it. But it's not over yet. He lets his burden slide from his back, to take the final risk, to pull himself up and, crouching as low as possible, still heave the burden—from which now come not screams but stertorous, heavy groans—up onto the bags and roll it over into the trench, trusting that someone will catch it before it crashes. And then, with what must be his last strength, mount the parapet and tumble in.

Now is when it will happen, he thinks; I hope it's my head, so I won't feel anything and won't live to be a cripple. At the instant I scramble up, that's when it will come.

But it doesn't come, and he is back after the last scramble, back on the floor of the trench, with his heart pounding so, he thinks he can taste its blood in his mouth, salty and sour.

His "burden" lies on the floor, faceup. The sky has gone abruptly black—that accounts for my escape, rather than bad aim, he thinks grimly—and the face is obscured. Anyway, everyone is staring not at the poor face but at the wound, a hole in the abdomen large enough to put two hands in. Blood leaks as if from a pouring spout or an emptying sack, while from the thing—was this a man?—the groans and gurgles are diminishing.

"The medics are on the way, sir," Koslinski says. Someone puts a rolled-up cloth, a makeshift pillow, under the head on the floor. It is a humane gesture, useless and unfelt. The groans grow fainter.

Someone thinks of asking Paul, "You all right, sir?"

"I'm sweating," he answers. "Soaked," and tries to pull away from the cloth that's sticking to his shoulder blades.

"It's not sweat, sir, it's the guy's blood," Koslinski tells him, and stares at Paul, looking puzzled.

The medics come hurrying down the communication trench and kneel to look. The sounds have now stopped. The thing on the floor is still, quite still.

"He's dead," the medic says unnecessarily.

No one answers. They put the body on a stretcher and go hurrying back up the communication trench. No one says anything for a minute. How many bodies have they seen? How many more will they see? Yet this one has been different.

Then someone brings hot coffee for Paul. He doesn't want it, but it's something to be doing. They stand around watching while he drinks it.

"Jeez," says "little" McCarthy, "he could have been a German, sir. You didn't know."

Suddenly Paul is too shaken to answer. The answer he would make if he could, would be, "What difference?" Some of them would understand that, and others would not. The way of the world.

They're in awe of him. He sees it in their faces. It's embarrassing. They've dispersed a bit, talking softly.

"He ought to make captain tomorrow morning," he hears.

"Captain? Commander of the Allied army!

Christ, what guts!" It's Koslinski's voice. "Not one in a million. Who'd ever think he—"

It's really embarrassing. Brave? First I was mad with fear, then numb with it. It was only that I couldn't stand the sound of that man's agony. Poor bastard! I wonder whether he felt much pain. They say you don't when you're hit like that, you're in shock. I don't know. Poor bastard. Yet . . . I wasn't a coward.

And suddenly he recalls one of Freddy's first letters from the war: "I was so glad to find out I'm not a coward," Freddy had written. And while Paul was moved by that, almost to the point of tears, he didn't truly understand it; it seemed so youthful, so naive. Now he understands it and sees with what unjustifiable arrogance he once judged the simple words: I'm glad I wasn't a coward.

Three years ago, that was. Ah, poor Freddy, where are you? But you'll be all right. Having escaped harm for this long, it means you're charmed and marked for survival.

Abruptly now, the sky lights up again with a blaze in the northwest. There is a distant rumble as in a summer storm, and again Paul has that flash, recalling a place he loved: the Adirondacks, and being a child safe in bed, with the fragrance of pine in the room.

"Somebody's getting it."

The men have mounted the fire step, poking their heads out into the night.

"How far you figure it is?"

"About forty miles, maybe."

"The Limeys getting it, then. Must be up near Armentières, I guess."

Paul raises his head toward the northern sky. Fountains of light erupt and cascade like waterfalls, like flowers, silver and scarlet, high, higher, over and over in unending splendor. Strange that it should be so beautiful, he thinks.

When those gorgeous lights die down over Armentières, it is clear that the tumultuous day has brought neither victory nor defeat, but only stalemate. Now it remains to get ready for the next day, repairing damage, bringing ammunition to the front, and carrying the casualties to the rear.

In the British lines, the wounded are being assembled for transport at the dressing station.

"This one has got it bad. Have a look."

"Leg gone."

"Blimey! Both of them, you think?"

"Sure. No question."

"Looks like that Yank chap, doesn't he?"

"I don't know. Well, maybe. What was his name?"

"Fred something, I think. Ross? Something like that."

"Well, look at the tags! We haven't got all night!"

"Wait, wait a second. Here it is. I was right. It's Fred Roth. R-o-t-h. Roth."

"Well, take him up. We haven't got all night."

4

Angelique's shocked disbelief had turned, with the passage of days, to indignation. "Where on earth has the man gone?" she demanded.

"He's staying in his room over the lab," Leah answered, glancing toward Hennie. "He told me to tell you if you asked."

"I haven't asked," Hennie said.

So he had returned to the room that had been his home; there Freddy had been conceived; the snow had sifted so high on the windowsill that one could see it from the bed without raising one's head; the shade had flapped in a hot summer wind; there the music had lain helter-skelter on top of the bulky old piano . . .

Suffer there! she thought. Mourn for your loss!

Angelique opened her knitting bag, closed it, and thrust it impatiently aside, as if to say: I am in no mood for anything as trivial as knitting.

"Charity!" the word was contemptuously thrown. "The great benefactor of humanity walks out, abandons his wife after twenty-three years!"

Hennie answered curtly. "He has not abandoned me. I sent him away. Let's get that clear."

"I don't understand. You won't talk. What is this all about? You won't talk—"

Very quietly, Leah said, defying Angelique's look of dislike, "Sometimes there are things people can't talk about."

"Thank you, Leah," Hennie said.

There was a Sunday afternoon staleness in the parlor, an air of limbo. We sit like three crones in the dusk, Hennie thought, and got up to switch on all the lights.

Angelique stood up too. "Well, since you won't talk, I don't see how I can help you. God knows I would if I could. Everything's crashing. It's this war. Everything crashes when there's a war. I re-member—" She checked herself and sighed. "It's getting late. I might as well go home."

"You won't stay for supper?" Leah asked, in the correct tone she reserved for Angelique.

"Not tonight. Maybe tomorrow. Let me know if you need me." And Angelique gave her daughter her dry, not unpleasant kiss, which smelled of her clear, flowery perfume.

To give her full credit, she had been coming every day since Dan's departure, had brought flowers and food. The poor woman was distraught. She had not even said, "I told you so," or "I warned you," which, in the circumstances, she could well have done. All of this had to be appreciated.

Still, it was less taxing when she did not come. Then Hennie ate in the kitchen; Hank in his high chair took all of Leah's attention, except for an occasional worried glance at Hennie, who ate her few mouthfuls in silence.

Only once Hennie looked up to meet the girl's full gaze and said, "Leah, you are a daughter to me." Then a terrible retributive anger brought from her a thing she would have sworn she could never say: "You know, he never wanted you."

"I know that," Leah answered calmly. She lifted the boy out of the high chair and removed his bib. "He telephoned today. He would like to see Hank."

"Let him come when he wants. I'll go to my room or be out."

Suddenly one day, Hennie's lassitude dissolved. The nerves at the pit of her stomach began to seethe like water at full boil. She couldn't sit still; she had to move. The tension became unbearable. She began to turn the house inside out.

Leah was astonished. "Surely you don't need to do everything all at once!"

"Yes, the place is awful. Never mind helping me. You worked all day, and anyway, I prefer to do it myself," Hennie told her as, in cap and long apron, she stood at the ready among her assembled tools: scrub board and wringer, dustpan and dusters; rug beater, camphor, tar paper, sponges, buckets, and beeswax. She swept the carpets with tea leaves; she aired the blankets, took the curtains down, scrubbed them, ironed them, and hung them back; she washed the furniture with vinegar and water and polished it; she washed all the china and emptied the drawers; she dusted every book on the shelves.

Exhausting herself, until her back ached so sharply that she was barely able to straighten up, she took solace from her exhaustion. Wronged and victimized, unvalued and shamed she had been, yet she could be proud of her strength and her will to survive.

After a while, when she could do no more, the frenzy died and the lassitude returned, so that she dragged through the days. In the afternoons she took Hank to the nearest scrap of a park and sat there, watching him play. Other women were there, watching other children, but she avoided them. And she felt that her loneliness must be visible to all, like those misty white halos around the heads of the figures in religious paintings.

She longed for a woman to talk to. Angelique was out of the question, so was Leah. She had, these days, many memories of her sister. Through half-closed eyes, watching Freddy's child scrape with pail and shovel in the hard earth, she was at the same time seeing and hearing vivid moments out of an old life that now, oddly, seemed secure and good.

Florence comes into Hennie's room, swirling the flowered ruffles of her first evening dress before the mirror. Florence wakes her at midnight to bring a napkin full of petit fours. Filched from the party just for Hennie, they are chocolate and strawberry pink. Farther back, much farther back, Florence and Hennie are scolded and punished. They lock the bedroom door and cry together. Then, forward again in time: Florence gives birth to Paul. Hennie is the first to hold the baby when he has been swaddled; she carries him to the light and studies the tiny face.

"Why, he looks like you," she tells Florence. He did, and still does. The patrician head and the calm air of noblesse oblige are all his mother's.

What will she say to Paul when he comes back and finds what has happened in this, his second home, as he always called it? What will she say to Freddy? He will be devastated. Yes, this business will devastate him.

Oh, it is better never to love anyone at all! If she had not loved Dan, she wouldn't be sitting here like this on this park bench, among the pigeons and noisy traffic and indifferent passersby. If she hadn't been wounded . . . And she was conscious of her hands, locked tightly together on her lap, with their dark blue veins bulging from the strain.

Summer came. The city smothered under a hot bronze dome. At night, people slept on their fire escapes, burning citronella candles to keep the mosquitoes away. Sometimes, when Hennie leaned on the windowsill, she could see people sitting up late, often a solitary man or woman on a stoop, staring into the darkness.

Other times, in the early evening, she rode the Fifth Avenue bus. On the dark Palisades across the Hudson a few lights gleamed. You could imagine the fragrant dampness among the trees over there. She rode the bus as far as it went and rode it back downtown.

It was always deep night on the backward trip; young couples sat with their arms around each other, sharing a scarf or sweater; around them, there was no aura of loneliness. What did they know? She saw them with pity and scorn. Better for them that they couldn't see ahead! She felt an urge to reach out and touch the young girl sitting in front, whose head rested so confidently on the shoulder of the man, to reach out and say—say what?

One evening she came home from her ride to find her brother waiting.

"This heat," he said, fanning himself with the newspaper.

He had obviously come from the office, dressed for business as he was, with his high stiff collar and, since Decoration Day had passed, a straw boater in place of the usual black derby.

"This heat! You look exhausted, Hennie."

"I'm all right." She had no wish for commiseration. "I've just had a bus ride. Why aren't you in the country?"

"We're going Friday, as soon as Meg's school is over. Hennie, how long are you going on like this? We're all so worried about you."

"Well, don't be. I'm all right, I tell you."

"Are you going to get a divorce?"

"There are no grounds for one. And anyway, I wouldn't want to make the effort."

"Well, then, will you ever go back together?"

"No, I won't go back."

Alfie clucked his tongue. "I'm sure I don't understand it all! I'd like to know what it's about! Then maybe I could make peace between you and Dan." His face wrinkled in distress. "Nobody talks to anyone anymore. That old business with Florence and you, what's that for? Emily and I never quarrel with anyone!"

"How is Emily? How is Meg?"

"Emily's fine. Busy packing the summer clothes.

And Meg takes all the honors in school. She certainly doesn't get that from me."

Hennie had to smile. "No, she certainly doesn't. Give her my love. I haven't seen her in so long. Haven't seen anyone," she murmured.

"That's just the point. That's why I've come. We'd like you to spend a week at our place. Cool off. Relax. Bring Leah and the baby, naturally. Do you all a world of good."

All that hearty jollity! She'd have to go on hikes, walk out to see the new colt, play croquet, and sit through convivial dinners. . . . Shaking her head, she demurred.

"I insist," said Alfie. "Make it the Fourth of July. You've never seen a bang-up country-town parade. We'll have just a small group. I'll ask Mama. Then there will be Emily's cousin, Thayer Hughes. He's an English professor, lost his wife a few years ago. A good sport. We always have him over the Fourth. And Ben Marcus is coming, he's a young lawyer, not from my regular firm, but I've been doing some real estate deals with him and we've gotten friendly, so I asked him to come out and look over some property in the area." Alfie was enthusiastic, trusting to his eagerness to keep Hennie from refusing again. "Yes, a very decent young fellow. He's got ulcers, or did have, so the army refused him. I think he feels humiliated because of it. So it's settled for the Fourth. I'll drive you out, so you won't have to lug the kid's stuff on the train."

"What a gorgeous car!" Leah cried. "A Pierce-Arrow, isn't it?"

She was delighted with everything, with her smart new duster, her goggles and veil, tightly fastened against the rushing wind. She could hardly sit still, and, to Angelique's annoyance, kept turning and twisting around to point things out to Hank, who sat squeezed between herself and Hennie.

"Look here, Hank, see these snaps?" She was showing him how the celluloid storm curtains worked. "You can close them when it rains, and here you'll be, all snug and dry!"

The car bumped onto the ferry. Belowdecks the engines rumbled and the boat began to move across the Hudson. Ahead lay the Jersey shore, faintly arched like the back of a tortoise and, like it, speckled brown and yellow-green. Alfie and Ben Marcus got out of the car to stand at the bow.

"I'm getting out too," Leah said.

"You'll be blown to pieces," Angelique objected. "Look how the wind's tearing at their coats!"

"I don't mind, I love it," Leah said, crawling out.

"Well, leave Hank here with us, then. It's dangerous having him stand near the railing. I declare," Angelique complained when Leah was out of earshot, "that girl can't be quiet for two minutes in a row."

They watched her walk to the bow, where the men moved to make room for her between them; the wind, catching the slit in her narrow skirt, blew it apart to reveal for an instant a sleek silk thigh.

"He's got an eye for her already," said Angelique.

"Mama! You don't mean the young man?"

"I certainly do. He's a foxy fellow."

"Well, he does look something like a fox," Hennie admitted.

Ben Marcus had a sharp, slender face; his hair was sandy red, with eyebrows and lashes to match. He had a keen look, not at all unpleasant; in his eyes there could be seen a readiness to laugh.

Angelique frowned. "And she a married woman. She ought at least to discourage him."

"Why? What is she doing? I'm happy to see her so cheerful. She's got enough on her mind."

Mama is positively prurient, Hennie thought; she would be shocked to know that she's prurient.

"You always think ill of Leah. Look at her now, just look at the pretty young thing."

For Leah had turned her back on the shoreline to lean against the rail, talking with animation; her hands moved gracefully as she related something that was apparently amusing, for both men were laughing.

"I've always told you I don't think she's pretty. Striking, yes. Attention-getting, yes, very definitely."

The sky grew wider on the Jersey side. Enormous puffy clouds floated westward with the car, over little rivers and through little towns one like the other.

After an hour or more through open country, they neared a county seat. The road widened; great elms met overhead to form a dark green roof. Farms gave way to the estates of gentlemen; behind wrought-iron gates and tailored hedges, one could glimpse courtyards and stables, carriage houses and conservatories.

Leah's head kept turning from one side to the other.

"That one on the right is supposed to be a copy of Hampton Court. Paul told us, I remember. And

Uncle Alfie, doesn't the one over there on the hill belong to Rowell Evans?"

Ben twisted around to see. "The railroad Evans?"

"Yes," Alfie said, "he raises prize Guernseys, they're his hobby."

The county seat still clustered around its eighteenth-century green; neat, prosperous shops on all four sides were busy with the afternoon's trade, as they drove through.

Halfway to the crest of a steep hill, they passed an unoccupied car. The owner had left a toolbox open on the running board; the tools, tire iron, blowout patches, and a shovel with a collapsible handle lay scattered on the verge.

"A Winston," Leah said.

Alfie heard her. "How on earth do you know that? Did you know it, Ben?"

"I don't know a thing about autos," Ben answered. "Living in New York, you don't really need one."

"That's true, but I love them," declared Leah.

"He's in plenty of trouble, whoever he is," Alfie remarked. "Four flat tires! Tough to get even one when you're going uphill, of all places."

"He was going down the hill," Angelique said.

Leah corrected her. "No, uphill. That's an antique he's got there. On those old models, the gas goes into the carburetor by gravity and it won't flow forward on a hill this steep, so he'd have to back up."

Ben was curious. "How do you come to know about things like that?"

"My cousin Paul told me once."

"By gosh!" Alfie cried, calling back over his

shoulder. "You've got a memory like an elephant, Leah." And, turning to Ben, "She's quite a woman, that young lady."

It was as Alfie had promised, a "real bang-up parade." The whole town and surrounding country-side had come to cheer. There were horse-drawn floats with the minutemen, and Washington crossing the Delaware; there were Betsy Ross and Patrick Henry. More than a dozen stalwart old men marched in Civil War uniform. Flags and bands surrounded the car that bore Uncle Sam in white chin whiskers and stovepipe hat; Miss Liberty, draped in red, white, and blue, carried aloft an appeal for Liberty bonds. The wheel spokes on the car were draped with daisies, poppies, and cornflowers, while the sun rained gold upon the happy warriors. All was triumph and jubilation.

None of this, thought Hennie, seems to have any connection with the trenches. And a trickle of cold dread seeped deep inside her, as if she had drunk ice water while standing here in the summer noon.

Beside her, little Hank rode high on the shoulders of Ben Marcus. The man and the little boy had taken to each other. Well, of course! The child needed and missed a man; she wondered whether it puzzled him that Dan wasn't in the house anymore to read a story at bedtime or keep him company over cereal in the morning.

"You're thinking of your son."

The gentle voice came from Thayer Hughes, who was standing on Hennie's other side.

"Well, yes, partly," she answered.

"Spangles and drums and hip-hip-hoorah. Still, I suppose it's necessary."

"I suppose it is."

"You have just the one son?"

"One child. To my regret," she said.

"I have none and my wife is dead. I sometimes think loneliness is a sickness."

"That's as good a way as any of putting it."

"Your husband and you are separated? Emily mentioned something."

Most surely she would have mentioned something.

"Yes," she said. "Separated."

She was not offended, as she might have been had some other person intruded on her privacy. For the man was mannerly, a true cousin to Emily. At first sight of him she had thought, with faint amusement, that he even looked like the popular image of a professor, thin and slightly stooped in his good tweed jacket. His thick hair, just touched with silver and in need of barbering, surrounded a face as serene as Emily's, with an added air of masculine authority.

"Are you shocked?" she asked him.

Thayer smiled. "No, not at all. That's middle-class morality."

Hennie's smile was inward. The man would only imply, being too well-bred to say aloud: I—we—are all of the upper classes. Dan wouldn't like him at all, she thought, and found him agreeable nevertheless.

"Would you care to walk back?" he asked her when the last of the parade had passed the firehouse and dispersed. "It's a good cool day for a walk."

"Why, yes, I would," she told him, while Meg said she would come too.

"It's going to pour before the day's out," Alfie warned. "Look at the thunderheads!"

"They're hours away," Thayer assured him. "We'll be home long before they get there."

So the three set out, Meg leading, while the rest of the party rode home.

"We'll cut off the main road and down this lane; it will take us to the tail end of our place and you'll be able to see the new hundred-acre piece that Dad's just bought," Meg directed.

They passed through the fields to the gardens, Meg explaining all the way. Neat rows of strawberries in white blossom lay alongside the delicate feathers of asparagus; to the left stood a grape arbor and to the right a row of raspberry canes.

Hennie paused; there was a sudden stillness in the air. "Feel how quiet it is," she murmured.

Thayer looked up at the sky. "I'm afraid it's the quiet before the storm. I miscalculated."

The sky had gone gray. Roiling clouds had come over from nowhere; a narrow gap of blue was closing fast.

"It's lovely, anyway. I've lived in the city all my life, and yet this does something rare for my spirit."

Thayer smiled. "Perhaps it's ancestral. The plantation memories in your blood."

"Oh, no, never that! That certainly skipped me! It's my brother who's got the feel for all this."

Hennie picked a handful of berries, pale rosy globes, segmented and veined, observing, "These look like onions, the skin's so thin."

"Gooseberries, Aunt Hennie. Awfully sour, only

good for preserves, really." Meg, striding always ahead, spoke with authority.

"There's something rather touching in the confident way she's taking charge of us," Hennie whispered to Thayer.

"You feel that too? But yes, you would understand."

"Why do you say that?"

"Because I see how soft you are. You're soft as Meg."

"Then you are probably 'soft' yourself."

He smiled, without answering.

Meg turned around. "I can milk a cow, you know. Would you like to go into the barn? We've two new calves."

Obliging her, they followed, touched the cows' rubbery pink muzzles and watched the calves nurse. When they emerged from the barn, thunder was just over the hill and overhead the livid sky flashed eerie green lights.

"Oh, Dad was right!" Meg cried. "We'll have to run for it!" And pulling her skirt up to her knees, she went leaping away from the path into tall, wind-bent grass, taking a shortcut through a hummocky field.

A sudden furious gust whirled barnyard grit into Hennie's eyes. Leaves flipped over onto their white undersides; a chill swept through the air, and branches, whipped by the wind, lashed dangerously about. The first rain spat.

"Run faster!" Meg, far ahead, called back. "It's going to pour!"

It was a long way to the house. Hennie's skirt

caught in stickers; tugging it loose, she ripped it.
One shoe came off.

"Go on, Meg, don't wait for me," she called.

Thunder now split the sky; lightning sizzled and
crackled.

"Not under a tree!" Thayer cried, pulling Hennie
by the arm. "That's the most dangerous place, don't
you know that? Here, this way, we can't make it to
the house." A rickety structure stood hidden, squat-
ting low in the shrubbery. "Here, into the gazebo—
isn't that what this thing is called? This'll be safe
enough."

The "thing" was a small octagonal space with
fretwork sides open to the weather; it had been neglected, but the roof was sound, and by standing in
the center one could keep out of the rain, which was
now coming down in torrents, flailing the earth.

"Sorry to be an impediment," Hennie apologized.
"Really, you should have gone ahead with Meg."

"Not at all. I wouldn't think of it."

"It's these shoes. Not meant for running." She
smoothed her dampened hair, caught her breath,
and, feeling a sudden awkwardness, sighed. One
could imagine oneself in a children's playhouse
here, or an explorer's jungle hut; in either case, what
could one do other than just stand, breathing close
together, waiting for the storm to pass?

After a minute or two she found something to
say.

"Alfie's been talking about fixing this up. With
the benches repaired, it might make a nice quiet
spot to read in, don't you think so?"

The rain, drumming on the roof, muffled her
voice, so that she had to repeat her words for him.

"Yes, rather nice," he said. "Do you do much reading?"

"I don't know that you'd call it much, compared with what you must do. Right now I'm halfway through *Sister Carrie.*"

Thayer's eyebrows went up. "Really? A banned book?"

"I know. It's supposed to be pornographic."

"Indeed. My cousin Emily mustn't know you've got such a thing in the house."

Dan said Emily was "lusty." This man sees her primness. Which is true?

Thayer said wickedly, "Come to think of it, I never see any books in this house at all except the Bible and Omar Khayyám on the table in the parlor. But then, every house in America has those side by side. A funny juxtaposition. I wonder they don't see the humor of it. So you're really reading *Sister Carrie?* What's your opinion of it?"

"I feel sadness and pity. I think it shows that women's lives can be very, very hard. Unfair and cruel."

The man considered her a moment before he answered.

"You looked very beautiful just now, saying that."

At least, Hennie thought that was what he had said, but the rain was still so loud that she was not sure, and so said nothing.

"I've just told you, you look very beautiful."

"Thank you." To her own ears she sounded shy and uncertain, like an awkward girl receiving a first compliment.

"You shouldn't be living in a vacuum," he told

her then. "You're in life, but you're not of it, and it shows."

She swallowed hard. She wanted to tell him she already knew that and that he should leave her alone, but her words did not come and the quiet, insistent voice went on close to her ear, under the roar of the storm.

"I said before that loneliness is a sickness. But the cure is at hand, you know."

A terrible crack of thunder shook the earth and sky; the little roof itself shook as though it would cave in. Hennie drew her collar around her ears and closed her eyes, while the crashing reverberated as though the very planet were being riven apart.

Suddenly she felt his hands on her shoulders. She felt herself being turned around, and her eyes flew open. He was pulling her to him, so that the length of her body, from shoulder to hip, was held against his, a supple, hard male body. There was a joining, a fitting, familiar and right; astonishing that it should instantly be so! That in a second should come a flash of realization: How she had been missing this, wanting this! How empty, otherwise! She pressed closer. Warm, warm . . . His mouth held hers; she inhaled from his flesh a fine aroma of cologne and pipe tobacco. For a long, reeling minute—minutes? they stood so.

Then something struck into the core of her brain and she fought loose.

"No—not here!"

"Of course not here. There's no place. But I can find one tomorrow."

The thing in her head expanded, quivered, vibrated. It took on a color before her closed eyes:

black, the color of fear. Wanting, not wanting, knowing one ought not to want, being afraid of oneself. She found voice, murmuring, "Oh, no! I didn't mean that—what you're thinking—"

The man's light twinkling eyes were amused. "Hennie, save your energy. Don't try to be indignant because you think it's expected of you. You know you liked it."

In the face of that rational calm, indignation would be absurd. Besides, she was not indignant, merely fearful, merely confused.

"But I'm not going to do it," she said.

"Why not?"

"I really don't know why," she answered wonderingly.

"I'll tell you. A thousand years of morality, that's why. Jewish morality. Oh, don't be insulted, I'm not anti-Semitic! It is Jewish morality, though. It started with you people."

"I can't help that," she murmured.

"Or is it that you still feel you 'belong' to your husband?"

Now anger did rise. "I don't want to talk about that. It's my affair."

He bowed. "You're right. And I apologize."

He flushed and turned his back to look out at the slackening rain. She understood that he was feeling the humiliation of her refusal. And she wondered what he was privately thinking of her: that she was a fool? I would never have suspected this of him, she thought. He didn't look like the kind of man who would—and yet that was absurd! What kind is a "kind of man"? It occurred to her that even young

Leah must know far more about the world than she
did.

Thunder, moving away, made a distant rumble
and slow drops splashed from the eaves of the gazebo. Only a fine steady rain grayed the air; the
storm was over. There was nothing left for them to
do but separate as soon as possible.

Thayer said formally, "We can make a run for it
if you're ready. I can give you my jacket to throw
over your head."

"Oh, no, oh, thank you, I'm fine," she told him,
and then, not speaking, they walked back through
drenched grass to the house.

Stretched in the high white tub, Hennie rested,
while a faint steam rose from the hot water, filling
the bathroom with the scent of Emily's geranium
bath salts. Under the water, clouded by the salts,
her legs rippled, while ten round toe-tops protruded
darkly pink from the heat. Her belly was flat, unlike
the soft jelly flesh of a woman who has had many
children. Her breasts were high, not pulled toward
the navel like the breasts of a woman who has
nursed many children. Her body was still young,
which was a sort of compensation . . . but its
youthfulness was wasted.

After a while she climbed out and began to dress
for dinner. The last time she had stood before the
tall glass in this room, she had watched Dan struggle with his collar studs and heard him grumble
about the idiocy of getting all dressed up just to eat.
It crossed her mind, as she examined herself, that it

would be a fine thing if he could know what had just happened to her this afternoon.

So that's the way it went! It was that easy. There it was; you didn't have to reach out to a man—if you were attractive, that is.

You're a lovely woman, he had said, or something like that. Oh, he might well have been just playing the game, probably was used to playing it, but he wouldn't have chosen her to play it with if she hadn't appealed to him! She examined herself more closely in the glass. Definitely, she was looking better, far better than she had for a long time. Maybe it was because of these few days of sunshine, or country milk or—or something. Or could it be only because of what had happened this afternoon that her eyes were so clear? The whites were almost blue and the irises were almost golden.

Your leaf-shaped eyes, Dan used to say. Like autumn leaves. Damn what Dan said! She could see for herself. But it was really irritating that he couldn't know she could do exactly what he could, if she wanted to.

Why hadn't she wanted to? A thousand years of morality, he'd said. She laughed. More like five thousand, Thayer. Was that the reason? Maybe. Part of it, anyway. And the other part? Oh, damn the other part . . .

Afterward, she remembered every smallest detail of that evening. The mushroom soup had been too thick; the asparagus, of which Alfie was so proud, had been perfect, as were his further pride, his everbearing strawberries. The new wallpaper in the dining room was royal blue, overlaid with medallions and arabesques; she would remember thinking that Leah, who knew about Syrie Maugham and the vogue for clear white, must be disapproving of it.

After dinner, as usual, the scatter rugs in the parlor were rolled away, for Alfie and Emily, who took lessons in ballroom dancing, liked to practice. Meg kept the Victrola wound.

In her awakened mood, Hennie was almost exhilarated. She watched Alfie and Emily's complicated maxixe, then Ben and Leah's jiggling turkey trot. Sharply observant, as if she had all of a sudden begun really to see other people again, she noticed that young Ben was especially clean and scrubbed; when he laughed, he showed clean handsome teeth. She decided definitely that she liked him.

Thayer Hughes had sat down with Angelique on a small sofa at the farthest end of the room, making it clear that he did not intend to dance, and clear, too, that he intended now to keep away from Hennie. One long leg was gracefully draped across the other as he leaned, inclining his elegant head toward her mother. Angelique would be overwhelmed by this attention. She wouldn't discern the man's dry irony and secret scorn, the scorn that implied that nothing mattered.

Yet his sensual touch had been a delight: locked, warm and curved—she could feel it still. Strange, because she knew now she didn't like him. Yet she owed him something.

Alfie and Emily were dipping and swaying in expert style. Emily's expression was calm; did she— and her cousin Thayer—just not believe in showing emotion, or was it not in them at all? On the other

hand, Alfie sweated and beamed as he threw himself
into the dance. He worked every minute of his life,
worked even at having a good time. He wanted all
the people around him to have a good time, too, and
to like him for making them have it. Still, one felt
good watching him. Even Angelique was uncon-
sciously tapping her feet.

The music stopped, and Meg, serious about her
job, went through the pile of records.

"How about a tango this time?"

"Make it a plain fox-trot," Alfie told her. "I want
to dance with Aunt Hennie and unless I'm mistaken, she doesn't know how to tango."

"You're not mistaken," Hennie said.

"Well, are you having a good time?" he demanded, and before she could answer, assured her
that she must be, because she was looking more like
herself.

"Like that painting over the sofa? It's new. A
Braque. Paul told me to buy his stuff."

Hennie considered. "I'm not a judge of art, but
it's interesting."

"Well, I don't like it at all and neither does Emily,
but he's already famous and it's a good investment.
I'll tell you something, Hennie. I wouldn't say this
to anybody else, but I'm making money hand over
fist with Dan's little tube. The company can't fill the
orders fast enough."

"War money, Alfie."

"Okay, but do you know how many German subs
have gone to the bottom because of those radio loca-
tors?"

Men gasped, gurgled, suffocated, screamed in
horror. The thing exploded, the waves closed over,

it plunged down into darkness: How far? Two miles down under the sea? Hennie shuddered.

"I know what you're thinking. But it's dog eat dog. Their men's lives, or ours."

"It should be no men's lives."

"Yes, when men grow wings. All right, I won't talk about it. What do you think of that fellow Ben?"

"He's pleasant. Honest, too, I would say."

"Turns out his younger brother was at Yale with Freddy. He remembers Freddy, met him a couple of times with his brother. He's smart as they come, he'll do well. I enjoy being with him. Pity I can't introduce him everywhere, though. He's a bit too Jewish, doesn't fit in with certain people, if you know what I mean."

Anger tightened Hennie's throat. She said carefully, "I'm not sure I do."

"Of course you do! A little loud, a little forward, wears flamboyant ties—"

By their neckties shall ye know them, she thought, not knowing whether to feel more sorry for Ben Marcus or for Alfie.

"For instance, he's not the type who'd be accepted at the country club."

"You don't belong to it, either."

"I'll get in soon. I've friends who are pushing for me. Prejudice dies hard, but with Emily being my wife—" Alfie did not finish.

Nor did Hennie make protest, since protest would accomplish nothing. But to think that he would tolerate membership among people who didn't want him, let alone seek it!

Then she remembered Freddy's love affair with

British aristocracy. Was that the same damaged ego of the outsider, longing to be in? She thought not: Freddy was too loyal a Jew for that. For him, it had more likely been a question of aesthetics, admiration for British refinement.

Strange that she had been thinking of Freddy at the very instant when the telephone rang. . . . Alfie picked up the receiver. Looking surprised, he turned to the room to say, "It's Dan."

For a few minutes he listened. Meg shut off the Victrola and everyone waited. Hennie's mouth went dry and her palms went wet. All the jollity seeped out of Alfie's face, like water disappearing down the drain.

"Legs?" they heard him say. "Yes. Well, I'll drive them back, first thing in the morning. There's nothing one can do tonight."

When he hung up, he spoke softly, looking from Hennie to Leah. "Freddy's been hurt. His leg. Or legs, maybe."

Leah's hand flew to cover her mouth. And Hennie steadied her voice, but it came out like a croak.

"How bad?"

"I don't know," Alfie replied.

He does know, Hennie thought, and can't bear to tell us. He does know.

5

There was nothing to say. On slat benches, they made a semicircle around Freddy in the wheelchair; Dan, Leah, Angelique, and Hennie, with strained false cheer all vied to talk to him—or, rather, at him —while trying not to see him.

Eyes wandered to the dazzling sky, the gloomy ivy on the walls, the hale young nurses walking briskly between the buildings or pushing young men in wheelchairs—anywhere but to Freddy.

"Why didn't you bring Hank today?" he demanded.

Leah bit her lower lip between her two slightly prominent upper teeth; she had developed the habit just since Freddy had come back.

"We thought perhaps he bothered you the last time. It's a long ride from New York and he's so cranky when he misses his nap."

"How can you think he bothers me? Bring him!" Freddy said angrily.

Early fall winds, blowing from the north, had scattered a few rusty leaves on the lawn. In deference to the chill, a nurse had brought a blanket to cover what remained of Freddy's lower half, but the government-issue wool, thick olive brown, might as well have been transparent, so clearly could one imagine the stumps.

"Obscene!" Freddy cried abruptly, bewildering them all before they could comprehend.

On the far side of the enormous quadrangle, two teams in wheelchairs were playing some sort of ball game.

"They keep trying to make me play, but I absolutely refuse. I was no athlete when I had my legs, so why should I be one now?"

There was no answer to that. And Freddy resumed, "Did you know I had a letter from Aunt Florence and Uncle Walter? They're coming to visit me. I guess it takes something like this to bring people together. It's rotten that grown people should behave like enemies over nothing. Nothing that matters a good God damn in the end."

Dan was staring straight ahead across the lawn. His lower lids were puffy, as though he hadn't slept. Well, of course he hadn't; who could? His jaw was dark. He hasn't shaved since yesterday, Hennie thought.

They hadn't spoken to each other during any of these visits; Leah and Angelique were buffers. She resented having to make the visits with Dan, but it couldn't be helped.

The rancor still burned, gnawing within her like an ulcer. An ulcer, however, with proper diet or surgery, could be cured; but where were the surgeons or diet to cure Hennie's burning?

One might think that, in the face of this new, far greater anguish, that other would be forgotten. On the contrary: It loomed larger. For what would it do to Freddy when he found out that they had parted?

Hennie felt tears gathering again, and, swallowing hard to stifle them, said, "Uncle Alfie said be sure and tell you they're expecting you in the country as soon as you—get better."

Freddy ignored that. "You haven't told me about Strudel; does he get along with Hank?"

Leah and Hennie glanced at each other. Leah spoke first.

"I'm sorry. We hated to tell you. He caught pneumonia last year—oh, it's more than a year, and we lost him."

"Didn't you take him to a vet, for God's sake?"

"Oh, yes, but it wasn't any use. I'm sorry, Freddy."

"Well, I want another dog, then. A dachshund just like him, brown with a black streak down the back."

Petulant, like a child, Hennie thought. He was so young, still so fair that his jaw looked as free of hair as a little boy's. And after all the agony, there were no lines in his face.

Oh, my God, my son, what's happened to you!

Leah, with shadowed eyes, nervously biting her lip, looked older and more troubled than he. It was going to be very hard for her, too. . . .

Hennie's heart kept fluttering: it slowed, it speeded, and frightened her. She couldn't afford to be sick now, with so much to be done. She wondered how it was that she was able to keep the tears from falling. Why, she had sobbed so that day when the dog was killed! But then, in Freddy's presence, she had to contain her tears. For her own sanity, she had to.

It was strange, too, that when you were here with him, you couldn't bear to get up and leave him, while at the same time you waited for the visiting period to be over so that you could get away.

The hired car waited in the parking area. Leah took Hennie's arm without speaking. Angelique was crying into a handkerchief, and Dan was silent, walking with bowed head.

Somebody called Hennie's name. A woman was stepping out of a limousine and coming toward her. The sky fell; it was too much, all in one day! And something tore apart in Hennie's chest, so that at last she could sob, while Florence, sobbing, too, opened her arms. . . .

She heard Florence murmur, "Hennie, Hennie, I don't know what to say to you."

Don't say anything, only let me feel the comfort of your arms.

When minutes later, they broke apart, they simply stood there looking at each other.

No one paid any attention, as cars and people came and went; in that place, in that time, tears were a common sight.

Around them, though, a civilized encounter had begun to take place.

Walter grasped Dan's hand. Dan said, a trifle uneasily, "You remember Leah, of course?"

And Walter replied with gallantry, "I remember a delightful little girl."

Then Angelique felt weak and had to sit down in

the automobile. Water was brought; her little spell of faintness forced a diversion from overwhelming emotion.

Walter cleared his throat. At once, Hennie remembered that he always did so when he was moved; she had not thought he could seem so familiar to her after all these years. He had scarcely changed, nor had Florence, in her dark red suit, soft veiled hat, and pearl choker.

"Are you satisfied with the care? If there's anything I can do, let me know. I have a cousin, a second cousin"—Walter corrected himself meticulously—"who's quite a name in rehabilitation."

"I suppose they're doing here whatever can be done," Dan replied. His voice was thick. "But yes, when the time comes, I'll ask you. He'll need all the help he can get."

Walter cleared his throat again. "It's terrible. When we heard it, we felt . . . a wretched thing, unspeakable." He took his glasses off to wipe them. "Paul's still over there, you know."

"I know. We—I think of him always."

"And he always thought of you. He used to say—" As if he were suddenly embarrassed, Walter subsided.

"Oh," Florence cried, "this awful, awful war! Paul writes that—but no, you've enough to think of without my giving you any more." She caught Hennie's hand. "I wish—I wish we could turn time back and start all over. And do things differently. We want to help you. Do whatever we can, only we don't know what. You'll come to us, will you? You and—"

But she did not say "Dan," so she knew. Of course. Mama would have told her in great detail.

"I will. Leah and I will come," Hennie replied. "Do you want us to go in to Freddy now?"

"He expects you," Dan said.

"We've brought some books," Walter announced. "We thought he might like a few novels, something light. And cookies. I don't suppose they get much of that sort of thing here."

Florence touched Hennie's cheek. "You'll manage, you've always been strong. And God will help you."

"God," Hennie said. "What good has He been? Where is His great compassion and love that we are taught to trust in?"

Her voice rose, keening, as if, having forgotten for a few minutes what she was doing in this place, she had suddenly remembered. It was the reference to God that struck her with horror. The earth reeled. She was caught between Leah and Florence. And she heard Dan's voice.

"Hennie, don't lose your faith. Now is when you need it."

Counsel from one who had never been a believer! She looked up, thinking for a moment that he might be ironic, but his eyes were filled with pity instead.

She looked away, and steadying herself, permitted Leah to help her into the car.

Dan tore through the streets. The odor of wet stone rose from the pavement where the street cleaners had just passed. Milk was being delivered; the horses clumped, the bottles jingled in the carriers. It was that early.

Not long after midnight he had awakened out of fretful sleep. From where had the idea come? From a startling dream? No matter where from, it had seized him on the instant like an unmanageable force, a command. He had then lain awake waiting for dawn, had dressed and been out soon after dawn. In a frenzy, he had walked and walked, all the way downtown past houses and factories and shops, coming at last into the sober, discreet streets where money was made and lost, borrowed and lent, where money was king.

The rush hour had barely begun, but Alfie had the habit of early rising; he would be in his office. Dan checked the scribbled address. Across the street it was, a tall building, twenty stories high. Alfie was on the ninth. The front was marble, dark gray, slick as glass, and the double doors were brass.

He saw himself reflected in the bank's window before crossing. *I look like a madman with flying hair. Damned hair always flies. Forgot to change my shirt—cuffs are filthy. Oh, well, Alfie knows me. Likes me anyway.*

The neat matron at the reception desk, behind the rose in the bud vase, was arranging her pencils for the day. He pushed past her astonished mouth and eyebrows. In the wide front room at his wide desk Alfie sat talking to a thin young fellow: *Who? Ben Marcus. Came to see Freddy at that place. Lawyer. Accountant. Business with Alfie.* Dan's memory clicked like a mechanical toy.

Alfie stood up. Immediate worry spread over his face.

"Dan! Has something happened?"

The rage that had been silent since midnight broke now, fired and scattered like bullets.

"I want the money! I want every damned cent of it!"

"What are you talking about?" Alfie stammered. "What money?"

"The money! All that stuff you—you sold—my stuff, those patents, stock—" Now Dan stammered too. His mind stopped clicking; it was blinded in a surge of anguish. "It's not for me, I wouldn't touch the dirty stuff, it's for him. For him, don't you understand?"

He was made aware that he was shouting at the top of his lungs when Ben Marcus shut the door.

"Please," Alfie said, "sit down and calm yourself. I don't understand. I'm ready to listen."

"They took his legs!" Dan cried. "They took his legs!"

"I know," Alfie said. He put a hot hand over Dan's. The manicured nails lay on the grimy cuff.

Quietly, Ben asked whether he should leave the room.

"I've nothing to say that you can't hear. I want my son to get something out of the lousy war, that's all I want. Something to compensate—" He put his head in his hands, then looked up bleakly at two pairs of pitying eyes. "Compensate. As if you could."

"No," Alfie said softly.

Suddenly Dan straightened, alert and alarmed. "You still have it? It's not all gone? Because I said I wouldn't take it?"

"It's in trust. You didn't think I could just throw

a bundle of stock into the wastebasket, did you? Yes, it's there, considerably grown since we last talked about it."

"Ah, yes. So it's a nice amount? Enough to keep him and his wife and child? The kid, Hank, with a crippled father, I worry—"

Alfie smiled. "Enough to keep them pretty splendidly, I should say. Incidentally, the War Department has renewed the contract." The smile twitched ever so slightly, ever so wryly.

A thrust. I-told-you-so. Well, let him. He's entitled to it. I must look foolish, reversing myself. Except that it's not a reversal. Not for me. Never. For my son. He needs it, no matter where it came from.

"How soon can I—he—have it?"

Alfie turned to Ben. "Tomorrow? Can you go over the figures that fast?"

Ben nodded. "Late this afternoon, as far as I'm concerned. The lawyers will probably need more time, for the trusts and—"

"I'll have them rush it. Ben's taken over as my accountant," Alfie explained, "and a damned good one too. His legal background's a real asset. Otherwise, I've stayed with my old law firm."

He stood up. Ben stood up. So Dan had to. Dismissal. Prerogative of the busy man.

"It really will be all straightened out by tomorrow, Alfie?"

"Come back tomorrow afternoon, late. No, meet at the lawyers'. Around four. You may have to wait; I've a closing at one-thirty and could be delayed. And Dan, now that everything's to be in Freddy's hands, he'd better be in touch with the lawyers and with Ben here. He'll need advice. I don't suppose he knows the first thing about money management."

"He's never had any to manage."

Alfie put out his hand; it shook Dan's, pumping it.

"Can't tell you how delighted I am that you've come to your senses about this. God knows, I wish the circumstances were different, but anyway—"

"Yes. Thanks, Alfie. And thank you, too, Mr. Marcus."

"Call me Ben. We'll probably be seeing a lot of each other."

"Ben."

Friendly face. Decent fellow. But canny. All these people who know about money. Keeping it safe. Making it grow. It's what they live for. Blood in their veins.

"Well, thanks. I'll see you both tomorrow, then. Thanks again."

He felt relief, sinking in the elevator. Something positive had been accomplished, like wrapping up a package in smooth paper, firm, taut, with a tight knot.

The air felt good out on the street. It would feel even better in the schoolyard again, with the kids screaming. Better in the lab, with the pigeons cooing, messing the windowsill. Cleaner and truer air than in this place, where money was king.

Still, Freddy needed it. . . .

Some weeks later, Alfie propped his elbows on Hennie's kitchen table.

"Yes, you should see him. He's been in a frenzy

ever since he came in demanding the money. Can you give me a sandwich or something? I'm starved, I haven't been home. He made me go look at the house he wants to buy."

Hennie cut bread and meat and spooned a helping of apple pudding while Alfie talked on in a disjointed rush.

"You know Emily and I would be glad to let them stay where they are in the wing with the little fellow. Lord knows, the place is big enough. The help's there all winter, and the country air would be good for Freddy. But Dan says no, they have to be in a place of their own."

"Well, I think that's so. And anyway, Alfie, they couldn't stay at your place because it would be too much for Leah to commute every day. It's really wonderful that her bosses have given her all this time off, but they do want her back soon, and she'll have to go if she wants to keep the job."

"Not anymore she doesn't. When your crazy husband refused to take his share, I took it in stock for him, and it's been piling up, quadrupled in two years. Freddy's a rich man, Hennie."

The words spun in the air and buzzed away with no real meaning. Hennie frowned impatiently.

"Where is this apartment? On the ground floor without steps, I hope."

"Not an apartment. A house, I said. You should see it! Right off Fifth Avenue, near the museum. Right in the midst of the fanciest German Jews. Below Seventy-ninth it's all gentile, of course."

The words began to take shape.

"A whole house?" Hennie repeated. "A private house?"

"Yes, aren't you listening? I tell you, I'm staggered! And you know I'm one who doesn't mind spending money. But this place! It's fit for a king. He's going to put in an elevator," Alfie added.

"How much does it cost?"

"The house? Hold on to your hat! Twenty-five thousand!"

"I don't understand . . . this money, this stock —what's it worth?"

"A little over a hundred thousand dollars, and that's only so far," Alfie said triumphantly. Taking a bite of the sandwich, he watched Hennie's reaction.

Certainly she had read in the public print about the fortunes that were being garnered in the war. Certainly she knew that there must be more of them that didn't come to public attention. Many were crooked, she knew that; but most were within the law, because, quite simply, waging war was expensive and those who could produce for it, made money. Yes, she knew all that, and still she was stunned.

It seemed as though there must be some trick to it.

It didn't make sense. All his life, the man had worked in a classroom, six hours or more a day, besides the evenings marking papers at home; year after year of early mornings he'd struggled through cold and dark to get to school; with a rueful grin, he'd told of clanging radiators, the smells of wet wool and boys; and all of that had brought nothing compared with this gadget he had played with; a puzzle, a toy it had been, a game to satisfy his curiosity. Yet a shower of gold was the reward for it!

She was dazed. "So much."

Alfie laughed. "Not when you think of Ford or Morgan's bank or U.S. Steel. But it's great, all the same. And the best part is, this outfit is going to keep right on earning when peace comes. I'll have to have a talk with Freddy, teach him how to invest. Build the pyramid. Listen, the closing's early next month, then I can show you the place while Dan's at work one day. I'm to have a key so things can be delivered. He's already been buying things right and left."

"What things?"

"Furnishings. Can you believe it of Dan?"

"He's furnishing a house for them and not asking Leah?"

Alfie shrugged. "He wants to do it his way. Says Leah can go to blazes if she doesn't like it."

Hennie stood on the sidewalk between her mother and Alfie, staring up. The morning sun fell white upon the brick-and-limestone facade of a fine Federal house, elegant and authentic; a pair of evergreens flanked the front door under a fanlight. The brass knocker gleamed like a gold coin.

Had Dan taken total leave of his senses?

"Wait till you go inside," Alfie said proudly, as if the house were his. "It's in splendid condition. And being so near to the park and the museum, it will be nice for Freddy."

He opened the door. The vestibule led through a second door into a circular reception hall, paneled in pale blond wood. The floor was marble; a dark red carpet covered the curving stairway.

Angelique took a quick breath, making quick appraisal.

"That paneling! It's all hand-carved!"

"I tell you, the place is a gem," declared Alfie. "Come on up."

On the second floor, at the front of the house, three tall windows faced the street. Painters had been at work, so that two walls were already finished in a subtle green, pale and fresh as the inside of a cucumber. A grand piano shone like jet in one corner near a window.

"A Steinway. Nothing but the best," Alfie said. "He wants Freddy to play again."

The perfect instrument, the one thing Dan had coveted and would have bought for himself if he had been able to afford one!

At the curve of the piano, in a large porcelain jar on a plinth, stood a thriving gardenia plant.

"Left by the former owners," Alfie said. "They left a few things when they heard about Freddy, the stair carpet and a handsome bookcase in the library. Awfully decent people. In fact, they hurried the closing out of consideration—although I'm sure it helped that Ben Marcus knows their lawyer very well and spoke to him for us. Ben's been really helpful, came out last Sunday to take Freddy for a ride. Guess this thing needs water, I think I saw a can or something downstairs," he recalled, and bustled away.

Hennie touched the keyboard, sending a tinkled note into the bright air. Standing by this piano, this object of exquisite refinement, she could look down on the refined street; she watched a governess walking two little girls in English tweeds, a nursemaid

veiled in navy blue pushing an English perambula-
tor and an upholsterer carrying a Chippendale sofa
into a house. An English decorum reigned. She was
overcome by confusion.

Angelique had collected herself.

"You know, Hennie," she said, in a low, indignant voice, "it's you who should be living in this
place instead of that girl Leah. If anyone has a right
to it—all your life you've had nothing."

"Oh, Mama, I'm tired, let's not start that again."

All my life I've been plagued by this sickly nostalgia for luxury.

"—won't even tell me what the trouble is between
you and Dan. It's really a shame that you won't
confide in your own mother."

Alfie had just come back with the watering can
when the doorbell rang. "Oh, that must be the girls!
I told them we'd be here." And he bustled away
again.

"Well, anyway, we have Alfie to thank for all
this," said Angelique. "Whatever else he may do—"

(Like joining the Episcopal church, Hennie
thought.)

"—you have to admit he's the best-hearted man
in the world. And as I always say, with the golden
touch!"

Hennie walked back to the piano. The sight of it
moved her to tears. If there were any possession that
might bring joy to Freddy, this one might. Here in
this airy room, he might make music again. That, at
least, was left to him. She slid her hand in a caress
over the slippery keyboard.

Yet one didn't have to live in a place like this to
make music!

Of course, Freddy would need money. The government's pension would hardly support his family, even with Leah working. So it was understandable that Dan would take some of what—because it was death's money, tainted and hideous, from sources that he rejected and fought all his life—he had refused before now. But this grandeur?

The women came babbling up the stairs. She recognized, in the voices of Emily, Florence, and Mimi, clear notes of surprise and admiration. And Angelique's again: "—the golden touch, yes, Alfie has it."

If I have to hear that once more, I don't know what I'll do, Hennie thought, gritting her teeth.

The women were followed up the stairs by two men lifting a desk, and these were followed by a smaller, fussy man who was apparently in charge.

"The desk goes here," he directed. "The two wing chairs in the back of the van are for here too. The pair of florals. And the clock!" he called, as the men started back down. "The gilt wall·clock. Bring something up to hang it. I don't want it lying around."

He turned to the women and introduced himself. "You're all family, I suppose? I'm Mr. Scaline, the decorator. I've not had the pleasure . . . Mr. Roth has been doing all the ordering alone," he explained, with a lift of the eyebrows to indicate that that was extraordinary in itself.

"But Mr. Roth has excellent taste," he assured the astonished women. "Excellent, indeed. I've had no problems with him at all."

"Now, who would think it of Dan?" asked Alfie. Hennie alone would have thought it. The others were judging him by his careless dress, but she knew his taste and was not surprised by it.

Now appeared a pair of handsome chintz-covered chairs, along with the clock and a Sheraton table. Mr. Scaline clapped his hands to his forehead.

"Dear me, I forgot about the table! And the lamp that's to go on it, of course! You must forgive me," he explained to the onlookers, "but Mr. Roth is so particular about rushing things through in a hurry that I find myself in a state of confusion. However, we're getting there, we're getting there," he finished with satisfaction as two Chinese ginger jars were brought in and placed on the mantel to flank the clock.

When the man had gone, Alfie took all but Hennie on the tour of the house. Left behind, she sat down on one of the new chairs. The scintillating sunlight played over the parquet floors, revealing an intricate golden grain, like the whorls on a fingertip. From the clock, which hung between two miniature gilt Ionic columns, there came a cheerful chime, as though the mechanism were aware that its duties in the new home must be promptly begun. Already the house was coming alive. Dan might have said that Leah could go to blazes if she didn't like it, but the fact was, Hennie was sure that Leah would. Its costly simplicity was what she would recognize. Yes, this was beautiful, no doubt of it.

Beautiful and wrong.

The voices came back, still babbling their amazement.

"It's elegant, Hennie," Florence cried. "Really elegant."

Far more so than her own dark brownstone off Central Park West.

"And on such a splendid street!" There was no envy in Florence's tone. "I hope it will be very, very good for Freddy," she said softly.

Mimi inquired who was to take care of such a large house—easily twice the size of her apartment.

Alfie explained, "The couple who worked for the former owner will stay on. A Mr. and Mrs. Roedling. Swedish. The man will help Freddy, lifting and—" He stopped, glancing at Hennie.

"And Dan has bought a car. Mr. Roedling knows how to drive," Emily reported. "There's to be a nurse for Hank too," she added in a tone of mild disapproval, "since Leah will not give up her job."

"I've spoken to her about that," Alfie said, "and so, I believe, has Dan, but she likes her work. She says she doesn't want to be dependent on Dan's money."

Angelique made a correction. "But it's Freddy's money now."

"Well, yes, but after all, Dan earned it," Alfie answered.

Earned it! Hennie thought. Dan wouldn't say so!

Alfie frowned at her. "You're so silent. Is something wrong?"

"I'm often silent. Haven't you noticed?"

"She's just thoughtful," Mimi said gently. "And why not? She has enough to be thoughtful about."

A silence fell momentarily upon the little group, a silence that seemed to echo, making the empty house larger and emptier. Into it, Mimi spoke again.

"It seems as if Paul's been gone a hundred years."

"They say the war will be over soon," Angelique said desperately.

"Oh, it surely will be. Any day now," Alfie assured them. "Well, shall we go?"

And they followed him, one by one, down the red carpet and out through the door of Freddy's sumptuous new house.

6

In the early spring of 1919, on an afternoon of blowing wind, Paul, having made his first visit at his parents' home, made his second one to Freddy.

A fire snapped in the comfortable library, a snug enclosure of burnished ruddy wood, Oriental rugs, and lamplight. Freddy's "man" having brought a tray with tea things, Mimi poured and served. The little sandwiches and iced cakes were the same as they'd always had at the Werner house and were quite familiar to Paul. It was just that it seemed so odd to be having them in a house that belonged to Freddy!

The wheelchair had been drawn up near the fire. Its warmth had caused Freddy to throw off the plaid rug, peppered with cigarette burns, that had covered him from the waist down, so that now what had happened to him could be seen in its full horror. Stumps. Half a human being, with the swollen broadening of the shoulders that comes from using crutches. Paul felt twinges in his own legs; a grimace pulled in his jaw and forehead; he couldn't bear to look and couldn't avoid looking. Mimi, more fortunately, was able to be busy with the tea things.

"You have your boy and Leah. They need you." Paul was ashamed of the cliché, yet what other way was there to answer Freddy's lament?

Freddy let the cliché pass. "Captain's bars, I see. What is it? Can't bear to take off the uniform?"

Paul winced. The sarcasm, if it was sarcasm, was so unlike Freddy.

"No, I've lost a lot of weight and my suits have to be altered."

"Mine too," said Freddy.

Mimi took another cake, remarking pleasantly, "I've got my appetite back since you've come home, Paul. They're so good! Have another, Freddy?"

"The thing is," Freddy said, "I'm of no use to the boy. He's a lively little kid, much more than I ever was."

I taught you to ice-skate, Paul thought, and said almost frantically, "But you are of use! There's more to life than sports. The real you is here, even though—" And he stopped short, unable to finish, "even though you've lost your legs."

"And Leah loves you," Mimi said.

"You've been wonderful," Freddy told her. "Your wife's come regularly, Paul, and brings me books." For a moment the old, soft, dreamy look passed across his face. "And Meg comes after school. She's only fifteen, but we can talk. Your mother comes, and mine . . . whenever she's sure my father won't be here. Whatever all that's about! Do you know?" he demanded suddenly.

"I don't think anyone does," Mimi told him.

"As if there isn't enough misery without making

more. . . . You knew when Uncle David died, I suppose."

"Yes, on Armistice Day," Paul answered.

"With all the crazy celebration in the streets and the whistles blowing. Do you remember New Year's Eve in 1900, Paul? Well, it was like that."

"Oh, I can remember," Paul said. "But can you, really?"

"Yes. I was lifted up to the window and my father said, 'He'll always remember this night.' "

Freddy's eyes were cast down toward the fire, which, flaring, made his pale lids almost transparent. What else was he seeing in the flames? No one spoke. The teacup clinked when Mimi put it down, jarring the stillness.

"What do you think of this house?" Freddy asked abruptly, looking up.

Paul was not sure whether he was supposed to have a favorable opinion or not; something in Freddy's voice made him unsure. He took, then, the cautious middle road.

"It's a fine, solid house."

"Well, you're accustomed to fine, solid houses. I'm not. Frankly, I don't know what to think of it and don't particularly care. Well, maybe it'll make a difference to my son someday. He'll be an American gentleman, almost as good as an English one."

Mimi and Paul, troubled by this terrible bitterness, exchanged quick glances.

And Freddy cried out, alarming the dachshund, who had been asleep in his basket, "The people who started this war ought to be shot! Wilson, too, the whole lot of them."

Paul said nothing. A sadness filled his chest. The

words that he could have spoken and would not speak, because they would have been too cruel, came to mind: And what about you? With your great crusade and your scornful attacks on pacifists like your parents?

"You know that line of Wilfred Owen's," Freddy said slowly, " 'These are men whose minds the dead have ravished'? At least I have got my mind left. Maybe that's not so good, though. I can remember too much. Mud and rats and bodies and rats eating the bodies."

Neither Paul nor Mimi stirred as he leaned forward and held them with a blazing stare.

"Do you know we fought three and a half months at Passchendaele? Fought in the mud, and lost a quarter of a million English boys? Yes, we fought. I learned to fight hand to hand. With grenades. They're more efficient than bayonets. Yes, and I remember Gerald's letters, his mother's too. 'Gerald died a hero,' she wrote." Freddy laughed. "Oh, yes, a clean, neat, instantaneous death with a bullet through the heart, or toppling gracefully from a white horse with your country's banner held high!" He subsided.

Out of the corner of his eye, Paul caught his wife's frail shoulders trembling. And he said very quietly, "Still, in spite of all, you know, the world would be a very different place if the Kaiser's side had won."

"I can't say it would, Paul."

No, it probably wouldn't matter to him. Without legs, nothing would matter very much. And Paul grasped at something else to talk about.

"You've a good head for detail. It's just occurred

to me"—actually it just had, and might or might not be such a good idea—"that maybe you'd like to study banking. Bankers sit most of the day. What do you think?"

Freddy's eyes went back to the fire, which was flickering into cinders.

"I can't think about anything yet. But thanks anyway."

Paul stood then. "We'll talk about it another time. I'm afraid we've tired you."

"No. I'm just tired, that's all. You didn't do it."

Intensely shaken, Paul and Mimi went downstairs, out onto the street, where a cold cheerful wind was blowing.

"I keep remembering what he was like," Paul said. "All that poetry, before he went away! Thanking God for this brave hour or that fine hour or something." He brushed his hand over his forehead, which ached. "What terrible innocence, I thought then. And now this bitter despair—it could break your heart."

At the street corner they met Leah, hurrying home. It was not until Mimi and she called out to each other that Paul recognized her; without that, he might possibly have passed her by. She had grown much older, and yet was young: her sleek bobbed hair was a cap worn under the peak of a small bright blue hat; two flat curls lay on her lightly rouged cheekbones, and her skirt was as short as the most daring fashionables in Paris had been wearing them before Paul set sail for home.

"Oh," she murmured, "so you've seen him . . . isn't it frightful?"

Paul kissed her cheek, from which breathed a warm perfume.

"Isn't it frightful?" she repeated. "What do you think of him? What's to happen?"

"Unanswerable questions, Leah."

"I know. He just sits there. Sometimes, oh, very rarely, he'll go to the piano and let his hands drift, not really playing anything. He won't let us wheel him into the backyard because he says people can look down from other houses on him. And here we are, only a few yards from the park, but he won't go there either, because people will see him and pity him." She sighed. "He'll only see people in the house."

"We'll keep coming," Mimi assured her.

"I know, you've been so good, Mimi. I must say that people really have been. Ben Marcus comes. He cheers Freddy a little, I think. And, of course, Dan comes. But that upsets Freddy some; he can't understand what's happened between Hennie and Dan. Nor can I, God knows! Everything's fallen apart."

"In spite of it all, you manage to look well," Paul told her. It was the only remark that came into his head.

"I have to. It's my job. That's the only thing that's going right. I've had a big raise and it feels good. Good not to be dependent on Dan Roth. I have to live under the roof he paid for, I can't help that, but at least I can support myself."

"I must go and see Dan," Paul said. "How is he these days?"

"Working, the same as always. But if you ask me, he's tormented. I think he must be remembering his

last words to Freddy before he went overseas. You
know what he said to him? He called him crazy, a
crazy damned fool. 'You're insane,' he said. He was
so angry, he was almost mad with it."

The wind blew around the corner where they
were standing.

"We're keeping you," Mimi said, and Paul knew
she wanted to get away.

Leah held Mimi's arm. "No, it's all right. I can't
ever talk to anyone about this, you see. It's pent up
in me. I can't be honest about my feelings, they're so
ugly. I can't tell Hennie, can I, that the day I first
saw Freddy in the hospital I had to run to the bathroom to be sick? It's not all because of pity, either—
although it's mostly that—but also, when he's undressed, I can't bear to look, and I'm so ashamed of
myself." She was pleading. "These are things you
don't say."

Mimi did not speak, and for the moment Paul
could not.

"And I can't talk to Freddy at all. He won't talk
to me."

Now Leah's round, intelligent eyes appealed to
Paul. Mimi had imperceptibly withdrawn. She was
not comfortable with the conversation; Paul knew
it, and probably Leah had sensed it too.

"You're a man, you've seen life, even before you
went to France and went through hell; you won't
shrink away from the truth even if it's ugly—will
you? Or shall I just keep still?"

"No. Say what you have to say."

"What's so awful is that sometimes I wish I could
disappear. Just vanish. Or, what's worse, that
Freddy would. When I think of all the thousands of

days of my life that will be like this, I don't want to
bear it, although I know I have to, and I will. And
then I'm ashamed to be the least bit sorry for myself, when it's he who—" Leah's face collapsed for
an instant into the ugly mask of grief, with lips
pulled away to show wet gums. Then she straightened it and raised her hand. "No, don't answer,
don't be comforting."

Paul answered gently, "We won't say anything.
We'll just try to be kind."

"Thanks. Well, I'd best go in. Thanks for listening." She took a few steps, and then turned around
with a question.

"Are you shocked?"

Paul shook his head no. He supposed that the
pity in him should all be kept for Freddy, and yet at
this moment it overflowed for her.

Mimi tugged the needle through the canvas, the final piece in the set of twelve chair-seats that she had
begun before Paul went overseas.

"I do think it's quite, quite awful what Leah said,
don't you, Paul? I haven't been able to get it out of
my mind all day. Poor, poor Freddy."

He wished she didn't have that habit of doubling
adjectives.

"How can she have said such a thing about wanting to disappear? It's not right, it's not loyal. I simply can't understand it."

Paul looked up from his book. The curtains had
not been drawn and in the low sky he was able to
see the reflection of city lights, a dull sullen pink
bleeding upward.

" 'Not right.' What did that mean?"

Was it "right" that he should be sound and Freddy crippled? "Right" that a president was elected on the slogan "He kept us out of war" and then promptly got us into it? Yet what else could the man have done? Was it "right" that the Werners' small bank, along with Morgan, Rockefeller, the Bank of England, and so on, and so on, should have prospered from war loans? Had Freddy and Leah's marriage been "right" in the first place? Dan had said no to it, but then, Dan was hardly infallible either. None of us is.

God knows I am no judge of anyone, Paul said to himself. And he could answer his wife only by saying that he thought Leah had not meant it the way it might have sounded to her.

Mimi put the needlepoint down.

"You know, you look absolutely worn out, Paul. I'll make some tea. It's a wonderful reviver."

"But I don't need reviving. Really."

She stood close to him. "Well, I don't know." Her voice quavered mournfully. "Heaven forbid if it had been you—I would love you so, Paul. Always and always. I love you so now."

He looked up at her. Tenderly, earnestly, her fine eyes looked back.

And he thought, assuring himself, Yes, yes, I have much to be grateful for after all. Poor Freddy. Poor Leah . . .

Marian's hand took his and held it with such firm possession that he felt the pressure of her wedding ring.

With this ring . . . until death . . . in the presence of this congregation . . .

As if she had read his thoughts, she smiled, and raised his hand to her lips and kissed it.

7

Freddy, having heard his father enter the house, swung away from the keyboard and propelled the wheelchair to the other side of the room.

Fresh air clung to Dan's clothes. In jacket and tie, he had come directly from school. He looked vigorous, filled with power, and ten feet tall.

"I heard you playing just now. Sounded like Debussy."

"Only chords. Nothing much."

Dan sat down on the sofa, crossed his legs, and lit a pipe; apparently he was settling in for a real visit. Well, why not? He owned the place.

"So. Enjoying the piano. That's great."

"It's a Steinway, isn't it? The best."

Dan didn't answer that. So transparent, Freddy thought, so genial and jaunty, never letting his eyes stray to where my legs ought to be, scarcely ever meeting my eyes, even, for fear of what he'll see there. So patient, so tactful. But not only he . . . all of them.

"Where's the boy? Still in the park, I suppose?"

"Yes."

He knew perfectly well that Hank was in the park, just wanted to make conversation, couldn't stand their silences. Not that there was anything new about that. Only more of the same.

Now Dan ran a finger over the surface of the end table.

"Keep the place nicely, they do."

"Yes."

Out of character, sloppy as Dan was. Never minded a bit of dust before; would just as soon have waded in it. Conversation again, that's all.

Dan sighed. He looked about at the sunny silk curtains tied back from the windows, at the flourishing azalea, the tawny carpet, the steady pendulum of the mantel clock, and finally up at the cornice in which plaster vines twined their way around the room. At the last, his gaze came to Freddy and rested a moment as if he were considering his next move. Then he spoke, asking directly, "Do you like this place, Freddy? The truth, please. I won't mind if you say you don't."

"Anyone would like it. Why shouldn't I? What makes you ask?"

"Then it must be my presence that you don't like. You hardly speak to me."

"I don't feel much like talking these days."

"I understand, of course. Still, you do manage a little with other people, I notice. But not with me."

"I'm no different that way from what I ever was."

"Possibly not. You just don't bother, or aren't able, to conceal it as well as you used to."

"Conceal what?" Freddy felt the frown gathering on his forehead; felt also an accelerating heartbeat.

"Freddy, don't fence with me. You're too intelligent, we both are, not to know that something's been wrong, or not quite right, between you and me from far, far back."

"Why are you bringing it up now? Why today?"

"I don't know. It's not always easy to say why suddenly we feel compelled to do or say something that should have been done or said long ago."

Dan's voice was hollow; there was a melancholy echo in it. And this melancholy quivered over Freddy's skin. He wished his father would go away; he wished it weren't necessary to answer.

"I've been upset about you and Mother." That was part of the truth, anyway.

"Naturally." Dan lowered his eyes. He cracked his fingers. "It's a tragedy. If only I—well, I can't. Can't do anything. Can't even tell you what it's about. She wouldn't want me to. Accept that, please."

He's weeping inside, Freddy thought. What the hell can it be? Whose fault?

Dan collected himself. "But there's more than that. You and me I'm talking about. What is it, Freddy? I want to know. I have to know. Because I made a fuss when you married Leah? No. It was before then, even."

The silences. They ring. They make the ceiling too high, the stairs too steep, the house too large. How do you break them? Do you, too, come to a moment when suddenly you say things that maybe you should have said years and years ago? Rather than let them seethe and burn in your chest?

He began. "It's never any one thing, is it? I always thought you thought I wasn't strong, wasn't enough of a man."

"Go on."

"I'm not at all like you. Rescuing that woman in the fire, all that hero stuff—"

"I never said—"

"I know you didn't. But it was there all the same."

"Is that all? Anything else?"

Now. Now. But why? So long ago, at the edge of childhood it happened. Yet, vivid it was, the lit bulb glaring against daylight in the lab, the voices upstairs, his knowledge that the bed was there and his knowledge of what was happening on the bed.

The memory swelled in his throat, wanting to be spoken. Dan was asking for it, asking. Give it, then!

"As I just said, it's never any one thing," he began. "So it's hard to put your finger on the right place. But—"

"But?"

"Well, there was a day, one day that mattered. I came to the lab after school to tell you something, and you weren't there, you were upstairs. There was someone with you."

"Someone?"

"A woman. I heard. I stood and listened, only a minute or two. Then I didn't want to hear any more. I ran out. I went home."

His father's face flushed. It looked scalded, as if it hurt. He was staring at his fingers.

"You never said anything."

"I couldn't."

Dan raised his head. His eyes were very bright, glistening. If he cries, Freddy thought, I won't be able to stand it.

"Freddy . . . I'm not a bad man."

"I didn't think you were."

"No, you must have. At least until you got old enough to know more about—about men and women. But that day you hated me, didn't you? You must have."

"Maybe."

"You must have thought I didn't love your mother. I don't blame you. A child—a boy—would think that. I loved your mother, Freddy. I still do."

Freddy's lips moved, making no sound: Stop it, you're all choked up, I don't want to hear any more.

"You can do things with your body that don't have anything to do with your heart or your mind. I don't say it's right. I don't say a man isn't very often sorry a moment later, and scared of being found out and hurting somebody he cares terribly about. Can you understand that?"

"I think so."

I'm expected to say I do. What he's asking for is forgiveness. Not mine to give.

"My mother never knew?" Freddy asked.

"About that day? No."

About that day, he answers. As to other days, he doesn't say. That's what has gone wrong between them, then? But they were always one in my mind: Mother-father, one. That's how they were. So he's messed things up. Women go to him. He's one of those chaps. No, don't say "chaps," you're not in England. Guys in the army were like that. Women can't keep their hands off them. They can't keep their hands off women. Can't help themselves. I wonder what it's like?

"I never wanted to hurt anybody, Freddy."

Huddled, almost, in the corner of the sofa, revealing himself, Dan looked smaller.

"I think I can understand," Freddy said again. Comfort was in order now.

"Yes?" Dan spoke quickly. "I'm glad. And I want to say—that sort of thing hasn't been the pattern of my life. Just now and then . . . sometimes too hard to resist an opportunity . . . my weakness. But not that often, remember. It was always"—he bit his lip, and finished—"always Hennie."

"Doesn't she know that?"

"It doesn't seem so."

"It's all too damned sad. Everything is."

"At least you have Leah. That's something."

"Not that simple, Dad." I can't remember when I last called him that. Did I have to feel pity before I could say the word again?

"I suppose it isn't, in the circumstances," Dan said.

Neither spoke for a minute. Then Dan said, "If there's any way I can help by listening, talking . . . but then, that's too personal, isn't it? To talk to your father about? A doctor, maybe?"

Freddy shook his head. "Please, not now."

"All right. But don't be too proud to ask advice, son. Remember, sex doesn't just go away." Dan stood up. He took Freddy's hand. "I'm sorry about that old business. Sorry about every unhappy minute I may ever have given you. I never meant to, Freddy, God knows. I hope you know it too."

"I do." Funny how the anger vanished. When he came in here an hour ago I was full of it. Now all I feel is the pulse in his hand, and I don't want to let go of it.

"Freddy . . . hell, let's not pretend. We've been plenty mad at each other. You haven't always been what I wanted, you've felt that. And I surely haven't been what you wanted or needed. But I always loved you and I do now and I always will. And I'm glad we had this talk, and I want to have more talks from now on." Dan's lips grazed Freddy's forehead. "Hey, let me get out of here before I start crying like a woman. See you tomorrow, maybe?"

"Tomorrow. Come back."

The swift tread went down the stairs, two steps at a time by the sound of it. And Freddy felt the break of a small smile, the first he had felt in months. Rising from someplace close to the heart, it lumped in his throat, and warmed him and spread and filled him, softly, with its grace.

8

Paul came out of Brooks Brothers and started on his way uptown. He had been feeling what he supposed was generally meant by the term "well-being." He had bought new suits; the uniform, cleaned and camphored, had been put away to be taken out as a curiosity some decades hence, like old Uncle David's Union blue, and shown to a curious admiring family: And what did you do in the Great War, Daddy?

Well, he had done plenty and seen things he would rather not think about, things that sometimes woke him out of sleep, so that he would lie for an instant blinking into the narrow slice of dark blue night, where the looped curtains separated; startled by the silver gloss of the mirror above the dresser, he would pull his mind back from the nightmare into the present safety of the room.

Now, passing a display of handsome foulards and regimental ties, he was brought up short; this was the shop where young Drummond had worked; he'd had a plaintive voice and a salesman's anxious glance, wanting to please. He was dead now.

This was the sort of recollection that could utterly destroy a sense of well-being.

Nevertheless there was an April feel in this last week of March, a soft, cool touch in the air; the sights of paper narcissi and straw hats in store windows, the feel of walking again on streets that now, in the second month of being home, were just beginning really to seem like home.

Having promised his father to pick up some papers at his parents' home for perusal while they were on a week's vacation, he swung west and north toward Central Park. Fifth Avenue was crowded with Saturday shoppers, readying themselves for spring. Moving briskly, he kept catching his reflection in plate glass. It felt good to see himself in a dark blue suit again. He was still a trifle too thin, but Mimi was taking care of that, plying him with thick soups and home-baked rolls and puddings, mothering him as though he'd been starved, which was hardly the case.

The word *mother* set his mind off in another direction, and kept it there as he crossed the park. There at the pond were the small boys he'd kept seeing in his mind's eye, a vision of sanity during the most insane hours of the war. Accompanied by parents or nursemaids, they were sailing their boats. Some things never changed; he could remember going there himself with a marvelous sailboat, sometimes he'd gone with his unlamented Fräulein and sometimes, so very happily, with Hennie. Probably that was why, when he thought of fathering a child, it was always a boy, and the pond was the place where he saw himself with that boy.

Mimi would be a conscientious mother. He could

imagine her worrying over a child as she now worried over him, fretting about wet feet and proper nourishment. She wanted a child so badly! And it was time, past time. Now that he was safely home, she'd be relaxed, he thought, and it would happen. True, she was not a vigorous woman, prone as she was to colds and sinus infections, but those, after all, were minor problems and should have no effect. . . .

That was a nice kid Freddy had, jolly and strong. He had a "personality," like his mother's, maybe like Dan's, but certainly not like Freddy's. And Paul had a vivid memory of taking Freddy to see *The Great Train Robbery* at the nickelodeon, holding his hand when, at the climax, the sinister masked robbers boarded the train. He could still see Freddy's scared white face.

"He sits there, staring at nothing," Leah says. "When you say something he looks up and gives you a vague smile. It's as if he'd forgotten you were there. He won't talk about anything."

Leah's naturally husky voice is roughened in a throat constricted by tears; the tone rises at the end as if asking a question, asking to be told what to do and whether it is always going to be like this. She wants, understandably, to know what is to happen with the rest of their lives.

Always one wants to know what is to happen. One imagines one would like to have the whole of life, from start to finish, laid out like a jigsaw puzzle on a table, so that one could be prepared. But if one knew, what then?

One day in France he had heard the sound of motors in the sky, an ominous thrumming growing louder and louder, until they came into sight, to battle there in the sleepy blue afternoon; circling, menacing, and retreating, they'd fought until one fell in a gush of fire, twisting like a wounded bird to the earth. He remembered now that he had had a vision then, and been horrified of his vision of another war, God forbid, in which hundreds or thousands of flying machines would fill the sky. . . .

What is to happen? Better not to know.

It all goes so fast. Everything speeds. There were almost as many autos passing him now in the park as there were carriages. The whole world was changed. Freddy had reminded him of the New Year's celebration in 1900, not quite twenty years ago; what would things be like twenty years hence? Look at the women, smoking cigarettes! Even Mimi had tried one, although she hadn't liked it. Leah liked it though. Leah would try anything new.

Only Paul's parents didn't seem to have altered their ways. They were the rearguard, dependable types holding on to the best of the old, making change slowly, with prudence and caution. He supposed it was good to have parents like his; they gave you a sense of place, of things holding when so much else was whirling. Yes, and his grandmother Angelique too. Her mind was still in the Old South. Chivalry on a veranda. He chuckled to himself, feeling the familiar mixture of exasperation and affection for her.

And here was the Dakota, rising on Central Park West, still the beacon that it had been for the small boy walking homeward after a day's play in the park. He came out onto Central Park West and entered the street of solid brownstones that, he supposed, would always be his symbol of home. There it stood, one out of an identical row, distinguishable from the rest by the carriage lanterns on either side of the door and by the heavy lace on all the windows from bottom to top. It was the white lace of cleanliness, order, and prosperity. He fished in his pocket for the key and climbed the steps.

His mother had left a note on the silver tray in the hall: *Paul, when you come for the papers, be sure to lock up carefully when you leave. The servants are away with us too.*

He stood a moment in the dim hall, holding the note. Then, mounting the stairs to the second floor, he went to his father's desk. Next to the folder that he was to take lay the telephone number at the shore, where his parents were staying. Something about the word *shore* then caught at his memory, and he was off into nostalgia, into childhood when he'd had saltwater taffy and pony rides on the beach. Perhaps he and Mimi should go away for a week or two. It would be almost balmy at the ocean late in April.

The doorbell rang. Now who on earth would be bothering on Saturday morning, with the family away? He went downstairs. The curtain over the glass upper half of the door showed a vague shape, a woman undoubtedly, because of the wide hat. He peered for a better look, praying it wasn't that garrulous old maid Miss Foster from next door; he'd have to ask her in and she'd talk him to death for half an hour.

Then he drew back. His heart lurched . . . he was seeing things! It couldn't be, for God's sake! The bell sounded again with a short, quick ring, as if a hesitant hand had barely touched it. He opened the door.

"Why, Anna," he said.

His heart pounded, pounded . . . he had a crazy thought: She had come to upbraid him, to call him the monster that he was. But after five—no, almost six—years?

"I have an appointment with your mother," Anna said, looking past him down the hall.

"My mother?" he stammered. "My mother? But she's not here. There's no one here."

"She told me to come this morning at eleven o'clock." Still the eyes looked beyond him.

"I don't understand. They went to the shore, to Cousin Blanche's farm. They're gone for the week."

"She told me to come at eleven o'clock."

Now he saw that her hands in their prim cotton gloves were twisting the strap of her pocketbook in distress, and grief pierced him as if someone had thrust a needle into him.

"Come," he said. "She may have left a note for you. We'll go look on her desk."

He stood aside to let her pass. Her skirt brushed him as she trod the step above. He remembered, or thought he remembered, the scent that came from her; not that of soap or perfume, but the healthy fragrance that comes from sweet grass or rainy air or young flesh. A linen collar was turned out over her suit collar; on its edge a row of homemade embroidery had been laid; over it had fallen a wisp of coppery hair, still worn long. Then he thought he must be imagining that he was walking again up the stairs, in this house, with Anna.

"In the morning room," he said unnecessarily, since Anna had already gone in.

In the white-and-yellow room, the blinds were down. He raised them and went to the neatly fitted little desk with its matching appurtenances: notepaper, blotter, calendar, and appointment book.

"No note," he said.

Anna was still twisting the strap. Her agitation affected him too painfully. He wished she hadn't come.

"Look, look here on the calendar! She's written it down. It's next Saturday. You're a week ahead of time."

Anna looked up. There was absolute desperation in her face.

"I'm sure it was today," she said.

"Well, then, it's my mother's mistake. I'm really sorry."

He understood that she had been thinking of things entirely different; he had been remembering their past, while she was beset by some deep present need, and he might just as well have been Mrs. Monaghan the cook, or anyone at all, rather than who he was, so great was that need and trouble.

He spoke very gently. "May I ask you what this is about? Is there anything I can do?"

"I was going to ask whether she would lend us some money."

"Sit down, Anna. Tell me."

"But I'm keeping you. You have your coat on."

"Then I'll take it off. I'm in no hurry."

She looked away again, down at the sewing basket on the floor, and at Paul's feet. He noticed, as she murmured, that her accent was much less foreign than it had been. Well, she had been learning since he saw her last. . . .

"My husband, Joseph, he's a painter, he works very hard. We have a little boy . . . he works hard for the boy's sake, you understand. He's ambitious. He and another man, an Irishman, a plumber, they work together on houses and they know a lot about building. They want . . . they have a chance to buy a house."

The voice ran on, pausing for deep breaths like sighs, and he saw that the telling of her story was agony.

"If he . . . if Joseph had two thousand dollars, he could buy the house and they would work and fix it up and sell it. That's how it goes, he says, that's how you begin. Oh!" she cried suddenly, almost angrily, "I didn't want to come here and beg! Why should people lend two thousand dollars to a person they don't even know?"

"I suppose the only reason is that one wants to." He smiled.

"You want to do it?"

"Yes. I'm sure Mother would, if she were here, so I'll do it in her place."

Anna's eyes were astonished. She had almost surely expected to be turned down; certainly she could not have expected such quick acceptance. Oh, but he needed to do something for her! To give, to prove that he had heart and knew contrition. . . .

"You have spirit and courage," he said. "That's why I want to."

His checkbook was in his pocket. He drew it out and took pen in hand. A good feeling came over

him, the powerful calm that comes when you have
bestowed comfort on someone else.

"What is your husband's name?"

"Joseph Friedman."

"Here you are! Two thousand dollars. When you
get home, have him sign this. It's an I.O.U. You can
mail it to me. No, mail it here, in care of my
mother."

She stifled tears. "I don't know what to say!"

"Don't say anything."

"My husband will be so grateful. I don't think he
really expected—it was just a last hope. We don't
know anyone else to ask, you see."

Of course it had been the man's idea. He would
have forced her to come. It must have been torture
for her to ring this doorbell. He remembered how
she had fled the house that morning. . . .

"He's really such a good man. The most honest,
good man you could know."

Relieved now, almost joyous, she was nervously
chattering. "But that's silly of me, isn't it? What
woman would tell you that her husband was dishonest?"

He laughed. "Not many, I imagine. But I do hope
this will accomplish what you want, Anna."

He thought: What are we talking about? What do
I care about her husband? I've held her, told her I
loved her, and now we're talking about her husband
and two thousand dollars. I've carried her picture in
my head, the way one carries a snapshot in a wallet.

The room was too warm. She had unbuttoned the
jacket of her suit. Two rows of spiral ruffles lay between her breasts.

"Tell me," he said, "tell me about your little boy."

"He's four years old."

"Does he look like you?"

"I don't know."

A smile curved her mouth. He had forgotten that her chin had a cleft, a shallow dimple.

"Red hair?"

"No, blond. But it will probably grow dark like his father's."

Something wrenched Paul's chest, almost taking his breath: a sudden vision of Anna and that other man in the act of creating a child. The word *husband* had not affected him before, nor touched him with its reality till this instant in which she said, "Like his father's." So she and this man had . . . they had . . . damn fool, Paul! What did you think? He stared at her, at the tiny pearls in her ears, the slight movement of her breasts under the thin white blouse, and the silk strands of hair that swept past her cheeks, hair that that man could unwrap, loosen, and kiss whenever he pleased.

His heart began to pound again. And he heard himself say, "You're even more beautiful than you used to be, do you know that, Anna?"

And he heard her answer, "Am I?"

Down below in the street, a horn blew. It was far away; the street, the city, the world, all were far away, removed from the hushed little space of this room and the couch where she sat, the feminine couch piled with soft, soft pillows. Again she had lowered her eyes; why, her lashes were dark, not red! Had he never noticed that before? Then it seemed to him that she was waiting, entranced; that the same possibility that in this instant had shot through his mind had also shot through hers, a passing dart. . . .

A shaft of sunlight quivered on the carpet. The next moment he thought: No, it's my vision that's trembling. The pool of light, an irregular oval, was steady on the rug. The silence made a high, thin hum like that of insects in late summer, rising, dwindling, and rising again while he waited, and could wait no longer. . . .

He knelt by the couch and buried his face in her lap. Her hand smoothed his hair. And he raised his head, or was it she who, turning to him, raised his face? The kiss was the longest and the sweetest . . . his fingers found tiny buttons hidden under the spiral ruffles. His fingers loosened the taffeta petticoat and the muslin. Slowly, entwined as they were with one another, all the encumbrances of her silks and his thick cloth were stripped away, slowly at first, and then desperately faster.

He lifted her into the center of the couch and pulled up the quilt that lay folded there, to cover and enclose them. Her warm hair, released from pins and combs, fell over the pillows. Her strong arms held him as he wanted to be held. Through half-open lids, her eyes gleamed, and then closed, and his closed, too, going down and down into the bliss that has no name.

When he woke, they were still loosely entwined and she was still asleep. Softly releasing himself, he slid away to see her better, to examine again the charming round of the shoulder where the quilt had been drawn away, and the delicate hollow under the collarbone. In what way were these so different from the flesh and bone of any other lovely young body? His pulse, which had quieted, began again to beat, not now with desire but with an ache of longing that was infinitely sad. He bent closer, as if to memorize the subtle structure of her face: the high bridge of the nose, the flat planes of the cheeks, the pure skin drawn over the bone, without flaw. But surely there were other faces as lovely? And again the sadness flowed over him.

He got up, dressed, and folded her clothes that lay in a heap on the floor. Then he went downstairs and stood for a long time looking out to the street. He felt drained.

There was a Latin saying: *Post coitum homo tristus est.* But this feeling was deeper than the natural melancholy that so often follows passion. Far deeper. And he stood there not really thinking, just letting impressions flow, as he watched a group of boys shoot marbles on the other side of the street, and a horse plod by with a wagonload of asparagus, rhubarb, and potted tulips.

Then he heard Anna flying down the stairs. Instantly, eagerly, he went to meet her. But with a stricken, wild expression, she fled past him.

"Wait! Wait! Anna, you're not angry?"

"Oh," she said, "angry . . . no!"

"What is it, then?"

"What I've done! What I've done!" she cried out.

He wanted to understand, and thinking perhaps that he did understand, he said, "Anna dearest, you've done nothing wrong. You mustn't think that

I—Anna, I respect you more than any woman I've
ever known."

Her voice cracked.

"Respect me? Now?"

"Yes, of course. Why not? You're the most enchanting woman . . . Don't you know this was the
most natural, beautiful thing? You do know."

"Natural! I have a child. A husband."

He tried to take her hands, but she pulled them
away.

"You've done them no harm. My dear, my dear."

"Oh, God!" she cried wretchedly.

"Listen. You were a girl, almost a child still,
when you lived in this house. I wouldn't have
touched you then. But I wanted you from the first
time I saw you. I know that now. And you wanted
me, too . . . you know you did. It's nothing to be
ashamed of. Remember that."

"I don't want to remember it. I don't want to
remember anything!"

She fumbled with the latch. "I have to get out!
Let me out!"

He thought she was going to be sick, and was
terrified.

"I can't let you leave like this! Please, sit down a
minute, let's talk. Please."

But she was frantic. The latch gave, the door
crashed open, and she flew past him, down the
steps. He started after her, and then restrained himself; she was half hysterical and in that state she
would only resist him; there would be a scene and
that would be worse for her.

Helplessly, he watched her race away. No doubt
she was going home.

Slowly, heavily, he trudged back up the stairs. In his mother's sitting room, he pulled the blinds down again, rearranged the quilt and pillows, and then stood looking at the place where, only a few minutes before, Anna had lain, all fragrant, pink and white. In a storybook, he thought, one would read: "It was like a dream"; but this was no dream; it was real and true, the truest thing that had ever happened to him. He felt a lump, a sob, in his throat.

Then he turned to go, and happening to glance at the floor, saw a bracelet lying there. He picked it up. Hers. A pretty thing, a cheap bangle. And, simply because it was so cheap and flimsy, it touched him. She had so little. She had nothing. He hoped he hadn't brought suffering and guilt to her just now; he hoped she would come to think of what had happened with joy, the deep joy she had felt as it was happening. And he thought: I will see her again. This isn't the end. It can't be.

He left the house and began to walk back home through the park. A taxicab passed and hesitated, but he waved it away. He was too tensed, stretched like a spring, and had to walk it off.

Her face had been illuminated in that moment when she had told him of her little boy. "Dark, like his father," she'd said, and once more that frenzy took hold, unreasonable rage at the unknown man to whom she belonged. He tried to picture him clearly, so as to hate him, and could remember nothing except he had seemed very young. He's probably about my age, Paul thought, yet I think of myself as being older. Why? Only because you are more fortunate, Paul, more powerful, since through sheer accident, it happens that you do not have to ask anyone for money.

True. But why should you feel guilty about possessing more? It's the way the world is, that's all. You could do so much for her. . . .

He hastened his steps through the park. His mind was sharply focused now.

You can persuade her to leave him, you know, Paul. You know she can be persuaded.

The maid came into the hall when she heard his key.

"Mrs. Werner said to tell you, if you came in early, that she'll be home at three. Will you have lunch, Mr. Werner?"

"No, thank you. I'm not hungry." He went into the library where *The New York Times* waited untouched; Mimi knew he didn't want to read a paper that had been disarranged. He picked it up and read the headlines without absorbing any meaning.

Then he took one of his art books from the shelf, and that was better. Opening it at random, he beheld a marvelous reproduction of Van Gogh's *Seascape at Saintes-Maries-de-la-Mer*. He'd seen the original at the Rijksmuseum in Amsterdam, and could remember how, standing before it that first time, he had known the magic of a masterpiece, a magic that was indefinable. It was something you could only feel. You were there, where the white froth lay scattered on the shallow waves, and the white clouds melted like puddled snow in the myriad blues of a sky that was here almost green, and there almost black.

He had now a total recall, not of the minutes when he had first seen the picture in a museum, but of the original reality; he stood on the southern tip of Provence; the sound of the surf went rushing around his head, so that his heart, which had been so unstable these last hours, began again to run faster and faster; he felt the start of the fresh wind, bringing its wonderful cool breath on that brilliant day, under the blazing sun.

And he stood there staring at the book.

All the grandeur and wonder of the world! And so little time! So long to be dead, and so many already dead, all young and able to love, who now never will. Never love, nor see the bright water.

Take it all, while you can! Take life!

9

"Do come with us to the antique show," urged Leah. "Alfie and Emily go every spring and it's fun."

"It's only a short ride, not six miles down the road," Alfie said.

Ben said, "I'll lift the wheelchair into the station wagon. No problem at all."

Freddy firmly refused. "I don't want to go, I said. But you all go. I don't mind."

Leah worried, "What will you do?"

He hated her worried look. Her eyebrows drew toward her nose, above which there were two vertical wrinkles. She made him feel useless, dependent as a baby. But that wasn't fair: he was dependent as a baby. If she hadn't worried about him, he would have resented that more, and he knew he would. So he made an effort to brighten his manner.

"Honestly, I'm not interested in antiques. I'll read. Look, I've three new books here on the seat."

"I'll take you for a walk to a different spot," offered Meg. "So you won't always have the same view from this porch."

"Good idea, Meg," her father approved with cheer. "All right, then, you'll be company for Freddy. We won't be long anyway."

Down the gravel path they went, along the garden's edge, where parallel strings stretched on wooden pegs marked the rows in which late-planted vegetables were germinating; early beans were already climbing up their poles and the earth smelled strong and sweet after the night's rain.

Apple orchards flanked the path: strong young trees in even rows, they formed diagonal alleys as far as one could see.

"I wouldn't mind having a working apple farm when I grow up," Meg announced, adding importantly, "I know all the varieties. I'd have some of each, russets, Gravensteins, Northern Spies, everything."

She lifted the rails at a gate to let them pass through. "This is the new piece Daddy just bought. Good grazing land, as you can see."

A dozen pale gold Jerseys moved head-down in the grass; among them a few horses foraged too. The dogs padded ahead, the tall setters prancing and the dachshund puppy panting to keep up with them.

"Strudel loves you the best, I can tell." Meg prattled with enthusiasm, determined to cheer him, Freddy knew, and because she was Meg, did not object. "Dogs do have favorites. I wonder how they come to decide who their favorite is to be? King loves Dad the best, while Lady loves me. I think dogs are very wise; you can tell it in their eyes. And I always think they laugh too, although people say they don't, but I think their mouths smile and, of course, the tail is really laughing when it waves. Don't you think so?"

Birds' song quivered in the trees, and the open air was laced by their swoops and darts. On the damp lawn, robins hopped, plucking worms. For a moment, before his life surged back upon him, Freddy felt the marvelous wealth of spring turning into summer.

Meg pointed. "See those five maples in a row? Our neighbor down the road—he's awfully old— was a young boy, hoeing corn, when somebody came along on horseback and called that Lincoln had been shot. So he ran to tell his father, who was planting those trees that very minute. Oh, I love this place! I'll always think of it as home, no matter where else I live. When I was little, I used to cry when we had to leave every September and go back to the city, and I still feel like crying. Do you think I'm silly?"

"No," Freddy said. "Tell me about it."

"Well, on warm fall nights when I'm in bed in the city, with the windows open, I can hear the rumble of the el from the avenue. It's such a melancholy noise . . . all those people packed together, rushing from one dreary street to another. And I think, here at the place, the Canada geese are floating on the pond; they always stop over for a couple of days on their way south. Oh, well, we're here now! It's getting too hot for you," she said brightly. "I know a good shady spot where you can read."

Meg placed the chair. Below, through a screen of moving leafage, the pond gleamed; flat as a silver plate it lay, decked with a ragged fringe of lilies.

Meg was satisfied. "There! Now you can enjoy your book."

"But you have nothing to read. I don't think you'd like any of these."

"That's all right. I'll just think."

She leaned her head against a pine trunk. Without seeming to watch Freddy, she could watch him. How unthinkable not to be able to run across a field, have a whole life like this ahead, knowing that nothing would get any better!

Only one good thing had happened, in the midst of his doom: the amazing new house, finer than Aunt Florence's, finer than the Dakota apartment. Meg was glad about that. If you had to spend your life in a chair or on crutches, it might help a little bit to do it in a beautiful place.

There was hardly a sound, except for the flick of a turned page every minute or two.

Suddenly, Freddy whispered, "Look on the other side of the pond."

A deer had come out of a thicket and paused. It was a young buck without antlers. One forefoot was raised: the delicate head was held high, as though he were listening. Feeling safe, he went to the water's edge and drank, then stood staring in their direction without seeing where they were hidden. For a minute he waited, quite still, with the sunlight glistening on his reddish satin back, then turned about and disappeared in the thicket as silently as he had come out of it.

"You know what makes me furious?" Meg made a fist. "Dad's friends who hunt deer. Dad doesn't, because he can't belong to their hunt club, but he tells me, and anyway, I can see them on the roads when we come here for the weekend in the fall. It makes me sick to see deer slung over a car, or heads on the wall in somebody's house. It's not as if those people needed them to eat."

"Yes, that's what Paul always used to say."

"It's revolting. Sometimes they use bow and arrow; when they don't kill, the wounds fester for days until the poor things die. And trapping is even worse. Sometimes, when a raccoon or a fox is caught"—Meg's voice trembled—"you find that it's tried to chew its own paws off to get free. I shall never wear furs," she finished.

Freddy closed the book. "I remember when you were born, Meg," he said softly. "The first day you got up and walked, it happened at my house. Your parents were visiting."

"Do you know? I always loved to go to your house. I would have liked to go more often. I love your mother."

"She loves you too. She thinks you're like her, inside."

Meg ventured to say, "I'm sorry about your parents. They're all trying to figure it out in the family."

"Let them figure, for all the good it will do them."

"I didn't mean to hurt your feelings or be curious."

"I know you didn't, Meg."

"I only meant—I love your side, Dad's side, of my relatives. I suppose I shouldn't say it, because Mother's people are really very nice, but I'm always more at home with Dad's, with you and Paul and Florence too. Only, my two grandmothers"—she began to giggle—"luckily, they hardly ever see each other since Grandma Hughes went back south, but when they do, it's so funny to watch them insulting each other so politely about their ancestry. They're both so proud."

Freddy laughed. "Oh, well, there's nothing new in that. Just human nature. Some people's natures, anyway."

A sudden recollection caused Meg to sigh. "I want to tell you something. It may be silly of them, but I wish I could feel as sure of who I am as my grandmothers do. And not only they. You're sure, and Leah is too." Her mind ran off then into another path. "Oh, Leah is so sweet, Freddy! I wish I had a sister like her. Isn't she the sweetest thing?"

"You were going to tell me something," Freddy replied.

"Oh, yes, I was saying . . . Mother's Episcopalian and now Dad's joined with her, but they hardly ever observe anything and I think they don't really believe very much. It's just something to be. And I get so mixed up, going to seders at Aunt Florence's and then Easter services at school. I still don't know where I am. At least you do, Freddy. Don't you?"

"Yes . . . it's the only thing that's stayed with me and hasn't changed."

"To celebrate Easter and a seder is to do nothing."

Meg sensed her father's confusion, which he denied. When he was with his new friends here in the country or with his wife's family, he didn't interrupt or contradict or laugh as loud as he did when he was with his own family or his New York friends, who were mostly Jewish.

Hesitantly, she had once told him so, saying simply that he had been "different," without saying precisely in what ways. He had widened his eyes in amazement and denied it.

"You're imagining things, Meggie! I'm the most natural person—whatever else my faults, I do know that about myself. No posing, no airs, that's me. No, I'm the same no matter where I am."

And she had seen that he believed it was so.

She repeated now, thinking aloud, "I really don't know who I am."

"I can understand that," Freddy answered.

"Am I boring you?" she cried, for he was gazing away from her.

"No, no," he said quickly. "Why should you think that?"

"Well, I thought . . . I'm only fifteen. We haven't much in common."

"Come here in front of me, Meg, so I won't have to crane my neck."

A ray of sunlight turned his fair hair almost white. He was a Greek youth; he had a statue's head, like those photographed in her textbook of ancient history: long, narrow, and elegant as a woman's. If his hair were longer, she thought, he would perhaps even look a little like a woman.

"If I had it all to do over," he told her now, "you'd be the girl I'd marry."

Caught between shock and embarrassment, she giggled again.

"We're cousins! It's illegal."

"All right, then, another girl like you. There must be a few others to find somewhere, if one looks hard enough."

She sought for something to say, and in confusion blurted, "But you have Leah . . ."

"That's true."

"Oh, she's so pretty! Mr. Marcus—Uncle Ben— he told me to call him that—says she reminds him of Pola Negri. Once, when they were at the opera, he heard somebody whisper that's who she was."

"I didn't know they'd gone to the opera."

"Yes, when you were in the army. They saw *Girl of the Golden West,* I remember, and Leah said it would have been better if it had been sung in English."

"That's probably so."

Freddy's tone was oddly flat. Meg hoped she wasn't annoying him. She thought maybe she ought to stop talking; yet the silence, which lasted for several minutes, was too uncomfortable, since he wasn't reading but only looking down at brown moss and old dried leaves. So she tried again.

"He's awfully nice, Uncle Ben is. Daddy says he's a very smart lawyer and he'll go far."

"No doubt he will."

Then she was appalled. To speak of another man "going far," when Freddy couldn't go at all—how unforgivably stupid of her.

Freddy looked very tired. He was her responsibility. It worried her to think that she might have worn him out and that he should probably be lying down.

"Shall I take you back now?" she asked anxiously.

"No, let's stay a little longer. This place reminds me of a summer afternoon in England. Oh, England was wonderful that summer! It was a paradise—a fool's paradise. And we'd have tea on the lawn and talk, good talk, even if, as it turned out, so much of it was fantasy. It was so innocent, all that bravery and sacrifice. I made the closest friend I ever had, in that month. I could say anything to Gerald and be understood—"

Abruptly, he returned to his book, and Meg lay back again on the pine trunk. The day drowsed. The dogs slept on their sides, twitching as they dreamed.

What an odd thing to have said, about marrying her! He must think she was awfully ignorant to believe such flattery. After all, he had Leah! He was always watching Leah; it was plain that he didn't want her out of his sight. And she was so lovingly careful of him, always fixing his pillows, fetching cold drinks or hot drinks or sweaters.

Leah was kind. When you were with her, she paid genuine attention and didn't treat you like a child from whom things had to be hidden. She was practical and gave practical advice, not sermons, but answers to questions you were ashamed to ask anyone else—certainly not Mother or even Aunt Hennie.

"Always let a man talk about himself. Men love that. Widen your eyes a little while you listen; it looks pretty and makes you seem to be fascinated. Take care of your hands, keep them white to show off the rings you will have someday."

And she'd laugh; her round eyes sparkled; she was frank and joyous; you felt that she wasn't afraid of anyone and you hoped you could learn to be like that.

Oh, how terrible it must be for her to see the man she loves come home to her like this! It would never —how could it ever—be romantic again?

The man I will love must be . . . will look like
. . . not Freddy, he's too . . . too slight. Someone
like Paul . . . Serious, with a gentle smile.

"I'm tired of reading," Freddy said. "Talk to me,
please, Meg."

"What shall I talk about?"

"Anything. Tell me what you've been thinking of,
with your eyes closed and that little smile that looks
so secretive."

"I was thinking I'd like to have a permanent
wave, my hair's so straight. I saw pictures of a girl
with long hair like mine, before and after. It comes
out all rippled. Leah says they started in Paris, and
now they do them here, too, only Mother won't let
me."

"Hush!" Freddy commanded sharply.

Twisting his head to one side, he strained to see
through the shrubbery. Surprised, Meg followed his
gaze.

"Oh, that's Leah and Ben, they're back—"

He turned on her. "Quiet, I said!"

Not understanding, she obeyed. The little breeze
had subsided; birds had gone to their afternoon rest;
nothing rustled or moved, and in the dead stillness
voices carried distinctly across the small pond.

"A magic spot, isn't it?" Leah said. "You would
think you were miles away from another human being."

"I wish we were," Ben answered.

"I know, darling, but it can't be, so there's no use
thinking about it."

Meg made a little sound in her throat. Freddy
grasped her hand, hurting it. His expression was so

—so awful! And rather than see what he was seeing, Meg stared at him.

When she did look back through the leaves, Leah and Ben were clasped together. She was frozen, horrified, and fascinated. For the first time she was seeing what she was used to imagining: the way they were actually folded into each other, the way their lips were fastened as though they were burrowing, tasting or eating; not that, at this distance, one could see as small an area as a mouth, and yet one knew that the joined lips did not want to come apart.

Meg's heart beat faster. She breathed faster and bent forward to see better, until she was recalled to the presence of Freddy by his painful grip on her hand. He was tightening it as if he, too, had forgotten everything except what they were seeing there in the dappled light between the branches: a picture of woods, pond, sky, and, at the center, the lovers.

Then came Leah's voice, high and clear. The two had separated.

"Not here, are you completely crazy?"

As they walked out of the picture the voices blew away, but not before the man's voice was heard saying something about "New York" and "Tuesday."

Freddy let go of Meg's hand. Her fingers were squeezed and whitened, so that she had to rub them; a terrible fear washed over her, trickling and shuddering down her back. She was ashamed to look at Freddy; it was as if she had caught him, rather than Leah, in a dishonorable act. What she ought to be feeling for him was pity. How could Leah? How could she? Then Meg remembered her responsibility.

"Shall we go back, Freddy?" she asked, not looking at him, and without waiting for his answer, turned the chair about.

The emerald grove was sinister. I will never be able to come down to this pond again without remembering, Meg thought: It has been spoiled. There was no sound now except the swish of the wheels and the padding of the dogs. She had still not looked into Freddy's face.

Should loving be so complicated or so dangerous? A recollection of Paul's wedding, the only one she had yet seen, came shimmering; so grave it had been, the vows so awesome. Leah must have made such vows. . . .

The silence, as they trudged, became unbearable. Not wanting to embarrass Freddy by forcing him to answer, since possibly he might be weeping or wanting to, she addressed the dogs instead.

"King, do be careful, don't step on Strudel! He's only a little fellow."

Freddy flung out an arm. Meg stopped and came around to see what he wanted. Red blotches had come out on his forehead. He clenched his fist, and involuntarily she stepped out of his reach.

"Don't you ever, Meg, don't you ever say anything to anybody about this . . ." The fist flailed the air.

"You're scaring the life out of me, Freddy! I won't tell, I promise I won't."

"Well, see that you don't. Because if . . ."

He did not finish. His arm dropped to his lap and his head drooped to his chest. The books slid to the ground.

Meg picked them up and slowly, with great effort, pushed the wheelchair up the slope to the house.

From the porch there sounded a pleasant babble and the clink of teacups. Leah's voice, cheerful and gay, rose over the rest.

"Goodness, where can Freddy be? Meg must have taken him on a sightseeing tour!"

10

Hennie, for months now, had been having vivid dreams. Often they were so oppressive that she woke with wet eyes. There was the dream in which Freddy was born: they showed him to her in the hospital, and he had no legs. Sometimes the dreams were sensual; she held a man's head to her heart, felt his weight and warmth with a suffusion of longing so tender and yet so elusive that the fear of losing it was as marked as the thing itself. Once she woke laughing. In some vague way that, once awake, she could truly not remember, Emily's well-bred, fine-spoken cousin Thayer had figured in the dream, and she had the airy sensation of being pleased with herself.

A rooster crowed far away; there was a plucky sort of cheer in the sound, as the creature prepared his welcome to the sun. It must, then, be almost dawn. A light rain began, then, turning heavier, struck at the windowpane and spattered on Alfie's famous maples, with their flat leaves broad as an upturned palm. She lay still, listening, caught for a

few moments in a trance of comfortable forgetful-
ness.

Reality swept back. In the room across the hall
lay Freddy; Leah and Hank were in a room apart,
for Freddy slept poorly and must not be disturbed.
What was to become of him? The same constant,
futile, senseless question! There was no answer to it.
Or else there was an answer all too clear: fifty or
sixty years more like this.

Sighing, Hennie fell back into half sleep.

Dreams again. Dreams.

The picnic cloth is littered with the remains of the
cake, on which *Happy Birthday* is almost eaten
away. The zoo is still uncrowded; people move easily along the path toward the haughty stone lions
who guard the portico of the Lion House.

It has been a lovely day. Walter and Dan are having a pleasant discussion, with no veiled argument,
while Paul is teaching Freddy to bat a ball.

The sun slides westward below the trees. People
stand up, fold their blankets, and collect their children. It is time to go home.

A girl in a yellow straw hat, who has been catching Dan's eye all during the afternoon, now drops a
bag of apples. As they roll in his direction he re-
trieves them for her, and she gives him a pretty
smile of gratitude.

"Why, thank you! Thank you so much!"

"Wonderful day," Dan says.

"Yes, wasn't it," responds Yellow Hat. "I love it
here. I come almost every Sunday."

"Dan, have you got Freddy's sweater somewhere?" Hennie calls.

Now, quite aware that she is dreaming, she can

remember how the familiar heat prickled her neck and can remember, too, having thought: *This sort of thing never happens to Walter.*

She woke up. A swath of light lay across her face; she watched it sway and flicker across the ceiling. The rain had stopped; there were voices below in the kitchen wing; the day had begun in Alfie's house. For a while she lay still, allowing a tentative comfort to wash over her.

And, following a habit left over from childhood when, scared or sad, she had needed to bolster her spirits, she began to make a mental list of things for which to be thankful. "Count your blessings," Mama had liked to admonish, forgetting how often she failed to count hers. (How strange it would seem when that rigid, carping, and yet loving mother was gone!)

So then, a list of positive things. One: Mama is still alive and well. Two: Florence and I are sisters again. Three: Leah has brought Hank into the world. Four: Freddy is with caring people.

The door to Freddy's room was being opened; someone, either Ben or Alfie, was coming to lift him into the wheelchair and prepare him for the day. She thrust the blankets aside and got up. The morning was cool and overcast, so she set out a skirt and a sweater, a bright one; she had some vague idea that it was important to be bright when one was with Freddy. His door was opening again; they would be bringing a breakfast tray. She hurried, pulling the sweater on—

A terrible cry tore through the house like a gale wind, and stopped Hennie's breath in her throat. Something went clattering, bumping . . . down the stairs? Thud and crash, smash as of ripping wood and screeching metal . . . and an animal howl . . . what . . . what . . .

She flung her door open; every door in the upstairs hall was open; people were screaming and scurrying; downstairs a door slammed; people came running. Hennie ran to the top of the stairs. Alfie in pajamas and Emily in nightgown and curlers were halfway down.

And at the bottom, oh, almighty God! At the bottom, heaped and crumpled and broken, lay the wheelchair with its wheels still spinning, while Freddy . . . Freddy lay still. Sprawled, bloody and still, with his arms flung out.

The cook dropped the breakfast tray, splattering broken crockery over the hall. Two young maids knelt moaning. One of the farmhands came running from the kitchen. Another grabbed the telephone. The staircase was clogged. Madness took hold.

Someone covered Hennie's eyes with a hand and forced her to turn away. Pinned to the wall, she fought to struggle free.

"What happened? How?"

"He was alone, he did it."

"Oh, my God."

"Leah, don't look, get back!"

"Meg, take Hank, close his door. Keep him away."

"Get the doctor! An ambulance."

"Whiskey! Brandy!"

"Cold water."

"Lift him."

"Don't touch him."

"He's gone."

Alfie rushed back upstairs. "Somebody take care of Mama—she'll have a heart attack. And Leah. No, Hennie, you can't go down, Ben and I will handle it, the ambulance is coming. You women, stay. No, Hennie, no! Jesus Christ, hold her!"

They held her; she heard herself screech and, knowing that she mustn't, that they needed all their wits to help Freddy, not her, she cut the cry short.

"Help him," she heard herself whisper.

Then there was Alfie's voice, quiet and sad, as he held her, still pressed against the wall.

"Hennie . . . he's dead."

Many people came. From her bed, she heard the house door opening and closing below; there was a constant traffic on the stairs. People stood around her bed, and someone—it must have been a doctor —said: "Take this, it will make you sleep for a while."

When she woke up, blinking, someone was sitting by her bed.

"It's all right. I'm here," Emily whispered.

Hennie's speech was thick, her lips were furry. "I have to go out," she said, rising up.

"No, no," Emily said steadily. "Lie back. It's the best thing for you, Hennie."

The telephone was ringing. She was aware of a subdued, continuing bustle in the house. Yes, of course: Freddy was dead.

"I don't believe it," she said.

Emily took her hand and stroked it, saying nothing.

"Where's Leah?"

"In bed too. The doctor gave her something."

"Poor Leah."

Still Emily stroked Hennie's hand; the touch was dry and warm.

"You're very good, Emily. You don't talk, and that's good."

"There isn't anything to say, except that we love you and we're here."

Hennie turned her face away into the pillow. A spasm shook her, but no tears. There was only a pressure inside, like air going into a paper bag, a terrible pressure that must be relieved if it was not to explode in her.

She jumped up, thrusting Emily away.

"I have to go out!"

"You can't, it's raining again, you mustn't, Hennie—"

She was already in the hall, going down the stairs, past the spot where he had lain in his blood. But they had cleaned it; a silky golden Oriental mat lay on the polished floor at the foot of the stairs.

Emily beseeched her. "It's pouring, Hennie. Where are you going?"

Then she heard Ben's voice. "Let her. She must need to. We'll watch her, not let her go far."

The rain lashed her. For an instant she stood bewildered, not knowing where to go, only needing to go. Then she ran to the shelter of trees in what Alfie called the woodlot. She flung her arms around a tree, leaning her cheek on the bark, not caring that it scratched and hurt but hugging it as if to draw the life from the tree into herself.

Dead! Crushed and dead. Then to rot, like the dark purple leaves that lie all winter where the wind has thrown them; like the poor bodies of little furry animals and birds who are flung at the side of the road.

Why? Freddy, we were caring for you as best we could. We would have cared for you always. Isn't life worth anything, even without legs?

Two hard hands took her by the shoulders. "You can't stay here all night, Hennie," Ben said gently. "It's cold, and you're soaked through."

She looked up at him. The humorous eyes were serious and soft.

"I want to stay here by myself," she said.

"You mustn't. You mustn't be sick now. We won't let you, my dear."

The voice was very firm, very kind, very—male. It was to be obeyed. She began to shiver. And in a fog, she allowed him to lead her back inside the house.

There was some sort of commotion in the living room; it stopped when Hennie and Ben came in. Cold and dripping, she stood in the doorway, wondering dully what else might have happened. Then she saw that Alfie had a piece of paper in his hand and that Leah was crying.

"What is it? Give it to me," Hennie said, for Alfie had tried to hide it behind his back.

"It's about Freddy, isn't it? I want to see it. Give it to me! You give it to me!"

There were only a few words in Freddy's hand: *I have lost everything. I hope you will be happy with Ben. He is more of a man than I am.*

"What does this mean?" Hennie cried.

No one answered.

Meg shook, with tears running down into her

mouth. "I didn't mean to tell! I didn't want to make trouble, but when they found the note it just came out, what I knew, what we saw yesterday at the pond—"

Leah spoke. "It's all right, Meg. You have every right to tell what you knew."

Hennie looked wildly from Leah to Ben. "Then it's true? You—you two?"

Leah pleaded, "It's not what it may seem. Awful as it is . . . the truth is that I would have stayed with Freddy for as long as either one of us lived. I would never have abandoned him. Did you really think I would?"

A great hot hand clenched its fist in Hennie's chest. She clutched the back of a chair.

That's Leah. Look at her, with the tears glistening in her big eyes and the earrings dangling. Face of a stranger. Cheat. What she did to my son. How can that be Leah? I don't know her.

"Abandon him?" Hennie stammered; her chest hurt. "You only killed him!"

"I would never have left him, I tell you! I was good to him, you know I was."

"You—you and your lover—do you think your lover would have waited forever? You would have left him to wither! You—I took you from nothing. Have you forgotten? You're a murderess. I gave you a chance, took you into my family, my home, and you do this? You and he, here—"

"You must believe Leah!" Ben said. "Yes, I want to marry her more than I've wanted anything in my life, but I would never have done so as long as Freddy lived. We would never have hurt him, as much as we love each other."

Hennie ignored him. "Oh, Dan will want to kill you! He was right about you, I have to give him credit for that much. He was right about you, Leah."

Her raging anguish mounted, and she moved toward Leah, not sure of what she wanted to do, perhaps to slap her or pound her. Alfie caught her arms.

"Hennie, hysteria won't help. There's a child in the house. Think of Hank. We must have some order and reason here," he said sternly. "Come upstairs with me. Dan has been summoned; he's the father and must take charge."

"I don't want Dan," she sobbed as he led her stumbling up the stairs. "Not Dan. I want Paul. Get Paul for me."

"Yes, yes, we're trying to reach him. I've left a message."

"I'll be out all day," Paul told his secretary, who, having just come in, appeared surprised to find that he had been there ahead of her and was already prepared to go out again. "I just came by to look something up; now I've got about six stops to make."

He was glad of a day like the one ahead, in which he would keep moving. His mind was prepared for the varied clients, bankers, lawyers, and brokers whose challenges he would meet and whom he would persuade to his point of view. It would be a kind of sparring. He was wound up, coiled tight. So it felt good to get out of the chair, the room, the office.

Before picking up hat and briefcase, he took a
quick glance over his domain. His eye fell upon the
new photograph of Mimi, which he had had made
for the office and had handsomely framed in leather
to match the desktop. It was a three-quarter pose
and she was wearing the kind of dress he most liked;
he had, for some unknown reason, always liked to
see lace on a woman, and this dress had a double-
tiered lace frill, worn high at the back, giving it an
Elizabethan look. In her ears were the sapphire pen-
dants he had given her on her last birthday. Her
head was slightly lowered in the unconscious attitude of modesty that was characteristic of her; yet
the arched nose, imperfect by the standards of the
northern European, was fully revealed; there had
been no attempt to camouflage it, and this candor
gave her a definite air of pride to offset the modesty.
A charming refinement was the result.

His distress was painful. He went out quickly and
shut the door.

Once downstairs in the street, the anticipation of
his first call filled his mind. The street was alive with
nervous speed; everyone was hurrying somewhere.
One by one, these narrow streets in the financial
district were turning into shaded canyons, as the old
three- and four-story houses were being replaced by
thirty and forty floors of limestone. The Werner
Building was already flanked by two such towers.
At the corner, Paul looked back at it: a holdout, it
was, and would remain so as long as he had anything to say about the matter. His three floors of
worn old brick looked like a countinghouse out of
Dickens, he reflected with satisfaction.

The day was crammed, and that was good. At

four o'clock he had finished the last call. He knew he ought to go back to the office, where surely a desk piled with mail would be waiting. Also, he could go home, having "earned his keep" for the day. Neither possibility appealed; the restlessness was upon him once more; he wanted the refreshment of open space and more motion.

At 59th Street, he entered the park, intending to leave it at Fifth Avenue at 72nd. The sun had hidden behind a ceiling of cloud, sagged like a top of a tent, and in the west the sky was livid. He guessed they must all be having a wet day at Alfie's place. He walked on through a soft gray mist, an English or Irish afternoon. Not many people were out. At the Bethesda Fountain there was no one except pigeons, mournfully cooing among broken peanut shells. His thoughts, the thoughts that he had controlled since the morning, now came swelling back.

They had been dammed up ever since that day (was it a lifetime past or only yesterday?) barely two months ago. The recurring images were dizzying, confused and contradictory. Anna on the couch; arms and moist lips; eyes gleaming under lids like petals. Anna rushing down the stairs, wild-faced. Rushing away down the street, with her hair falling out of her hat. So terrified . . .

But later she must have calmed enough to think it over, to recollect and weigh. Surely in these past weeks she must have been thinking and, just as he was, asking herself: What is to be done? Is there not something to be done?

For she had wanted him. There was no mistaking that it had been a totally mutual thing between them from the very beginning, from the day when, coming into his room, he had found her with duster and apron, looking through his art books. He felt himself smiling at the recollection, and a lady with gray curls, walking her dog, looked up in affronted surprise at the impertinence of his smile, whereupon he burst out laughing.

An instant later he sobered angrily. Everything, everyone, the whole damned world, conspired to keep apart two people who only wanted to be together! From that beginning, all had conspired! And now, even now, when he had told his mother about the visit and the loan, she'd looked startled and questioned him sharply, dared to question him as though he were a boy.

"You were alone in the house with her? It wasn't wise of you, Paul. That girl had her eyes on you."

Furious, he'd answered her coldly. "Mother, excuse me, but that's a shameful thing to say."

Whereupon his mother, still unshaken and determined, had insisted, "No, Paul, just realistic. You were a catch for someone in her circumstances and married or not, you still are. Let us, as your father says, put all the cards on the table." And she had looked him straight in the eye.

Well, then, he would just lay them on the table, that was all! They wouldn't like what they were to see, and he could feel sorrow about that; to hurt anyone was the last thing he ever wanted to do, but there were some things one had to have, no matter what. And Anna was one of them.

He had been puzzling, scheming, and discarding schemes. She had no telephone. A letter was obviously too risky. He'd even had a faint foolish hope, knowing better all the time, that Anna might make the first attempt.

Yet there must be a way; somehow it must be done. Carefully, oh, so carefully! Doing, please God, a minimum of damage to anyone.

When he opened his front door, Mimi was waiting in the hall. All the world's sorrow was in her face as she came to him.

"Darling, darling, I don't know how to tell you. Freddy is dead."

11

Periodically, after work, and during these last few months since Freddy's death, Paul had been going downtown to visit Hennie. Once descended from the trolley car, he had to walk through a neighborhood that was almost unrecognizable from the one he had known when he was a child. Gone downhill, it was poorer and dirtier, more crowded and more noisy. Old homes now held shabby ground-floor stores; others had been completely turned over to commerce; trucks filled the street with fumes and racket; innumerable children dodged the trucks. To be sure, there were far worse places on the globe, yet anyone who could possibly do so ought to leave it. Certainly Hennie could, but she chose not to.

Paul, trudging up the dark stairs, was assailed by the smells of international cooking; Italian sauce was unmistakable, as was some sort of sickening sweet spice, definitely Indian.

Hennie opened the door. He kissed her cheek.

"How are you, Hennie?"

"I don't know. I keep living."

They sat in the dim parlor. He had a feeling,

without being able to see whether it was true, that
the place hadn't been dusted. The shades were
askew on the double windows, one of them up
enough to admit the bleak light that was trapped
between the buildings, while the other was halfway
down. The ivy, once so exuberantly green, was dying.

"What are you thinking?" he asked gently, for
Hennie, who had not spoken, was staring out of the
window at the gray wall.

She smiled wanly. "Do you really want the
truth?"

"The truth, of course."

"I was thinking of the funeral. The cemetery.
City of the dead. All the separate faces. I didn't
know that day that I was seeing them at all; I didn't
know anything that day. Yet I must have seen them,
because I remember them now. Your wife was holding your arm, and I thought she was thinking how it
could have been you who came back from the war
like that."

Paul threw up his hands. "Thrown dice, that's
what war is. Who happens to be standing where and
when and what bullet strikes. The most hideous
gamble of all."

"Yes, that I understand. That, in the end, comes
down to a simple grief. You can put your hand on
your chest and feel the place where the sorrow lies.
But when I think of this death, I can only cry: Why?
Was she worth it, Leah? Worth taking his life?"

"Ah, a dark mystery, all of it. How can we
know?"

He knew no comfort to give. Is life always worth
living? How could he know otherwise when, for

him, in spite of everything that weighed so heavily upon him, the future loomed gloriously because— because he would make it be so? No, it must remain a mystery for anyone who hadn't been where Freddy had been. One could only puzzle over it. Every man who had suffered as Freddy had did not kill himself. Maybe, in those dreadful seconds, shoving off and hurtling down the stairs, Freddy had even wished to undo and turn back. Who could know? Paul only knew that he was sitting here with a poor woman who wanted an explanation, and he had none to give.

"You're alone too much," he said abruptly. "Something has to be done about you." He came now directly to the thing he had been wanting to say, and, out of discretion, had put off saying: "You won't tell anyone what went wrong between Dan and you. It can only be something unforgivable . . . but for me it seems hard to imagine Dan doing anything unforgivable."

His silly habit of flirtation? Exasperating to a woman, he supposed, infuriating even, but hardly reason enough to separate after all those years: it was merely a flaw. And Paul wondered what his own most serious flaw might be: love of beauty, to a fault, or else that tendency to overrationalize, both other people's motives and his own.

He said again, since Hennie had not responded, "I can't imagine Dan doing anything unforgivable."

For the first time in his life, Hennie's face closed against him, hard and cold.

"Forgive me," he said.

He saw that she was instantly sorry. "And you,"

she asked. "You're so concerned about me, but how are you?"

He heard himself saying suddenly, "I've seen Anna." He had no idea why he had said it.

"Anna? How is that? What happened?"

"Nothing . . . she has a child."

He wished Hennie would ask him more, not that he knew what he would tell her, certainly nothing of any significance, for he was not yet ready to make disclosures. Maybe he only wanted to say and hear Anna's name.

But Hennie asked nothing. She was absorbed in herself.

"I long to see Hank," she said. "I haven't seen him since—since it happened. But I will not go to that house. I despise her, I can't look at her. That's one thing Dan and I have in common," she finished, clipping the words with an air of defiant, bitter satisfaction that did not suit her.

This unfamiliar coldness in his beloved Hennie dismayed Paul, and angered him, too, so that he replied almost harshly.

"You'll be surprised to learn there's been a great change. He visits there almost every day."

"I don't believe it! He's not forgiven her, has he?"

"I don't know anything about that. We haven't talked about it."

Forgiven her, he thought. So they had done, all of them in the family, if one could call a discreet silence on the subject of the "other man" a forgiveness. And he thought that they—meaning his parents, his grandmother, and his wife—if they had not been so impressed by Leah's renunciation of the money, might not have done so. Ah, money! Voluntarily to give up what was legally yours, ah, that was impressive indeed! That could outweigh many another transgression, if you wanted to call a love affair a transgression.

"Leah has given up all her widow's rights to the money," he said now. "Everything has been put in Hank's name, even the house."

"I don't believe it," Hennie said again. "The way Leah loves money."

Once, Paul recalled, she had praised the girl for her ambition and industry. We see only what we want to see. . . .

"But it's true," he said. "Hank is a rich little boy and will be a rich man."

"Nothing makes any sense . . . rich! It will ruin him."

"Wealth isn't necessarily ruination, you know." He added, "Leah wants to move, but Dan won't allow it. He wants the house kept for the child."

She was defeated. Her gaze returned to the gray wall, now turning black as the sun moved away.

"I should so like to see my little boy," she murmured after a while, as if she were speaking to herself, ignoring Paul. "He must have forgotten me."

The words fell away into the mournful room: *forgotten me.*

And quick pity rose in Paul, as a composite picture darted and flickered: Hennie marching; Hennie, twice his height, holding him by the hand; Hennie with Dan . . .

"Do you know what I'll do? I'll arrange a time when Leah won't be home and you can see Hank. And I'll meet you there," he said.

* * *

He had Dan's habit. Hennie watched the boy push back the glossy dark hair that fell like a bird's wing over his forehead. He had Leah's round, curious eyes and her snub nose; he had—she stopped, impatient with herself. A child is who he is; why must we always itemize and compare?

Right now Hank was on the floor with Paul, building a tower of blocks. Autumn sunshine fell over the corner in which they sprawled, warming the bright room, a child's world. On the headboard of the painted bed sat Humpty-Dumpty; Mother Goose flew on the footboard. Everything was proportioned to a child's dimensions, from the red chairs and table before the fireplace to the toy shelves and the closet rods on which hung rows of little pants and jackets, leather leggings and a velvet-collared overcoat.

I suppose he goes to parties: whose? Hennie wondered.

Yes, it was a child's paradise. And she thought that every child born ought to have such a clean, quiet room.

"Let me show you how I can catch." Hank scrambled up and took a large ball from a shelf. "You stand over here, Uncle Paul. No, you're too near. That's a baby throw."

"Can you catch from this far away?"

"I can! You'll see I can!"

Paul tossed the ball and Hank caught it neatly. "I told you I could!" He shone with glee.

"Who taught you how?" Paul asked him.

"Uncle Ben. He takes me to the park and we play ball."

That stranger, taking his father's place! But Freddy had hated games when he was little; when he was grown, he'd tried tennis for sociability's sake, because Paul had urged him to, and he hadn't liked it. . . .

Hank interrupted Hennie's regrets and doubts.

"Uncle Ben's going to buy me skates for my birthday. He promised."

"Oh, that's wonderful!" Paul agreed. "Now, tell me, would you like me to buy you a boat? A sailboat? And let me take you to the pond?"

"For my birthday when I'm four?"

"Maybe we won't wait that long," Paul told him, tossing the ball back.

When the clock struck, Hank put the ball away.

"It's time for my lunch. Want to know how I know? It's because those two things, see, when they both stand straight up that means twelve, and lunch. I'm hungry, too."

"You're always hungry, you are, bless your soul."

A neat woman of middle age, who wore a white uniform and moved briskly, had come in with a tray.

Paul made the introduction. "Mrs. Roth—Scotty. She's really Miss Duncan, but she likes to be known as Scotty."

In uniform, Angelique had reported, with a navy blue cape when she takes him out. Very kind, but correct too. He's being well brought up. The Scots know how to do it.

It is all so odd, thought Hennie, acknowledging the introduction.

"Come now," said Scotty, setting the tray on the table. "Here's your nice lamb chop and Mrs.

Roedling made ginger cookies just this morning; they're still warm. Now go into the bathroom, like a good boy, and wash your hands."

Curious, no doubt, about the grandmother who had up to now been hidden, Scotty smiled at Hennie. She had a good face, this woman who had taken Hennie's place, who now did for the boy what she had always done. Yes, a good face.

Impulsively, Hennie said, "I'm glad he has you, Scotty. Especially since he has a mother who spends no time with him."

"Oh, no," Scotty said, surprised. "His mother is wonderful with him. And when you consider that she goes to business—why, I've been with families where the mothers don't do anything all day but go to luncheons and tea parties, and don't do half as much with their children as Hank's mother does."

Thus politely rebuked, Hennie flushed, and was about to sit down with Hank, disregarding the nurse, when voices came floating up the stairway.

Paul started. "Oh," he said, "I don't understand! What happened?" For unmistakably, the voices belonged to Leah and Dan.

Hennie was furious; this was his trick to get me here, she thought, following Paul as they skimmed down three flights of carpeted stairs.

"How could you have done this to me?" she whispered angrily to his back.

"I swear I had no idea! There's been some misunderstanding over time. I swear it, Hennie."

Leah and Dan looked up from the foot of the stairs, under the glittering chandelier. Hennie had a quick impression of Leah, sober and delicate in slender dark gray, a kind of half mourning. She had a quick impression of Dan, looming in an attitude of protection. For a moment, a frozen moment, in which the flesh shrank, no one spoke.

Then Paul said, "We were just leaving," adding unnecessarily, "we came to see Hank."

Hennie moved toward the front door. She was shaking; there was a bolt and a double lock that she didn't know how to work.

"You're not coming up to see Hank today?"

She heard Leah's question and Dan's reply.

"Tomorrow. I can't now. I only wanted to deliver these for you to sign. They're the final papers. . . . Hennie," he said.

Almost automatically she turned about, thinking in the same instant, I don't have to answer his summons; he doesn't belong to me anymore.

"Hennie, I think you ought to know that, with these papers, Leah is signing away her rights to everything, including this house. It's all to belong to Hank."

"I know all about it. Paul, open this door for me, will you?" she demanded, for Paul was standing there ineffectually, looking from one to the other.

"I thought you should know what Leah has done," Dan repeated.

"Yes, admirable of her. Isn't that what I'm supposed to say?"

Leah said quietly, "I don't care anymore about your good opinion, Hennie. I know I've lost it. And life's too hard to struggle to be where you're no longer wanted."

She gave a little shrug, a gesture of regret, wistful and rather charming; then she turned about and went up the stairs.

Grand lady, Hennie thought.

The three walked eastward toward Madison Avenue; Paul went between Hennie and Dan.

"I'll never forgive you for this," Hennie muttered, knowing that Paul must have heard, although he went on talking volubly to Dan.

It was Sunday. Women in furs and men in Chesterfields and tall silk hats strolled and greeted and swung their malacca canes. And here was Dan in the same old winter jacket, treading these streets on which he didn't belong! All these things that he had scorned, while others coveted and gloried in them, all these he now wanted for the child!

"Any place around here to eat lunch?" Dan inquired.

Paul said, with some hesitation, "Not many in this neighborhood, but you can get a very nice lunch just a few blocks down. It's in a hotel, but—"

Dan grinned. "A bit fancy for me, you're saying, but we'll try it anyway."

"I'm not in the least hungry," Hennie said.

Did he actually think she was going to sit at table with him? Bold and brash as ever, he might just think he could make her do it, and anyway, why? They had nothing to say.

"You need to eat, Hennie," Paul remonstrated, "and I'm hungry too. Mimi's gone to her parents' and they won't be expecting me. So come on."

He had a hand on her elbow, steering her down the street. She felt his fingers, pinching.

The hotel's lobby shimmered with flowers and smelled like spring, oblivious to the rising chill outside. Hennie felt tired and dowdy; her black coat was four years old.

Paul propelled her into the dining room. More flowers and a white gleam of tablecloths. It was too intimidating. But she was almost pushed into a seat.

Immediately a waiter came, hovering with pad and pencil.

"I'm not hungry," Hennie said again into the vacant air. "I don't want anything, really."

Dan ignored her.

"The lady will have a small steak, medium rare. A baked potato without butter. And French dressing on the salad."

She was miserable and humiliated. Dan was trying to meet her eyes; she wouldn't allow him to. Paul was considering the menu, hiding his face behind it. There were no windows in the room. There was no place for Hennie to direct her gaze except at the back of a feather-festooned hat nearby; it crossed her mind that young Meg would be outraged by the feathers.

Dan was not to be put off. "Well, Hennie, I hope you're surviving."

"I'm surviving."

"We're lucky to have Hank. He's all that's left."

How am I supposed to answer that? Don't I know what's left and what isn't? Paul's so awkward, so unlike himself, not helping me at all. This whole morning is his fault. Of course he's terribly sorry. He imagines he knows how I feel, but how can he know? He's got a smooth life with Marian, with that other old business long blown over, long forgotten. How can he know how this is for me?

The waiter brought rolls and butter. No one touched them.

"Well, isn't anyone going to say anything?" Dan asked.

Now she looked over at him. The vertical lines in his forehead were deep-cut grooves of anxiety and anger. And she was moved to speak.

"Yes, I'll say something. I don't understand this business between Leah and you. After what she did to Freddy, how is it possible that you can forget? You, who never cared for her anyway? All the times I felt you were too hard on her, you found fault with her for being frivolous, domineering—I can't begin to remember all the things you said—that she was all wrong for Freddy— And now it turns out, much as I hate to admit that you were right, it turns out that you were. So I can't understand you now."

"I wasn't right and I wasn't all wrong, either. I wonder whether you can understand that? Because with you things are either black or white; nothing in between. Would you, would any one of us, have expected Leah to turn down her inheritance?"

The waiter came back. In silence, impatiently, they watched him serve the vegetables with skill and care, as though the task were of enormous importance. When he had gone, Dan continued.

"Yes, one of us, only one." He raised a finger. "Alfie wasn't surprised. She wants to be independent, he told me. Wants to thank no one for anything from now on. That's what Alfie told me. And I know it's because he recognized something of himself in her."

"The part you despise."

"I don't think I can say that, exactly." Dan's body drooped as he held the fork, contemplating the food; he had abruptly gone tired. "I have to admire the drive such people have. I'm incapable of their success. Alfie had a goal and he's reached it. I've spent my energies, shouted my lungs out for justice and peace and accomplished nothing—"

Paul interrupted. "Not so, Dan. Remember the tenement laws? Why, I can name—"

Dan interrupted him. "No, no. Not nearly what I hoped to do."

His eyes were sad; the pang of pity that they aroused in Hennie made her exasperated with herself, so that she had to attack.

"She took away my son's last reason to live, she broke his heart, and you make a saint of her simply because she doesn't want your money!"

"I make a saint of Leah?" Dan grimaced. "Hardly! We see the world too differently. She was proud of Freddy's going to war, and I'll never forget that. She stood for things I didn't stand for and still don't. Never will, either. But hell, do you have to love a person and approve one hundred percent to give him a chance? Fair is fair, that's all."

"So now it's you who've become a saint."

"God knows I'm not! You surely know I'm not. Only try to remember what it is to be young, Hennie. It's not so long since you were young yourself. Now this fellow Ben comes along . . . can't you feel for her? Flesh and blood, man and woman . . ."

Leaning across the table toward Hennie, he urged and appealed in a low, passionate voice.

"Don't make a spectacle of yourself," she warned.

"The flesh! You don't understand it! But I do!"

"Yes, well you do. Every woman you see . . . all

the years, wherever we were, you thought I didn't notice. I've been so humiliated by your silly flirting—"

Dan threw up his hands. "What are you talking about? I was never aware of doing anything!"

"Not aware? It was even noticed by other people, I know it was."

"Because I talk to women? Sure, I'm drawn to a beautiful woman! What do you think? But it was always harmless, I never meant anything by it."

"But I hated the way you behaved . . . I hated it."

"Why didn't you say so? Why didn't you kick me under the table or give me a dirty look?"

"I had too much respect for myself. I wouldn't lower myself."

"Ah, you see what I mean? You're not like other people! The average woman—Leah, while we're talking about her—would have spoken her peace, gotten mad, been honest about her feelings."

"Leah again. The woman who killed our son."

Tears came stinging. She pressed her lids shut; damned tears again, here in this public place! She strained her lids wide and looked around the room, everywhere and anywhere except at Dan or at Paul, who had been watching her with concern. Two good-looking couples were coming in from the cold, rubbing their gloved hands; they were having a festive Sunday. A pair of elderly ladies with wholesome pink cheeks were chuckling over a joke. At another table sat young parents with three little girls in flounced dresses. All of these were people who belonged in this place: They were happy.

"That's not true," she heard Dan say. "You don't know. It wasn't her fault."

"Not? Whose was it, then?"

Dan sighed. "I shouldn't tell you. Frankly, I don't think you'll understand." His mouth was twisted. "I don't think, knowing you, that you'll even want to understand."

"I didn't come here to be insulted." Hennie flung her resentment at him as though it were one of the plates or cups on the table. "I didn't want to come in the first place."

"Hennie, please," whispered Paul, who was miserable.

And Dan said, "Yes, he lost his legs. Yes, she took a lover. It was all that, but at bottom it was because he despised himself."

"What do you mean?"

Dan lowered his eyes. He cracked his fingers, a habit that, rarely used, and then only in extreme agitation, sent shudders down Hennie's back. And she waited.

At last he spoke. "It was because . . . because he was less than a man. Before he lost his legs. He was not good with a woman. He found out . . . it wasn't women that he wanted."

She felt ill. The sight of juice, oozing out of the meat, turned her stomach. When she could manage to speak, she said, "If you mean what I think you mean, then I think it's revolting."

"The meaning couldn't be clearer, could it? But it's not revolting. It's only a fact, a sad one, but a fact."

"I don't believe it!" she cried out, so loudly that a woman at the next table turned around in annoyance. She lowered her voice. "How do you come to know such a thing?"

"Leah told me. She had to let somebody in the family know the truth and I was the logical one, I guess. That's what he meant in the note, you see, about Ben being the better man. They'd talked about it, Leah and Freddy. Talked about it a lot. It wasn't the legs. . . ."

"She lied! She lies to excuse herself! Do you believe this, Paul? Can you imagine such a thing?"

Paul opened his lips to speak, closed them, and opened them.

"Yes," he said. "I have to confess that, in one way or another, it did cross my mind, and then I was ashamed to be thinking it."

With this acquiescence, she lost her ally. And she faced the two men.

"This is the vilest slander. To say that Freddy did anything like that! You disgust me."

"I didn't say he did anything. I think it was that he came to despise himself. He hated being the way he was. And I feel it was our fault. All right, maybe mine alone. Because I saw it years ago. We're so secretive, so afraid of anything we think is ugly, and I'm as guilty as anyone," Dan said. "We can't even say the right words straight out. As if he could help it. As if it were a sin."

Paul put his hand over Hennie's. Quiet, he is saying, don't let this tear you apart. I'm here. She drew her hand away.

"And when," she asked, pursuing Dan, "when did you make this discovery?"

"Years ago, I realize that now. But I wouldn't allow myself to think it through. I was impatient

with him, instead. I loved him so much that I didn't
want to see— Perhaps, if we could have talked to
each other, I could have helped him. Perhaps, even,
he wouldn't have gone to war when he did, with his
false dreams of what it takes to 'be a man.' " Dan
gave a dry, forlorn laugh.

There was a long, stark silence until Dan resumed.

"So I went a little crazy over the house, buying
things for him, giving him what he would like instead of foisting my ideas on him. Let him have
something, anyway. The comfort of money . . . all
this." And he looked around at the sheltered room,
the soft nest.

Hennie reeled. She clutched at the table's edge.
She could not have stood up. Within her, denial
raged. Yet at its core there lay something hard and
lead-heavy; she was not ready to recognize what it
was, but at the same time knew she would one day
have to: the truth.

The waiter, a courtly, gray-haired European,
leaned toward them anxiously, for their plates, except for Paul's dabbling, were untouched.

"Is everything all right?"

Paul frowned. "Yes, all right."

"Too much hidden," Dan said. "Too righteous,
both of us, afraid of a truth that wasn't beautiful.
Even our own affair, Hennie. If I could have dared
to tell you the truth in the beginning— I'm willing
to wager you've never told anyone why"—and as
Hennie in spite of herself gave him an intimate
warning look to remind him that Paul was present
—"Paul can hear, as far as I'm concerned. He'd
open his mind."

Dan looked steadily into her eyes. She looked back; let him be the first to look away.

And he turned to Paul.

"I once did a terrible thing to Hennie. She can tell you if she wants to."

Flushing, Paul shifted uncomfortably in his chair.

"For a woman so practical in so many ways, my wife is a childish romantic. She thought I was a knight on a white horse and I was only a fallible man."

"Please," Paul said. "I don't know what this is all about."

"You know something," Dan said, "sometimes I think I don't know either. Anyway, I hope Leah marries Ben. Maybe they'll be luckier than we, and last their lives out together. He's a decent sort. He's lending her money to open a business of her own, and he loves the boy; he'll be good to them both."

"You hope she'll marry Ben!" Hennie cried. "And Freddy not three months in his grave. She left him when he needed her, even if what you say about him is true."

"You left me when I needed you, Hennie."

"I left you! This is outrageous!"

"Not here in this place," Paul remonstrated. "You've got to postpone it."

Dan touched Paul's arm. "You're right. It's not fair anyway, dragging you in."

"Paul, I must get out of here. I must," Hennie insisted. "You shouldn't have done this to me."

Dan stood up. "Never mind. I'm leaving. Just one more thing, Paul. That business between your father and me. I thought I was right at the time and I still think I was right. I'm sure your father still thinks he was. Yet it shouldn't have been allowed to go on all those years. We could have agreed to disagree and made peace. So that's that. I'm going."

"Finish your lunch." Paul looked pitying. "Don't go like this, Dan."

"No, here's my share for the lunch."

Dan drew some bills from his wallet, the same old wallet he'd always carried, Hennie saw. He looked down at her; she felt huddled in the chair, felt that every eye in the room must be on them.

"Wake up, Hennie." He spoke very quietly now. "Be human, learn to forgive. I don't give a damn about myself anymore, but Leah—she's suffered, she's got courage and guts, and she's the boy's mother. Will you shake hands, Hennie? Never mind, you don't want to." For Hennie's hands were knotted together in her lap. "Paul, will you remind your parents—I've already asked them—to look out for Hennie? She needs them."

They watched him walk away. A few heads turned to follow him, whether because he was still an impressive man, or because people were aware that something interesting, or maybe scandalous, had been going on at their table, one could not tell. Hennie quivered. It was like being in an accident, at the core of horror, while at the same time one was outside the event, observing it.

"Well," Paul said after a moment, looking at the untouched food, "I don't suppose you care to finish lunch."

"I'm sorry."

"I'm sorry too. It was my fault. I shouldn't have insisted."

They walked out onto the prosperous avenue. All

was calm. People were strolling, on their way to pleasant places, or coming back from pleasant places.

"Would you like to come to my house?" Paul offered.

"No, thank you. I've had enough for one day. I just want to go home."

She didn't stir from the apartment all that week. She slept, got up to make some tea, and slept again. Sometimes she went to the window and looked out. Things wavered before her: the white arc of a ball in brilliant light, or the wet top of a truck sliding through the rain.

It had taken the rest of that Sunday for wrath to spend itself, and now there was only a tiredness so profound that she had no will. Occasionally she talked to herself, even speaking the words aloud; that's what happened to people who lived alone.

It has to be admitted that some of the things he said were probably right. Yes. We had a strange child. I always felt he was, and I worried, not knowing what I was worried about. And I thought it was my fault, that he was like me. I should have talked about it. The boy might have been less isolated if we had. I don't know. I wanted everything to be perfect and look perfect. Our marriage . . . I cringed to think that there were things hidden. Then came the day I found that letter and couldn't hide from myself anymore.

In front of Paul he'd said, "I did an awful thing to Hennie. She can tell you if she wants." That was decent of him, because he cherishes Paul's good opinion, and still he was willing. But he has never been afraid of the truth, as when he used to say of Leah, quite frankly, that he never liked her. He made no excuses for his feelings. And why not, when you come down to it? It made as much sense, I suppose, not to like her as my having been drawn so strongly to her when she was only a little child. Yet he was always kind to her, kind and fair, until it came to her marrying Freddy. Now he even defends her. . . . He asks me to remember what it was like to be young. I'm not that old now, am I? Why should he think that I can't remember? Does he think I'm dried up, and feel nothing for anyone but myself?

She said she would never have left Freddy. I didn't believe her. Still, maybe she wouldn't have. She was never a liar. I guess I know her as well as a mother can know a child, and whatever else she does, she doesn't lie. So she would have stayed with my son and had her lover too. It's done all the time, isn't it?

What a terrible thing, to live without loving or being loved!

Why did you do that to me, Dan? I was so happy with you. Whatever else went on around us, still I was happy with you. That's where the center was. . . . You looked so lonesome walking away from Paul and me. I hated you last Sunday, and still I could see how forlorn you were. Your eyes reproached me.

I have that look in my eyes too. I see what I am and I'm afraid of what I see. I don't like to look. I'm just forty-five, but I'm stern-faced and straight-lipped, a woman who sleeps alone and knows no desire, only the memory of it. Such women used to come to the settlement house sometimes to work; they were charitable and respectable, they were good women, I knew, but only half alive, I used to think. They were so righteous. . . .

And yet I have it in me still to bloom, to desire. That day at Alfie's, that terrible day when we got the news about Freddy, there was that man Thayer, in the gazebo, in the rain. I refused him. But with part of myself I didn't want to refuse. A second time I might well not have. I felt so young. . . . Because it was wonderful, yes it was, without loving the man, or even liking him. So it could have been that way for Dan and that girl, couldn't it, just as he said it was? So long ago . . .

And if, like Leah and her young man, you do love, how much harder to deny, to refuse.

And why should you, after all?

So she spoke to herself, frowning with the effort of thought as she paced the floor; on the bare wood between the rugs, her heels struck like a shock into the silence.

A ball rolled out when she chanced to bump into a chair. Hank's ball, left behind in the move. When she picked it up, she remembered how his hands looked, how the short fat fingers clutched.

She walked into the room that had once been Freddy's. Nothing had been changed in years. Dim in the lamplight, it looked like a tomb in which all the possessions of the dead had been stored to accompany him to the next world. She turned off the lamps and raised the shades to let in the daylight. It fell over the austere bed and over the table where the last books he had been reading before he left still lay: a text in Greek, a translation of Euripides, and the poems of Emily Dickinson.

She stood there stiffly.

What am I doing?

Terror was at her back, lurking in the empty rooms. And she flung the window open as if to escape it. From the street below, life came sweeping up: harsh cries, the sound of quarreling, a child crying, an engine being cranked, and an ashcan clattering. And the peal of laughter. Even here in this ugly place, the sound of laughter and life.

Oh, God, what have I done?

She went to the telephone. Her voice quavered and cracked so badly that the operator had to ask her to repeat the number. And when the connection was made, she could scarcely whisper.

"Dan. Please come back."

Afternoon sunlight, turning toward evening, lay over the bed where they lay. They had loved, they had slept, and now at last could let words flow as they wished, random and free.

"And did you really intend to kill yourself that night?" he asked. "I haven't been able to get that out of my mind."

Had she? Or had she been playing with the idea, beholding herself as the central figure in a tragedy? Would Freddy, too, have turned around if he could have?

"I don't know . . . I just felt as if the world had no place for me anymore."

"Your place—your place is here. You know that now, don't you?"

"Yes, yes, Dan."

It would not be exactly the same as it had been in the beginning. How could it be? But it would suffice, and would more than suffice.

"I hope I didn't make too much of a fuss for you and Paul that day."

"It's all right. I guess if we hadn't met there, I wouldn't have started to think as much as I have, and we wouldn't be here in this bed together."

"I'm so glad to be in this bed again, Hennie."

The hall clock rattled and struck the hour. The sound that had been so ominous that morning was merely friendly now.

"I'm thinking, Hennie, that maybe it would be nice to move away from here. We could find a good small apartment uptown in Yorkville. They don't cost much if you can do without an elevator. We'd be only a few blocks away from the boy. What do you think?"

"I think I'd like it."

"We don't need all the rooms we have here, so it would probably cost no more than this place does. And I'm due for a raise next semester anyway. I could give the little fellow piano lessons, when he turns four. That's not too soon to start."

She got up on one elbow and looked at Dan. The grooves had been miraculously erased from his forehead; he looked boyish.

"Hello!" he said, laughing.

"You're home again! Aren't you hungry?"

"I haven't had anything since breakfast."

"Then I'll get up and make you something. There isn't much in the house, just some eggs, but I'll see."

* * *

When they had eaten their supper in the kitchen, he in his old place and she in hers, he went to his usual chair and read the paper. She went to the desk and began to write.

After a while Dan put the paper aside and got up. "What are you writing?" he asked.

She covered the paper with her hand. "Nothing much. A couple of weeks ago I started to write a poem about Freddy. I wanted to tell about his gentleness . . . well, I tried, but nothing happened. I had the love and the intention, but not the gift. The words were dull in my mouth when I read what I had written."

"Let me see it anyway. May I?"

"I tore it up. This thing is about myself, clarifying my thoughts. I thought it would be good for me."

"Will you let me see this, then?"

"You may not like it."

But she removed her hand, and over her shoulder, he read:

"He's a lone man, for all his boisterous gaiety, a frustrated musician and a disappointed reformer. I suppose he feels powerful when women turn to look at him. I must keep reminding myself, because I really know, that it is truly without meaning for him.

"And as for that other thing long ago, I believe it was pretty much the way he said it was, although maybe he would have married her instead of me if he could have . . . but also I must remember that I am the one he has loved all the years since.

"Oh, yes, I can still be bitter when I think of it; I'm not all that magnanimous.

"We own nothing and no one. Our children grow up and go away, and sometimes they die before we do. Yet we continue to live. For these few years are all we have. So let's take what there is, since we can't make more. I had a son. I had a wish for perfection. What was, was. I had a lover, too, a large man, brave and good, who has done good things in the world, and I have him still. I don't want to be without him ever again. I . . ." The writing trailed away.

Dan pulled her from the chair and opened his arms. His eyes were wet.

"Has it helped you to write it all out?"

"I think it has."

"Then tear it up and throw it away. Oh, Hennie, Hennie, it's a new start."

On the sidewalk outside of the restaurant, Paul had parted from Hennie in deep distress. Watching her walk off, he was tempted to go after her, and stood for a moment struggling between that temptation and an equal need to get away alone.

Such bite and bitterness in her! So unlike the Hennie he had known all his life!

And Dan so subdued . . . Paul had a quick flash at the front of his mind, an instant recall of Dan standing high up someplace and people crying out, people clapping; was it only that he had heard the story so many times that it had become vivid to him, or did he actually remember it?

Courage Dan had. Courage to have said what he did just now about the awful thing that had come between the two of them. It must have been an awful thing for Hennie to be like this.

Still, they were destroying each other. As if Freddy's death were not enough to bring them together.

And yet, how can I judge? Paul asked himself. Someone looking at me wouldn't guess the first thing about what's happening inside me.

A little boy, walking between his parents, went past with a sailboat in his arms; they were going to the park. He must remember to buy one this week, rather than wait for Hank's birthday; too much of life was spent in postponement.

From the thought of Hank, his mind traveled farther: *She* had a boy the same age. Her boy wouldn't be sailing a boat in Central Park, though. He didn't think there was anyplace to sail a boat in the part of the city where she lived. Then his mind recorded the name of the street where she lived, and the address from which the husband's I.O.U. had come. He hadn't intended to memorize the address on Fort Washington Avenue, but it had obviously stuck in his memory.

He walked on, going east toward his home. It was a brisk day with a wind that tossed the trees, the kind of vigorous weather that he liked, the kind that drove some people indoors and brought others outside to brave it. The lofty sky shone like blue glaze. It was a perfect day for a ride in the country, to get out on some side road perhaps, and hike a way, then drive to some old inn and have a drink. But not alone . . .

He looked at his watch; it told him that the afternoon still had a long way to go. The garage in which he kept his car was just down the street from his house. He stood in front of it uncertainly. Of course, he could go to his in-laws', where they were entertaining some visiting cousin who had recovered from a desperate illness. The thought of the overstuffed apartment and the family gossip oppressed him. The day had already been such a miserable one, between other people's troubles and his own. . . .

Suddenly the decision made itself and he went into the garage to ask for his car. It was important to use the motor, he argued. One so seldom needed an automobile in the city; the last time he'd taken it out was to drive to Alfie's place, weeks ago.

He got behind the wheel, put on his driving gloves, and swung westward. He opened the window and let the air blow in. It felt good. He came out onto Riverside Drive. On his left, the river sparkled where the wind chopped the water. Thin clouds appeared in the sky that had been without flaw; the wind pulled them, drawing them on like kites' tails.

Three great gray battleships were anchored in midstream. Let's hope we've seen the last of those, he thought.

He brought the car to a stop at the Claremont Inn, thinking he'd go in for a while and watch the river over a drink. Then he remembered the Volstead Act—stupid and unenforceable for very long, he'd wager; the only drink he'd get was coffee or tea. So he drove on, turning northward; he'd go through The Bronx and on up to Westchester a little way for a look at open fields. Maybe the sight of their peace would clear his head.

He went up Broadway, keeping a careful eye out

for Sunday strollers, who tended to amble across the avenue, and for children who darted across. Suddenly, Fort Washington Avenue slanted up on his left. If he hadn't been going so slowly, he wouldn't have noticed the street sign. He became aware of his leaping heartbeat. And he kept going. He went on for five more blocks, and ten. Then he thought how odd it was that, born in this city and living here all his life, he had never been on Fort Washington Avenue. It wasn't more than thirty minutes away from his neighborhood, or forty at the most. Strange, when you thought about it! And without really intending to, he made a U-turn and went back.

It was a foolhardy thing to be doing. Besides, it made no sense: The chances of seeing her among all the hundreds of families who lived in these houses, packed side by side, were almost nil. And it was Sunday; the husband would be home. Still, he thought, I'm here and how can I pass her street without stopping for only a minute, just to look and to feel the atmosphere of the place where she lives?

He parked the car on the opposite side some distance down from the house whose number was etched in his mind. He watched the comings and goings on the street; old people sat on camp chairs in their doorways, out of the wind; big boys on roller skates dodged the light traffic; families were out together with baby carriages and dogs on leashes, looking the same as they did downtown, except that the clothes were different.

He glanced up at her house, wondering which of the windows were hers, which the kitchen where she worked, and (did she sing while she worked?) which her bedroom—their bedroom.

A crazy feeling came over him; he felt like a thief, snooping and sneaking. He wanted to see her and was afraid that he might. It was foolish to sit there any longer; he'd already been there for twenty-five minutes. And glancing through the rearview mirror, gauging the space to back away from the curb, he saw her.

She was walking up the little slope; her hand was lying in the crook of her husband's elbow; their little boy was pushing a tricycle. He ducked his head as they passed. He was shaking. They went ahead and crossed the street. The wind blew her hat loose and she took it off to refasten the pins; her red hair glistened before she covered it again. He saw her laugh, turning her mouth up to the man's answering laughter.

Then the man picked the child up and set him on his shoulder. The child reached for his mother's hat, teasing, but she drew out of his reach, still laughing and shaking her head: No, no! She picked up the tricycle, and the three of them stood a moment with their faces turned to the sun, as if they were trying to make up their minds whether to go back inside or go on. Then they moved up the street and climbed the steps of their house, the man, the woman, and the child.

What is she thinking when she looks up at her husband like that? Paul wondered. How does she feel when she remembers that morning when we went mad together? And he sat unmoving behind the wheel of his fine car, at which more than a few men stared, appraising it as they passed; he sat with his arms gone limp.

Was it really quite simple, after all, a matter of

glands, an abundance of health, so that the joy of untried flesh is irresistible? Especially when what is forbidden is the most irresistible of all?

Secrets. Like having a hole in your sock under a bright new shoe.

Up there behind one of those windows, Anna would be getting the supper ready. The husband would probably be playing with the boy. He wondered whether the real estate deal had gone through. The fellow was certainly ambitious, he was trying. One had to give him credit for that. He was thinking ahead for her and for their child.

Christ, how can you just walk in and blow the man and his hopes sky-high? How can you do that? Take his home . . . take his child . . . a little boy like Hank . . . Christ!

Paul put his head in his hands; then, remembering where he was, and that such a posture would make him conspicuous, he forced himself to put the car in gear and move away. Feeling a painful grimace, he composed his mouth, and smoothed his forehead. The blowing air cooled him.

Oh, the turmoil! The turmoil! Hennie and Dan; Leah and Freddy and Hennie; Anna and—

Anna wouldn't. She wouldn't do such a crazy thing, wouldn't make chaos out of order. How well he knew her! He felt as if he could crawl into Anna's mind and know what was there.

It was all an aberration.

No, Anna, sweet Anna, we don't belong in each other's lives.

He brought his car back to the garage and went home. Mimi had just come in. She hadn't yet taken her hat off. It had a feather on one side, something like a whisk broom, so that he had to guard his eyes from it when she kissed him.

"Well, how was your day?" he asked.

"All right. Dull, without you there. And yours?"

"Upsetting." And he told her about Hennie and Dan.

"I'm so sorry, darling. There's been too much trouble around you since you came home, with Freddy and all this business between Hennie and Dan. I know how much you love them. I'm sorry, darling. I hope they straighten themselves out."

The wind had put a becoming flush on her cheeks. Her eyes were wide with concern, and this concern, along with the baby-pink flush, gave her a look of extreme tenderness; he could imagine how she would look if he were ever to do anything to wound her.

"You'd think," she said now, shaking her head, "you'd think we might all have learned something at least from the war, if we didn't know it before."

"And what is that?"

"To be better to each other," she answered simply.

Something struck at his heart and he cried out, "Oh, Marian, dear girl, I'll never hurt you!"

Her eyes were puzzled. "Hurt me? Of course you wouldn't."

No, no. My first love. Your braids dangling over the algebra book. The blue ribbons on your dancing dress. Your bridal veil and the bouquet trembling in your hands."

He laid his cheek against her hair.

"Choose life, that thy children may live."

The ancient words, high poetry from the prayer

book, shot through his head. Nourish and build, they meant. Keep tranquil places. Heal, they meant. Inflict no pain. All that are born under the sun, let live to flourish under the sun, and disturb no peace.

12

The birthday cake stood on the dining room table between two crystal bowls filled with jonquils.

"Four candles," said Leah, "and one to grow on. There'll be a children's party tomorrow," she told Hennie, who stood next to her. "But today I wanted the whole family alone together."

Leah looked around with satisfaction at the lovely room, whose lattice wallpaper made a green-and-white garden wall. It was Elsie de Wolfe's decoration of the Colony Club that had started the vogue, she had explained quite seriously to Hennie. Of course, Leah knew all about such things; she was fashionable and knew how to live in rooms like these, while I, Hennie thought, have never been and am not now at ease in them.

"And now, Great-Grandmother will cut the first piece," said Leah.

Angelique was pleased; she loved the house, as well as ceremonies of any kind. She gave the first piece to Hank and beamed while everyone sang "Happy Birthday."

"Did you know you were named after your great-grandfather, darling?" she asked Hank, whose cheeks were immediately smeared with chocolate frosting.

"I never knew that," Leah whispered to Hennie. "I thought I was naming him after my father."

"Shush." Hennie put her finger to her lips, and they both giggled.

"How the world has changed since he was a little boy like you!" Angelique exclaimed. "It was another world when he was young, when I was young—" She faltered, and her eyes went blank, looking away into some ancient distance.

It had been happening more often lately, this wandering back into the past with recollection of dread days, like the one on which the Union soldiers had come and her father had been killed. Shaped by that war, Hennie thought, as we have been—as little Hank will have been—shaped by this last one.

"I was just thinking," remarked Dan at her elbow, "it's too bad Uncle David couldn't have lived long enough to see this."

Hennie nodded. Uncle David would be glad to know that she and Dan were all right together. Yes, really all right this time.

"The world changes minutely every single day," Paul observed. "It's not noticeable, of course, but go back twenty years and you'll realize what's been happening while you slept. Why, look at you, Leah! Would you ever have dreamed, five years ago, that you would be opening your own establishment on Madison Avenue?"

Leah answered promptly, "Yes," and everyone laughed.

"I've hired away two seamstresses and two tailors

from downtown," she explained. "Offered them more money and nicer surroundings. And I'm to be known, in business, that is"—she made a little self-mocking moue—"as 'Léa.' Please do not forget the accent, people. One has to be French to get anywhere in my business. But it's going to be really beautiful, thanks to Ben's generosity."

Ben grinned. "I'm not really all that generous. After all, it will be mine, too, since we're being married next month."

"Well, it evens out," Leah retorted. "I'll get the benefit of free legal advice."

"There's one clever girl," Alfie said to Hennie. "Never went to college either, any more than I did. It just goes to show you."

Meg had brought her plate of cake and ice cream and drawn up a chair next to Hennie.

"I don't know what it goes to show," she complained, when her father's attention had been directed elsewhere. "I've been accepted at Wellesley and I want to go, Aunt Hennie, I really do. Mother doesn't think girls need college. She wants me to go to a finishing school, in Switzerland, maybe. Her fashionable friends all send their daughters. Worse than that, she'd like me to be a debutante; she's trying her darnedest, but it won't work anyway. I'm not the type."

No, Hennie thought, regarding the girl's large bony frame and sweet earnest face. It's true you're not, any more than I was. And she said sympathetically, "I've always been sorry I didn't go to college. Let's talk some more about it. Maybe I can persuade your parents. Oh, they're opening presents, let's go inside."

Ben was holding Hank aloft, carrying him to the library. The boy's arms and legs were swimming in the air and he was crowing.

Leah's boy, Hennie thought, with an instant's jealous dismay. Still, he had Freddy's luminous smile, caught at moments like skimming clouds reflected in a lake; she strove for a simile, strove to bring back and never to let elude her even the most subtle detail of the living Freddy; a mole on his left cheek midway between his nostril and jaw; a barely noticeable separation between his two front teeth; remember those, not the bloodied body at the foot of the stairs.

You will be happier, little Hank, you and your mother will be happier with Ben than you could have been—oh, forgive me, Freddy! Forgive me, but it is so.

Dan was on the floor, opening toys. There were so many beautiful things! Trains and cowboys, wonderful books, puppets and Indians and a huge stuffed kangaroo from Florence and Walter. There were no toy soldiers, though. Dan forbade that.

How strange it is, Hennie thought as always, to see Dan here in this rich room, with the glossy boxes and the tissue paper strewn among all the expensive presents. The money was coming in floods, most from Dan, but some would be coming now from Leah, too, who would also, indirectly, be making money out of the war, out of a new class of rich women.

Money coming in floods. And she hoped again that it wouldn't affect the lovely child. Still, it hadn't changed Paul! And she glanced over at the sofa where he was sitting with his wife. The baby was due any day now. They looked very happy; around Mimi lay the peaceful aura that can make a pregnant woman so beautiful.

Paul caught Hennie's glance. He looked from her to Dan and back and he was glad for them. Whatever their trouble had been, plainly it was over. He watched them all; his parents were talking to Leah and Ben, and he smiled to himself, reflecting that his mother would be one of Leah's best customers. And there was Meg. He remembered that Freddy had said Meg was so kind to him. He would have to get to know her better, now that she was grown.

Yes, this was a day to be glad of; the family was together and healed. And he thought of Freddy, with his gentle ways; he would be glad, too, if he could know.

Hank was dancing, holding the kangaroo by the paws. And the thought of having a child of his own like him, very soon now, filled Paul with a gratitude that seemed too much to contain. He caught and held Mimi's hand.

Dan struggled up from his knees.

"A beautiful boy," Paul said. He was expected to say it; the question was in Dan's eyes. But Paul meant it, nevertheless. "A beautiful boy!"

"Yes, and he'll never suffer his father's fate." Dan sighed. "Thank God we've seen the last of the wars. Never again will young men go off as my son did, puffed up with false heroism." He sighed again. "We'll have the League of Nations this time. Did you know Hennie's been making speeches for it? I heard her the other night. She was marvelous."

"I had a letter the other day from my cousin Joachim," Paul said. "The first I've heard from him.

He philosophizes. You know those wordy Germans! He had a stomach wound, got the Iron Cross, too, but he feels fine again and he's very optimistic. The country's a shambles, but it will pull out, he said. The German spirit will build it up like new."

The dachshund came in from the dining room with a stolen piece of cake and crawled under the piano, reminding Paul of the day they had bought that other dachshund. They'd selected it from a litter of yapping puppies, carried it back to the inn in Freddy's pocket, and gone out for beer. A hundred years ago, that was.

"I'm optimistic too," Dan said. "Man is learning. Civilization is advancing. The whole working-class movement is advancing all around you. One can see and feel it." And he waved his arm around the room. "Yes, a better world," he concluded.

Paul questioned himself: Why do I think he is naive? Am I any wiser than he?

"Yes, I really believe you're right," he said.

Mimi shifted heavily on the sofa. Immediately he was concerned.

"Are you feeling anything?"

"No, nothing yet." She smiled at him, and he thought he had never seen her look as beautiful as she was now. "Nothing yet, but soon, I'm sure."

It was growing dark. Someone turned up the lamps and a tender pink light flowered. It circled the room to touch each member of the gathering, each so separate and distinct from every other, joined now in one of those rare, quick moments when amity and hope and love are fulfilled.

One's heart had to go out to them all.